The B
By L.K. Hill

Discover more titles by Author Liesel K. Hill on her Author Website[1] or her blog, Musings on Fantasia[2].

---

1. http://authorlkhill.com

2. http://musingsonfantasia.blogspot.com

Table of Contents

This book is a work of fiction. Names, characters, places, and incidents either are products of the author's imagination or are used fictitiously. Any resemblance to actual events or locales or persons, living or dead, is entirely coincidental and not intended by the author.

Copyright © 2015 by L.K. Hill

Cover design (c) 2016 Christopher Loke

All rights reserved. Except as permitted under the U.S. Copyright Act of 1976, no part of this publication may be reproduced, distributed, or transmitted in any form or by any means, or stored in a database or retrieval system, without the prior permission of the publisher.

First Paperback Edition: April 2015

The scanning, uploading, and distribution of this book via the Internet or via any other means without the permission of the publisher is illegal and punishable by law. Please purchase only authorized electronic editions and do not participate in or encourage electronic piracy or copyrighted materials. Your support of the author's rights is appreciated.

To my big sister, Erica, who's been my companion for most of our lives and made me love law enforcement and everything surrounding it. Love you, Sis!

Get L.K. Hill's Starter Library for FREE!

Signup up for the no-spam Story Squad and get 4 free reads plus tons of exclusive content.

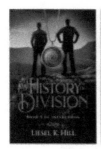   

Dystopian Romance   Historical Romance   Crime & Mystery   High Fantasy

www.authorlkhill.com/storysquad

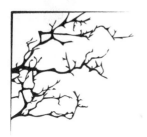

Chapter 1

PROVO, UTAH

The flashing red and blue lights in Alex Thompson's rear view mirror were not the first indication of trouble. She'd sensed something amiss before, as the sun disappeared and the blue of the sky siphoned away after it, but she was too caught up in her own crisis to pay attention. Where had he come from? He couldn't have been following, or she'd have seen him sooner. She'd been alone for hours, isolated with her thoughts and the cool easterly wind on this potholed, prolapsed stretch of highway.

She glanced down and found exactly what she'd expected: she wasn't speeding, unless the limit had changed and she hadn't known it; it had been seventy-five for the past hundred miles. Turning on her signal, and wiping her tear-streaked face, she pulled to the right.

As she decelerated, she passed a dark mound, her headlights glaring briefly over the metal plaque on the front. One of those historical monuments, no doubt—the kind that were out in the middle of nowhere, where no one saw them or remembered what they stood for. It reminded Alex how far she was from civilization.

The road stretched out before her, a gray ribbon through the desert. As darkness edged in, the highway had grown darker, too—a black stripe on a blacker animal. It was eleven o'clock, and the light was long gone.

Only what could be seen in the field of her headlights was visible. If she gazed to the right or left, she could just make out the tips of the looming mountains in the distance, blocking out the stars, but beyond that it was just her and the squad car.

A soft alarm bell clanged inside her head. Her parents could probably guess where she'd gone, but she hadn't actually told anyone. She'd just taken off.

As soon as the door of the squad car opened, something clenched down tight in Alex's stomach, but she didn't know why. Then he was standing next to the window. It was already down, and the cop stayed slightly behind her so she couldn't look directly at him.

"License and registration." His voice was a scratchy whisper. It sent chills down her spine. She wondered why she felt fear. It was just a cop.

Trying not to sniffle, Alex pulled her driver's license and Conceal and Carry Weapons Permit from her wallet, and reached across the seat to get the registration from the glove compartment. She handed them to Officer Raspy with the CCWP on top, then craned her neck around, trying to get a better look at him.

He was tall—more than six feet, she was sure. He had a thick mustache with some kind of dark line under it, as though someone had drawn on his face with a ballpoint pen. The line stretched down over his lips and part of his chin. His hair was dark, but she couldn't see much beyond that. The spotlight from his car made him look washed out, and his eyes were in shadow. His police uniform was filthy, and he looked like he hadn't bathed in weeks.

Welcome to Hickville, she thought.

He looked at what she'd given him, and his eyebrows went down.

"What's this?"

She didn't answer. Once he read it, he'd know what it was. It was the reason it was legal for her dad to keep the loaded nine-mil under the seat. After a moment, he thrust the permit back at her.

"I don't need that."

A little confused, Alex took the permit back and tucked it into her purse.

"May I ask what the problem is, officer? I don't think I was speeding."

She felt his eyes on her, and the sense of danger intensified. It was a long time before he made any reply.

"Where'd you get that bracelet?"

She wished he would stop whispering. "What?"

Immediately there was a flashlight beam in her eyes.

"It's sweet. Just wondered where ya got it." His voice was almost serpentine.

Alex looked at the silver bracelet, covered with magnolia charms, on her left wrist. She hadn't thought of the bracelet or its significance when she ran out of her parents' home up north several hours earlier.

"M-my mother gave it to me."

"Do you know where she got it?"

"No. It was a gift."

A long pause followed, then his raspy whisper reached her ears. "Cordelia."

"I'm sorry?"

The cop stepped closer to her window and every fiber of her body screamed at her to get out of there, but what was she to do? Run from a cop? She'd never been in trouble with the law before. Deciding her nerves were due to what she'd learned this morning, she told herself to breathe and willed the cop to just give her the ticket and let her go.

He leaned his forearms on the window, his face close to her ear. His breath was acrid, and, even from the corner of her eye, she could tell his teeth were cornbread yellow.

"And where's a pretty young girl like you headed this time of night?"

Something told her to lie. She glanced at the GPS. She'd turned off the audio, but kept the map up for reference. The next town she would drive through was seventy-five miles away; it was called Mt. Dessicate.

"Mt. Dessicate. I'm meeting my . . . someone there."

She was going to say husband, but she choked on the lie. Did her license say she was single? In her fear, she couldn't remember whether marital status was printed on driver's licenses. She'd never been a good liar anyway. As though reading her thoughts, he chuckled softly—a hoarse, grating sound—before answering.

"You don't look old enough to be married. Who ya meetin'?"

"M-my boyfriend. I've been driving a long time, and he's meeting me there so we can drive the rest of the way together."

The cop sighed, and then was silent for a long time.

Alex clutched the steering wheel with white knuckles to keep her hands from shaking. The minutes on the car's digital clock changed twice before he moved.

He stepped backward—not toward his own car, but out from hers, backing up until he stood in the middle of the road. He looked in the direction she was headed, then back the way she had come, as though debating with himself about something.

When he stalked back toward her, hiking boots thudding on the ancient pavement, it took every ounce of self-control she had to not throw the car into drive and slam her foot down on the gas.

"You weren't speeding," he finally whispered. "I'm looking for two suspects who might be passing this way, and your car matches the description of theirs."

Alex's eyebrows jumped. "Really?"

"The outside does. The inner upholstery of theirs is red leather. He played the flashlight over her back seat. "And we're looking for two men. *You* can go."

He practically threw her license and registration papers back at her and, without another word, swaggered back to his cruiser.

Under the pretense of adjusting her mirror, Alex tried to get a better look at him. He was tall, husky, and walked with a slight gimp. When his silhouette was swallowed by the blinding spotlight, Alex adjusted her mirror for real and put on her left signal to pull out.

As distance opened up between herself and the squad car, she breathed easier. Maybe the situation hadn't been odd at all; maybe it was just her nerves and the isolation of the open road.

The highway was relatively straight and flat in this part of the desert, so even after several miles, she still had a clear view of the cruiser's bright—albeit smaller—headlights. Then, suddenly, they blinked out.

Another anomaly. Why would he turn off his lights? He hadn't backed up or turned the car around. She would have been able to tell. He was still sitting where he'd parked behind her and had simply turned his lights off.

She supposed it made sense if he was waiting for two specific suspects to drive by—and perhaps that explained why she hadn't seen him before he'd appeared behind her—but why hadn't he repositioned his cruiser before turning off his lights? Was he just going to sit there, in that same position on the side of the road?

Alex shivered and hit her power lock, even though the doors hadn't been unlocked since she left the house. As she drove on, she couldn't shake the feeling that the cruiser was following, just far enough back to be cloaked by the darkness.

The sensation of being preyed upon perched in her chest. She eased her foot down on the accelerator until her speed gauge read well above eighty.

She didn't care.

MILES AWAY, SITTING high up in the mouth of a cave overlooking the desert, the Artist watched the civilian car be pulled over. He was too far away to tell the age of the driver or see if there were any passengers, but he didn't need to. The details were irrelevant. It always ended the same way.

He sighed, running his hand through his thick hair. He was too young to have such a silver head, but this was exactly why he did.

For a while he tried closing his eyes, but it didn't help. He could never escape the images. Eyes open or shut, asleep or awake, laughing or crying, he always saw them. There was nothing he could do, so he sat and watched and waited for the inevitable.

Then something happened that hadn't happened in all the years he'd dwelt in this place. The civilian car pulled out onto the highway . . . and drove away.

The Artist jumped to his feet, moving as close to the mouth of the cave as his shackles would allow him to go. He watched the car until he couldn't see the taillights anymore. Then his eyes went to the cruiser. It sat there for a long time. Then the lights winked out, and he couldn't make it out anymore. Mudface had let the civilian go! What happened? Knowing he had just witnessed something monumental, and probably useful, the Artist sat awake at the cave's mouth for a long time, searching the night sky for answers.

AN HOUR LATER ALEX drove into the unassuming little town of Mt. Dessicate. It seemed modern enough, but was very small. Main Street was synonymous with the highway, and from one end of town, she could see the other end, where it became desert and open road again. It looked like the man-made structures came and went in under a mile. A sleepy passenger could blink and miss the town all together.

Originally, Alex had planned to stop here for the night, find a motel or inn to catch a few hours' sleep before going on. She was exhausted, and earlier she'd wanted nothing more.

After being pulled over, her outlook had changed. Her adrenaline was still pumping and she didn't think she could deal with the solitary shadows of a hotel room. The next town was nearly eighty miles away, but she didn't feel remotely tired, so she opted to drive straight through Mt. Dessicate and keep going, letting the lingering fear spur her on.

Despite only covering a short stretch of highway, the town sprawled right and left, tapering off into residential areas and probably outlying farms after that. Several blocks off the highway, a well-lit sign announced the grand opening of Mt. Dessicate's Walmart.

So, perhaps this wasn't a complete hickville after all.

On her left she passed the only building on Main Street that still had lights on. It was nearly midnight and sleepy little towns like this generally didn't stay awake past supper time. As she passed the building, she read the brick sign in front: Mt. Dessicate Police Station.

Then Alex did something she'd never find the logic for in later years: she made a U-turn. She had to report what had happened to someone. She didn't know who, or why, or what she expected anyone to do about it, but she had to tell *someone*. It was too unsettling to keep to herself.

Pulling into the six-car lot, where two spaces were already in use, she parked and got out. The second she put all her weight on her feet, she nearly fell over. She'd been driving non-stop for nearly five hours. There was a miniature cooler belted into the passenger seat with food, so she wouldn't have to stop in every other city, but she'd been too upset to eat or drink anything, so she hadn't had to stop for bathroom breaks either. Her legs didn't want to work.

She staggered into the tiny gift box of a police station, and was greeted by a professional atmosphere and a round, homely woman behind the front desk. She didn't look pleased to see Alex.

"Can I help you?" It wasn't a happy question.

"Yes. Thank you. I have something I'd like to report. Is there someone I can talk to?"

The woman looked pointedly at her watch and then up at the large, flat clock ticking loudly on the wall.

"Honey, you know what time it is?"

"Yes, but—"

"Detectives won't be here until morning."

"Okay, but I'm just passing through. *I* won't be here in the morning. Can't someone take my statement now?"

The woman pressed her lips together and sighed loudly. She put her head back and opened her generous mouth. "Oliver!"

From the back corner of the room, a head popped up from behind a cubicle. The woman stabbed the air over her shoulder with her pen.

"Go see him. He'll do your report."

Alex hesitated a moment before walking around the desk. "Through here?"

The woman waved a hand in the general direction of the man in the corner, but didn't bother to look up from her paperwork again. Alex wove her way around several desks before coming to stand in front of the man.

With sandy blond hair and a baby face, he looked like he could be younger than her twenty-one years, but she knew you had to be at least twenty-one to become a cop, so obviously he was older than that. He might have been handsome if his face wasn't screwed up into a grimace.

"What do you need?" he asked.

"She said you'd take my statement?"

He looked over her shoulder and yelled toward the front of the room.

"Really, Rose? I have eight hours of paper work that I have to get done in five. Can't you do this?"

Rose's voice drifted to Alex's ears, muffled but understandable.

"Sorry, kid. You're the rookie, so you get the crappy shifts. I'm off in ten and I'm *not* staying late again, so you get to help the young lady file a report."

The man, whose nameplate read Officer Cody Oliver, sighed loudly, just as Rose had, and then grudgingly motioned to a chair next to the desk he was working at.

"Have a seat."

She did, feeling like a total intruder.

The baby-faced cop pulled out a bunch of papers and sat down behind his desk with another long-suffering sigh.

"What's the nature of the complaint?"

"Well, I'm not really sure it is a complaint."

"Then what?"

"It's just . . . something odd that happened. Strange behavior. I guess I'm not sure what it is."

"What?"

Alex told herself to keep her temper. She noticed a road map of the local area on the wall and walked to it. "Is this entire map part of your . . . district?" She hoped that was the right word.

"What?"

Glancing at the scale measurement in the corner of the map, Alex did a mental calculation of how far she could have come in an hour and ran her finger up the straight line on the map that represented the highway until she came to approximately where she thought it had happened. "Is this part of your jurisdiction?"

He stood up and walked over to the map, looking at her with surprise for some reason. He was much taller standing directly next to her than she'd realized before.

"Yes, it is." He looked more genuinely concerned than he had since she'd walked in. "Why? What happened to you there?"

"I got pulled over."

Immediately his eyes took on a flat, annoyed quality. "You're here to complain about getting pulled over?"

"No." She fought to keep her voice calm. Why did this guy have to be such a jerk? "I'm not going to *complain* about it. The guy didn't even give me a ticket."

"Then why are you here?"

"Because it was *weird*. He acted strangely, and I just thought I should run it by someone."

Officer Oliver still looked annoyed, but he sat down in his chair again, going back to the papers.

"All right, tell me what happened."

She started at the beginning and told him every detail she could remember, emphasizing the things she thought constituted odd behavior in a cop.

"When I handed him my concealed-weapons permit, he looked confused, almost like he didn't know what it was, and then he handed it back to me. He said he didn't need it."

Officer Oliver frowned.

"Is there any reason a cop wouldn't care that I had a weapon in the car?" she asked.

"No. That *is* strange . . . but he must have had a reason for it. Keep going. Then what happened?"

When she talked about the cop asking about her bracelet, Oliver's frown returned, deeper this time.

"Did you notice this cop's name?"

She thought for a moment. "No. Actually, now that you mention it, I didn't see a name tag at all. But then with the spotlight on, half his body was completely in shadow. Maybe I just didn't see it. I don't know."

He nodded, making notes on his papers.

"And then I told him I was meeting someone here." She paused for emphasis and Oliver raised a questioning eyebrow. "It was a total lie. I wasn't even planning on stopping here. But I felt like if he thought someone would miss me soon, I'd be in less danger."

He frowned some more, but didn't comment.

She finished the story, ending with the lights blinking out.

"Is that everything—all you remember?"

She leaned forward in her chair. "I don't know if this is something you can write down in your report, but I felt something strange."

"*Felt* something strange?"

"Yes. I felt like I was in real danger. It was only a feeling, but it's the real reason I came here to report this. He didn't actually *do* anything wrong I can point to, but I felt like something very wrong was going on out there."

He pressed his lips together. "Look, ma'am, I can write that in the report, if you want me to, but it's less likely to be taken seriously if I do. We can't investigate people's gut feelings. As for this cop, he acted very unprofessionally, but that's all. It's exactly like you said: he didn't actually *do* anything wrong. Maybe he really did like your bracelet. A cop who completely ignores a CCWP is an idiot, but it's only his own safety he's putting in jeopardy. So I'll agree with you that he was being stupid, but chances are his department won't write him up for that."

When she didn't answer, he sighed again. "Can you describe him to me? What did he look like?"

"I can't tell you much. There's no moon tonight—it's just too dark out there."

"What about his spotlight?"

"Yeah, but that threw him half into shadow and made the other half look washed out. I can tell you that he had dark hair—"

"Dark?"

"Yeah, either dark brown or black, and his hair was darker than his skin. I'm positive he wasn't African-American, but he might have been Caucasian, or Latino, or something. I couldn't see his eyes at all. Oh, but he had a mustache, and I think there was a scar coming out from under it. It was small but it went down over his chin. And he was tall—probably an inch or two taller than you."

He was frowning at her now, and not writing anything down, she realized.

"I'm sorry," she said, exasperated. "I *know* that's a vague description, but it all happened so fast and he stayed behind me for most of the time and—"

"It's not that. The scar and the mustache are good identifying marks, though the mustache could be shaved. I'm just thinking that there are no cops in our department that match that description. We're a small town, and every cop in the precinct knows each other well. That isn't anyone I know."

She breathed a sigh of relief. "Then it wasn't a real cop."

Oliver immediately hedged. "Why are you so happy about that?"

"I'm sorry. I didn't mean to cause offense. It's just that if he wasn't a real cop, then something really was going on. I'm not crazy."

"Look, ma'am. There's no one that far out that could have pulled something like this off. The only things that live out there are cow tippers and sage brush. No one that could have gotten a hold of a uniform and fake badge, much less a squad car."

Her temper flared. Snatching up her purse she got to her feet. He looked up in surprise.

"Look, *officer,* I came in to report this because I felt like something strange was happening, but I'm finished now. I'm just passing through this town. I've done enough to clear my conscience. Do whatever you want with the report. You don't have to file it. Tear it up when I'm gone, if you like, but it's on you now if something sinister is going on out there."

"Look, ma'am—"

"And I swear if you 'look ma'am' me one more time, I going to file a complaint against *you!* Good night."

With that, she stalked away, past the desk where Rose still sat, and out into the night.

CODY OLIVER WATCHED her go in complete confusion. The story she'd told was strange—he'd give her that—but could it really be true? He had been sure she was going to want to talk to the sheriff in the morning, create a whole stink, demand something be done, yada yada yada.

But now she was just leaving? That alone lent her a lot of credibility. Feeling guilty for being curt with her, he got up and followed her into the parking lot.

"Ma'am—" *What was her name?* "Ms. Thompson, wait."

She was already pulling out of the parking lot. She didn't stop or even slow down, but whether because she didn't notice him or simply didn't care, he couldn't be sure. He watched her headlights shrink into the darkness, and then Rose was standing beside him, coat and purse draped over her arm.

"Smooth."

He rolled his eyes. "I suppose you heard all that?"

"I did. Creepy story."

"Yeah, but who could possibly be doing something like that clear out there? We're talking the middle of nowhere, Rose. Sagebrushville."

"The Pushkins."

"What? Are you serious?"

"It's a bit before your time, kid, but a few years ago, the oldest three boys somehow got a hold of some firefighter equipment. They had a suit, mask, even a used up oh-two tank. They started going around to businesses in town, saying a fire alarm had gone off. They were stopping work in the middle of the day, scaring the daylights out of people, causing all kinds of chaos. Their daddy got the sheriff to agree not to press charges if they did community service. I'm just sayin', if anyone is out there, impersonating cops and trying to scare travelers, my money'd be on them."

"Impersonating a cop is a felony, Rose."

"I know that. Could be you'll never prove who it was one way or the other. Of course, if you drove out there, talked to some of the locals, maybe casually mention that you're looking for cop impersonators, and said impersonators will do some jail time, it might scare some sense into them. Solve your whole problem."

"Is that what you think I should do?"

"I think you should talk to the sheriff in the morning, let him decide."

Cody nodded, then realized Rose was throwing him side-long glances. "What?"

"She was kinda cute."

He chuckled softly, then shrugged. "Okay, I guess."

"Just okay?"

"Yeah, she was kinda chunky."

A soft crack again the back of his head jerked it forward.

"Ow." He rubbed the nape of his neck. "What was that for?"

"She was *not* chunky, young man. I weigh twice what she did."

"Well . . . I . . . uh . . . really? You two looked exactly the same to me."

She peered up into his face, scrutinizing it for signs of a lie. Then, satisfied, she looked straight ahead again, even lifting her chin a little. She gave one quick nod.

"Nice save. See you tomorrow."

He watched her get in her car and pull out of the lot, waving as she did. Then, chuckling to himself and shaking his head, he went back into the station.

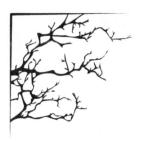

Chapter 2

FOUR YEARS LATER

Colleen Hinkle let the letter drop into her lap and leaned her head back against the wooden rocking chair her husband had carved with his own hands. She was near the end of her life, it seemed.

The sun was sinking down behind the horizon, and her chair made a rhythmic thud against the wooden slats of the wrap-around porch. Colleen glanced down at the white braid that lay over her shoulder. She'd lived in this house on the outskirts of Mt. Dessicate for the better part of forty years. The rural, desert-like atmosphere of Southern Utah suited her well after so many years. Her will said the house would pass to her eldest son upon her death. That was fitting. He already lived in it with her, along with his sweet but headstrong wife and their two children.

Colleen had buried three husbands in her time. She'd married at eighteen to please her parents, but her first husband, Bob, had been unpleasant at best and downright abusive at worst. When he died in a mining accident, she was afraid she'd go to hell for being relieved he was gone.

Three years later she'd married again. His name was Connor, and he'd been the love of her life. Their relationship had passion, romance, friendship, respect, and children. They'd been together more than twenty years. Then Connor had gotten sick. Tests at the university hospital up north had revealed leukemia as the culprit. By the time they knew anything was wrong, it had already spread so thoroughly through his body; the doctors said nothing was to be done. They gave him six months to live; he died one hundred and seventy-two days later. It had been the greatest grief of her life.

At the time, she'd figured forty-five was old. Now, looking back thirty years later, she realized that she'd still been young. She and Connor had had four children together. When he died, three were teenagers, the third only barely, and the youngest was ten.

It was another five years before she married Edgar. Edgar was sweet and soft-spoken. He didn't have Connor's fire, nor Bob's temper. Their marriage had been one of convenience. She was a widow, he a widower, both with teenagers to raise and not enough money to do it with.

Despite the necessity of their arrangement, Colleen came to have such a deep respect and trust for Edgar that she couldn't help but love him. He was good to her and loved her children. The two of them became the best of friends; the perfect companions for each other during their twilight years. Eventually, they'd even spoken at length about their earlier partners. Edgar had felt about his wife much the same way Colleen had felt about Connor. Their empathy with one another allowed them to talk about the previous relationships, look back with affectionate nostalgia, and chase away the loneliness together. They playfully agreed that whoever died first would find the other's previous spouse in the next world and keep them company until they could all reunite.

Then, three years ago, Edgar had succumbed to liver disease. Apparently he'd done a lot of drinking in his younger years. He'd told her often that he'd been a mean drunk and done a lot of things he wasn't proud of. Colleen simply couldn't picture it. He'd been so sweet and . . . sober when she'd known him. But perhaps it was the booze itself that had changed him.

She'd been nearly seventy years old, then, and had no desire to marry again. When Edgar died, she simply hoped that she could find joy in life, and that God wouldn't make her wait too much longer to reunite with the men she'd loved. Today, that prayer had been answered.

She'd begun getting headaches several months ago, but had ignored them for a long time. When her oldest son, named Connor after his father, realized she was in pain, he insisted on her seeing the doctor. Their country doctor could tell her very little, but he seemed worried when she described her symptoms. He recommended she go up north to the fancy university hospital and get an MRI.

Colleen put it off as long as possible, but last month she'd finally gone. They'd discovered a mass in her brain during the first round. She'd gone back two weeks ago for a biopsy, and the letter resting casually on her knees included the results of that test. It wasn't good. Of course, this news hadn't been delivered by letter, not at first. The doctor had called her several days ago, begging her to come north for treatment. She'd refused. When she stopped answering his calls, he sent the letter to beg her again.

He claimed if she got treatment, she might have a chance to shrink the tumor before it metastasized the way Connor's leukemia had. The problem was that there were no guarantees. Colleen was seventy-two years old and had no desire to go through horrible radiation treatments. She'd lived in this small town most of her life. She was surrounded by her children, grandchildren, and even a few great-grandchildren. She would rather spend her days with them, and let the cancer take her, as it had taken the darling of her life all those years ago. She would set her affairs in order and be with her family as much as she could. Then she would go gladly and with no regrets.

She cork-screwed her mouth into a grimace, as though she'd eaten a sour grape.

No, that wasn't true. There was one regret—one thing she wished she could go back and fix. It happened just after Connor died, nearly thirty years ago. She'd been more distraught—in a darker place—than she'd been during any other part of her life. Though she'd been sure that what she'd seen that afternoon was important, she hadn't had the strength or know-how to push through her grief and act on it.

Even now, she was sure it had been important. But it was twenty years ago. Who would know or care *now* what she saw then?

The sun disappeared behind the mountains and darkness seeped over the sky like spilled ink. The wind carried squeals of laughter to her from up the road. They came from four houses away. The Caraways were in their forties, but they hadn't married until their thirties, so they still had young kids at home. And a trampoline in their backyard.

Colleen smiled, but the sound of the children made her sad. She would have to call her kids together and tell them the news. There would be tears and anger at her decision. She was sure they, especially her stubborn youngest daughter, would try to force her to get treatment, but she'd hold her ground.

A shooting star streaked across the sky and Colleen knew she ought to make a wish, but for what? She'd led a good, long life. She'd been blessed. There was nothing she wanted. All her prayers had been answered.

After a moment, she settled on the regret. With the star's last twinkling, she asked God for the chance to put right what she'd kept silent all those years. She had no idea how it could be put right, or if it even mattered anymore, but it was the only thing in her life left undone.

Colleen got to her feet, letting the doctor's letter fall to the ground. The wind picked it up the next minute and carried it off the porch and into the grass. Colleen let it go. She didn't need it anymore. The east wind would carry it away and God would see it. Perhaps it would end up just a soggy piece of paper in a ditch somewhere, but Colleen fancied that perhaps another would find it, and it would inspire a story or a positive life change.

Colleen chuckled to herself. She was a silly old woman, letting flights of fancy take her mind, but how else was she to fall asleep at night?

Still smiling, she went into the house. The wind followed and wrapped itself around her as she slept.

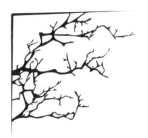

Chapter 3

"HEY CODY, THINK FAST!"

Detective Cody Oliver caught the torpedoing can of soda only inches in front of his nose. He rolled his eyes, knowing he wouldn't be able to drink it for at least ten minutes now.

"Thanks a lot, man. Trying to expand on my scar, are we?"

His partner of three years grinned. "Meeting with the captain in ten." As Tom walked by his desk, he picked up the soda Cody had set down and shook a few more times, just for good measure.

"Gimme that." Cody snatched it away, and Tom chuckled.

Tom had been tall and lanky in his younger years—Cody remembered because he grew up across the street and gone on a date or two with Tom's oldest daughter—but as his hairline receded, his belt line expanded. He would always be tall and lean, but along with his graying hair, he'd developed what his fellow detectives affectionately referred to as a baby bump. Tom always threw things at them when they said it to his face, but he didn't seem to mind the teasing; or at least, not enough to get himself into better shape.

"Where're we meeting, anyway?" Cody asked. "Isn't the conference room still being re-done?"

"Oh, come on, Cody," Frank Dannel said, striding into the room. He was more than six feet tall, and it was all in his legs. He flipped his head to get his chestnut man-bangs out of his face and flashed Cody his signature, rogue smile. "A little noxious paint vapor never hurt anyone. Where's your sense of adventure?"

Cody smiled but didn't comment. He knew better than to get into an argument with Frank, even a friendly one.

"Captain's coming here," light-haired Court announced, plunking down at his desk across from Frank. He was the smallest of the four of them. "We'll be ghetto today and just huddle around the desks."

"Long as we're not cuddling around the desks," Frank answered cheerfully.

Cody tuned them out. He was trying to check his voicemail, and kept having to repeat the messages because he was listening to the other detectives.

A call from Melissa (she was cancelling for Friday); a recorded message from a telecommunications company; and his mother, asking him to drop by for dinner.

"Your father and I would love to see you. Oh, and bring chips."

Cody groaned. He loved his mother's company, but all he and his father did lately was argue. He'd been a cop for six years; why couldn't his dad give it up, already?

Tom's chair creaked loudly when he collapsed into it at the desk across from Cody's. He didn't seem to notice. He glanced over at Cody on his phone, and Cody quickly amended his sour expression, but he wasn't quick enough.

"Trouble with the ladies?" Tom grinned.

Frank swiveled his chair around so fast he almost fell over. "Cody? *Ladies?* You holdin' out on us?"

"You actually got a girlfriend, Cody?" Court asked, feigning shock.

Cody adopted a look of mock-hurt. "Is that so hard to believe?"

"Well, who is she?" Frank scooted his chair closer to Cody's. "Is she pretty? Upstanding? Could *my* wife take her?"

"Want us to pull her over?" Court asked.

"You three are like the teenage brothers I never had. You know that?"

They ignored his comment but leaned forward, eager for information. Cody sighed. "I've been on exactly two dates with her, and she just cancelled on me for tomorrow night. I don't think that constitutes a serious relationship, do you?"

"What's her name?" That was Tom.

"Until it *does* become more serious, I'm not going to tell you."

Frank looked hurt. "Why not?"

"Because you'll do a background check on her."

Frank's face froze, then slid slowly into a grin. "Yeah, I probably would. But"—he adopted his most obsequious expression—"just a hint? I wouldn't shake your soda can quite as much next time."

Cody sighed but was saved from having to answer because the captain walked in. Several inches taller than Cody and solidly built, Captain William Brecken always seemed . . . serious. Even when he was sharing one of the detectives' jokes. He had deep, pale blue eyes and his dark hair was thinning, but had yet to lose any of its color.

"Morning, all. How is everyone?"

Various mutters of "fine, sir," and "good" followed. Frank jerked a thumb in Cody's direction. "He's got a girlfriend."

The captain frowned, his eyes shifting to Cody, who promptly studied the pencil sharpener on his desk.

"That's . . . great," the captain muttered. Without another word, he produced a two-foot stack of file folders. All four detectives groaned as he handed each of them roughly one quarter of the stack.

"I don't get it," Court said. "We have a town of, like, twenty people. How can there be this much crime?"

"Two *thousand* people," the captain corrected, "and it's not all crime." He paused to thrust a meaty finger into Court's face. "Don't go around telling people it's all crime, 'cause it's not." Court gave him an exaggeratedly innocent look.

"You know," Frank chimed in, "Court told me he especially likes being assigned to walk old ladies across the street. Most fulfilling job he's ever had, according to him."

Court picked up his stapler and chucked it at Frank. The captain pretended not to notice. Cody smirked as he opened the top folder the captain had placed on his desk and began scanning it.

"One more thing before you go to work," the captain said, silencing them all. "We have a maggot case."

Frank and Court dove under their desks. Tom wasn't that lithe anymore, but he jumped to his feet, announcing a sudden urge to relieve himself. Cody wasn't paying attention; he was still studying his folder.

"Will you relax?" The captain put up his hand to stop Tom from leaving. "It's Cody's turn."

Cody looked up from his folder, terrified. "Me?"

"You."

"But . . . they haven't—" He motioned to the others.

"Hey, that's true. He hasn't had one in a while." Frank came out from under his desk, confident once more. "I had the crazy stoner in the swamp thing, remember?"

"I had to look into the weird smell down by the refinery," Court said.

Cody looked at Tom, his last hope. Tom shrugged. "I'm still looking into the haunted library thing."

"About that," the captain said. "Any progress there?"

Tom shrugged. "Just a lot of mothballs and thick glasses, Captain. We're expecting them to attack any day now."

"The mothballs or the glasses?" Frank asked. Court seemed to think that was hilarious and laughed so hard he knocked his soda over.

Tom shrugged. "Either one would prove the librarian isn't crazy. She swears the place is haunted, and not in a good way. Books keep going missing and some of them—not all, mind you—have turned up in odd places. She says she feels an ice-cold presence, like she's being watched. Personally, I think she's either losing her marbles or someone's pranking her."

"Did we ever do a drug test on her?" the captain asked.

"Yup," Tom said. "She's clean as spit."

"If you don't find anything in the next week, put the case to bed, Tom," the captain said. "We have better things to be doing with our time."

Frank had opened the top folder on his desk and was scanning it skeptically. "You sure about that, Cap?"

Cody let his head fall back against the wall. They were right. It *was* his turn. All of them had done one more recently.

They called these cases maggot cases because they were creepy, gross, and hard to pin down. Cody didn't know if it was just the curse of the small town, or something else, but every couple of months like clockwork they would get a case that made absolutely no sense. The last one he'd worked, about a year ago, involved a homeless guy that insisted women in his area were being abducted by aliens. His proof of this was that they were leaving used feminine napkins in their wake. He insisted that they were ascending so violently into the "mother ship" they were leaving . . . things behind. As it turned out, a garbage can had fallen over, depositing much of its goods onto the ground, including the used napkins. The hobo was a chronic drunk, and probably a little crazy to boot. He'd seen the napkins and his mind had just filled in the blanks.

These ridiculous, disgusting cases made all four of the detectives shudder, but that didn't mean they could ignore them. If a report was filed, it had to be followed up.

Cody looked fearfully up at the captain. "So, what is it?"

The captain held up a clear plastic bag that made Cody cringe. It was enough to silence the other three detectives as well, which didn't happen often.

"Comes with a mutilated doll," the captain grinned.

"Great," Cody muttered.

"Two hikers found it up Hydra Mountain. There's a trail called Hy-Hydand-dera—?"

"Hydrandra Trail," Court finished for him. "Yeah, I been up there. You take it up to the fork and if you go left, it takes you to the waterfall."

"Is there really a waterfall up there?" Frank asked.

It didn't sound plausible to Cody, either. He'd never been up that particular mountain, but they were in the southwest corner of Utah. Not much outside the city limits but dust and sagebrush. A waterfall just didn't seem likely.

"Yeah. I mean, it's more like slobber on a burner, this late in summer, but it's there."

Frank nodded knowingly as the captain went on.

"Well, according to the report, they went right, not left. Two young lovebirds, just exploring. Then they found the doll."

"So some hiker's kid dropped it," Cody said. "What's so special about a doll?"

The captain tossed the bag at Cody, who caught it above his head.

"Why don't you press the hand and find out."

Feeling the urge to scratch his scalp, Cody carefully removed the dirt-covered doll from the bag. Most of the hair had been pulled out, one eye was permanently shut, and the faded pink dress it wore—it may have originally been red—was ripped and unraveling.

Reaching over and taking a tissue from the box on Frank's desk, Cody squeezed the doll's right palm. Then he hunched his shoulders, waiting for something to happen.

Nothing did.

The captain had put on his reading glasses and was studying the report in front of him. "Other hand," he murmured, not looking up.

Cody pressed the other hand. This time, a jovial, high-pitched, little girl's voice came out of the doll.

"I'm a whore," it announced cheerfully.

Cody almost dropped the doll.

Frank gasped and slid his chair several feet away from Cody.

Cody glanced at him, annoyed. "Well *I* didn't say it, Frank."

"I'm sorry," Tom said from across the room, "an old man's hearing starts to go. Did that thing just say, 'I'm a whore'?"

The captain looked up at them. "Press it again, Cody." His look told Cody it wasn't just to repeat the first phrase. Against his better judgment, Cody pressed the palm again.

"I like it when Daddy touches me," the doll announced in a *way*-too-happy voice.

Cody did drop the doll this time, chills running down his back.

"What"—Court also scooted away from Cody—"the *hell*."

The captain gave them a grimace of a smile. "Now you know why the hikers turned it in. Look"—he removed his reading glasses—"before you all go getting worked up about it, I want you to try and keep this in perspective. It may be nothing at all."

"No offense, Cap, but how could that be nothing?" Frank asked.

Cody was about to agree, but the captain held his hands up. "Think about it. This thing is battery powered, which means there must be some sort of computer or recording device in there. You know how smart kids are today, especially with electronics. This may simply be the case of horny, teenage boys screwing around with this thing and thinking it's hilarious. It was abandoned near what I understand is a popular high school hotspot."

"And if it's not as innocent as that?" Tom asked.

The captain sighed. "Worst case scenario: there could be a domain nearby."

Cody groaned. So Tom got crazy-librarian-telling-ghost-stories and he got a pedophile case. Fantastic.

"Cody, I want you to go up there and have a look around. If you can't find anything, consider it a dead end and file it away. I don't want you wasting a lot of time on this."

Cody nodded at the captain. That was fine with him. He wanted to spend as little time on this as possible.

"That's all, then," the captain said. "Let's create some order out there."

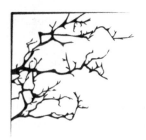

Chapter 4

CODY KNEW HE WOULDN'T have time to check out the twisted doll case that day, especially with his mom expecting him for dinner. He usually liked to get the nastier aspects of his job over with quickly, but he wasn't at all sad about putting his hiking trip off until the next day.

After leaving the precinct, he dropped by the grocery store to pick up some sour cream 'n chive potato chips—his parents' favorites—then went home to shower and change. Glancing at his appearance in the mirror before leaving, he ran his fingers over the now-familiar scar.

It ran from above his right eyebrow, down over his eye, and part-way down his cheek. The fugitive who had given it to him had made sure it was deep enough that only plastic surgery would fix it, and his insurance didn't exactly cover that. Now it stared back at him daily, a reminder of why he did the work he did, and the price that sometimes had to be paid.

The drive to his parents' house was a pleasant one. The traffic wasn't bad for rush hour, and Cody enjoyed a casual spin past the places he'd grown up. Mt. Dessicate was a tranquil little town that in recent years had blossomed into a small city in the desert. It was a mining town, and new caches of mineral had been opened about ten years before. That had brought more people, which in turn brought more modern businesses. Mt. Dessicate may have been just a bump in the road compared to some of the bigger cities up north, but it was still much more urban than it had been when Cody was a kid. Gone were the days of knowing everyone in town by their first names—the population was too large for that anymore—but Cody still knew the majority of them; if not personally then by acquaintance.

Pretty much everything in Cody's life was within a twenty minute ride of his home, most things much closer than that. The streets of Mt. Dessicate were clean and wide. Children played basketball and rode their bikes in the residential areas. Commercial streets were much busier, of course, but not unsafe.

Cody had been north to the larger cities plenty of times, but he wasn't someone who longed for big city life. There had always been plenty of diversions for him in Mt. Dessicate, even as a teenager, and besides, all his friends and family were here. He didn't mind working in a big city—he might wind up in one someday, for some part of his career—he just hadn't found incentive enough to leave yet.

At six-fifteen, he knocked on the front door of the house he'd grown up in. No one answered, but it was unlocked, so he let himself in. The knock was really just a courtesy anyway.

The parlor and living room were empty, but when Cody followed the narrow hallway that led to the kitchen, he found his mother rinsing spinach in a colander. Diced tomatoes and cucumbers leaked juice onto a cutting board beside her.

"Mom?"

"Oh, Cody. You made it." She wiped her hands on a dishtowel and met him half way across the kitchen.

"You really shouldn't leave the front door unlocked, Mom. Any screwball could have walked in here, and you wouldn't have known you were in danger until he was in the kitchen with you."

"Oh." She waved her hand dismissively, going up on her tip toes so he could kiss her cheek, which he did. "I knew it was you, dear. And don't say screw."

Cody smiled and held up the chips for her inspection.

"Sour cream and chives? Your father'll love those."

"We'll see," Cody muttered, plunking himself down in one of the wooden chairs that ringed the kitchen table.

His mother shot him a disapproving look.

"Where is Dad anyway?"

"He's outside at the barbeque. I know he'd love it if you said hi."

Cody didn't think his mother knew any such thing, but he didn't say so. Seeing his expression, she brandished a salad fork at him.

"Your father's in a good mood, Cody. Don't ruin it."

"Good mood? What about?"

"Well . . . I . . . it's his news to tell, but it's part of the reason we invited you over tonight. I'm sure he'll tell you over dinner. Go out and see if he needs any help, and try not to ruin the happy-family-togetherness thing."

Smirking, Cody got to his feet and went out onto the back deck, sliding the heavy glass door closed behind him.

"Hey, Dad."

Norman Oliver had been handsome when he was younger and now, with salt and pepper hair and a well-groomed beard, he looked like a distinguished gentleman. Today the image was marred by the floppy chef's hat settled precariously over his ears and the grease-stained, hot-dog-print apron that covered his polo shirt and cargo pants.

"Cody! Great to see you."

"Thanks. You too."

An awkward silence descended and Cody's father went back to his grill.

"Can I help?" Cody asked.

His father turned. "Why don't you bring me that seasoning there?"

Cody turned to where his father pointed and picked up the bottle of Smokey-BBQ Seasoning. He took it over to stand opposite his father on the other side of the grill. The hamburger patties had already been seasoned, but his father opened the bottle and sprinkled a little more on for Cody's benefit.

"So," Cody said, "Mom said you had some news?"

"I do. I'd like to wait 'til we're all around the table, if that's all right."

Cody nodded. "Speaking *of*, how much longer 'til the meat's ready? I'm starved."

His father grinned proudly. "Any minute, now."

Fifteen minutes later found them all around the table. After saying grace, they dug into the food. Cody definitely missed home-cooked meals. Detective work was often synonymous with bad take-out.

Around mouthfuls of flame-kissed hamburger meat, he asked his mother about her scrapbooking business. She launched into a thirty minute tirade about trouble getting acid-free slip covers from her vendor, because they were trying to charge her twice what the larger company in Salt Lake was getting.

"I mean, I know it's a bigger company and they order more than I do, but they promised me the same pricing agreement. If the price of the covers themselves hasn't gone up, then they have no reason to charge me more, right?"

Cody nodded along, making certain to take his mom's side in every detail, or risk not sampling dessert, which he'd glimpsed when she asked him to get the soda from the fridge. It was some sort of fruit pie. He didn't even care what kind; he just wanted some.

By the time she'd finished, Cody and his father had cleaned their plates, though due to her chatter, his mother hadn't come close.

"So." She tried to kick her husband in the shins under the table, but missed and kicked Cody instead. He didn't think she realized, so he didn't tell her. "About time for your news, isn't it, dear?"

Cody's father nodded. "I suppose it is. Cody, you know I do most of my consulting from home. The internet allows me to do most of it online, via email, or over the phone, which has worked out beautifully since my shoulder started acting up again."

Cody nodded. He knew all of that. "Do you use that video phone of yours much?"

"Much?" His father's grin widened. "I told you it was the telephone of the future, didn't I? *Most* of my telephone conferences are also video conferences now."

Cody smiled at his father's enthusiasm. His mother was right; he *was* in a good mood.

"So what's changed?" Cody asked, and his father became serious again.

"A larger consulting firm, based out of Denver, has approached me. They've heard my name in the industry and seen some of the work I've done."

"Your father has a reputation for honest dealing and hard work. He gets a lot done in a shorter time and with more efficiency than most other consultants do." His mother chewed her salad, looking proud.

Cody's father gave her an appreciative smile.

"So did they offer you work, Dad?"

"Actually, they want to buy me out. They want me to write a book on my techniques and use it to expand their own company."

Cody sat back in his chair. "Is that something you're interested in?"

His father shook his head. "I'm not interested in retiring. Not yet."

Cody nodded, knowing his father's fiftieth birthday was still six months away.

"So," his father continued, "we worked out a deal. We're going to merge. Actually, their huge corporation is absorbing my small business, but I'll become a partner. I'll help them expand and they hope over the next ten years to become a national business."

"Wow. Dad, that's great. Congratulations."

His father beamed. Cody's mother looked between her husband and her son happily. She was probably pleased they were getting along so well.

"Thank you, Cody."

"So, will you two be moving up north then?"

"We won't sell this house," his mother answered. "We love it here too much. If nothing else, we want to come back here when we retire. Even before then, we'll keep the property so we can visit you weekends and summers. But we wanted to let you know what is going on, and to tell you that you're welcome to live here if you want."

Cody thought about it for a few minutes. "Well, thank you. I appreciate the offer. I don't know that I'd take you up on it right away. This is kind of far from the precinct. It's easier to live in my apartment, close to town. It's nice to know it's here, though, if I ever need it or get into financial trouble."

His mother nodded encouragingly.

"Cody," his father said, "that brings me to something I wanted to ask you."

His father's tone made Cody wary. "What's that?"

"Your mother and I will probably take a house up north so I can work up there for a while. This merger comes with a bump in pay that means we'll be able to afford both properties without a problem. But I'll be working with that larger branch of the company for the next few months. I won't have time to do anything else. There are still several dozen small businesses down here, in the southern part of the state, that rely on me for my services. I don't want to leave them high and dry.

"Despite the fact that you decided not to follow me into consulting, I know you know how to do it. I taught you how. I was wondering if you would consider taking over my duties down here for the next several months, just until the transition to the larger corporation is complete."

Cody tried very hard not to sigh. There it was. It would be one thing if Cody needed money, or a job, or was not happy at his, but he was, and his father knew that. This wasn't a loving gesture. It was an I-don't-approve-of-your-work-and-would-rather-you-do-what-I-did gesture.

Cody's anger flared, but it had been a good visit and he didn't want to fight with his father, so he told himself to remain calm.

"Dad, I appreciate that you're going to need help during this transition, but I don't think I'll have the time. My job keeps me really busy and—"

"Oh, nonsense," his father broke in. "It'll be a lot of work—there's no point sugar-coating that—but I'll make sure you're paid well for it. It'll be eight hours at your day job, then, granted, probably another six or eight hours consulting, but you aren't doing anything else. It's not like you're dating anyone or anything."

Cody's anger flared again, hotter than before. It wasn't the line about dating anyone that made him mad—up until a week ago, that had been true—but rather the presumption that his father knew *anything* about his job. Despite how many times Cody had tried to explain to his dad the ins and outs of the work he did, his father still seemed to have some bizarre image of him sitting around, cuffing and un-cuffing bicycle thieves all day. He had no interest in what Cody's work actually entailed, and no appreciation for it.

Cody wanted to lash out at his father, but in his furious haze, he couldn't think of where to start.

"How do you know I'm not dating anyone?" he asked lamely.

His mother immediately perked up. "Are you?"

"Well . . . I . . ." His head swiveled back and forth between them. "I've just started seeing someone."

"Really? What's her name?"

"Uh, Melissa. Dad, look, I—"

"Melissa Cornish, the reverend's daughter?" His mom's eyes lit up.

Cody turned back to her. If he was thinking of the right person, he'd only met the reverend's daughter once or twice, and she'd seemed like a prattling, holier-than-thou princess to him.

"No."

His mother looked crestfallen. "Oh."

He turned back to his father, who looked about as annoyed as Cody felt. "Dad, if I had the time to spare, I'd be there for you, but you don't understand what I'm trying to say. It's not that I don't date because I'd rather cuddle up to my TV. I don't date because my job keeps me working around the clock. I don't have the amount of time that you're talking about to commit to this."

His father took a deep, controlled breath. "Well, perhaps you could leave your job for a few months, just to help me out."

His control deserting him, Cody jumped to his feet. "Why does it always have to come to this, Dad?" His dad looked up at him in surprise and Cody moderated his tone. "I respect your work a great deal, Dad, but it's not what I want to do. Why can't you respect mine?"

"That's not fair, Cody," his mother said calmly. "Your father and I *do* respect your work. It's just . . . we're worried about. . ." She studied her fork. "Your safety."

"My *safety?* In *Mt. Dessicate?*" When his mother still wouldn't meet his eyes, he turned back to his father. "Is that really all this is about, Dad?"

His father's mouth settled into a stony line. "That's part of it."

"What's the other part?"

His father rose slowly to his feet. "You're throwing away your potential, Cody, on these negative scumbags who don't deserve your time. You ought to be creating something, putting something positive out into the world. Instead, you waste your talents hauling criminals from one cell to another."

"*I* don't think so."

"Neither do I. I *know* so."

"Norman." Cody's mother's voice held a warning, and his father backed off. A little. He didn't take back what he'd said.

Chest heaving, Cody placed his hands flat on the kitchen table. "Dad, if you need help moving, adjusting, getting things in order, or help that only requires a few hours a week, that I can do. *That* I'm willing to do because I'm sure this will be a hectic transition for you. But that's all I can manage."

"You mean that's all you're *willing* to manage."

"Yes."

His father sat down roughly in his chair. "Typical," he muttered. "Just like your Uncle."

That made Cody's eyebrows jump. "I thought you and Uncle Clyde were close growing up."

"That doesn't mean I want you to be just like him. He wasted his life, too!"

Cody suddenly knew this visit was over. He turned stiffly to his mother. "Thank you for dinner. It was delicious. If you'll excuse me, I have a busy day tomorrow, and I need to brainstorm a few more ways to waste my life before I hit the sack."

He threw the back of his calves against his chair so hard that it screeched across the kitchen floor and hit the opposite wall. Cody didn't care. He stalked out of the house, leaving his father looking ready to flatten a puppy and his mother ready to cry.

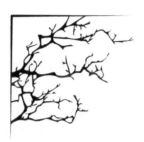

Chapter 5

THE NEXT MORNING, CODY decided to hike up Hydra Mountain in the morning, while it was cool, and hopefully make it in to work by noon with nothing to report.

It had been awhile since he'd actually gone outside the city limits. He packed a backpack with a few bottles of water and some food, and brought a bandana with him. Then he headed north. He'd called Court the night before for directions. The base of the canyon was a forty minute drive from town. Once he reached it, he found a large sign map with the words "Hydandra Trail" written in big letters over a line that twisted and curved its way up, ending in a picture of a waterfall. "5.3 mi."

The trail was obviously well used, wide enough for two cars to pass one another and paved. Cody drove until he reached the fork. The waterfall was to the left, but the hikers had gone right, so he did as well.

The hikers reported camping below an M-shaped mountain. It sounded vague to Cody, but when he saw it, he knew it was the right one. The top of it looked like a perfect McDonald's arch.

The road became gravel, then dirt, then completely impassable. Cody pulled his car off to the side of the trail, parking it in the shadow of the mountain, and began his trek on foot.

The path took him between rises and into the shadow of the M-peak. It struck Cody how treacherous the hike was. As a cop, he was required to keep in good shape, and had grown up in this part of the country, but for the inexperienced hiker, this kind of terrain could be downright dangerous. More than once he slid on loose gravel, barely catching himself from sliding down the face of the mountain.

Beneath the M-mountain, he found evidence of recent campers: a haphazardly constructed fire pit rimmed with small rocks, and deep grooves in the dirt where he imagined a tent had been set up. He even found a discarded yellow tent stake.

The campsite was nestled in what he could only have described as a tiny valley, surrounded on all sides by small rises. The valley floor couldn't have been more than a quarter mile square, and the rises that fenced it in, though not more than a few hundred feet in altitude, were made of sheer, rocky faces with almost no vegetation whatsoever, even of the desert variety.

Cody spiraled out from the campsite to cover ground in every direction at once. Inevitably, his spiral led him to the rocky inclines, forcing him to scale them in order to move out from the site. Several caves high up in the rock looked down on the campsite and he knew he'd have to check them.

Cody found, to his relief, that there was not much to see. Most of the caves were not big enough to be called caves, but rather were just deep gouges in the rock, reaching back only ten or twelve feet.

When he'd glanced into the last one, he decided he'd done his due diligence. It was already almost noon—this had taken longer than he'd planned—and the sun was radiating what felt like volcanic temperatures. He'd donned his bandana long ago to keep the sweat out of his eyes, and his food was completely gone. He had only a few swallows of warm water left in his second bottle.

Preparing to head back to his car, he glanced around to make sure he hadn't missed anything that might be important, and made mental notes of what to put in his report.

Then something caught his eye.

Though the southern and western rises had looked like two different formations, he could see from this high up they were connected. The mountain he was on fell away into a bridge of land that looped around and connected with the western rise on the opposite side than the one the camp site was on.

Wondering what could be seen from over there, he decided to take a quick look before heading back. He knew the highway was in that direction, though it was at least a couple of miles from the mountain's base. If there were other mountains in the way, he wouldn't be able to see it anyway; he was just curious.

He followed the bridge of land and found that it was a relatively easy route to the other side of the mountain. He scrambled over a few boulders and one fallen tree, but that was all.

When he reached the other side, he found that he *could* see the highway. It stretched across the distant horizon, a glimmering silver ribbon in the midday sun. He did a three-sixty, and saw the first strange thing he'd observed all day. Thirty yards above where he stood, five wooden planks were set up against a hole in the rock.

The hole looked like yet another cave-like gouge in the mountain's face. The planks made it reminiscent of how old, unused mining shafts were boarded up. Picking his way up to it, Cody found that the hole was a shaft and it was small—tiny, in fact.

Each plank was held in place by small stones around the base. The stones didn't give way immediately when Cody pulled on them. He had to dig the dirt out from around them and push them aside to remove one of the planks.

He ran his flashlight over the inside of the shaft. He doubted he'd even be able to sit up on his knees in there, much less stand. He'd have to pull himself along on his belly. He couldn't see how deep the shaft was. It stretched for twenty feet before disappearing around a curve to the right, and sloping slightly downward.

If, as the captain had half-heartedly theorized, this was the hideout of sexual predators, Cody supposed they might be willing to scoot along on their stomachs for a while if the shaft eventually opened into a larger chamber where they could go to do their twisted, masochistic rituals, but he doubted it.

Other than the campers, who were probably looking for some serious alone time and found it in the secluded little valley between the rises, he didn't think anyone had been out this way for years.

The idea of crawling into the bowels of a mountain on his belly, especially without knowing if the shaft was structurally sound, made him claustrophobic. And even if he wanted to, he didn't have the supplies for an adventure of that scope.

Cody replaced the plank, scooting the rocks up around it as before, and turned. Something else caught his eye.

Directly below him, a small pocket of land lay in the natural shadow of the mountain. He couldn't have seen it from where he was before; in fact, he couldn't have seen it from anywhere but the mouth of the unused shaft, which looked directly down on it.

Perhaps it was because the small, almost eerily square pocket of earth was in shadow, but the soil itself didn't look like desert. It was dark brown, almost black, as though it had a layer of the fertile topsoil on it. A line of tall, perfect tulips grew in two straight lines in the shadow of the mountain.

These, Cody knew, were not desert flowers. For them to be here was just . . . unnatural.

Though he wasn't feeling lightheaded, he thought perhaps the sun was getting to him and he was hallucinating the flowers. Taking out his water bottle, Cody chugged the last of the warm, fetid water. It tasted gritty, like he'd backwashed dirt into it at some point, but he didn't care.

After drinking the water, the flowers were still there, not ten feet below him. Skidding his way down the rock, he let his body slide over a small precipice that overlooked the bizarre flower garden. He hung by his fingers so that his feet dangled only five feet above the flowers, then dropped the rest of the way.

Falling into a crouch, he scooped up a handful of dirt. He was right; it was not parched dirt but soil, and it was wet, as though it had been recently watered. Cody looked around. Who was nurturing a garden this far out here? And with what? There was no hose, no irrigation system, not even a watering can, and no evidence that anyone had been here recently.

His eyes went to the boarded-up shaft. No one could be living in there, could they? A damp, slithering sensation crept into his middle.

He moved over to the nearest flower to examine it more closely. Now that he was looking, each tulip sprouted out of a small mound of dirt. All of them were a pale blue color that had looked white from a distance. Each had two perfectly shaped leaves that connected to an eighteen inch shaft where stem met soil.

Spinning on his toe to take in a full view of the place, Cody frowned. Painted in black on the inward-sloping wall below the boarded-up shaft were the words, *"Shakespeare's Girls."*

A soft, deep foreboding filled Cody's stomach, but he pushed it away. Bizarre, yes, but that was all.

Wondering why the flowers were planted in mounds, rather than flat earth, he stood. Cody was no gardening expert—far from it—but weren't tulips bulbs? Putting his foot down on top of the mound, next to the flower but not close enough to disturb it, he put his weight on it, stepping on top of the dirt mound.

The soil was soft and his foot sunk two inches. A sickening sensation radiated through him when he both felt and heard crunching beneath his boots. Whatever the mounds concealed, he was sure it wasn't rocks.

He hadn't brought any gloves—he hadn't thought to. Taking off his backpack, he scrounged around for something to cover his hand with. He only found the sandwich bag his food had been in. Deciding that would have to do, he stretched it over his hand and began digging at the mound of dirt. He only dug a little at a time, trying not to disturb the tulip.

Finally he reached something solid. It felt like sticks—thick twigs embedded in the ground. Soon he'd moved most of the dirt away, but still couldn't see it clearly. He leaned down and blew the excess soil off with one huffing breath. Then he sat back on his haunches and sighed, letting his head hang for a moment.

The white, carpal remains of a human hand glared up at him from its bed of dark soil, its fingers spread out as far as they could go. A skeleton was waving at him from the basement of a manmade oasis.

Cody looked at the other mounds: twelve of them, in two rows of six. He'd stumbled onto a mass grave in the middle of the desert.

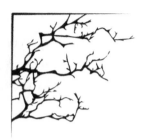

Chapter 6

ALEX HAD BEEN HOLDING her cell phone to her ear for so long that her arm was beginning to ache. She wanted to strangle the lady that kept telling her that her call was important and to please stay on the line.

She'd been watching the news for hours, long enough that everything they had on the mass grave found in Southern Utah had repeated several times. Though the police had released no statements yet, the reporters were musing that so many victims going missing in one place would have been noticed, so they must have been snatched from various places and brought from afar.

Snatched off the highway, perhaps? *Alex thought.*

The instant Alex saw it, she knew. She hadn't stopped thinking about that night since it happened four years ago—not completely. She'd always been certain something strange was going on. Now, four years later this news report stated that twelve bodies had been found not far from where she'd been pulled over.

The local community was banding together to try and catch the killer. The police were insisting that the hills be searched by professionals—both because they were worried the killer might be hiding under some rock out there, and because they didn't want civilians who didn't know any better trampling potential crime scenes. None of the victims had been killed where they were buried.

Instead, the local volunteers made signs, got the media involved, brought in meals for the local police—which were more numerous than normal, as reinforcements from other jurisdictions had been brought in to pick up the grunge work—and they set up a tip line.

Alex had been on hold with the tip line for more than an hour. According to the news, tips were rolling in by the thousands. Everyone who ever had a loved one go missing, and thought they might have passed through that part of the desert, was tying up the line, trying to speak with the detectives. The detectives weren't speaking to anyone calling in. They were following leads recorded from the tip line and assuring people that as soon as autopsies had been completed and DNA profiled, the families of the victims would be notified.

Then she saw him.

She let the phone drop from her ear and leaned forward so that she was inches from her parents' LCD flat screen.

That was him; she was sure of it. The same cop she'd talked to that night kept walking across the screen. She couldn't remember his name, and he looked different than she remembered. His hair was longer in back, his face more weathered, and a jagged scar reached across his right eyebrow and over the upper part of his right cheek. She was certain he hadn't had that the last time she'd seen him, brief though their meeting had been.

The reporters tried to get his attention, tried to get a quote from him. A spokesperson for the department finally stepped forward, assuring the reporters that a press conference would be held as soon as possible, but that the detectives were making no statements at this time.

So, he was a detective now. With a sigh, Alex looked down at her phone and made a decision.

"Your call is very important to us. Please stay on the—"

Sure it is, she thought. *Which is why I've been on hold for an hour.* Alex clicked the PWR/END button on her phone and got up from the couch. Her mother watched with anxious eyes from the loveseat four feet away.

"Alex," Deirdra Thompson's voice was wary. "Where are you going?"

She knew her mother would object, but she just couldn't sit around anymore. "I've been waiting almost ninety minutes, Mom."

"They'll get to you eventually," her mother muttered, but Alex ignored her.

Alex pointed to the man on the TV screen. "See him?"

Her mother glanced at the screen, but Alex doubted she really saw the detective.

"He's the cop I filed the report with."

Her mother's eyes widened and darted to the television screen. "Really? But I thought you said he was just some amateur uniform."

"He was, but that was four years ago. Things change. If I can talk to him, I think he'll remember me." She started for the stairs.

"How are you going to talk to him if you don't stay on the tip line?"

"That's just it, Mom. The detectives aren't talking to anyone on the tip line. Volunteers write down what you say and pass it on to the cops."

"Then what are you going to do?"

By now, Alex was calling over her shoulder on her way up the stairs. "I'm going to drive down there and find him."

She heard her mother's gasp from behind her and, as she entered her own room, the unmistakable stomp of her mother coming up the stairs.

Alex grabbed her duffel bag from its usual place hanging behind the door. She yanked out stale gym shorts and dumbbells, replacing them with clean clothes, toiletries, and her MP3 player. She also tucked in a couple of books and her wallet. She'd moved back in with her parents a few months ago when her mother's health had taken a turn for the worse. With her father traveling as much as he did for work, it was just better for someone to be around to help. Yet, Alex worked so much that a dozen unpacked boxes still leaned against the far wall, waiting to be dealt with.

She was almost done packing when her mother finally huffed into view.

"You aren't supposed to be going up and down the stairs, Mom. Your hip will act up."

"Don't really," Dierdra panted, "give me much . . . choice, Alex. You just . . . walked away."

Alex glanced patiently at her mother while putting her travel bag together. Her mom leaned over, bracing herself on her knees and catching her breath. Alex knew as soon as she could, her mother was going to give her best lecture.

"Alex," she finally said, "I don't want you going down there. I don't want you mixed up in this."

"I'm not going to get mixed up in anything, Mom. I'm just going to tell them what I saw."

"You already did that. You filed a report two hours after it happened!"

"That was four years ago." Alex stuffed three rolls of socks in beside her intimates. "What are the chances anyone will remember or dig it up again?"

"Don't you think they'll be looking into old reports of the area?"

"Maybe. But even so, it could be weeks before they find it. And what if whoever looks at it passes over it, decides it's not relevant?"

"They're the cops, Alex. We should let them decide what's relevant. You don't even know if your experience has anything to do with this."

Alex zipped the duffel bag up, then stared at her fingers drumming on the top of it, trying to figure out how to explain what she was feeling to her mother.

"No, Mom," she said calmly, "*you* don't know that my experience has anything to do with this grave. *I* do."

Her mother gave her a scathing look.

"Come on, Mom. I've been talking about it on and off for four years. You know how disturbed I was by it. I was sure something sinister was going on, but I couldn't prove it or do anything about it. Now, seeing this . . . I feel like there's a connection. I could be wrong, but I have to go down there and talk to someone—to ease my conscience, if nothing else. I promise, all I'll do is tell them about what happened, make sure they pull the old report, and then I'll let them take it from there, okay?"

The duffel bag was packed to the rafters, making it difficult to keep up on her shoulder, but Alex tried anyway. Her phone was on the desk. She snatched it up along with her keys.

"Will you be okay by yourself here tonight?" Alex asked her mom. "Dad's flight comes in tomorrow morning, but Tony's picking him up. He should be back by ten or eleven. I can have Mrs. Drescher come stay with you tonight if you want. She said if I got a gig, she would."

Deirdra shook her head. "No, I'll be fine. But I may just sit up all night worrying about you."

Alex smiled and then reached over to hug her mom. "Don't do that. I'll be fine, too. I'll call you when I get there. I'll probably end up staying in a motel overnight, but if I can get in to speak with someone right away, I'll be able to drive back tomorrow. This is just something I have to do."

After a moment, her mother nodded, though she still looked far from pleased. "All right, then. Let me make you some food for the road."

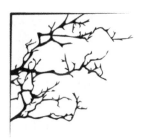

Chapter 7

LARS STIEGER SIGHED, trying to decide what to do. He'd been trying to speak with the lead detective on the case—Oliver was his name—for two days now. It just wasn't happening. He wondered if he could get the man's home address. He supposed it wouldn't be hard; he was a PI after all, but perhaps it would be easier to simply wait until midnight and then approach the police station. In his experience on the job, cases like this kept their detectives up into the wee hours most nights.

Stieger wanted to go through the county records. The bodies were found in the middle of uninhabited desert and Stieger was curious about the history of that land. Did it mean something to the killer? Why did he choose it for the grave site?

It wasn't that Stieger needed permission to look through the records—he had no problem taking the initiative and doing it himself—but he wanted to be sure no one else was. That would just be wasted effort.

He supposed he could inquire at the records office if anyone else had looked through them. At least he would have something to do, and something to report to Claire.

With that in mind, Stieger jammed a baseball cap on top of his salt and pepper hair, donned a pair of sunglasses, and got in his car.

As he made his way through the crowded streets of downtown Mt. Dessicate, he took in details, storing them up for future use. As a PI, details were often the most important part of his work. Cases were made or broken based on the nuances of life. Mt. Dessicate looked very different than he remembered. The last time he'd visited had been nearly ten years earlier, and of course all the press and extra uniforms were absent then. Still, Mt. Dessicate was growing, not by leaps and bounds, but a little at a time. If the growth continued at this slow and steady rate, Mt. Dessicate might be a metropolis in its own right in another twenty years.

At his last visit, there'd been a sheriff and his deputies. Now there was a department with detectives. That alone was evidence of the population growth.

Ten years ago—it didn't seem like it had been that long. They were saying that this desert predator may have been operating for several decades, which meant that the last time Stieger had visited the small town, the killer was already pulling people off the highway. The thought made him shudder. Thirty-five years in law enforcement didn't give a man immunity from monsters.

The courthouse was larger than Stieger would have expected for a county this rural. Once inside, he realized it doubled as the only public school around. Kindergarten through twelfth grade met in one of four classrooms. A playground and sandbox were out back, and a multi-purpose room served as lunch room, assembly hall, and gymnasium. A small, stuffy-looking courtroom occupied an entire wing of the building, while the record office shared a room with a pathetic school library.

On his way out of town, Lars had picked up a box of donuts, wolfing down one of the custard bismarks in two mouthfuls. He left the rest of the box untouched. As he approached the receptionist in the courthouse, he hid the donuts under his coat.

The woman behind the counter was middle-aged. White streaks weaved through her brunette hair, and small half-moon spectacles rested on her nose. She smiled politely when Lars leaned against the counter, but the smile seemed strained.

"May I help you?"

"I hope so, ma'am. I need access to your county property records."

The woman, whose name tag read, "Helga," eyed him suspiciously. "You investigatin' that business that's been all over the news? Those skeletons found in the desert there?"

"I'm part of that investigation, yes, but I'm only looking into one lead of many. Could you show me to where I can find the information I need?" He *was* investigating that case, so it wasn't a complete lie. He just hoped she didn't call the Mt. Dessicate Police to check and see if they had a man going through county records.

The woman made no move to help him. "Don't suppose you have a warrant now?"

Lars smiled. "No, ma'am. Past property ownership is a matter of public record. I don't need a warrant, just directions."

The woman looked like she'd just swallowed a sour plum, but she came out from behind the counter. "Follow me."

Helga was a small, plump woman who waddled crookedly as she walked. Her shoes had toothpick heels that ticked out a muffled staccato, even on carpet, as they went.

"Has anyone else investigating this case asked to look at any records?" he asked as they walked.

"No."

She showed him where the records were kept, and pointed to a card catalog for references. Lars sighed. He supposed he shouldn't have expected a dusty, rural county like this to be on the cutting edge of technology.

"Ma'am?" She'd started back toward the lobby, and when he called she turned slowly, as though she couldn't believe he had another question. "I was hungry this morning and picked up a box of donuts on my way. One was enough for the sugar fix I needed, though, so if you want to set this out in the lobby for any hungry employees, you're all welcome to them."

She walked up beside him and looked down her nose at the full box. After a moment, she took it from him. "Know how to butter up county employees, eh?"

He grinned at her. "Yes, ma'am."

She tried to look stern, but her mouth was turning up a bit at the corners. "I'll be at my desk if you need anything."

"Don't think I will for a while, ma'am, but thank you."

She gave him the scantest of smiles before turning to go. After she was out of his sight, he could hear the flapping of the plastic-and-cardboard box as she opened it in the hall.

Lars smiled to himself as he turned to the records. Worked like a charm.

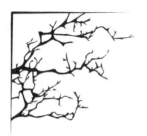

Chapter 8

THE DRIVE SOUTH WAS long and boring. Despite leaving at ten in the morning, Alex didn't make it to Mt. Dessicate until after four.

The town used to be sleepy, but now it was hopping with activity. Dozens of police cruisers lined the streets, all with the names of different cities painted on their sides. Mt. Dessicate had called in help from nearly every jurisdiction in the state. The natives were outside their houses, despite the scorching July heat, chatting over fences and pointing at all the alien things that had shown up in their small city in the last forty-eight hours.

Every parking lot, curb, and red zone was filled with cars from all over the country. Alex saw a lot of license plates from neighboring states—Nevada, Idaho, Colorado, New Mexico—but then there were some from up north and even a few as far away as Georgia and Ohio. These were the people who were hoping or fearing—perhaps a little of both—to find word of their lost loved ones among the victims of the mass grave.

Of course there were reporters on every curb, hoping to corner a cop or get a quote from a grieving family member.

Alex drove around for twenty minutes before finding a parking space in front of a general store. She noticed several cart boys scanning each car that entered the lot suspiciously. It occurred to her that perhaps they were ticketing non-customers who were parking here.

Pulling a smaller purse from the backseat of her car, and putting her wallet inside, she walked into the store, swinging her purse ostentatiously. For honesty's sake, she bought a soda and a candy bar, making sure to pocket the receipt for later, and then slipped inconspicuously out the side door, making sure the boys didn't see her leave.

She glanced back and saw a huge black truck parked in the spot next to hers, completely obscuring her car from the cart boys' views. Hopefully that would buy her enough time to find the detective and get back without being cited.

She walked around downtown Mt. Dessicate—which was smaller than the smallest suburbs up north—for another fifteen minutes before locating the police station. The massive sprawl of squad cars and uniformed officers made it difficult to pinpoint the central hub.

Finally she arrived at the police station, only to find a human, blue-uniformed barricade had been set up in front of the main doors. It was probably to keep the media from entering the station, but Alex was suddenly not sure she would be able to get in.

She approached one of the uniforms. He was tall and lean, Caucasian, but with a large, square jaw reminiscent of Native Americans, and chocolate-brown eyes. He might have been handsome if not for the resemblance to a horse Alex once met.

"I'm not a member of the press," she said quickly. "I just need to get inside."

The suspicion didn't leave his eyes. "Who are you? A cop?"

"No, but I need to talk to one of the detectives. I've spoken with him before and have some urgent information for him."

The cop looked indecisive. "Is this about the Shakespeare case?"

"What?"

"The mass grave they found."

Alex didn't answer right away. Something told her that if she said yes, he wouldn't let her in. Her silence was enough, though, and he shook his head.

"You'll have to speak with the tip line." He pointed down the street to his left. "Second building down, the one with the big white pillars. That's where the tips are being processed. Most are on the phone, but I'm sure someone in there can take your information down and pass it along. I can't let you in the station, ma'am."

Alex sighed. She would rather talk to that detective than to a civilian volunteer, but she supposed she wouldn't get anywhere by putting up a stink. She thanked the man and went in the direction he'd pointed. As she passed the station, she noticed a narrow alley that ran along its left side. She glanced back at the man who'd directed her, but he'd moved on to the next hopeful trying to get into the station.

Alex ducked into the alley, wondering why the press wasn't all over this crevice.

When she got to the end of the alley, she understood why. Two heavy metal doors bridged the station to the alley, but neither had knobs on the outside, so they were either service exits for the night crew—or the type of alarmed doors only used in emergencies.

Alex walked to the back of the alley, but it didn't extend around to the back of the structure, instead dead-ending after running the length of the building. With a sigh, Alex turned and headed back in the direction of the street. Just as she reached the two double doors again, one of them opened, and two men walked out. She was walking close to the building, and they turned for the street, not noticing her.

Knowing this was perhaps her only chance to get into the station, Alex ran as quickly and silently as she could, praying the two men wouldn't turn and see her. She caught the door just before it shut. Its weight slammed heavily against her fingers, and it was all she could do not to cry out. She pulled the door carefully back out and managed to slip inside just as the two men turned onto the street.

Alex found herself at the end of a skinny corridor that had half a dozen personal offices attached on either side. The air-conditioned interior was a relief. Not wanting to speak with any bureaucrats, she hurried past the offices, not even glancing to the side to see which ones were occupied.

Exiting the corridor, she found herself in the lobby of the tiny police station. Despite having been there before, it was hard to recognize the interior of the structure. It had been quiet, sparse, and uncluttered the last time; now it reminded her of the central office of a political campaign.

People in temporary work spaces were packed cheek by jowl, and all of them seemed to be in an inordinate hurry to do something. Phones rang, people ran or power-walked zigzags across the room, others shouted to coworkers who were across the building. There were only enough computers for half the people in the room, and everyone was sharing—a.k.a. fighting—over them.

Amidst the chaos, no one noticed when Alex entered from the corridor. Wondering who to speak to, and understanding why the tip line was necessary, Alex soon located the building's front desk. It was hidden under papers, boxes of files, messages, and a dozen phones, and surrounded by desks and busy people.

Alex found a void in the smaller desks where she could approach the large one. She thought the short, plump woman behind the desk might have been the same one who had worked the night shift when she filed her report four years ago, but she couldn't be sure.

"Excuse me, could you—"

"You'll have to give me a minute, honey."

The woman, whose nametag read Rose Mitchell, had gathered up an armload of manila file folders and practically ran out from behind her desk with them.

Alex blew out her breath and rested her arms on the counter. Five full minutes passed and Rose still hadn't returned. Alex didn't know what to do besides wait. She was sure if she tried to go anywhere, she'd be trampled.

Out of the corner of her eye, she saw someone walk by on the other side of the desk, but didn't pay any attention. She was keeping her eyes peeled for any sign of Rose. A moment later, she realized the person was still standing there, and turned her head to look at him.

The detective from the news, the same one she'd spoken to four years ago, was staring at her. He was mercifully carrying only two file boxes, rather than the four that seemed to be the rule here, and looking at her like a puzzle he couldn't figure out.

When she looked at him, he came toward her.

"Do I know you?"

She smiled briefly, surprised he had some recollection of her.

"No, but we had occasion to meet about four years ago." When he didn't answer, she went on, telling herself to look at his eyes rather than his scar. "Actually, you're the person I came in here looking for. I just didn't think I'd actually be able to speak with you."

He set his boxes down on the desk that was between them. "*Who* are you?"

Alex stuck her right hand out. "Alex Thompson."

He shook her hand, but still looked confused.

"I drove through your town, filed a report in the middle of the night." His brow was furrowed. "I had been pulled over, but thought the cop was acting strange? Ringing any bells?"

He was still staring blankly at her. Finally he shook his head. "I can't say I remember the incident, but you look very familiar to me."

"Look." Alex leaned on the counter again. "I know the detectives aren't supposed to take tips, except from the hotline, but I'd really love to speak with you. It won't take more than five minutes. If now isn't a good time, I can come back later today or tomorrow?"

"You have a tip about *this* case?"

"What happened to me that night, the thing I filed the report about, may be related."

It was then that Rose came back to the desk and heard Alex's last statement.

"If you have a tip, the building you're looking for is down the street, honey. You aren't supposed to be in here."

Alex sighed. "I know."

Rose frowned. "You *know?*"

Alex put her hands up. "I've been trying to call the tip line, but there are so many I can't get through. I was on hold for more than an hour this morning, so I just drove down instead."

The detective's eyes widened, but whether because he was impressed or annoyed, she couldn't have said.

"Even if I go through the tip line, it could take weeks before anyone gets to mine, and I feel very strongly that this may have something to do with your case."

Rose was shaking her head. "I'm sorry, but we can't just—"

"Rose."

Rose stopped and turned surprised eyes on the detective.

"It's fine. I'll speak with her."

Rose opened her mouth to protest, but he talked over her.

"I know we can't do it for everyone, but she's here now. It'll only take a few minutes."

After a moment, Rose looked Alex up and down, then shrugged. "Whatever."

After hours of work, Lars leaned back and rubbed his eyes. A visit to the john would reveal shrunken pupils and red streaks, he was sure. That was one problem with looking through county records: hours of work and burning eyes could get results, but they were small potatoes. With these kinds of records, the information payoff wasn't worth the weight and time of the work, but that didn't change the fact that the research had to be done.

Lars had found some intriguing things, even if they didn't give him a complete picture.

The land south of Mt. Dessicate on which the mass grave had been found was owned by the county, and had been for decades.

The last time it had been sold to a private owner was in 1946, to a man named Alastair Landes. Lars couldn't find any records for Landes or his family before that year. From what he could tell, Landes simply showed up in town, picked a spot, bought some land, and began a life for himself. He'd started a ranch and been a profitable, upstanding man for the next decade and a half. After that, Lars found a number of liens that had been put against the man's house for non-payment of property tax. Landes always redeemed the lien long before he lost the property, but obviously he'd had some troubled years.

The property records couldn't tell Lars much else, except that an heir had been listed when Landes died who could have claimed the parcel but never did. There might be any number of reasons for that.

Lars's next foray was into the birth and death records.

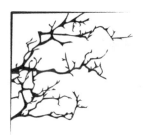

Chapter 9

THE DETECTIVE DIRECTED Alex around the main desk and through the obstacle course the lobby had become. He took her to a quiet back-room office. His desk was part of a group of four that all faced one another. Every patch of space was covered with more boxes.

With a quick apology, he moved two boxes from a sliding chair, stacking them atop four more against the wall, and ushered her into the seat. He then took the one vacant chair behind the desk.

When he turned, looking for something amidst the clutter of his desk, Alex nudged one of the many folders aside so she could see his nameplate. Cody Oliver. Grateful she wouldn't have to ask, she waited patiently for him to get to her.

"So." He finally turned his navy-blue eyes on her. "You passed through here and filed a report a few years ago?"

"Four years ago, yes."

"And you say I'm the one you talked to?"

"Yes. You still don't remember me?"

He smiled apologetically. "Afraid not. I just saw you out there and knew I'd seen you before. Do you remember the date the report was filed on?"

"March sixteenth."

His eyebrows went up. "You seem quite certain of that."

Alex nodded. "It was a red-letter day for me. There was a specific reason I was passing through your town that day."

When she didn't elaborate, he smiled. "Is the reason important to the case? Was it part of the report you filed?"

She shook her head. "No, just a family thing, but I do remember the date very specifically."

He seemed to accept that. "Well, that will make it easy to pull the report. Can you tell me in a nutshell what happened?"

Alex leaned forward, making sure to look him straight in the eye. She needed him to believe what she was saying and feel the urgency she felt about it.

"I was pulled over out on the highway. The officer acted weird. It wasn't anything concrete, just a strong feeling I had that something sinister was going on."

"Did you feel threatened?"

"Yes, very much so. I kept thinking he would try to . . . do something to me. He never did, but I definitely felt afraid."

He remained silent, face unreadable, and Alex remembered all too well what his objections had been four years ago.

"I'm sorry," she found herself needing to explain, "I know it was just a gut feeling, but I really felt like—"

He held up his hands to stop her. "Please, there's no need to explain, and no need to apologize for a feeling. I believe you."

Alex sat back in her seat, taken by surprise at the completely opposite reaction from what he'd given last time. The scar was not the only thing the years had changed about him.

"All right." He stood. "Why don't you sit tight, and I'll go try and pull that report?" He gave her a sheepish grin. "You'll have to excuse our computer system. It's pretty ancient, and I can't access reports that are more than twelve months old from this computer."

Alex nodded, and Detective Oliver gathered up what seemed to her were random papers, before heading out the door. Then he stuck his head back in.

"You want something to drink? Soda?"

Alex's throat was parched raw from the heat outside. "Do you have bottled water?"

"Sure, coming right up." He gave her a toothy grin.

While waiting for him to come back, Alex thought about where she'd stay for the night. She probably should have gotten a hotel room before coming here, but she'd been too anxious to talk to someone.

Suddenly it occurred to her that the small town was full of visitors from other places—far more than it was used to—and a town this size wasn't likely to have many places to stay to begin with. It wasn't exactly a tourist attraction.

A short search ended with Alex flipping through a local phonebook from one of the adjoining desks. The list of motels was alarmingly short—and no hotels. She pulled out her cell phone and called four of them before finding one with a vacancy, but she managed to secure a room without any trouble.

Heaving a breath of relief, Alex looked around the police station. Each of the four desks held photos with distinctly different people in them, so she assumed each desk belonged to a different person—different detectives, perhaps?

Cody's desk held only two photos. One was of him with two middle-aged people. Cody had the woman's shape of face and hair color, but he unmistakably shared eyes with the man. Alex decided they must be his parents.

The second photo showed a teenaged Cody with his arm around a man in a police uniform. Alex wondered who'd been the idol in Cody's life that prompted him to join the police force.

"Hey Cody, did you ever find that file from Salina—oh." A stocky man with chestnut hair came in and noticed her. A mischievous grin slid onto his face. "You're not Cody."

Alex smiled. "No. He stepped out for a minute."

"Mmm." The man came over and rummaged around in the desk next to Cody's. The nameplate on the desk read Frank Dannel. "Do you know where he went?"

"He's looking for a report. Said he can't pull any older than twelve months from this computer."

Frank grinned at her, his eyes twinkling. "How old?"

"Four years."

Frank thought for a moment. "That'd be the east-wall computer. Thanks!"

He bounded from the room. Alex chuckled.

In all, it was more than twenty minutes before Cody returned.

"Found it," he said as he sat down.

"Did Frank find you?"

The detective looked worried. "Frank talked to you?" His voice was wary.

"He was looking for you. He seemed to know where to find you, but . . ."

Cody waved his hand dismissively. "He probably got distracted. There are a lot of pretty women in the lobby he's never met before."

Alex laughed softly, and Cody grinned.

"So, I read through this, and I do remember it now. Vaguely." He set the report down and leaned back in his chair, looking straight at her, as she had at him earlier. "I seem to remember not being very nice to you."

Alex shrugged. "I think we'd both had a long night."

Cody nodded. "Still, that was no excuse. I apologize for it."

"I appreciate that."

"Why do you think this guy had anything to do with these murders?"

"I can't be certain of anything. I know something weird was going on with him. I felt like he meant me harm. And I know it happened—that is, I was pulled over—less than a quarter of a mile from where you found those graves."

Cody's head snapped up. "What? How do you know that?"

"They showed a map on the news of where the graves were found. It was roughly a quarter mile from that historical landmark you have out there. I was pulled over right next to that."

Cody looked troubled. He skimmed the report again. After that he straightened, staring at nothing and thinking. Alex watched him, but didn't interrupt his thought process, willing him to decide to investigate her lead.

When he nodded, it was more to himself than to her. His eyes focused on her again.

"I know we have *this* report, but it's old. We may need to take a new statement from you. Would you allow us to do that?"

"Of course."

"I'd also like to bring my captain in to hear what you have say, if that's all right with you."

Hope swelled in Alex's chest. "You think this could be important."

Cody studied the clutter on the desk in front of him. He seemed to be choosing his words carefully. "I think it's too much of a coincidence to dismiss." He looked up at her and smiled. "It's like you said: there's no way to tell. It might be nothing, but I'd rather be certain. And I'd like to get my captain's input."

Alex nodded.

Cody stood again. "I need to get some things and . . . people together. It may take a few minutes. I apologize for the wait. Can you bear with me?"

"Of course. It's fine."

When he hurried from the room once more, Alex practically slumped in her chair with relief. For the first time in two days, her thoughts turned to happier things. She'd talk to his captain, give her statement, get plenty of sleep in the motel, and then head back to her mother tomorrow, with her conscience finally cleared after four years.

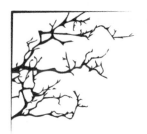

Chapter 10

AS EVENING GAVE WAY to dusk, Lars went to the bathroom to splash water on his face. So much reading was making him sleepy, and he was willing to wager that the courthouse would shut down with the sun, which didn't give him much time.

A more complete picture of the Landes family was emerging,

Alastair Landes had married a local woman in 1948, two years after buying his ranch. Her name was Gertrude Alder. These were the years when Landes paid his taxes and was profitable, so, on paper at least, the marriage seemed to be a happy one. Their first child wasn't born until 1957, which in a time when birth control was only just coming onto the market and most religious folk considered it a sin, bespoke fertility problems in the marriage. Still, a son named Jonathin Landes was born in '57. Lars noted the odd spelling of the first name, but that could have been due to the illiteracy of the times.

Sadly, Gertrude died in childbirth, or perhaps a few days after. The death certificate was dated three days after Jonathin's birth certificate. It was in the next few years that liens began appearing against the property. Lars wondered if the negligence was more due to emotional problems than financial ones. A sad tale.

Oddly, Lars could find no record that Alastair's son, Jonathin, had ever bought, sold, or held any property in the county. He never seemed to have held a job or made any purchases that would leave a paper trail. Granted, when Jonathin reached adulthood, it would only have been the mid-seventies, which meant that most transactions—and even most jobs—were paid in cash. Still, the lack of records, coupled with the fact that Jonathin never laid claim to the substantial property after his father's death, made Lars believe that perhaps Jonathin had died as a young man.

But there was no death certificate. There were no records at all. Jonathin was born; his father had some financial difficulties; and by the time of Alastair's death in the late eighties, all sign of Jonathin had simply faded away.

There could be many explanations. Jonathin might have moved away to make his fortune. Perhaps he and his father had a falling out. Jonathin might have left and simply never returned, never knowing of his father's death or the property he could have claimed. A more extensive search would be required to see if Jonathin Landes was still alive somewhere.

Lars leaned back to consider. Jonathin was born in '57. If he was still alive, he'd be in his mid-fifties today. Still young enough to manage a sadistic operation like the one out in the desert? Perhaps. It would depend on the man's health, but it wasn't implausible. The Vampire of Brooklyn had operated well into his eighties before being caught. Granted, that was snatching helpless children, not grown women out of cars on the highway, but still.

Helga stuck her head in the door. "We're closing in fifteen minutes. I expect each of those records to find its home before then."

"Yes, ma'am. Say, Helga?"

Her head had disappeared, but popped back into view when he called. She seemed considerably less grouchy than she had this morning, but then closing time was in fifteen minutes, so that might have accounted for it.

"Do you by any chance remember a family by the name of Landes?"

The rest of Helga's plump body appeared as she meandered into the room, eyes on the wall while she thought. "First names?"

"Father was Alastair. Looks like he died in '87. Might have had a son named Jonathin."

"The family name sounds familiar to me, but I don't know anything about them."

Lars nodded. "Well, thank you anyway. Is there anyone you could point me to in town that might remember more?"

Helga regarded him suspiciously for a moment before shrugging. "You been to the bar on the corner a block down?"

"I passed it on my way here."

"There's a gaggle of old timers who frequent it. They smoke their cigars and drink their beers and reminisce—you know the type. Most of them set up shop in Mt. Dessicate about the time the dinosaurs went AWOL. They may be able to tell you something. But"—she wagged an index finger at him—"I didn't send you, you hear? They won't appreciate an investigator pestering them with questions, so leave me out of it."

"They're a tough group, eh?"

"Yes. It may be hard to get anythin' out of them."

Lars sighed. *Great.* "Any suggestions?"

"Got any more donuts?"

Lars grinned. "That depends, Helga. Have *you* got any more donuts?"

Helga put her nose in the air and sniffed loudly. "*Everything* had better be put away before you leave, or I won't be so nice next time."

With that, she spun and marched crookedly from the room.

FROM HIGH ATOP THE mountain, the Artist chewed his non-existent fingernails with worry. Though he was too far away and too high up to be seen, he had a clear view of what was happening several miles over. He wasn't sure what they'd found—probably bodies, but then old Mudface didn't keep him informed, so it was hard to be sure. If they began roving searches of these mountains, they could find him. They could expose the entire thing.

Despite his fear for his daughter, that was exactly what the Artist wanted. To be free, to see her again after all these years. He closed his eyes and let the immortal line run through his mind.

'Tis a consummation devoutly to be wished. To die, to sleep . . .

No! Perhaps not. If the police could find him, could do this right, without getting everyone killed, he might actually have some hope of rescue.

For the first time since this entire thing began—so long ago now—he didn't long for death.

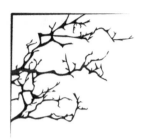

Chapter 11

ALEX WAS IN THE PRECINCT for another two hours. She met with the police captain and was introduced to the other detectives. They took a second statement, compared it with the first, and asked her endless questions.

Before she left, they asked her to stay in town for a day or two while they checked out her lead, just in case they had any follow-up questions.

Her mother wouldn't be pleased, but Alex agreed. She'd made the decision to travel to Mt. Dessicate; now she'd have to deal with the inconvenience.

It was getting dark when they finally released her, taking her cell phone number, as well as the name of her motel, and telling her they'd be in touch. Cody walked her out. "We'll try to get you on your way as soon as possible. Unfortunately, with as many leads as are pouring in, this may take a little bit of time."

"I understand. I'm not in any particular hurry to get home. I just want to make sure this gets checked out."

"No husband or job?" He grinned, and she could tell he was teasing her.

"No husband, but I'm a freelance photographer. I have a job lined up early next week." She pretended to look stern. "So you definitely don't have me longer than that."

"Fair enough. Where's your car?"

"A general store two blocks down."

Cody winced. "They may cite you for that."

"I went into the store and bought something. I'm hoping they think I'm still in there."

Cody grinned. "Good luck."

She asked for directions to the motel she was staying at. He gave them, cautioning her to watch out for lost pedestrians. When she laughed, he raised an eyebrow.

"Detective, I've taken jobs from L.A. to New York and everywhere in between. Trust me: the biggest cities are *way* more congested than your little town here, even with all its extra visitors."

He quirked a smile and nodded. "Well, it's getting dark, so be careful anyway. And you may as well call me Cody. Get some rest. I'll call you when I know anything."

She thanked him and headed down the street.

The motel turned out to be middle-of-the-road. It wasn't up-scale, by any means, but it wasn't of the flea bag variety either. Alex was just glad to find somewhere clean.

She knew she ought to find something to eat, but she was exhausted, and the heat was suppressing her appetite. Kicking off her shoes and flopping onto the bed, she picked up the remote. Two full cycles through the channels—and there weren't very many—showed absolutely *nothing* on TV.

With a sigh, she clicked off the twenty-pound television set. Deciding that fourteen hours' sleep was exactly what she needed, she pulled a pillow out from under the comforter, curled up, and, without bothering to undress or get under the covers, fell asleep.

The dream was one she hadn't had in years. In it, she sat in a cold, red room crying. Bone-chilling screams could be heard from beyond the walls, and a deep voice—that of a man, she thought—wailed and begged for mercy from the room adjacent. She couldn't see the man or tell what he was saying, but she pictured a kindly face crying, while the more feminine shrieks sounded from unknown, ubiquitous places.

In the dream, she always shut her eyes and clasped hands over her ears, but the screams and the man's wails only became louder. Then she would get a whiff of something she couldn't identify. It had a sickly-sweet odor, like fruit just beginning to putrefy, but it scared her more than the screams did. She smelled the odor and startled so violently that she woke herself up.

Alex kicked awake from atop the motel comforter. Her hand was hanging over the side of the bed, and she knocked her knuckles hard into the bedside table. Groaning at her own stupidity, she pulled the aching hand into her stomach as she rolled herself upright.

Sitting up was like pushing through a veil. Her dream immediately faded. She'd had disturbing dreams on and off her entire life, but she usually couldn't remember the details upon waking. She'd often wondered if they had to do with the time of her life before memory had taken hold, with her biological parents, but her waking self never had much desire to pursue the subject.

She thought she'd fallen asleep around 9:30 and it was now just after eleven. She knew she ought to rest, but the ninety-minute interval felt like a power nap, and she wasn't tired. The dream left a yoke of fear over her, and she was afraid of dreaming it again.

She swung her legs over the side of the bed. The hotel room was too quiet, foreboding in its solitary shadows. Deciding that a midnight drive with the cool desert air was just what she needed, Alex grabbed her car and room keys and headed out the door. Having a purpose made her feel better, and by the time she reached her car, the oppressive pall of the nightmare was gone.

Being the middle of July, the air in the desert was not as cool as Alex would have hoped, but it was refreshing nonetheless. She took the same highway out of town that she'd taken in. It was the one that ran right through the center of Mt. Dessicate—the same one she'd been pulled over on that night, come to think of it. Though she was going in the opposite direction, Alex identified the historical landmark as she passed it. A chill went down her spine, but she put the memory from her mind.

The cool air, empty road, and solitary blackness of the desert soothed her nerves. After half an hour, she decided to head back. She wasn't ready to sleep yet, but she was getting there, and she didn't want to become exhausted and still have an hour's drive ahead of her.

It wasn't difficult to do a U-turn, as there were no other cars on the highway, and as she headed back, she told herself that she was fine and would be able to sleep now.

She passed the historical landmark once again, and wondered vaguely how she would react if cop lights appeared in her rearview mirror. Chuckling to herself about her own neuroses, Alex pushed down on the accelerator.

It was then, with a deafening pop and sickening jolt, that one of her tires blew out.

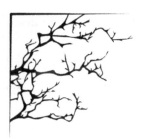

Chapter 12

"SO JONATHIN DIDN'T die as a child or a young man?" Stieger asked.

Ronnie Martin, a white-haired man with striking dark eyes and a spare tire around the middle, shrugged. "Lived to be at least seventeen."

"What happened after seventeen?"

Ronnie gave Stieger a conspiratorial smile. "That there's the question, isn't it?"

Stieger smiled indulgently. Ronnie had stories to tell—boy did he ever—and obviously he seldom got to tell them to anyone who hadn't already heard them a hundred times, so Stieger let him ramble. Stieger hadn't been a patient man in his youth, but age and PI work had taught him better. Patience always got the payoff.

It was getting late but it was a weeknight and the bar wasn't busy.

"They say"—Ronnie set his empty beer mug down on the bar and went on without any urging—"that Jonathin and Alastair had a fallin' out."

"What kind of falling out?"

Ronnie shrugged. "Who's to say? Alastair 'as a mean old cuss and he and his son didn't get along." Ronnie leaned forward and dropped his voice to a whisper. "When Jonathin up and disappeared, lots o' people said Alastair might've flown into a rage and killed his son."

"Isn't it possible that father and son had a disagreement, and Jonathin simply left home—struck out on his own?"

Ronnie leaned back, resuming his normal voice and looking disappointed. "Yeah, I guess that's a possibility, too. Actually, a few people say they sawed him marchin' out o' town, knapsack over one shoulder and wearin' his best hikin' boots."

Stieger took a draw on his beer to hide a smile. Despite the macabre excavation going on in the desert, the truth was generally less juicy than local gossips liked to believe. So Jonathin had left town, which explained why he never owned land here and—if he had passed—why there was no death certificate for him in the county records.

Stieger glanced down the bar. A middle-aged woman with rumpled clothes and greying hair pulled back into a loose bun was watching them. She'd been watching and listening since Stieger had first started talking to Ronnie. A fit, thirty-something bartender polished glasses behind the counter. He was listening, too.

"Still," Ronnie persisted, "it was odd that people saw him leavin' town, but no one saw him after that."

"Why is that odd?"

"Well more people *should've* seen him. There was farm houses he'd have to pass, goin' that way, people goin' in and out of town." He leaned forward again. "Folks said maybe he tried to leave, but never got far. Maybe Alastair couldn't stand the thought o' his son tryin' to leave him. Maybe Jonathin's ghost haunts the old Landes farmhouse to this day."

Stieger frowned. "Is Alastair's house still standing?"

"Yup. The old place is still creakin' away. It's a shell of a place now. Junior high kids go there on Halloween to tell ghost stories. High school kids go there to get frisky. One o' those places, you know?"

Stieger chuckled. Most likely Jonathin had simply left the main roads, not wanting to be seen or harassed by lifelong nosy neighbors.

"And then"—Ronnie almost knocked his glass over—"there were the rumors that Alastair's transient had something to do with it."

Stieger's ears perked up at that. This was not something he'd heard before.

"What transient is that?"

"So get this." Ronnie turned fully to face Stieger so he could gesture with his hands. "One day this man just walks into town—no expression, no personality, no identity. Gives everyone the creeps, like some phantom come out o' the desert. No one liked him at all. But Alastair gives him work."

"Doing what?"

"Workin' his ranch. Some folks said Jonathin didn't like that too much, that Alastair favored this transient over his own son. Plenty o' people thought maybe they got in a tiff and the transient killed Jonathin."

Stieger frowned. "Forgive me, but if Jonathin felt this man was threatening his home, his father, his . . . place, wouldn't he have more incentive to kill the transient, rather than the other way around?"

"Sure, but no one liked the transient. They thought he was weird, and Jonathin's the one that disappeared."

"Did this transient have a name?" Stieger asked.

"Sure he did. I just don't remember it."

"How long did he work for Alastair?"

"Oh, a handful of years—seven? Eight maybe?"

"So the town would have gotten pretty used to seeing him, then."

"I s'pose. He didn't come into town much, though. And never by hisself. Only when Alastair needed help carrying supplies or some such."

"Did he have many friends?"

"None that I knew of." Ronnie leaned back far enough that Stieger wondered if he'd fall off his bar stool. "We townsfolk are pretty set in our ways, especially old timers like me. We're superstitious and don't take much to outsiders. It's what the young people these days call cliquish."

Stieger thought Ronnie probably meant cliquish, but didn't correct him. "You seem friendly enough."

Ronnie tried to take another swig of beer, but missed his mouth. He wiped it, but succeeded only in smearing foam all over his goatee. "Ah, but I'm the only one you've found who's willing to talk, aren't I?"

Stieger grinned. That was true enough. He'd been shut down by people all over town. No one wanted to answer questions about Alastair Landes. They just looked at him suspiciously and shut their doors. He suspected the only reason Ronnie was being so liberal-tongued had more to do with the drink he was nursing than with his being a friendly guy, but he didn't say so.

"You know your neighbors well, Mr. Martin."

Ronnie lifted his cup in a toast. "I ought to. 'Ve lived here most o' my life."

"So no one liked him, this transient?"

"He was a strange sort—loner, kept mostly to hisself. I don't know. Don't think he actually did anything bad, just sort of rubbed everyone the wrong way, you know?"

The scraping of a bar stool on his other side brought Stieger's head around. The middle-aged woman from down the bar had taken the stool next to him.

Stieger smiled politely. "Ma'am."

"Why were you asking if Jonathin died as a child?" Her eyes were bloodshot, her mouth screwed up in a scowl.

"I didn't mean anything by it, ma'am. I was searching county records. I had a birth certificate for Jonathin, but nothing after that, so I wondered if he'd died young. Ronnie, here, tells me my theory was wrong. Jonathin left town."

"He told you we don't know if Jonathin left," she said sharply. "Lots o' folks think he never made it out of town."

"Yeah, but he still wasn't a child, Janie," Ronnie put in.

"Seventeen isn't a grown man," Janie snapped. Her voice softened. "Anyway, if he did die young, he wouldn't be the first." Her eyes focused on Stieger and she gave him a sad, faraway smile. "Children die in Mt. Dessicate all the time, Mr. Stieger. The graveyard in the desert wasn't really shocking to anyone." With that, she spun on her stool, hopped off it, and marched out of the bar.

Stieger gaped after her a few moments before turning to let his gaze shift between Ronnie and the bartender.

"Ronnie," he said when he'd found his voice. "What was that about?"

Ronnie waved a hand dismissively. "Ah, don't mind her. That's just Crazy Janie."

"Ronnie." The bartender's voice had a warning in it. "Be nice. Janie's not crazy." He came forward to stand in front of Stieger and stuck out his hand. "I'm Blaine Mr. . . . Stieger, is it?"

"That's right." Stieger shook his hand.

"Janie isn't crazy. She just never got over her daughter's death."

Stieger leaned back. This town was more interesting by the minute. "When was that?"

"Long time ago. More than twenty years."

"How'd the girl die? Could she be among the dead out in the desert?"

"Aw, no," Ronnie piped up. "Nothing like that. Janie's daughter drowned."

"Drowned? Out here? In the desert?" Stieger asked.

"About five miles north of here there's a river," Blaine said. "And by river, I mean a meandering little creek. It's not much to look at most of the time. Women let their toddlers wade in it without worrying. But that year, as the story goes, there'd been an unusually large amount of rain and snow. When the spring runoff came, that stream became a full-blown river. It was probably the most excitement Mt. Dessicate had seen for some time. Janie's daughter—what was her name, Ronnie? Julie? Julia?"

Ronnie shrugged and took another swig of his draft.

"Anyway, she was twelve and playing with two friends by the river."

"She fell in?" Stieger asked.

"Yeah."

Stieger glanced over his shoulder. Janie could be seen walking crookedly down the hill. At least she had the good sense not to drive. "Poor woman."

"Yeah," Blaine agreed. "She never got over it, probably because she never got closure."

"Why's that?"

"They never found a body."

Stieger's eyes narrowed. "How's that? I thought you said she drowned."

Blaine saw Stieger's expression and smiled, leaning his forearms on the bar. "Please understand, Mr. Stieger. It was a dangerous spring. No one was used to having a large, rushing body of water around. As you said, we're desert folk. Four children went in to the river that year. I know because one of them was my kid brother. Luckily, they fished him out in time. He had a mild concussion from hitting his head on a rock, but that was it. Another of the victims was his best friend, who went into the river at the same time he did. His friend drowned. Now, they were able to revive him with CPR on the bank, but his brain had been deprived of oxygen long enough that he was mentally handicapped for the rest of his life."

"How old were you when that happened?"

"Twelve. Janie's daughter was the third victim. A fourth was a boy I didn't know. They found his body, but only because it snagged between two boulders." He shrugged. "Janie's daughter weighed less than him. The current must have just kept on carrying her. After two deaths and two near-deaths, people smartened up, kept their kids away until the water levels went down. The river's never been that high again."

"But, if they never found the body, how do they *know* the girl went into the river?"

"She was with two playmates. They said she was standing on the bank. They heard her scream. She was there and then she was gone. There was nowhere for her to go but into the river. They found her cardigan and one of her shoes tangled in riverside brush an hour later, forty miles downstream. The only way she could have gotten so far so fast is on the currents. A child couldn't have hoofed that."

Stieger nodded.

"It wasn't rocket science. Don't read too much into what Janie says." Blaine picked up his polishing towel again. "She's not crazy; she's just had it hard. She did okay until her husband passed a few years ago. Since then, let's just say she's been a much more loyal customer of mine."

"Or she's just gone crazy." Ronnie let out a wheezing laugh at his own joke and wiped tears from the corners of his eyes while Stieger and Blaine looked on.

"Well"—Stieger addressed the bartender again—"I'd like to find out all I can about Alastair, and possibly this transient he employed. Any suggestions?"

"I don't know about the transient." Blaine said. "I was only a kid when Alastair passed, but when you were talking about county records and Alastair's land earlier, I thought of Neil Griffith. He's retired now, but he used to be a lawyer. If anyone handled Alastair's legal affairs, it was probably him."

"You know his phone number?"

"No. I'm not well-acquainted with him, but I can write down his address for you."

"I'd appreciate that."

Just then the door to the bar opened. An elderly woman with a thick white braid lying over one shoulder shuffled in.

"Evening, Colleen," Blaine said.

"Hi, Blaine. I came to pick up those parcels for John."

Blaine nodded. "I'll get them." He disappeared into the back room.

Ronnie tried to stand up, but he fell off his stool and barely kept his feet. "Colleen," he called to the woman, "you should come over and meet my friend, uh . . . uh . . ." He scratched his head.

"Lars," Stieger supplied.

"Yeah, Lars." Ronnie turned to him and dropped his voice. "If you wanna know more about Alastair," he whispered, "you should ask Colleen. She's lived here longer than *I* have."

Colleen came up beside them, a reserved smile on her face. "Hello, Ronnie."

Stieger stood and held his hand out. "Lars Stieger, ma'am. Nice to meet you."

"Likewise. What brings you to Mt. Dessicate?"

"He's asking about ol' Alastair Landes," Ronnie chimed in. "Wants to know about that transient that worked for him. Remember, Colleen?"

The instant Alastair's name was out of Ronnie's mouth, Colleen's expression went from warm and inquisitive to utterly still. Stieger watched her closely, gauging the reaction. He'd been a PI long enough to recognize when a person had something to say, but desperately wanted *not* to say it.

The next moment, Colleen realized he was watching her. She pasted another smile on her face, though it never touched her eyes. Just then, Blaine brought two large boxes from his back room for her.

"Well, isn't that nice?" she said. "Could you bring those to my car for me, Blaine?"

"Sure, Colleen."

"You gentlemen have a nice evening. Nice to meet you Mr. Stieger."

She was out the door before Stieger could react. He turned back to Ronnie. "Did she know Alastair or his family, or the transient very well?"

"Dunno."

"Will you excuse me, Ronnie? I'd like to catch her before she leaves."

"'Course."

Stieger hurried toward the parking lot, nearly colliding with Blaine at the door, coming back in. He ran out to where a late nineties model geo metro was just pulling away. He waved his hands for Colleen to stop. He could swear the old woman looked at him in her rearview mirror before putting her eyes forward and disappearing in a shower of dust and pea gravel.

Stieger twisted his lips in dissatisfaction. That was one woman he'd have to track down.

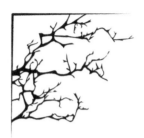

Chapter 13

CODY RETIRED A LITTLE after midnight. He was ready to drop. It had been an exhausting day and he knew tomorrow would be worse. He was following up on several leads at once, by far the most interesting of which was Alex Thompson's.

He didn't know what to make of her. She had a quiet confidence about her, a dignified form of self-possession that made him want to trust her.

As he got into his jeep, he dialed her number to go over some clarifying details that were overlooked during preliminary questioning. Not until the phone started ringing did he get his car started and glance at the digital clock, which read 12:18. He immediately tried to hang up, but before he managed it, she answered.

He cringed. "Alex, it's Cody. I'm so sorry. I wasn't thinking about how late it is. Did I wake you?"

"Oh, detective. No, you didn't wake me. I . . . haven't gone to bed, yet."

"Oh," he was relieved. "Night owl, huh?"

He heard the measured hesitation before she answered. "Not exactly."

He waited.

"Just . . . you know . . . strange place and all."

He decided not to pursue it. "Well, will you be up for a while?"

Again, the hesitation, before her noncommittal, "Probably."

"I have a few questions to ask you—just some clarifying points. Would it be possible for me to drop by your motel? Or would you like to meet me somewhere?"

She was quiet so long he thought perhaps the call had been dropped.

"Alex?"

"Yes, I'm still here. The truth is detective—and try not to be angry at me for this—"

"What?"

"I know I promised not to leave town . . ."

"You left town?"

"I just went on a drive. I took the main highway just to get some air, and I blew a tire."

"Are you okay?"

"Yes, fine. But I'm kind of stranded. I have a spare but not a jack. I don't suppose there's any good roadside assistance to be had in Mt. Dessicate?"

"Well"—Cody was pulling out onto the highway—"there's a towing company, but they're not much good after six o'clock."

"Why not?"

"Happy hour."

"Oh."

"I'll come and get you. Just turn on your hazards and tell me where."

After hanging up her phone, Alex got back into her car, which she'd successfully navigated onto the dirt shoulder of the highway. Her forearms ached from gripping the wheel so hard when the tire blew. She wished she'd never left the motel.

She was half an hour from town, which meant it would be at least that long before Cody reached her. She pulled her mp3 player from the glove box. Her charm bracelet caught on the corner of the glove box door, and she reached over with her other hand to untangle it. She was never without that bracelet, and she knew it was only a matter of time before the clasp broke.

Making a mental note to look into having the bracelet cleaned and reset, Alex turned on her mp3. Jamming the buds into her ears, she got out of the car and walked around for a few minutes, letting her favorite country singer's ballads sooth her. When she tired of that, she sat on the hood of the car, sliding back far enough to stretch her legs out in front of her and leaning against the windshield. She gazed toward town, willing the headlights of Cody's car to appear, and tapping her foot to the rhythm of the music.

Nothing moved. There was no wind, no tumbleweeds, no nocturnal desert creatures. It was as though the scenery around her was a three-hundred-and-sixty-degree plastic panorama.

Alex didn't know what alerted her to the presence of something other than herself in the still desert night. There were no lights, but perhaps it was a movement of air, or the sound of tires on gravel penetrating the ear buds. Either way, she twisted around to look behind her, yanking out her headphones.

A dingy, ancient-looking squad car pulled up directly behind her on the gravel shoulder. Her stomach did a summersault as she flashed back to that night four years ago when she'd been pulled over in this very spot.

There was no doubt in her mind this was the same squad car. Though she couldn't have made the connection back then, she realized now how old a model the boxy, gaudy cop car was. The eighties probably wanted it back.

The driver's side door opened, and the man that stepped out filled Alex with icy dread. It was the same man; there was no mistaking him.

Alarm bells clanged in her head, signaling danger, just like before. But what could she do? Run? Despite being very tall and stocky—he could probably hold her down with his little finger—he didn't look particularly athletic. She was sure she could outrun him. The problem was he had a car, and she couldn't drive on her rim.

Jumping off the hood of her car, she planted her feet to face him. It made her feel more in control. As he sauntered toward her, taller than she remembered and exuding just as much menace as he'd shown four years ago, every ounce of that control slipped through her fingers like oil.

He kept walking until he was only a few inches from her, and she had to crane her neck back to look up at him. She refused to back up. They stared at one another for several seconds before he spoke. "Havin some car trouble, are ya?"

She jumped. His voice was still a raspy whisper.

Alex swallowed and willed her voice to be steady. "Yes, officer. I blew a tire."

His eyes went casually toward the shredded left front tire of her car, then returned to her.

"Waitin' for prince charming to drive along and rescue you?" He had a slight lisp when he said his s-sounds, but he was trying so hard to cover it, they came out more like a hiss.

"I've already called somebody. He's on his way." She emphasized the "he" part, hoping that knowing another man would soon be here would intimidate him somewhat.

He laughed softly—the same, sinister sound she remembered from before—and Alex had the sneaking hunch he wasn't intimidated in the least.

"Well." He stepped toward her, and now they were toe to toe. "Maybe I can keep you company. Until he gets here."

Alex did step back now. Not only was he way too close for comfort, but his breath was horribly foul. She started to put a hand to her nose to block his stench, then realized that might offend him. She covered by running her hand through her hair.

"That won't be necessary. I'm sure he'll be here any min—"

The massive cop grabbed her wrist and yanked it toward him. She yelped before she could stop herself, wondering what on earth he was looking at. It took a moment for her to realize he was staring at her bracelet.

Then she remembered. That night he'd first pulled her over, he had remarked on the bracelet, asked where she'd gotten it. Now he was looking at it again.

He studied the silver charms for several seconds, then a light dawned in his eyes. They shifted to her and she shivered violently.

He remembered her.

Breathing raggedly, she yanked her arm away from him. He didn't try to keep it, but his eyes had taken on a predatory glow.

"Cordelia?" he hissed, stepping toward her.

She stepped backward, but he followed her, step for step. They were locked in a deadly, linear waltz now, and she knew she had to run.

She understood then. The thought pealed more clearly in her head than any she'd had in her life: this man was going to kill her.

She didn't know if she could get away. He could get in his car and run her down easily. She still couldn't see headlights in the darkness, but the highway wasn't a straight line. It twisted and turned around hills and rises on its way south. Cody should be coming around that far bend any minute now. Perhaps, if she could stay near the road, she could run out and get his attention when he got near.

Knowing she should have done it five minutes ago, Alex spun on her toe and leapt away.

Even as she began her first sprint, strong fingers dug into her scalp. She screamed as he yanked her backward by her hair and slammed her head into her own car window.

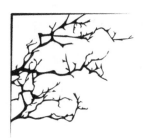

Chapter 14

CODY HAD TO TAKE THREE different detours to get out of the city. With all the extra people, large sections of town had been blocked off. Consequently, it was nearly thirty minutes before two flashing hazard lights came into view in the distance.

As he came level with Alex's car, he couldn't see her, but he figured she was lying down in the back seat. It was nearly one a.m. after all. He parked on the other side of the road.

"Alex, I'm here," he called, getting out of the car. He got into the back of his jeep and rummaged around until he found a flashlight, a tire iron, and a jack. He crossed the deserted highway, wondering if she had headphones on, or was just a deep sleeper, and noticed the driver's side window for the first time.

The glass was thick and tempered, not easy to break, but a fist-sized, circular crack was in it. Spider web splinters spiraled into its center and grew out of the crack, and a dark substance dripped from it.

Suddenly wary, Cody stepped up to the car and ran his light over the front and back seats. Alex wasn't in there.

Knowing he ought to be wearing gloves, but not caring at this particular moment, he touched the dark substance and brought his finger up to study it in the concentrated beam of the flashlight. It was red—the bright, arterial kind.

Blood.

Whirling around, Cody brought his flashlight up to his shoulder, turning in complete circles.

"Alex. Alex!"

When he stood on the staggered stripes of paint that divided the two-lane highway, he dropped into a crouch, looking under her car. Nothing. He circled the perimeter where she was parked, letting his light play over the uneven desert just off the highway, casting tall shadows behind the dirt mounds, peppermint bushes, and sagebrush.

"Alex!"

What could have happened to her? The desert held plenty of predators, but none that would have wandered into the yellow, blinking lights of her car, slammed her into the window, and then dragged her away. Cody's heart pounded. Where was she?

His light hit something tall and dark off to the side and he did a double take. It was the historic monument she mentioned in her report. Cody's hands went cold. This was almost the exact spot she claimed she'd been pulled over four years ago. He looked over at the blood on the window, then at the monument.

It loomed, twelve feet tall, dark, and ominous, about a hundred yards from where Alex's car was parked, the kind of historic monument that had to be protected, even though no one could remember what it commemorated. Cody thought it might have something to do with where the town had originally been established. No one he knew could say for sure.

He was only ten feet from where he had parked, but he'd already been completely swallowed by the darkness. The beam of his flashlight was his only salvation. He kept it on the ground, looking for anything that might trip him up as he made his way to the monument. He knew he'd have to leave the paved road and that meant treacherous footwork.

As he moved onto the shoulder, he noticed a track from a large tire with a wide tread. It transected the highway—a strange way to drive. Cody played his light over the road and found small, crushed dirt clods that had probably come off the same tire that made the tread. Following the trail with his light, he realized this vehicle had been parked directly behind Alex.

Whirling back to the shoulder, Cody followed the track with his flashlight. It led into the desert. Feeling a sudden, desperate urgency, he ran back to his jeep. After slamming the door, he belted himself in, grabbed his radio, and blessed the car gods that had invented four-wheel drive.

Turning on the spotlight that was situated just outside his window, Cody spurred the jeep onto the rocky, virgin terrain.

"Dispatch. Dispatch, this is Detective Oliver. Respond."

The radio crackled for a few seconds before a voice came through.

"You're supposed to use your identification number, Cody."

"Shut up, Dave, and listen. I need back up."

At least five seconds passed before a response came, and Cody could just see the nighttime dispatch officer scratching his head.

"What's wrong, Cody?"

"I think we have a 207a in progress."

"A 207a? Of who?" Dave's voice was incredulous.

"Alex Thompson. She had a lead in the Shakespeare case. Her car is parked on Route 24 with the hazards on, just past mile marker forty-one. You know that old historical monument?"

"Is that old thing still standing?"

"Yes! Send people out that way. Her car is parked facing south. Tell them to turn west when they get there and head into the desert."

"Now wait a second, Cody. I can't just wake people up and tell them to go for some midnight off-roading."

"Dave, this is serious! There's blood on her car and tire tracks that lead into the desert. Get me some back up. Make sure they come in vehicles equipped with four-wheel drive, got it?"

Another short pause.

"They're on their way. Be careful, Cody."

Cody followed the track for more than fifteen minutes, keeping his spotlight trained on it so he could carefully imitate its twists and turns. The view of the terrain from the road was deceptive. It looked like there was only a few hundred yards of ground flat enough to drive on, even with off-road capabilities. After that, steep rises became tall plateaus and mountains.

In actuality, the ground rolled so much that he kept dipping down steeply enough that he no longer had a view of Alex's parked car. Then he would crest the next rise and see it again in his rear-view mirror. There were hundreds of places to hide in the shadows out here, and he couldn't have been more than a quarter mile from the road.

The thick tread was heading for a mountain that loomed straight ahead, blacking out the stars. It seemed as though the vehicle had driven in a straight line to the base of the mountain, but Cody's headlights were bouncing off that base now and there was no one in sight. The driver must have driven to the base of the rise, then turned and driven along the length of it for a while. Cody would have to follow the tread all the way in to determine which direction it would go.

Something moved in the corner of his eye, coming from the right. His head snapped in that direction, but neither his headlights nor his spotlight were pointed there, so he couldn't see much of anything.

Then, without warning, his headlights illuminated a figure. The bright color of the person's clothing, made neon by the concentrated light, was a shocking contrast to the muted tones of the desert. Cody recognized Alex right away and, sucking in his breath, slammed his foot down hard on the brake pedal, but it was no use. She'd run so suddenly into his path that, at the speed he was going, he couldn't stop in time.

Alex's legs thumped sickeningly against the jeep's grate. Her body popped upward like a Tiddlywink, rolling over the hood and halfway up the windshield before sliding up over Cody's side mirror and careening across the driver's side window. Cody's window was still rolled down, and he had a reflex to grab her, but it came too late and he missed completely. She landed with a hollow thud.

The jeep came to a stop with such a wrenching jerk that Cody hit his chin on the steering wheel. Cursing, he leapt from the car to find Alex.

She'd landed ten feet from the jeep. Even as he jumped out and ran to her, she was trying to get up. He immediately pushed her back down.

"Alex, don't move. What're you doing? You need to lie still."

She was breathing hard, almost gasping, and her eyes were wild.

"We have to go! He's coming!"

"Who is?"

"*He* is. He's gonna . . . he's trying to . . ."

"Alex, lie still. I hit you going really fast. You might have a neck injury." Despite the calmness in his voice, which he'd been trained as a cop to put there, no matter how he really felt, Cody reached down and quickly un-holstered his gun. "There's help on the way, but I need to call them and tell them to bring an ambulance. Lie down—"

"No! We have to go. If he finds us—"

"Who?"

"It's him! The guy that took me . . . the same guy from before. He's gonna kill me. We have to go!"

"Stop shouting!" It came out more harshly than he'd intended, but her panic was infecting him. He took a deep breath and rested his hand on the joint between her neck and shoulder, pressing down gently to keep her shoulder blades on the ground. It was only then that he realized she was trembling violently and her behavior was probably a result of adrenaline. She was terrified. From what he'd seen, this woman was calm and deliberate, with very little drama. Now she was on the verge of hysterics.

"We...have...to...go. He'll come back." Her voice shook and her eyes shifted every which way; she looked like a cornered animal.

He leaned over her. "Alex, look at me." He waited until her eyes locked on his. "If he comes back, I will kill him."

She froze, staring up at him with tears in her eyes.

He held his gun up so she could see it. "Okay?"

After a moment, she nodded, and all the tension drained out of her like unstopped water. She slumped back onto the ground and lay there shivering.

"I have a first-aid kit in my car with a space blanket. I'm going to get it for you."

He stood and went to the jeep. After grabbing the kit, he took the opportunity to play the spotlight over the mountain, running it along every crevice and nook in the terrain. Only shadows and sagebrush revealed themselves, and there was no sound at all.

A soft crunch of gravel made him swing the light to one side, but it revealed only a loping jack rabbit that turned its back to him, stuck its tail in the air, and kept going.

Cody radioed in his position, told Dave to send an ambulance, and then went and wrapped Alex in the space blanket.

He sat by her, gun cocked, listening for any void in the silence, and prayed that her injuries weren't serious.

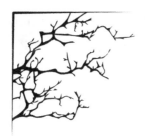

Chapter 15

AN HOUR LATER, THE silent, desolate corner of desert was crawling with cops and emergency vehicles. The captain and other detectives had been awakened. When word got around about what was happening, many of the uniforms who'd come to Mt. Dessicate to help with the Shakespeare investigation had shown up as well.

One of only four ambulances in town had come to pick up Alex. A plump but capable paramedic whose nametag read "Bob" directed his much-younger partner in putting Alex in a c-collar and strapping her to a backboard. Cody held her hand, assuring her that he'd be right behind her, and the ambulance sped off for the hospital.

While the crime scene unit scoured the desert, Cody, Frank, Tom, Court, and the captain congregated around Cody's jeep. They didn't have to lower their voices; no one was close enough to hear them.

"Okay, Cody." The captain's hair pointed in every direction and the right side of his face still looked vaguely pillow-squished. "Let's hear it from your lips. Tell us what happened."

Cody recounted the night's events for them. When he finished, they all gaped in stunned silence. Frank whistled.

"What do you think?" Cody wasn't addressing anyone in particular.

"Well," Tom finally ventured, "there's the track from the tire. And she couldn't have gotten so far from her car on foot in twenty minutes, so there must be another vehicle involved."

"Yeah," Court said, "but that doesn't mean she didn't orchestrate it somehow."

Cody's eyebrows had risen with Tom's comment, but they jumped higher at Court's. "You think she's making this up?"

They all looked at him like *he* was nuts.

It was Tom that spoke again. "It's quite a coincidence, Cody, if she's not. She shows up, talking about a particular incident, and then she, of all people, just happens to blow a tire in the same spot, and have an encounter with the same man, who—by the way—no one else has ever laid eyes on? She seems pretty normal, but that stretches the bounds of the believable, don't you think?"

Cody sighed. When put that way, he could see their point, but it hadn't even occurred to him that Alex might be lying. Her terror had been too real. The whole thing had been so bizarre, so shocking. He tried to look at it from their perspective, but ultimately shook his head.

"I understand why it sounds strange, but I don't think she's making it up. I don't think she has any more idea what's going on than we do. You didn't see her. She was petrified."

"She could just be one hell of an actress," Court put in, and when Cody looked at him, he put his hands up. "I'm just saying. We've seen them before."

"Or maybe," Frank added, "Cody wants to believe her because she's pretty."

Cody scowled at Frank. He wasn't in the mood for his jokes. He endured them most days, but he'd been present when this happened. He knew what he was talking about.

"And she what? Beat the hell out of herself?" he asked.

"Actually, I think you helped her out on that count." Frank grinned and, though Cody was in no mood to grin back, it made him less annoyed. Slightly.

"What do you think, Cap?" Tom asked.

The captain was scrutinizing Cody, but Cody met his gaze. He had nothing to hide.

"I think we ought to forego any concrete conclusions until we have the evidence to back them up. Maybe something very strange is going on here; maybe there's an explanation. Maybe this has nothing to do with the Shakespeare case; maybe Alex is a little crazy. Let's just take the evidence one piece at a time. Cody, go to the hospital and take a formal statement from both Alex and her doctors. Frank, Court, follow up with the CSI report first thing in the morning. Tom, go home. Your wife always gives me an earful about your heart condition when I keep you up all night. We'll have a meeting tomorrow morning."

"You mean *this* morning, Cap?" Frank asked, staring pointedly at his watch.

Cody glanced down. It was nearly three a.m.

The captain stared at Frank blankly for a few long seconds, then without a word, turned on his toe and walked to his car. The others headed for their respective vehicles.

Frank turned to Cody, hesitating. "Are you pissed at me?"

Cody sighed, letting his chin rest on his chest for a moment. "No. Sorry, man. Just coming down off an adrenaline high, I think."

Frank grinned. "I been there. I don't know how women do it every month."

Cody stared at Frank. "They don't have *adrenaline* once a month, Frank."

Frank shrugged. "Same diff. Anyway, I was just making a joke at your expense. I know you'd never jeopardize a case for a pretty girl." With a floppy grin, Frank hurried toward his own car.

Cody smiled after his friend, but if felt forced, and Cody wondered why. Nothing was going on between him and Alex, so the jokes shouldn't bother him. Feeling troubled, Cody got into his jeep and headed for the hospital.

ALEX LAY ON A GURNEY in the emergency room. IVs sprouted from both her arms and her shirt had been replaced with a hospital gown, though she still wore her jeans, which had a large tear in the front right thigh. At least the uncomfortable c-collar had been removed.

When Cody breezed through the swinging doors into the trauma room, she sat up.

"Please." He put a hand up. "Take it easy."

She croaked rather than speaking. "The doctors say I'll be fine. No head or neck injuries."

He looked relieved, but when he came up directly beside her, his frown returned, deeper this time. She knew why. After the c-collar had come off, she'd been allowed to use the restroom, which had a mirror. Under the harsh ER lights, her injuries looked more pronounced. Her eyes were both red and black-rimmed. The red was from crying. The black was because she had been beaten about the face, and developed raccoon eyes as a result. Redness, blemishes, and scratch marks covered her face, neck, and shoulders as well as her hands and arms. And finger-shaped bruises stretched around her throat.

Suddenly, Cody looked uncomfortable. "I'm here to take your statement, but if you want me to come back, so you can rest . . ."

She shook her head. "I should tell you now while it's fresh."

Cody found a stool underneath a fluorescent x-ray reader and dragged it noisily over to Alex's bedside. "Tell me," he said.

"I was sitting on the hood of my car, waiting for you."

Cody pulled out his notebook.

"And he came up behind me in that ancient squad car."

Cody's thumb was poised to click his pen but it froze in the air above the clicker.

"He was in a squad car again?"

"Yes."

"What did it look like?"

"Old, boxy, with a boat on the front."

Cody thought about that for a moment before nodding.

"What is it?" Alex asked.

"That makes a bit more sense. This guy could more easily be impersonating a cop with an ancient cruiser. It wouldn't be simple to steal and replace one that was being used. If he's restored one that's been out of commission for years, no one would miss it."

She told him everything the cop had said, and how he'd fixated on her bracelet again, and finally, how he'd smashed her head into the window, knocking her out.

"Where were you when you came to?"

"In his car. I was in the front seat and he was driving."

He nodded. "Go on."

Alex came awake by degrees. The ground below her rumbled violently and an engine in desperate need of a new muffler roared in her ear. She had no idea where she was, but as her eyes slowly opened, she registered the dull throb in her head and the large vomit-smelling cop in the front seat. It all came crashing back to her.

She panicked, lunging for the car door. She yanked the lever back twenty times, but the door didn't budge. Of course it didn't. This was a police cruiser. The back doors were criminal proofed. There was no grate between the front and back seat, but whether because the older cruisers didn't have that feature or because her assailant had removed it, she didn't know.

Her next thought was to try to crash the car. She lunged for the wheel, and actually managed to grab it, but that was as far as she got. One gargantuan fist came around and hit her squarely in the face. The impact was enough to slam her against the back seat and keep her there for several minutes while the interior of the car gyrated around her.

When they came to a stop, she told herself to think rationally. She wasn't even tied up, which meant he was confident she couldn't get away. Considering the back doors of the cruiser, he was right to be cocky. The front doors, though . . .

She'd have to move quickly. Alex took a few deep breaths to clear her head, but she didn't dare wait until it was entirely clear. The car was moving fast—probably thirty or forty miles per hour—and each second took her farther away from civilization.

She flipped onto her stomach and pulled her knees up under her, but kept her chest on the seat so that he wouldn't suspect she was about to pounce. All in one motion, she threw herself over the seat and into the front beside him, lunging for the door.

Something sharp dug into her shoulders and arms as she went over, and she had the far away thought that perhaps the grate had been cut out after all, leaving behind tiny, biting nails.

Her blitz action took him by surprise. He inhaled sharply and leaned away from her.

As soon as her torso found the front seat, she reached up and grabbed the lever on the door, swinging it wide open, while simultaneously kicking with her feet. She grabbed the metal that made up the top of the door and used it to pull herself toward the exit, until her head and shoulders were outside the car, looking across the roof.

By then, Psychocop had recovered and wrapped his right arm around her knees. His grip was as uncompromising as cement. She could still kick with her feet but her knees wouldn't budge. She kicked as hard as she could, and even connected with flesh a couple of times, but the hold around her knees remained locked. Her fingers were slipping on the metal.

With a sharp yank he pulled her back into the car. Reaching over with one long arm, he wrapped fat, solid fingers around her throat. He was trying to pinch off her airway, to make her pass out again.

Alex wanted to put her thumbs through his eyes, but his arm was too long, and she couldn't get her hands anywhere near his face. She lashed out with her feet and landed a solid kick, which made him release her throat, but her legs were still practically across his lap. She twisted around on the seat, pulling herself toward the door, then around again so she could see him. She did a one-two punch with her feet. The one he evaded easily; the two connected solidly with the nape of his neck, throwing his head into the steering wheel. The horn let out a staccato *honk*. It was enough of a distraction for Alex kick her way out of the car.

The next step was letting go. During their struggle, the car had slowed considerably, but it was still moving faster than she would have liked. If she broke a leg, she'd never get away from him. For some reason, it didn't occur to him to use speed to keep her in the car.

The next moment he lunged across the seat, trying to grab her again. She hung onto the top of the door, feet dragging on the ground. If he grabbed her again, her chances of getting away were slim to none.

He lunged for her. She let go.

She didn't so much feel the impact of her body on the ground as of her organs against her ribs. The thump was solid and jelly-like at the same time, and left her stomach heaving.

For an instant, the black star-strewn sky became a brilliant white with shades of gray at the corners. As it faded back to black, Alex knew she needed to run. She couldn't remember why, only that she did.

The sound of tires braking on gravel spurred her into action, and she rolled onto her stomach. It took a few seconds to get to her feet, but once she did, her head cleared almost immediately, and she found herself sprinting.

She ran along the foot of a dark, towering mountain for perhaps a hundred yards before his harsh headlights threw her shadow out in front of her. She was on foot; he was not. There was no way she could outrun him.

Then, off to her left, she saw something: bobbing lights. Headlights! Another car. She didn't know who was in it—she didn't dare hope it was anyone coming to her rescue—but she didn't think anyone could be worse than the guy that had just abducted her. It could be campers or thrill seekers out for some midnight four-wheeling.

Whoever they were, they could help her. She had to get their attention.

With a new goal and possible salvation in mind, Alex found a second wind and ran with everything she had for the lights. She knew she wouldn't reach the path the vehicle was on in time to signal them. She could only hope that perhaps she would get there at the same time and manage to slap the back window.

To her surprise, she did make it out in front of the vehicle—not a four-wheeler after all—and had to jump up to avoid braking her knees on the front of the car. She did, and went up over the hood and across the driver's side window.

Another sickening thump. When she looked up, it was into the eyes of Detective Cody Oliver.

"And he didn't say *any*thing?" Cody asked.

"In the car? No. He was sort of . . . eerily silent. But before . . ."

Cody quirked an eyebrow. "What?"

"He called me Cordelia. I'm pretty sure he did that four years ago, too."

"Why would he call you that?"

"You think I know?"

"That wasn't in the report."

"I'm sure I didn't tell you. I didn't register it before, but when he said it tonight, I remembered him saying it last time. Do you think he's mistaking me for someone else?"

"It's possible," Cody admitted. "Though probably not in the way you're thinking."

"What do you mean?"

"I'm sure there's someone he thinks you are, but not literally. If this is our killer, he's obviously psychotic. Whoever it is may not even be real. There's no way to tell."

Alex nodded. "He zeroed in on my bracelet again."

Cody's eyes went to her wrists, but the nurses had taken her watch and her bracelet when they'd put her in the hospital gown. All her belongings were in a plastic bag beneath her gurney.

"Are you sure?" Cody asked.

"Yes. He asked me about it four years ago. Tonight, he looked right at it, and I'm sure he remembered me."

"From four years ago, you mean?"

"Yes."

"What do you know about your bracelet, Alex?"

"Not much. It's got part of a serial number on the back. My dad tried to look it up for me, once, but it didn't give us any useful information."

"Would you mind if I looked at it?"

Alex hesitated, suddenly possessive. She had never in her life been without that bracelet, but she trusted Cody, so she directed him to the bag under the gurney. He studied it for several minutes, as though trying to memorize the pattern of the charms. He turned it over and wrote down the number engraved into the largest charm, then handed it back to her.

Cody made several scribbles on his notepad before looking up at her. "Where did he go? I didn't see anything at all after I hit you. No headlights, nothing."

Alex shrugged. "When he came up behind me on the road, he didn't have his lights on. Either time. I think he has a habit of driving without them to hide himself. Maybe he saw you and realized he wouldn't get to me before you did, so he turned off his lights and backed off."

"Maybe." He sounded doubtful. "Alex, this is going to sound like an odd question, but, do you have any . . . proof . . . that this happened to you as you've said?"

Alex furrowed her brows at him. "You think I'm lying?"

He put his hands up in a placating gesture. "No. I believe you, but you've got to understand the way this sounds to other people. No one else has seen this guy. No one has ever reported him for anything. Now, twice, on the same stretch of highway, he attacks you, only to disappear into the night? It sounds kind of weird, and we only have *your* testimony to go on."

Alex opened her mouth to protest, but Cody stood, took her hand, and looked candidly down into her face. "I want you to know that I believe you; I'm on your side in this. But you're going to be under a lot of scrutiny until we find some evidence to stand on. Can you think of anything that might prove your story?"

Ales threw up her hands. "Why would I make up something like this? Don't you think this might be the guy who killed those women in the desert?"

Cody sighed and leaned back against his stool. When he did, it slid several inches back, and he had to catch himself from falling onto his rump. Alex pretended not to notice.

"It's possible, Alex, but we can't be sure."

Alex crossed her arms and huffed, looking at the opposite wall. When she looked back, Cody's expression was empathetic.

"Look," he said, "I think it would be too much of a coincidence for this guy to not have any connection to the grave in the desert, but until we have evidence to connect them, we can't officially assume they're related. As of right now, these are two separate incidents."

Alex sighed. She tried to see his point, though she resented being called mental after she'd just been beaten to within an inch of her life.

"I don't have proof. When it gets light, can we go out and follow the tire tracks? See where they lead?"

He nodded. "We're planning to do that anyway."

"Until then, you'll just have to take my word for it."

Cody stared at her for another few seconds before nodding.

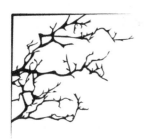

Chapter 16

CODY ASSUMED ALEX WOULD sleep most of the day away, and she was already unconscious before he left the hospital, but he felt strange leaving her by herself. He trusted the hospital staff, but made a mental note to ask the captain to allow him to post a guard at Alex's door.

The doctors admitted her for a mild concussion. Though they assured her it wasn't serious, she needed to be awakened every two hours for the next twenty-four, and as she was staying in town alone, the nurses would have to do it. It was nearly six a.m. before they got her tucked away into a tiny room, so she would be under the nurses' care until the following morning.

Cody knew he ought to go home for a few hours—sleep, shower, shave. But he didn't want to. He knew the captain would call an early meeting, and Cody was curious to know what everyone else had found.

He drove to the station and curled up—or as close to that as his six-foot figure would allow—in the back seat of his jeep, setting his watch alarm for 9 a.m. That meant less than three hours' sleep, but he'd survived on less. As he drifted off, he wondered if his Uncle Clyde had ever worked a case this complicated.

When his watch alarm chimed, he could have sworn he'd been in the jeep for five minutes. Hoisting his heavy eyelids up, he was surprised to find sunlight streaming through the jeep windows.

He uncurled himself, finding that every muscle was stiff, and staggered out of his car, walking directly into the one parked next to his. Luckily it was just Rose's battered Oldsmobile; she'd never been very particular about her ride.

Gathering his things and slapping his cheeks repeatedly so as not to surrender to the already-stifling morning heat, he headed into the station.

The lobby was already hopping with people, many of them unfamiliar. As he passed the front desk, Rose's voice drifted to him.

"You know my car is made up of matter, right Cody?"

"What?"

"Which means you can't walk *through* it?"

Cody cleared his throat, glancing around to see if anyone else had noticed his little parking lot mishap. "Uh, yeah. Sorry about that."

Rose didn't bother to take her eyes off her computer screen as she talked. "More worried about you than it, honey."

Cody grinned and wove his way through the chaos until he got to the room that housed his and the other detectives' desks, wondering if anyone had gotten more sleep than him. He got his answer when he walked through the door.

Frank and Court both sat at their desks, chins on their chests, breathing slowly and loudly. Tom also sat his desk, but his head had fallen back between his shoulder blades. His mouth was open and a sound like that of a quiet power drill was emanating from it. The noise didn't disturb the two younger detectives.

A presence came up behind him. He turned to see the captain chuckling.

"Glad you made it in, Cody," he said softly. "I need to address all four of you. Care to do the honors?"

He flung his hand out to the side of the room, indicating a particularly large box of files, which Cody knew to be very heavy.

Cody grinned and hurried over to his desk, careful not to make any noise or bump anyone. Then he went and picked up the box the captain had indicated. After clearing a space on his desk, he hoisted the box up until was level with his nose . . . and let go.

The resulting *bang* was at least half as loud as a gunshot, and the effect was extremely satisfying. Frank actually yelped—the sound of a frightened little girl. Court fell backward, chair and all. Tom's head snapped up, eyes looking like bloodshot CDs, and had to slurp to keep from depositing any of the drool crawling out of the corners of his mouth into his lap.

Court was on his feet almost the instant his chair hit the ground, leaving Cody to suspect he'd awakened mid-fall. When he got up, he clasped one hand over his right ear, stomped his foot, and turned in a circle, face contorted in pain.

The other three detectives watched him with tired, passive eyes. The captain, as usual, was pretending not to notice the pranks his detectives pulled on each other, though Cody suspected he enjoyed them as much as the next guy. Even now, he was conspicuously reading the report in front of him, Cody thought he could see trembling at the corners of the captain's mouth.

"What's the matter, Court?" Frank finally asked. "Having nightmares about Mike Tyson again?"

Court glared lightning bolts at Frank, but his gaze quickly moved to Cody.

"Thanks a lot, *Cody*."

"Yeah," Frank chimed in. "How was *your* beauty rest?"

"Hey." Cody put his hands up. "I've been sleeping in the back seat of my car for the last two and a half hours. I wouldn't call that beauty sleep."

"True." Tom was looking at Cody. "I gotta say, Cody, your eyes look kind of bloodshot. Have you been smoking pot?"

"Gee, Tom." Cody didn't miss a beat. "Your eyes are looking kind of glazed. Have you been eating donuts?"

Tom threw a pencil at him. Cody tried to duck but sleep deprivation made his reflex come about eight seconds too late, and the pencil hit him in the cheek.

"Back seat of a car, huh?" Frank was muttering. "Sounds hot."

Cody rolled his eyes. "Not when you're in there by yourself." He glanced up in time to see Franks eyebrows go up and down several times in quick succession.

"Well that depends—"

"All right." The captain cut him off. "Listen up. I know I said we'd meet first thing, but I'm going to push it by an hour. Linda just called, Cody. She's finished her autopsies of the Shakespeare bodies. She wants to give you her report. I'm coming along to listen in. The rest of you, we'll have our meeting as soon as Cody and I are finished in the morgue. Wake up and find some good news to give me.

"By the way." The captain put one foot back into the room. "News of the flowers has been leaked to the press. They've named him the Botanist."

Cody's groan was echoed by the other three detectives.

"Fantastic," Frank murmured as Cody followed the captain out of the room.

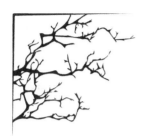

Chapter 17

"SO WHAT BRINGS YOU down here, Mr. Stieger? Not enough excitement in the big city?"

Stieger chuckled. "Not at all. I have a client who wanted me to come down and find out if her loved one was among the dead in your mass grave. Unfortunately there's been little to do yet but wait."

Griffith smiled. He had fine crow's feet around his eyes and a pot belly, but little enough white hair for his age. "I'm sorry for your client's loss. What can I do for you?"

"I'm looking into the history of the land out there. I understand it used to be owned by a man named Alastair Landes. I was told you might be able to help me learn more about him and his . . . circumstances."

Griffith frowned. "You don't think Alastair had anything to do with that mass grave do you?"

"I'm not sure," Stieger answered, choosing his words carefully. "That's what I'm trying to determine one way or the other. Perhaps the land's history will have some bearing on this case, perhaps none." He spread his hands. "Anything you could tell me would be helpful."

Griffith leaned forward, resting his clasped hands on the mahogany desk between them. "I knew Alastair Landes very well, Mr. Stieger, for most of my life. He was a decent man. Old school, perhaps, but not the sort that would have done this."

Stieger nodded. "All right. Since you seem to have known the family better than anyone else I've spoken to, I'll take your word on his character."

Griffith sat back in his chair, shoulders relaxing. "What do you want to know about him?"

"I understand he and his son didn't get along. They had an infamous falling out?"

Griffith nodded. "Jonathin was too much like his mother."

"What do you mean?"

"Gerty was a sweet girl. She was dreamy and artsy, always creating things. She was into horticulture and cooking and crafts. Alastair loved her to high heaven, but I think he saw such things as feminine work. He was the man of the house. He had a ranch to run."

Stieger nodded. When Griffith said old school, he wasn't kidding. "So the son was more like the mother than the father?"

"In every way. Jonathin wanted to go to art school. Alastair was well-to-do and could have paid for it, but he refused. He didn't see it as manly work, didn't think his son could support himself that way. So Jonathin left."

"Where'd he go?"

"He planned to join the army. He knew they'd pay for school."

"When he was seventeen?"

"Jonathin didn't leave 'til he was twenty-two. He'd probably been talking about the army since seventeen, but he was a good kid at heart—felt guilty abandoning his old man. But, when at twenty-two, Alastair was still trying to run his life, I guess Jonathin finally decided he'd had enough and took off."

"And you're sure he made it out of town and to the army?"

Griffith raised one white tufted eyebrow and Stieger spread his hands. "Just trying to be thorough."

"I know he made it out of town because I saw him myself," Griffith said. "Beyond that, I couldn't say. I was acquainted with Jonathin—well-acquainted, even—but the boy didn't confide in me. Far as I know, no one in town heard another thing from him after that. He left us all behind—the entire town, not just Alastair. The problem wasn't that Jonathin left; it's that he never came back. That's what started all the rumors."

Stieger nodded. "I hear tell from some people in town that Alastair hired a transient to help him work his ranch. What can you tell me about him?"

Griffith steepled his fingers. "I remember who you mean, but I haven't thought about that chap for years. He just came into town one day looking for work."

"I understand not everyone . . . liked him."

Griffith shrugged. "That's to be expected. He was a transient, a strange sort. People are bound to be suspicious, but Alastair hired him without pause. He was getting on in years by then, and Jonathin certainly wasn't being much help. Alastair needed someone he could trust to run his ranch."

"This transient have a name?"

Griffith thought for a moment. "I want to say he called himself Charles, but the last name escapes me. If you give me a few days, I could look it up for you."

Stieger arched a brow. "You have his name on file somewhere?"

"He made a claim for the land after Alastair passed, but he had no legal right to it. He would've had to buy it, if he wanted to own it privately, and he didn't have any money. I'm sure I have his name in one of my old files, but it's in storage somewhere; I'll have to fish it out. Might be faster to check county records for it."

Stieger nodded. "I'll do that. But to clarify, this Charles came to work for Alastair *before* Jonathin left?"

"Yeah. Just before, if memory serves. Jonathin didn't get along with his father, but he wouldn't have left his father in a pinch. Once Alastair had a surrogate son, one who was much more like him and could take better care of both him and the ranch than Jonathin cared to, Jonathin didn't feel so guilty leaving. I think he saw it as a sign that he was meant to live a different life. The next blowup they had, he packed his bags."

"So Charles tried to claim the land after Alastair died . . . and then what? What did he do when he was denied?"

Griffith shrugged. "Beats me. I think he moved on. Don't think I ever saw him after that. Probably fell back on his transient lifestyle and went to another place to live. You're right that no one liked him, and with the ugly rumors circulating, I doubt he could find any other work in this town. Truthfully, I don't think he tried. Just disappeared."

"Mr. Griffith." Stieger sat forward. "I don't want to offend you, and I certainly don't want to cast a shadow over a family you once knew well, but I have to ask. Was there any abuse going on in the home?"

"Alastair's home? Nah." Griffith hesitated briefly. "Well, I suppose you'd have to define abuse. As I said, Alastair was old school. He had acres of land, and the house is several miles outside of town, but it was said that when he and Jonathin fought, the people in town could hear them yelling."

"Is that true?"

"I doubt it. It's just what *they* say, but I can see that Alastair might have been verbally abusive. Jonathin himself told me that Alastair often said he wasn't a man, wasn't good enough, that sort of thing."

"But nothing physical or sexual?"

"Definitely not sexual. Alastair might have cuffed Jonathin every now and again for disobedience, but understand, Mr. Stieger, that Jonathin was a teenager thirty years ago. Times were different. How do your daddy and his daddy's discipline compare with people today?"

"I understand, but there was nothing out of the ordinary? No violence, no pattern of abuse?"

"No, nothing like that."

Stieger nodded, thinking, while Griffith peered at him. The old lawyer leaned forward, resting his forearms on the desk once more.

"Why these questions, Mr. Stieger? What are your theories?"

Stieger smiled. "I'm not sure I have any, Mr. Griffith. I thought—with all that ugliness out in the desert—that perhaps the killer had some tie to the land. Alastair was the last one to privately own it, so assuming the killer isn't more than a hundred years old, any connection would have to be to the Landes family."

When Griffith frowned, deep lines appeared around his mouth. They weren't there when he smiled. "But why do you assume there's a connection at all?"

"I'm not assuming anything." He smiled, hoping to reassure the lawyer. "I may be barking up completely the wrong tree here, Mr. Griffith. Like I said, I had some time to kill, so I thought I'd find out what I could on the off chance that it might be relevant. Indulge an old PI in his conspiracy theories?"

Griffith returned the smile. "What other questions do you have?"

"Just one. From what you remember of them, do you think either Jonathin or Charles is capable of this?"

"Of what?"

"The bodies in the desert."

"Of *murder*? On *that* scale?" Griffith's eyes widened to the size of saucers. "No, I can't say I do."

Stieger tried not to sigh. Questions about murder could be a lot for anyone, and he couldn't help but think that the town of Mt. Dessicate, collectively, was in a state of shock over the discovery of the bodies.

"Mr. Griffith, I'm not accusing anyone, or anyone's memory. I'm not asking *you* to make any accusations, but remember back. Based on what you knew of these two men, is either of them capable of it? Is it *possible,* in your opinion, for one of them to have done this?"

Griffith shrugged, swallowed, and loosened his tie. He studied his desk for a long time before answering. "Mr. Stieger, I haven't seen either of them in almost thirty years. For Jonathin's part, I'd have to say no. He was a good kid, but that many decades could change a person, incomprehensibly. As for the transient, I never knew him to begin with. I think I *saw* him once when I went to visit Alastair, but Alastair didn't even introduce us. I couldn't say anything at all about his character."

"What about your neighbors? None of them liked him. Why do you think that is?"

"That was based largely on suspicion, as I said before. He was an odd-looking transient."

"Odd how? What did he look like?"

"He was tall, intimidating. And his face was scarred."

"Scarred? How so?"

Griffith shrugged. "I never got a good look. Not anything out of the common way—he wasn't disfigured or anything—just scarred. But it fueled the gossip and made people that much less trustful of him." Griffith opened his mouth to speak again, then snapped it shut, throwing Stieger a suspicious look.

"If you have anything else to tell me, Mr. Griffith, now would be the time."

Griffith stared out the window for a moment. Then his shoulders sagged. "I suppose it's all ancient history anyway. I truly didn't know the transient and don't know anything about his character. I don't wish to defame him in any way. Truthfully I always felt sorry for him—thought he got an unfair shake from the town. But I could be wrong. Perhaps there was something sinister about him but I never had occasion to observe it. That said, I did warn Alastair about him once."

"Warn him? Why? About what?"

"Being primarily a property lawyer, I know county employees pretty well. A couple of weeks before Alastair passed—and this was several years after Jonathin left, you understand—a friend of mine called me to say that a strange man was asking questions about how to go about claiming Alastair's land after his death. By her description, the man was Alastair's transient, Charles. I felt kind of strange about it, so I went out to see Alastair."

"Did you suspect anything sinister?"

"Not at all. I just thought Charles would try to disinherit Jonathin upon Alastair's death. I told Alastair what I'd learned and urged him to draw up a will. He didn't have one at that point. I told him that if he wanted Jonathin to have his land, he needed to make it legal."

"And did he?"

"No. He flat-out refused. He expressed remorse about the way he and Jonathin had parted. He truly wished he could see his son again, but he said if Jonathin couldn't forgive him enough to come back, then so be it, and let the chips fall where they may."

"Had he tried to reconnect with Jonathin before then?"

"I got the impression that he had, but hadn't received a reply. It made him angry, or maybe just sad. He also confided to me during that visit that he was much sicker than anyone in town knew. Even *he* didn't think he'd be around for long. He said Charles was just helping him get his affairs in order."

"Did you believe that?"

Griffith shrugged. "I thought Charles's motives were more selfish than Alastair believed, but it also occurred to me that if Alastair was sick, Charles was the only one who knew that. If he knew Alastair was on the brink, that might be why he was asking after the land. Either way, you can't force someone to draw up a will, so I left. Two weeks later, Alastair was dead."

"And no one ever suspected foul play?"

Griffith waved his hand dismissively. "Nah. Alastair had sent Charles on a supply run up to the north, so Alastair was alone when he passed. There was no reason to believe anything other than a natural, peaceful death had occurred."

Stieger turned it over in his head while the other man peered at him. After a moment's silence, Griffith leaned forward, clasping his fingers together.

"I really don't see that there could a connection of the sort you're looking for, Mr. Stieger. This was all so long ago, and this psychopath is operating *now*."

Stieger smiled. "I'm sure you're right, Mr. Griffith. I'm sure this will just end up being the way I entertained myself for a few days waiting for DNA confirmation of the victims. I understand Alastair's home is still standing?"

"Still standing, yes, but it's not much of a home anymore. Just a shell of a shack, hardly fit to get out of the rain in. It's a favorite hangout spot of our young people, though technically they aren't allowed to visit it. But you know how kids are."

"So I've heard. I'd still like to put an image to the place I've learned so much about in the last couple of days. Could you direct me to it?"

Griffith smiled and got to his feet. "Let me get you a map."

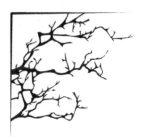

Chapter 18

THE MORGUE WAS AN EXTENSION of the funeral home, and Cody knew Linda hadn't had this much work in years. She'd worked in an L.A. crime lab for most of her career. Though she was only in her mid-forties, Cody knew Linda considered her move here two years ago a form of retirement. Her husband had a bad case of asthma, so he needed the lower elevations and warm temperatures the southern part of the state provided. Though she was still a coroner, her workload was a fraction of what it had been in L.A. The only time she had customers was when someone died, and in a place like Mt. Dessicate, that was mostly the elderly.

Cody wondered how she was handling having twelve bodies to autopsy.

He and the captain made the ten minute walk to the funeral home in silence. They entered through the front door and the air conditioning was an immediate relief. Cody followed the captain through the foyer, the vacant viewing room, and back into the space that served as Linda's office.

The captain knocked on Linda's open door, and she looked up from her desk. She kept her sandy-blond hair short, but wore a lot of makeup. Linda was one of those women who always gave the impression that, if she just switched her lab coat for a dress, she'd be ready for a dinner party.

Today she looked a bit peaked with just a hint of darkness under each eye.

"Cody and I are here for your report, Linda," the captain said. "Whenever you're ready."

"How are you doing, Linda?" Cody stepped into the room. "You don't look so good."

Linda sighed as she got to her feet. "I've been autopsying these victims for three days, Cody. At this point, I desperately need to come up for air."

Cody felt something clinch in his stomach. "Is it that bad?"

She eyed him steadily. "It's pretty bad, and you know I've seen bad. Consider yourselves warned."

They followed her into the small assessment room. Normally, there were only two examination tables in the morgue, and another all-purpose table that could be converted. In other words, it was only big enough for three victims at once.

For the Shakespeare case, Linda had somehow turned all three of her tables in the opposite direction, and brought in nine more. Some were makeshift tables that had been dragged in; others were gurneys that had been borrowed from the hospital; the two on the end looked like stacked crates with sheets draped over them.

All twelve skeletons were laid out in two rows of six, heads all facing in, with an isle down the middle. Cody was reminded of how the burial mounds had looked in the desert, but he pushed the thought aside; it was too haunting.

"There is very little flesh left on any of them," Linda began. "Most of them have been in the ground long enough that it's all decomposed, so it's hard to say what the cause of death is with any certainty. Some have broken hyoid bones, which suggests strangulation; others have injuries that suggest blunt-force trauma. Still others have fissures in places that suggest stabbing. Overall, no two of them is similar *enough*."

"For what?" Cody asked.

"To assume they all have the same cause of death."

"He doesn't have a consistent MO?"

"Not that I can tell. Cody, come here. What do you see?"

Cody came up to stand across the slab from Linda. The captain remained at the body's head, watching. The skeleton was long, suggesting a tall woman. There was some kind of inky residue on the forehead, but Cody assumed that was due to some test the coroner had run. The thing that most distinctly caught his eye was the condition of the rib cage.

It looked . . . warped was the only word that came to mind, as though the bones were made of plastic that had melted into twisted shapes, then hardened again.

"The ribcage. It's deformed." He looked up at her, a few particular B-horror flicks coming to mind. "Is that due to . . . radiation?"

She shook her head. "It's from breakage."

"Breakage?" The captain sounded as skeptical as Cody felt. How did one break a bone into that shape?

"Yes. Take this bone, here." She pointed to one of the lower rungs of the rib cage that looked more like a squiggly line than a rib bone. "This bone has been broken at least eight times. Each time the bone tried to heal, but it was broken severely enough that it healed crookedly. This is why doctors set bones. The body will always try to heal itself, and if the bone isn't straight, it will just heal in whatever position it's in. If this woman had been brought into a hospital, they would have done surgery, re-broken the bones and inserted pins to make them heal straight. Unfortunately for this woman, she died before receiving medical attention." Linda swallowed before continuing. "But it's not just her ribcage. Her ankles are a mess, too."

Cody squinted. Sure enough, there were deformities in the ankle bones as well. Linda walked over to the next victim. She pointed at an obvious groove and large bulb in each of the victim's clavicles. Her arms each had three fracture lines, two of which on the right arm were spiral breaks, reaching all the way around the humorous bone. A third skeleton had major deformities of both bones in her legs, below the knees. Her feet appeared to have been smashed, the bones crushed almost into powder at some points.

"So." Cody stopped her from going on to other victims. He'd seen enough. "You're saying he tortures them by breaking their bones?"

"That's one of the ways."

Cody clamped his mouth shut, trying to summon the courage to ask the obvious question. He wasn't sure he wanted the answer. The captain asked it for him, though.

"What are the other ways, Linda?"

Linda came over to stand next to the body Cody was closest to. "As I said, there's almost no flesh left, no specimens to collect, so we can't exactly do a rape kit. Any alien DNA left on the bones has been too denatured by the soil to tell us anything. However, all of the victims have marks on their pelvic bones."

"Marks?"

"Dents, crevices, fissures."

Cody frowned. "What does that tell us?"

"Something like rape with objects."

"But," the captain said, "these are evidence of something dug into the pelvic bone. Even object rape . . . doesn't . . ."

Linda was nodding. "Doesn't usually produce that kind of result," she finished. "You're right, captain. What this tells us is that it was more of a stabbing gesture than anything else. Look." She pointed to the pelvic bone of the victim in front of them. "This mark here is both long and deep, and it has a beveled edge."

Cody and the captain leaned in. The mark was four inches in length and had cut into the bone itself at least a quarter inch. The highest point in the cut had a small pile of calcification, as though the bone tissue had been scraped out of the groove, pushed up, then packed into the highest corner.

"This mark was probably made by a serrated blade."

Cody waved his hands around, trying to make sense of what she was saying. "Are we talking about him stabbing them . . . between the legs?"

Linda looked very haggard. "Yes."

Cody passed a hand over his eyes, trying to get a handle on the horror of it all, but it was too much. He took two steps back from the table, feeling claustrophobic.

Linda and the captain both set their eyes on the skeleton in front of them, saying nothing, and Cody knew they were waiting for him to regain his composure. He'd always been good at taking whatever weird or macabre things his job presented him in stride, but he couldn't catch his breath this time. Twelve women . . . this kind of torture . . . the cold, creeping feeling he'd gotten in the desert. . . .

Resting his hands on the table, he leaned over and let his head fall forward. He took a few deep breaths, telling himself to pull it together. After the drama of last night, and going on only a few hours' sleep, some discomposure was to be expected. But this, too, would pass.

When his head cleared, he stood up straight and stepped back toward the table. Linda looked up at him as he did. When their gazes met, he understood the dark circles under her eyes. How lonely a coroner's job must be when they had to work alone on *this* kind of case.

"What else?"

"I kept seeing groves and markings on their foreheads, but they were faint. I couldn't tell what caused them. Then, one of the victims over here"—she led them to the body in the far corner—"had grooves that looked distinctly like the number five. I used some colored ink to get a better look. The number turned out to be fifteen. I did the same thing on all the victim's foreheads. I think they're all numbered, but some of them are so faint that they're almost undetectable."

"So what are they?"

"I think he carved numbers into their foreheads. He carved it into the flesh, so it didn't always go through to the bone. From what I can tell, these are victims thirteen to twenty-four."

Cody sighed. This was getting worse by the minute. He rubbed his forehead, but it didn't dispel the tension gathering there. "That suggests the killer is burying them in batches of twelve. If this is graveyard number two, there are at least twelve more victims out there."

Linda nodded gravely.

"Let's hope there isn't a graveyard number three," the captain said, "or anything beyond that."

"Anything else?" he asked Linda.

"Only that, despite the fact that all of the victims are Caucasian females, there's more of a range of values on other things than I would have expected."

"What do you mean?"

"Two of the victims have injuries, but they didn't get much chance to heal. They died too soon after. Of course, that could be chance. Perhaps they weren't very strong or healthy and they went into shock from the injuries and simply died before the killer meant them to. My point is that some were only kept for days after the injuries started, others for weeks, and still others for months.

"Then there are the ages. From what I can tell, the oldest one isn't quite old enough to be considered middle-aged, but probably late thirties or early forties. On the other side of the spectrum, the victim behind you was not fully pubescent, probably twelve or thirteen years old. It's a wide range for a serial killer."

Cody nodded. Then again, it was also true that serial killers were so ruled by their own individual psychoses, that there really was no "norm" for anything they did.

Linda handed him a thick manila file folder.

"The detailed reports on all twelve are in there. Let me know if you have any questions." She turned to the captain. "Unless you have any objections, I'm going start the process of getting the bodies moved to the Salt Lake morgue."

The captain gave her a tight smile. "No objections."

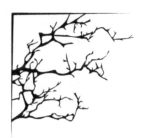

Chapter 19

CODY FOLLOWED THE CAPTAIN back through the funeral home and into the bright sunshine. They walked side by side in silence toward the station. One block from their destination, the captain turned to Cody.

"Are you all right, Cody? You seemed . . . out of sorts in there."

Cody faced the captain. He took a deep breath before answering. "I'm fine, sir. Better, now. I guess I just didn't expect it to be so . . . brutal."

The captain nodded. "It never gets easier. I can tell you that. Is that all that's bothering you?"

"What do you mean?"

"I know your folks are planning on moving up north. I also know you and your father still don't get along too well. I thought maybe that had something to do with it."

Cody had to look down at his shoes to keep himself from chuckling. In recent years, their small town had become a small city. Still, the captain knew everything about everyone. It was in large part due to his socialite wife; the captain obviously made good use of her gossip. Cody supposed he ought to be used to it by now.

Seeing Cody's reticence, the captain put his hands up. "I don't mean to pry. I'm sorry if I'm being too personal. I just need to know that your work has your full attention right now. This is a big case, Cody. Press from out of state are already showing up. It's bound to be national news. I need to know that you're completely focused. If you have other things—family tie-ups and such—I understand. I can work with that. But if that is the case, I should probably make one of the other detectives the lead."

Cody immediately shook his head. "No, Cap. My work is my first and only priority right now. My dad's taking a job up north, but that has nothing to do with me. I'm here. One hundred percent."

The captain looked relieved. "Good. Your instincts are better than just about anyone I've ever worked with. You're the most valuable investigator I have."

Cody couldn't keep his eyebrows from rising. The captain had never said anything like that to him before. Cody didn't think he was any better than Frank or Court, and certainly not better than Tom, who'd been on the job for twenty years.

"Thank you, captain."

The captain gave him a good-natured punch in the shoulder, but thanks to his meat-hook hands, it felt more like being slugged with a dumbbell. Then the captain turned toward the station again.

"Uh, Cap? About my instincts?"

The captain turned back.

"Could I have your permission to assign a uniform to Ms. Thompson?"

"You mean a detail?"

"Yeah."

The captain frowned.

"I know my priority is the Shakespeare case, and we can't assume that it and her case are related without more evidence, but this man went after her very aggressively. Provided she stays off that highway, she should be safe, but I'd feel better if we had someone guarding her."

The captain still looked indecisive.

"Cap, we've got all these extra cops in town, looking for some way to help. Why not put them to work?"

That seemed to sway him. He nodded.

"Put someone on her."

"Around the clock?"

"Yes, but Cody, if the case drags out, as they usually do, interest will start to waver. All the extra cops will go back to their own jurisdictions. At that point, we won't have the manpower for it anymore."

"I understand, Cap. Hopefully it won't get that far."

They returned to the station to find that none of the other detectives had gone back to sleep. They were busy following leads and making phone calls. The captain pulled them all into the back room for a quick meeting.

"Frank, what did CSI have to say about the attack on Ms. Thompson?"

"They took molds of the tire tread. Followed it for miles. They say it eventually went up onto some rock, where there wasn't a track anymore, and they lost it. We still have people scouring the area, looking for anything that might help, but other than the track, there's not much to find."

"All right, keep me apprised." The captain made notes in his ubiquitous notebook. "Court, how about the Shakespeare case?"

"The flowers are common tulip bulbs that can be bought anywhere. The topsoil was probably brought in, so we're trying to narrow down where it could have come from. There was very little trace evidence at the scene. A few hairs, but we're waiting for DNA to rule them out as belonging to any of the victims. There is one interesting fact, though."

"What's that?"

"The tulips were a pale blue color."

"Yes."

"They weren't that color naturally. They were actually white."

"What made them blue?"

"An easy botanist trick. Apparently, if you put the stem of white flowers in water that has blue food coloring in it, it will suck up the color with the water and turn the flower pale blue. From what I was told, you can even cut a stem in half, put half in regular water and half in blue water, and only half the flower will change color. Now, granted, the lab guy said he'd only seen it with roses, but these were growing that way. My point is that this guy is going out of his way to make these flowers look how he wants them to."

"You're saying he has a green thumb?" the captain asked.

Court shrugged. "I'm saying he's taking a lot of time with these grave sites. Who knows where he got the know-how?"

The captain nodded and added more notes. "Anything else, you three? Tom?"

"Just following more leads, sir. Nothing's panned out, yet. Although, we are getting an influx of people who've had loved ones go missing in the area."

The captain groaned. "How big an area?"

"Pretty much the entire intermountain west. The good news is that most of these people have been looking for said loved ones for years. Many of them already have DNA in the system, so once the autopsy results come back on the vics, it'll be easy to rule most of them out."

"What about the ones it doesn't rule out?" Frank asked quietly. No one had an answer.

Cody cleared his throat. "Actually, autopsy results are already back."

He tossed the folder Linda had given him toward Tom.

Tom looked at it pointedly. "And?"

"It's about as gruesome as they come."

The other detectives groaned.

"Everyone read it when they have time," the captain said. "Cody has asked that we put a guard on Ms. Thompson for her safety."

Cody turned sharply toward Frank, daring him to make a joke. But instead of his usual mischievousness, he looked impressed.

"You'll get that all set up, Cody?" the captain asked.

"Yes, sir."

"Good. Let's try and make some order out of this chaos."

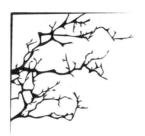

Chapter 20

THE INSTANT CODY PARKED his car behind Tom's in the driveway of the modest middle-class home, a smile meandered across his face. Tom had asked him to dinner with his family, a warm invitation Cody would've said yes to anyway, even if spending the evening alone after the day he'd had wasn't such a bleak alternative. Soft orange light shone out from every window in the place, and the blinds in the front room windows kept plastering themselves against the glass as tiny, playing bodies from within ran into them.

"Cody!"

Tom's youngest son was eight years old and had enough energy to wear out the family's two Labrador puppies on a daily basis.

"Hi, Hank. How's it goin'?"

"Great! I taught Sugar and Flour to roll over. Wanna see?"

"Yeah, sure."

Cody followed Hank into the living room where the boy got down on his knees in front of the dogs. He made a circular motion with his hands and commanded, "Roll over." He had to do it three times, but both dogs finally did it.

Cody applauded. "Good job, bud. How long did it take you to teach them?"

"Three days. Are you staying for dinner, Cody? Mamma's makin' meatloaf."

Cody laughed. "Yeah, I'm stayin'."

"Of course he is." Margaret breezed into the room. She wore an apron covered with various streaks of food over blue jeans and a plaid, button-down shirt.

Cody straightened and kissed Margaret's cheek when she came up to him. "Thanks for having me."

"Of course. Hank's been asking about you for days. Hank, take Cody upstairs so you can both wash up."

Cody followed Hank around for another twenty minutes before they all sat down together. Tom's three older kids weren't as enthusiastic as Hank was to see Cody, but they were polite and friendly as always. His oldest son, also called Tom, was seventeen. His two younger daughters were fifteen and twelve respectively while his oldest daughter was up north finishing her degree at the university.

After the meal, the likes of which Cody was sure only married women like Margaret and his mother knew the secret to making, Margaret chased Hank upstairs to get ready for bed, hollering over her shoulder for Tom to start the dishes. With a sigh, Tom got up to clear the table.

While Cody helped with the dishes, Hank tried to argue his way out of bedtime, Tom Jr. found an excuse to go to the market—a.k.a. an excuse to use the car—and Margaret argued with Jamie, the older of the two girls, about going to a friend's house on a school night.

When things settled down, Cody and Tom went out on to the porch to talk. Tom sat on the front steps while Cody perched on the railing in front of the bay window.

Of course, Hank had to make one last-ditch effort, and his whining, followed by Margaret's stern voice, could be heard in muffled tones.

Margaret stuck her head out the screen door. "Tom, little help here?"

Tom put on what Cody called his "mean dad" face—brows down, eyes narrowed, and jaw set—and raised his voice. "Hank, do as your mother says!"

"But Da-*ad*," came Hank's tiny, disembodied voice. "Why?"

"Because I said so," Margaret said. The screen door slamming muffled Hank's reply.

Tom kept the stone-dog face on until Hank's pre-pubescent squeaks could no longer be heard. Then he grinned at Cody, who chuckled.

"So," Tom said, when they'd savored the silence for a few minutes, "what do you think, Cody?"

"About what?"

"The case. All of it. Off the record."

"There's a lot of 'it,' Tom. Which part do you want my opinion on?"

"Well, Ms. Thompson, for example. Do you think she's staging this?"

Cody sighed. "No, I don't. I know there's no evidence either way, but I believe her."

"Why?"

"I was there when she was running from this guy. I don't think she could have faked that kind of desperation."

"We've seen people fake it before."

"Yeah, but this was different. People can fake it, but to do it so convincingly, they'd have to be stark raving lunatics. She's too, I don't know . . . together? Too grounded."

"Too believable."

"Yeah. I suppose I can't explain it very well. It's just a gut feeling."

Tom seemed to accept that. "We'll know soon enough, I suppose."

"What do you mean?"

"When she gets out of the hospital tomorrow, we'll have to start investigating her. If what she says is true, we need to figure out who this guy is and what she is to him. If there's anything shady in her past, we'll know about it before long."

"Did you get anywhere on her bracelet?"

Tom sighed. "Yes and no. I found a database that lists expensive pieces and their serial numbers. Mostly it's there to track the pieces in case of art theft. If anything emerges on the black market, you can look up its history. It also establishes history so buyers can be sure they aren't buying blood diamonds—that sort of thing."

"And Alex's piece was in there? I thought she told us it wasn't expensive."

"It's not; that's one thing that's strange. Alex's piece is middle-of-the-road. I'm no appraiser, but from what I can tell, most of the pieces from the collection it came from are probably worth two, three, maybe four hundred dollars."

Cody considered. "I bet she doesn't know it's worth that."

"Probably not," Tom agreed, "but even so, the other pieces housed in that database are worth tens, even hundreds of thousands of dollars. It's odd to find such a low-price piece among them. And what are the chances that Alex's piece would just happen to be in a database like that? It wasn't difficult to find at all."

"What do you think it means?"

"I'm not sure, but I don't think it's a coincidence."

"So what information does the database give?"

"Not much. It says the designer of the collection was named Daniel Nath Jones."

"Nath? Odd middle name."

"Yeah."

"Any information about him?"

"None. Just the name and the fact that the pieces in his collection all sold on the east coast about thirty years ago."

"Which would have been just a few years before Alex was born," Cody put in.

"I Googled him," Tom said. "Couldn't find a single stitch of information about who he is, where he lives, his work, nothing. Not that I'm done with this lead, that's just what I found out today. I'll keep you posted."

Cody nodded.

"What about our Shakespeare guy?" Tom asked.

"Now *there's* a lunatic. Did you read the autopsy report?" Cody sipped his soda.

"Yeah. Lots of contradictions."

"Such as?"

"He's beyond brutal with his victims, yet he's gentle enough to get flowers to grow a specific color for him? The bodies show no signs of reticence or remorse, yet he gives them a beautiful burial and even irrigates the soil?"

"Probably for the sake of the flowers," Cody said.

"Yeah, but still. Our killer is chock-full of contradictions like that."

"The psychotic ones generally are."

Margaret came out to the porch and sat on the wooden swing behind the door. Both men fell silent. She looked back and forth between the two of them.

"Sorry. Did I interrupt you two talking about your case?"

"How did you know we were talking about the case?" Tom asked.

"Whenever you guys work on a particularly disturbing case, you have a habit of ending conversations when I come close enough to hear."

Tom grinned up at his wife. "Sorry, honey. We don't mean to be condescending."

Margaret laughed her quiet laugh. "Don't be sorry. You have the right of it. If either of you"—she included Cody in her gaze—"need to talk, I'm happy to listen. But, that said, I'd just as soon avoid the grim realities if I can." After a short silence, she addressed Cody. "Are you having trouble with your dad again?"

Cody threw Tom an accusing glare. So, Tom *had* noticed Cody's reluctance to see his father. Tom suddenly found his shoes fascinating.

"He and my mom are moving up north. He wants me to cover his business while he's away."

"That's out of the question now, isn't it? With this new case and everything?" Margaret asked.

"It was always out of the question. He just wants to get me out of cop work."

"Why is that?"

Cody sighed. "Margaret, I've been trying to figure out the answer to that for—what—six years? Everything I know about my father's childhood, everything *he's* told me, says that he was close to his brother. They were best friends growing up. Yet, when I announced I would follow in my uncle's footsteps and become a cop, my father was completely against it."

"Perhaps the two of them had a falling out as adults."

"If they did, I can't get him to tell me a single thing about it."

"Maybe he's just being a parent, Cody." Margaret pushed a stray lock of hair out of her eyes. "Just worried about your safety, you know? Being a cop can be dangerous."

"In *this* town?"

She gave him a flat-eyed stare. "A psycho in a barn nearly killed you two years ago, Cody."

Cody's cheeks heated. Why was it so easy to forget about that? Not that it ever left his mind, but he just didn't see it as a reason not to do his job. He sighed. "Maybe you're right. I don't know. He never says that, though. I always get the impression there's more to it."

"Well." Margaret leaned back, and the porch swing swayed gently in the warm evening breeze. "Don't be too hard on your father, Cody. I'm sure there's a good reason for the way he feels about this."

"Then why won't he tell me what it is?"

"That I don't know, but perhaps he will in his own time. Besides, it's natural for men to want their sons to follow in their own footsteps. After all, you're the only son he'll ever have."

Cody didn't particularly share her sentiment. If he was the only son his father would ever have, shouldn't his father be proud of him no matter what profession he chose?

After a few minutes of companionable silence, Margaret got up. "Well, I'll let you two get back to discussing your gruesome case. I'm going to bed."

She kissed Tom goodnight, and Tom murmured something about coming up in a while.

Cody got to his feet as Margaret disappeared into the house. "Go up now, Tom. I should get home, anyway."

"Do you need to talk about this thing with your dad more?"

Cody shook his head. "No. He's mad at me, I'm mad at him. There's not really much more to say."

Tom smiled empathetically. "I'm sorry he's giving you a hard time, Cody, but you've got to know what a good detective you are. You're one of the best we have. Do you know that?"

Cody studied his soda can. "The captain told me that today."

"He did? Good."

"You're the best detective this town has, Tom. I don't deserve the sentiment yet."

Tom leaned back against the railing and grinned. "Yeah, I am pretty good, aren't I? But I'd say we're neck and neck."

"If I can crack the Shakespeare case, maybe I'll be there."

"If you can crack the Shakespeare case, we'll all sleep a little better at night."

"'Night, Tom." Cody headed down the stairs toward his jeep.

"See you tomorrow, Cody."

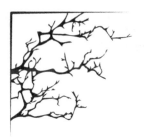

Chapter 21

THE DREAM CAME AGAIN. Alex was in a large cavernous room with walls painted a color somewhere between brown and red. The edges were blurry. She couldn't make out the dimensions very well. High pitched screams bounced off the space around Alex's head and echoed in her ears. The sickly-sweet, putrid smell invaded her nostrils, and she tried to plug her nose, but she couldn't do that *and* clamp her hands over her ears to block out the screams.

"*Please. Please! Leave her alone!*" The voice was a man's, and it sounded familiar somehow, but she couldn't place it. Something wet dripped onto her bare leg and she looked down. She was sitting cross-legged and wearing a dress that didn't quite cover her knees. It took her moment to realize the water droplet had come from her own face.

Another loud screech came from behind the walls, and Alex abandoned her nose and wrapped her arms around her head, using the length of her forearms to cover her ears. The smell was bad, but for the moment the screams were worse.

A presence next to her. A hand on her forehead. She looked up. Her eyes traveled up an impossibly tall frame. It seemed the person's head must be miles above her. He had something—mud, perhaps?—caked all over his face. As he turned toward her, the same scar, those same eyes, glared down at her. It was the cop from the highway. He bent, his face descending rapidly toward her.

A throaty whisper, "Alexxxxxx . . ."

Alex kicked awake with a yelp. The nurse bending over her jumped back in surprise, cursing softly. It was dark in the room, but a shaft of light from the open door had draped itself down the room's center, and faint light was beginning to come through the windows.

Only an instant after stepping away, the nurse stepped back up to Alex's bedside. It had been the nurse's hand on her forehead, not the cop's.

"I'm so sorry, honey. I didn't mean to scare you."

"Not your fault," Alex breathed. "Nightmare."

"Oh. You okay?"

"Yeah. What time is it?"

"Early, a little after six. You should try and sleep some more."

Alex nodded, deciding not to argue. This was a new nurse. The night nurse, Thelma, had awakened Alex every two hours all night. Alex remembered Thelma saying something about getting off at six, so this woman must be her replacement. Each time she'd been awakened, Alex had startled awake in a similar fashion. She'd had the same dream over and over.

At the last awakening—four a.m.—she'd decided that she simply wouldn't go back to sleep, but would lay awake so the nightmare couldn't return. But her body was so exhausted from the trauma it had suffered over the last few days that she simply couldn't keep her eyes open.

Now it was six, though, a time that Alex generally rose in the mornings. And it was starting to get light. Confident that she could stay awake this time, Alex settled back against her pillow to think . . . and promptly found herself in the brownish-red room.

After scaring the tar out of the nurse again, Alex awoke to find a young officer stationed outside her door. After the doctor spoke to her about taking it easy for the next week or two, the nurse brought in her personal items and helped her change. Once she was in her own clothes, Alex invited the unidentified officer into the room.

His name plate read Officer Shaffer. He had the face of a twelve-year-old, complete with peach fuzz on the upper lip, but he moved with the same easy grace she'd noticed in Cody and the other detectives that spoke of prowess with a weapon and confidence in his own abilities.

"You been here all night, Officer?"

"Yes, ma'am. Since about nine last night."

"Who set that up?"

"Detective Oliver, ma'am. Said the Mt. Dessicate PD would feel easier about your safety if we kept a detail on you for the time being."

Alex nodded. Officially she was offended that they didn't think she could take care of herself. Really, though, she was glad to have a police presence nearby. The fact that Cody Oliver was the one who'd set it up for her was even better.

"So what now? They're letting me out in about an hour."

"The captain wants me to take you to the station, ma'am, so you can talk to the detectives some more. I believe they're preparing a safe house for you to stay in until this is resolved."

Alex nodded. She noticed the letters on the side of his uniform were GPD, rather than MDPD. "Where you from, Officer Shaffer?"

"Gunnison, ma'am. A ways north of here."

"Well, thanks for watching over me. I appreciate it."

When the young cop spoke, his voice was soft. "Of course, ma'am. It's my job."

Alex smiled.

An hour later he helped her into the back of his patrol car. Though she hadn't actually broken anything, her ribs were badly bruised, she had bad road rash on her arms, knees, and belly, and then there was the concussion. A glance in the mirror of the hospital bathroom had revealed a checkered scrape on one cheekbone, a split but healing lip, and two colorful but healing eyes—one black, one purple and yellow.

To say that she had to move carefully was an understatement.

When she was safely in, Officer Shaffer shut the door and went around to the driver's seat. Suddenly, Alex felt claustrophobic. Memories of the previous night invaded her mind. Now, with the grate intact and the knowledge that she couldn't get out unless someone let her out, she felt the same panic rising in her chest.

She told herself to breathe. Officer Shaffer had been sent by Cody Oliver, who she trusted. Besides, it was only a five minute car ride to the station. That was all.

She told herself not to be such a ninny. She would not have a phobia of cop cars or back seats for the rest of her life. She couldn't live like that. She would get through this short car ride and the next one would be easier.

In spite of her resolution, by the time Shaffer pulled into the Mt. Dessicate Police Station, Alex was on the verge of a meltdown. Her hands shook in her lap, and she focused on keeping her breathing even. Shaffer parked and got out of the car, and Alex willed him to move faster to her door. She was behind the passenger-side seat, but she had the urge to scoot across the back seat and bang on the door until he opened it.

She didn't.

As he went around the back of the car, the door to the station opened, and Cody Oliver came out. He was talking on his cell phone, oblivious to her and her neurosis. It looked like he might have come outside the station for quiet so he could make his call.

Something about him being there instantly calmed Alex. Even if her worst imaginative fears came true—if Shaffer suddenly turned into psycho-cop and tried to abduct her—Cody was *right* there. He would see her; he would help.

Alex took a deep, calming breath and by the time Shaffer opened her door, her hands were hardly shaking at all.

"So, Ms. Thompson," Tom said when Alex was seated at his desk in the back room of the station. Office Shaffer was chatting with some of the other uniforms in the lobby, while Tom and the captain questioned her. None of the other detectives were investigating her case, but Cody, Frank, and Court had conveniently found things to keep them at their desks when Tom's questions began. "I've gone over both the statement you gave us when you got here the other day and the one you gave Cody last night about your abduction. I've compared them. The one thing that sticks out to me about both accounts is that this man zeroed in on your bracelet. I'm looking into the serial number Cody pulled off the back of it, but I haven't come up with anything conclusive yet."

Alex nodded. "I thought of that."

"Is it valuable?" the captain asked.

Alex looked down at the silver charm bracelet slung around her lower forearm. She'd worn the bracelet almost every day for as long as she could remember, but she'd never thought to have it appraised.

"I don't know. It's not heavy."

"You didn't buy it?"

"It was . . . given to me."

Tom frowned. He could probably tell she was being evasive. Alex realized she'd have to tell them about her true reason for being on the highway outside Mt. Dessicate four years ago. It was personal, which was why she'd been reluctant to tell Cody about it the first day she arrived, but she supposed that was irrelevant now. After two days, she knew the detectives a bit better and, if they were going to help her, she'd have to tell them the whole truth. Besides, it wasn't anything to be weird about, just something she didn't volunteer in conversation with people she barely knew.

"Detective?"

"Tom."

"Tom. Are you going to be digging into my past?"

Tom scrutinized her face for a few seconds. "Ms. Thompson, I'm not convinced that this has anything to do with you personally. I still think it may be a wrong-place-wrong-time scenario. Granted, those scenarios don't generally happen twice, but if this guy's been pulling people off this highway for years, and you're his victim-type, it's not completely implausible. On the other hand, if this does have anything to do with you personally, we need to find out what. His attention to your bracelet is the closest thing to a lead we have. Unless there's something else you'd like to tell me?"

Alex sighed. "I don't know why he would come after me specifically, or why my bracelet caught his attention. I don't mind if you dig around in my personal life. I have nothing to hide. But you may as well start calling me Alex, if that's the case." She glanced around the room. "All of you."

Despite being apparently busy with paperwork, the sides of Court's mouth went up. Frank wasn't even pretending to work. He grinned over at her and winked. Cody's back was to her, so she couldn't see if he was listening or not.

"So." Tom hesitated but when she didn't go on, continued, "What do you have to tell us?"

"Only that I was adopted."

Tom sat back with raised eyebrows. Even the captain looked up from his notebook, mild surprise written on his face.

"Oh," Tom said.

She shrugged. "I didn't know about it growing up. Even when I was eighteen, my parents didn't tell me. Not until I was trying to get a visa to go down to Mexico for a job and there was a problem with my birth certificate did I have any inkling. That was the real reason I was on your highway four years ago. I confronted my parents, who fessed up. Then I got really upset, totally overreacted, and sort of stole my dad's car."

A guffaw from behind Tom said Court was still listening. Cody and Frank had abandoned all pretense of work and were watching and listening intently.

Alex ignored them. "I have an aunt in Arizona. She's the one I always talk to about things I can't talk to my parents about. I was going to see her." She shrugged again. "That's when the Botanist first pulled me over."

Tom gave her a wary look and, from the corner of her eye, she saw Cody and Frank exchanged glances.

"What?" she asked.

"We don't know for certain that they're the same man, Alex."

Alex studied her hands a moment before giving him a tight smile. "I understand that *you* don't know that yet, Tom. But I do. I'm sure of it."

Tom sat deep in thought for a moment, processing what she was saying. Alex didn't interrupt his contemplations. Finally he leaned forward. "Okay . . . and the bracelet?"

"I've had it for as long as I can remember. My mom always told me it was a christening gift but she never found out who it was from. When I found out about the adoption, she told me the whole story. Apparently I was found wandering on a highway as a toddler. Someone stopped and picked me up, took me to the police station."

"You were wandering on the highway as a *toddler?*" Tom looked flabbergasted.

"Yeah, I know. I was really lucky I wasn't killed. I could barely walk, and so was too small to be seen above the hood of a car. If I had crawled into the middle of the road, even if by some miracle the driver saw me, it probably would have been too late to stop. Luckily, that didn't happen. A trucker saw me playing in the dirt on the shoulder."

Alex glanced around the room. All five men looked shell-shocked. Frank and Court's mouths hung open slightly, though she didn't think they realized it. Cody didn't say anything—and his mouth stayed shut—but his eyes were the size of saucers.

"I don't remember this," she offered, "at all. The earliest memories I have are with my adoptive parents."

"And you"—Frank was still trying to recover—"didn't think this was important enough to tell us before?"

That confused Alex. "No. Why would it be?"

"Frank, get back to work," Tom said over his shoulder, looking annoyed.

"But Tom, think about it. Maybe this has something to do with her birth parents. Maybe *he's* her birth father. Maybe she's his long-lost daughter and he gave her the bracelet so he'd be sure to recognize her again and—"

"Frank!" It was the captain that yelled at him, while Tom rested his forehead in his hand.

Alex shifted uncomfortably in her seat. This psychopath had better not be her father. How awful would that be?

Frank looked mildly surprised at the captain's rebuke, but then he glanced at Alex and seemed to check himself. He cleared his throat. "Uh, sorry, Alex. I get carried away sometimes."

Alex smiled in spite of herself. Even when Frank was being insensitive it was endearing. She glanced at Cody, who was watching her.

"Oh, Frank." She looked back at him. "Please don't ever say that again. If my life is really some kind of Star Wars psychodrama, I must be a lot more messed up than even *I* realize."

Frank grinned at her, and she smiled back. The mood in the room lightened palpably. The captain looked relieved that she wasn't offended.

"Now if I can get back to questioning *my* witness." Tom spread his glare around the room. Cody, Frank, and Court went back to what they were doing, looking chastened, but Alex was sure they were still listening.

"Where were you found, Alex? What highway? What state?"

"I'm . . . not sure. It was here, in Utah, but beyond that I don't know. I never thought to ask which highway it was. My dad told me it was farther south, but we live up in Cache Valley, which leaves pretty much the entire state below us."

"Can you find out?"

Alex sighed. "Yeah, I *can* . . ."

"You don't want to?"

"If I call my parents and start asking questions about that, they're going to know something is wrong."

"You haven't told your parents about all of this yet?" Cody burst out.

Alex chuckled under her breath. Yeah, lots of work getting done over there.

Tom glared at Cody, but Cody ignored him.

"You really ought to have a support system, Alex," he said.

She gave him—all of them, really—her best pleading look. "I'll tell them. I promise. But my dad just got back into the country, and my mom just had hip replacement surgery. They don't need this kind of stress. I would just like to have more answers for them first."

"Alex." Tom threw another annoyed look Cody's way. "Was there an investigation into where you came from?"

"Yes. Search parties went out on the highway, apparently, looking for my family. I think they were afraid I might have wandered away from an accident or something. They never found anything. They figured my parents were either junkies and didn't even realize I was gone, or that I was deliberately abandoned. How else would I have gotten out there?"

Tom nodded. "As I said, I think there's a good chance that this was random. You said it yourself: your assailant is psychotic. His attention to your bracelet may be no more than thinking it was pretty and wanting it, and that's why he decided to attack you."

"But then why let me go the first time?"

"Who knows? Psycho, remember? Now, adoption records are sealed, but as you were an abandonment case, I don't see that it makes any difference. I'll try to dig up the old police report, if you can just supply me with the date?"

Alex nodded. "Sure."

"Good. That will tell where you were found and some other details. That way you won't have to bring your folks into it. We'll go from there."

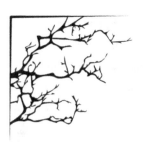

Chapter 22

CODY TRIED NOT TO SIGH as he put the receiver down onto the ancient phone's base. "Tom?"

"Yeah?"

"They're not sure if they can get it for us today."

"What?" It was a bit muffled. The next instant Tom appeared from around the corner, and Cody understood why. Tom's lips were clamped around a donut and a cup of some steaming drink was balanced precariously atop a stack of files he was carrying.

Tom made it to his desk and managed to set the files and the Styrofoam cup down safely. Only then did he remove the donut from his mouth. It came away with a huge, smile-shaped bite missing. "Why not?" Tom asked around the mouthful of sugar.

"The secretary says they're really busy. She's got someone working on it, though. If they can't get it to us today, they'll fax it over first thing tomorrow."

Tom grumbled under his breath about computer databases and email, but Cody stopped listening. He was combing through reports: CSI reports, search and rescue reports, environmental reports. Every report under the sun that might have something, even obliquely, to do with the Shakespeare case had made its way to his desk this morning. He had to read and retain them all. He had a long evening ahead of him.

Alex had been at the station for most of the morning. Around noon Shaffer had taken her to the safe house. Cody knew it well. It was one of only two the police department had within the city limits. It was the larger, nicer one, so they used it first, by default. He knew she'd be comfortable there.

With a sigh he scanned a report about tire treads. It confirmed what Alex had already told them: the tread belonged to the same kind of tire that was used on squad cars in the eighties. They were hard to find nowadays, but not impossible.

There were so many things that bothered Cody about this case, aside from the obvious. Everything they had was discontinuous—bits and pieces of information, but nothing coherent. They had leads; they had bodies; they had a phantom killer somewhere out in the desert, but they didn't know where to start looking for him. Just random pieces of a puzzle they didn't even realize they were constructing until a few days ago.

Cody picked up yet another report and skimmed it. His eyes burned from reading so many pages, but he plowed on, hoping something would strike a chord or point to a lead.

This one was about the land the mass grave was on. The last private owner of that land was named Alastair Landes, but he'd died in the eighties. The county had liquidated Landes' ranch to pay the back taxes, which generally meant the man had died without leaving any legal instructions or heirs to take on his debts.

Cody didn't see how that would help the investigation. The land was now just another plot of undeveloped public desert. Anyone could have gone out there, chosen a spot, and started digging graves. With a sigh, he put the report down and picked up another. There was no end in sight.

A voice, strangely high-pitched for the back office, cleared its throat, and Cody looked up to see Melissa standing in the doorway.

"Hi, Cody. Rose said I could come back. I hope that's okay."

Cody was instantly on his feet, mind searching for why she was there. Had he told her to come? Had they planned a date he'd forgotten?

"Melissa. What . . . are you doing here? Did I forget something?"

"No, nothing like that." She glanced nervously at the other detectives and ran a hand through her dark brown hair. "I just wanted to talk to you. I've been calling you for three days and couldn't get you on the phone. I even left a few voicemails."

Cody sighed. "Sorry about that. My phone's been ringing off the hook for two days. I'm sure I haven't gotten to all of my messages. Actually, I don't think I've gotten to *any* of them. I didn't mean to ignore you."

Melissa gave him an understanding smile. Cody almost asked her to have a seat, but thought better of it. Tom and Court were both studiously reading reports, but Cody was sure their ears had never been more open than at this moment. Frank didn't even bother trying to look busy. He grinned at Cody and gave Melissa a coy little wave.

"Why don't we walk?" Cody said.

Melissa nodded.

They walked out the back door and toward the parking lot to avoid the press. It was only 5:30, but even the reporters were learning that Mt. Dessicate more or less settled down with the sun, and most of them went to their hotels about that time. If Cody tried to walk past the cameras with Melissa, they'd mob her for information as much as they would him.

Cody didn't speak until they stood beside her light green sedan in the otherwise deserted parking lot.

"I'm sorry, Melissa. I don't mean to be distant. It's just that . . . this case is . . ."

"Huge. I know, Cody. I've been glued to the TV just like everyone else. I can see how they have you running around. I'm not angry. I just wanted to make sure you're okay. Are you?"

Cody sighed, thinking about his state of okay-ness for the first time since this all began. "I'm exhausted. And really busy. And stressed out. I've never run an investigation of this magnitude before. It's . . . overwhelming. But, it is what it is. It's work. Yeah, I guess I'm okay. I'm handling it."

Melissa nodded. She unlocked her car with the keyless entry and ducked into the backseat, re-emerging with a paper bag.

"I brought you some food. I'm sure you're eating all kinds of nutritious take out, so..."

"You didn't have to do that."

"I wanted to."

"Thanks." He knew he ought to leave it at that, but he couldn't. The truth was that he hadn't even thought about Melissa in days, and that might not change for a while, not until the case cooled down a bit. And that wasn't fair to her. "Melissa, listen. I don't mean this to sound like I want to break up, because I don't—"

"I don't think we've been together long enough to actually 'break up,' Cody."

A small sedan pulled into the parking lot of the station. Cody looked over, but didn't recognize the driver, so he turned his attention back to Melissa. The driver exited the car and went into the station.

"Okay, but I don't want you to think I'm ignoring you. I don't mean to, but it may feel like that for a while. This case has me going in circles. It's taking up every waking minute and . . . I don't think I can do anything else right now."

The sound of the station door opening and closing came from behind him, but Cody barely registered it. Melissa stared at him for several seconds before nodding. "You know, the semester is almost over for me, which means finals are coming up. I have way too much to do right now, too. Maybe it would be a good idea for both of us to put this on the backburner and let our professional lives take over for the time being. When things get easier, we'll see where we are."

Cody smiled. Melissa was getting her Master's degree. Despite not working, being a full time student did keep her very busy. Still, she was being entirely too reasonable, and he felt guilty. "You're too good to me, Melissa."

She grinned and stepped closer to him. "Only because it works for me, too. But I intend to remind you of that the next time you try to blow me off."

He opened his mouth to object but she put a finger to his lips, then went up on her tip toes to kiss him lightly on the mouth. He returned the slight pressure, and then she turned and got into her car.

She rolled down the window. "Cody?" She buckled her belt as she spoke. "Take care of yourself. I get that you're busy. Trust me, I know a thing or two about pulling an all-nighter, but you aren't going to catch a killer smart enough to say off the cops' radar for so long on two hours' sleep and a ninety-nine cent chicken nuggets meal."

He smiled. "I'll take care of myself. I promise. You do the same."

She nodded and he stepped back as she pulled forward. Just before pulling out of the lot, her hand appeared out the window and she twiddled her fingers at him. He raised an arm in farewell. Then she was gone.

A rumble sounded behind him as a deep voice cleared its throat. Cody turned to see a man he didn't know—the same one who'd pulled into the station two minutes ago—standing a few feet away. The man was tall, broad shouldered, but lean at the waist. He had middle-aged jowls, deep crow's feet around his eyes, and salt-and-pepper hair and mustache.

"Forgive me," the man said. "I didn't mean to interrupt, but are you Cody Oliver?"

"That's me."

The man nodded. "I spoke to your captain and he said you were the lead detective on the case. I have some information for you, about the case. I'd really like to speak with you, if you have the time."

"Who are you?"

The man stuck his hand out. "I'm Lars Stieger, PI I've been digging through county records for the last few days. There are some things I think you should hear."

"PI, huh? And you're investigating *this* case? The Botanist?"

Stieger spread his hands. "I'm not here to step on any toes. Will you allow me to explain?"

Cody nodded, then looked from the bench to the station. "You wanna go inside so I can take an official statement?"

"I'm okay with the evening air if you are."

They walked to an abandoned bus bench and sat down. "I have a client up north," Stieger said, shifting a thick file he was holding to his other hand so he could set it beside him on the bench. "Name of Claire Pert. Her daughter disappeared almost ten years ago."

"You think she was one of the Botanist's victims?"

"It's possible. I'm retired from the SLPD, Detective. Thirty years on the job. I started doing consultations after that, and eventually started doing my own PI work. Mrs. Pert hired me ten years ago to find her daughter. Daughter's name was Miranda. She was nineteen."

"Cold case?"

"Not much of a case at all, actually. The girl disappeared while on a road trip, impossible to say exactly where. I don't have to tell you that no one's going to spend time and resources on a case like that, especially if they don't know for sure that she went missing in their jurisdiction. Private investigation was the only avenue Claire had available to her."

Cody nodded.

"Miranda called her mother about two hours south of here. That was the last anyone heard of her. I was actually here a decade ago. I poked around, asked some questions, but no one had heard of her and not a single person recognized the picture. I could only conclude that she'd driven through, probably didn't even stop for gas. So, I moved on. Never found any sign of her. Eventually I had to change her status to 'presumed dead.' As soon as the discovery of the mass grave hit the airwaves, Claire called me, begging me to come down here and find out if Miranda was one of the victims."

"They haven't released the names yet, have they?" Cody asked.

"No, not yet. Maybe not for another week. As you can see, I had some time to kill. I thought of something—just a curiosity, really—but working beats waiting around for MEs to release their reports any day. Besides, that way I could tell Claire that I was working on something."

Cody nodded, understanding. "What did you expect to find in the county records?"

"I wondered if anyone had looked into the history of the land out there. Sickos of this caliber tend to exist in their own warped universes. It was a long shot, but I thought maybe your guy had ties to the land once upon a time."

"It's a good idea," Cody agreed. "And we did some cursory checking on the land, but it hasn't been privately owned in decades."

"True." Steiger reached for his file. "But I still found some interesting things."

Cody leaned forward.

"The land out there was last sold as a twenty acre parcel in 1946 to a man, name of Alastair Landes. He put down roots and started a ranch."

"Cattle?"

"Sheep and horses. Two years later he married a local girl, but their first son didn't come along until nine years later, in 1957. His name was Jonathin."

Stieger kept talking, but Cody fixated on the name. Something about it was standing out to him. Jonathon. Jonathon. Jo*nath*on."

"Detective, are you following me?"

"Sorry. That name, Jonathon Landes, is it spelled traditionally?"

"Uh, no actually, the end of 'Jonathin' has an *i* instead of an *o*."

"Do you have a pen and paper I could use for a minute?"

"Sure." Stieger pulled scratch paper out of his file and a pen from his shirt pocket. "You want me to write the name down for you?"

"Would you?"

Stieger did, and then handed Cody the paper and pen.

Jonathin Landes. Jonathin Landes. Daniel Nath Jones.

Cody started crossing out letters.

J̶O̶N A T H I N L A N D̶E̶S̶

D A N I E L N A T H J O N E S

The problem was that there were two *e's* in Daniel Nath Jones and only one in Jonathin Landes.

"Did this Jonathin Landes have a middle name?"

"Uh," Stieger rifled through his file. "Edgar."

Ah. There it was: middle initial *e*.

Stieger watched with interest but cocked an eyebrow when Cody was finished. "What is it, Detective?"

Cody glanced up. As Stieger wasn't a working cop, Cody probably shouldn't give him information on the case, but this man had given him a viable lead concerning Alex's involvement in it. Cody made a decision.

"A would-be victim has a certain piece of jewelry that the killer keeps fixating on. The creator of the jewelry line is named Daniel Nath Jones, but we've been unable to find any information on this man. His name is an anagram for Jonathin E. Landes."

Stieger's eyebrows rose steadily as Cody talked. "Really?"

"Does that mean something to you?"

"Not particularly, but it's interesting. Let me tell you the rest of what I've found."

"So Jonathin was born and Alastair's wife died in childbirth, but after that, there are no records for Jonathin. He never bought or held property in the county. No marriage certificate, no birth certificates for further Landes descendants. When Alastair died, his land went unclaimed until the county absorbed it."

"So what happened to Jonathin?"

"I talked to some local old timers who had some intriguing stories. Jonathin and his father butted heads. Alastair wanted his son to grunt and sweat and run the ranch with him. Jonathin was, shall we say, more artsy.

He wanted to go to art school, but his father refused to pay for it. Jonathin packed his bags and ran away to the army."

Cody waited but Stieger didn't go on. "And?"

"And nothing. That's it. He left and never came back. When his father died, people tried to locate him—sent out letters and legal notices and such about the property—but he never responded and he never showed."

"Just fell off the planet, huh?"

"Seems that way."

Cody digested what he'd just learned.

"Well, it's interesting, but there's no obvious link to the case."

"Doesn't seem so, does it?"

Something in Stieger's voice made Cody turn. "You think there is?"

Stieger shrugged. "Nothing concrete. If Jonathin Landes is still alive, he would be in his mid-fifties. I'm not sure about his looks or stature—didn't find any photos of him—but he could be our desert grave digger."

"Is there anything in the history to suggest that he might have been psychotic?"

"Not yet, but this is hardly comprehensive."

"Stieger, how would you like to become a temporary employee of the Mt. Dessicate Police Department?"

Stieger grinned. "Get paid for my work? Revolutionary idea, that."

Cody smiled. "Can you access military records? See if you can pull Jonathin's personnel files? If he was off his rocker, military tests might have revealed it. He may have been discharged or even rejected as a military candidate. Talk to some more locals as well. See what else you can find out about the family. Maybe part of Jonathin's flight had to do with some kind of abuse going on in the home."

"It won't be easy to get the old timers to talk about that, even if they knew it was going on at the time—I've already tried. They're from the era of hiding dirty linen behind white picket fences."

"I don't envy you the task. Just do the best you can. Also, see if you can find anything linking these two names: Jonathin Landes and Daniel Nath Jones. It could be that Jonathin just used a different name for his business. On the other hand, he might have legally changed it, which is why we can't find any background on Jones. If that's the case, maybe he didn't want to be found, which begs the question of why."

"Or who he was hiding from," Stieger said, nodding.

"Exactly."

"I found one other strange thing, and I'm not sure what to make of it."

"Tell me."

"I looked through some old reports and newspaper articles from when Alastair died. There are some things that don't add up, but I'm hoping more digging will help me understand."

"Like what?"

"First of all, there's a police report and a coroner's report on him."

Cody arched an eyebrow. "Did the police suspect foul play?"

"I'm not sure. Like I said, I need to dig some more. Jonathin was long gone before his father died and Alastair was alone at the time of his death. Perhaps it was just a matter of finding a dead body, and needing to make sure that the death was natural. That *was* the conclusion that both the ME and police came to. Alastair also hired a transient to help him do ranch work. No one in town liked the guy. There are some pretty sinister rumors about him."

"What do you suspect?"

"I honestly don't know. I found out that Alastair's old ranch house is still standing. It's a ruin, but I thought I might go check it out. Care to join me, Detective?"

Cody glanced back toward the station. He knew he shouldn't. He ought to stay and absorb more of those files, but a quick field trip and some fresh air was too much to resist.

"Actually, yeah. We should take separate cars, though. I might get called back sooner than you want to come."

Stieger nodded. "Do you know where it is?"

"Yeah. I'll meet you there."

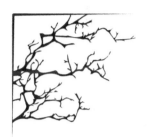

Chapter 23

CODY SIGHED. HE STOPPED at a red light and took the opportunity to lean his head back against the car's headrest and shut his eyes for a few seconds. The details of the case swirled inside his skull like debris in a tornado, but he was so tired he couldn't grab on to any of them. There weren't many tornados in Utah.

The light turned green and Cody sat up straight and accelerated. He glanced to the right. In a small parking lot a sign that read *"Janet's"* was lit up. *Janet's* was a ma-and-pop convenience store that had been operating since before Cody was born.

Something struck him.

Many of the more seasoned uniforms were being used for leg work: following leads, collecting information, talking to people, that sort of thing. Just before leaving the station for the evening, Cody had come across a report that said all the local grocery stores had been visited, but no one could remember any strange customers who might have bought a lot of blue food coloring. A list of the stores visited was at the bottom of the report. Now, thinking back, Cody was sure *Janet's* wasn't on that list. He supposed it made sense, but it was exactly the problem with having out-of-towners do leg work in Mt. Dessicate: they didn't know the area. They didn't know what to search for, didn't know what was normal and what wasn't.

Whoever had done the investigating had probably used a local phonebook and looked for all the grocery store chains, but *Janet's* was a tiny, family-run business. It wouldn't be under "grocery" in the yellow pages, if it was in the phonebook at all. And the name didn't exactly scream food.

It was probably close to closing time, and Stieger was waiting for him at the Landes place, but Cody decided to stop in anyway. It couldn't hurt.

A bell nailed to the top of the door tinkled as Cody entered. A woman in her thirties stood behind the single register in the place. She glanced up from her novel, but went back to it before speaking.

"If you're gonna shop, do it quick. We close in five."

Cody walked toward her. "Actually"—he got out his badge —"I'm not here to shop. I wondered if I might ask you a few questions."

The book dropped to the counter, forgotten, and the woman, whose hand-written nametag read "Marg," folded her arms atop the counter and leaned forward, studying Cody with interest.

She looked him up and down. "You look familiar. You been on TV?"

Cody felt his cheeks warm. "Uh, yeah." He cleared his throat. "There've been a lot of cameras around lately. I'm Detective Oliver."

"You aren't the one that actually found the bodies, are you?"

"Actually, I am."

Her eyes got wider, if that was possible, and her mouth worked soundlessly for several seconds. She looked at the counter, then back up at him, but still said nothing. Cody thought she was trying to be both curious and tactful at the same time, and what that amounted to was a complete loss for words.

"Well, uh," she finally managed, "how's that goin'?"

He smiled. "We're working on it, day and night."

Marg shivered. "It's so scary. I never been one to lock my door, Detective, but the second I saw the news, I made my husband march right out and buy a deadbolt."

"That's understandable. It *is* scary. But don't you worry. We'll get the guy, and make the town safe again."

Marg took a deep breath, as though to calm herself, then put on a polite customer service smile. "So what can I help you with detective?"

"Actually, I'm not sure that you can. I know I'm not supposed to ask a woman her age, but you look too young to help me."

Marg's smile lit up her face. "Well, you sure do know how to lay on the butter, dontcha, Detective?"

Cody chuckled. "How long you been working here, Marg?"

"Since I was about fifteen."

"Hm. Do you remember any customers who might have bought a lot of blue food coloring?"

Her smile faded a bit. "Huh?"

That was answer enough, he supposed.

"Well, Colleen Hinckle always buys a bottle or two around the holidays. That's more than most. How much is a lot?"

"More than a bottle or two. I'm talking by the case, or with constancy. This person may not have been in for years. If that's the case, he would have stocked up. If no one buys it more constantly than Colleen, it would probably have bought many cases years ago. Ring any bells?"

Marg shook her head. "Nothing comes to mind."

Cody nodded. It had been a long shot to begin with. "I don't suppose there's anyone who's worked here longer than you? Say, twenty or twenty-five years?"

"My dad has. My grandpa opened this store when he first married my grandma. My dad started working here when he was a teenager, same as me." She grinned proudly.

Cody smiled. "Is there a way I can get in touch with your father? Ask him a few questions?"

"He's in the back doing inventory. I'll get him for you."

"Thanks."

She walked the length of the counter and disappeared through an ordinary-looking door. Cody leaned on the counter to wait.

Minutes later she reappeared with a shorter, plumper, balder version of herself. Her father was heavyset and wore horn-rimmed glasses, but had a kindly look about him.

"Hullo, Detective." The man shifted his clipboard to his left hand and stuck out his right. "I'm Greg Coleson, owner. My daughter tells me you're working the Botanist case and have some questions for me."

"Nice to meet you, sir. Just one question, and it's an odd one, to be sure. In your recollection, did you ever have a customer that bought large amounts of blue food coloring?"

Mr. Coleson smiled at first, as his daughter had, at the absurdity of the question, and opened his mouth to speak, but then he stopped, frowned, and looked down at the counter. He turned his head and studied the wall. "Actually, I have."

Cody's heart leapt into his throat. "You *have?*"

Coleson shook his head slowly. His smile was one of quiet awe. "You know, Detective, I haven't thought about that man in years."

Cody's pulse pounded, his exhaustion forgotten. "What man? Who was he?"

"I never knew his name. This was . . . twenty years ago, maybe more."

"What can you tell me about him?"

"He was a strange man; no one in town much liked him. He got work over on the Landes farm. Ol' Alastair was the only one didn't seem disturbed by him."

"Why were people disturbed?"

"Don't know. He was just a strange sort; made the hairs on the back of your arm stand up, you know? I remember my wife waiting on him once, then telling me if he came back in she wanted me to do it. He creeped her out too much."

"And he bought a lot of food coloring?"

"Tons. Actually, that's all he bought. Back then the stuff only came in glass bottles, in cases of twelve. He would come in when my truck arrived and buy the entire case. I started holding two or three bottles back in storage until after he came so there'd be some for other customers who wanted it. Even if I brought in two or three cases a week, he'd buy 'em all."

"Whatever happened to him?"

"Don't know. After Alastair died, he disappeared."

"Can you think of anyone who would know his name?"

"Anyone who knew Alastair well might remember," Coleson said with a hint of apology. "I knew him by reputation, but I couldn't even call myself an acquaintance."

"Anything else you remember about him that you could tell me?"

Coleson thought for a moment, but shook his head.

"Well, thank you Mr. Coleson, Marg. You've been very helpful."

Cody smiled and turned to leave, but stopped when Coleson addressed him again.

"Detective?"

He seemed hesitant, and Cody stepped toward him again. "Yes? What is it?"

Coleson shrugged uncomfortably. "I never knew much about that man, but that's because I didn't want to. He was the kind of guy that just gave you a cold feeling, you know? If he's somehow involved in that . . . ugliness out in the desert . . ." Coleson trailed off and looked out the window in the general direction of the mass grave. He shuddered, then met Cody's gaze again. "You just take care of yourself, detective."

Cody smiled, though his stomach had gone cold. "I will, sir. Thank you again."

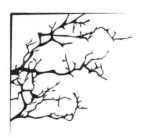

Chapter 24

AN HOUR LATER, CODY sighed and rubbed his face with the heels of his hands. The description Griffith had given Stieger was all too accurate: the two remaining buildings on the Landes property were barely fit to be called buildings. The house had been gutted. Only two walls were left standing. Mildew and mothballs garnished every surface. The smell of rotting wood permeated the air.

The barn held up better. Most of the structure was still there, but the roof, as well as the east wall, had several man-sized holes in them, and there was nothing inside but some black straw on the ground and old, rusted tools.

Cody had been studying in circles for the past half an hour. If he hadn't found anything by now, he never would. Grateful to move into fresher air, he headed farther out on the property to join Stieger. He found the older man staring out over a fence made of wooden posts and barbed wire. Beyond it was a meadow of greenish-yellow grass, and tiny, light blue flowers that grew in concentrated, random clumps.

Stieger turned his head when he heard Cody's footsteps. "Find anything?" he asked when Cody was beside him.

"Lots of initials surrounded by hearts carved into the walls. Dust bunnies to keep the mothballs company. That's about it. You?"

Stieger jerked his chin toward the field. "Dirt. Grass. Shrubs. Flowers."

Cody was about to suggest they head back to the station when something occurred to him. He frowned.

"What is it?" Stieger asked, seeing his expression.

"These flowers. I haven't seen them before. They're not desert flowers."

"Maybe they're imported."

"Exactly. You aren't from around here, don't know the climate. Only desert shrubs will grow out here naturally. Anything else has to be specially cared for."

"Are you saying the Botanist cultivated these?"

"I'm saying he's a creature of habit."

Cody fell into a crouch, but even that was not enough. He leaned forward, resting his weight on his knees and laid his cheek against the ground.

There it was.

The densest concentrations of flowers were atop small mounds of dirt. They were so small and the meadow around them rolled just enough that they were hard to distinguish except from ground level. He looked up to find Stieger frowning at him quizzically.

"Join me down here, Stieger. Look at this."

Stieger quirked an eyebrow at Cody, eyes shifting from right to left.

"Trust me," Cody said. "This is something you want to see."

After a moment, Stieger shrugged. He knelt where he was, put his cheek to the ground and gazed in the same direction Cody was. He let out a soft gasp. "More mounds." He raised his head to look at Cody. "Do you think they're more human bodies?"

Cody sighed, sitting back on his heels. "They're awfully small, but I suppose it would depend on how deep he buried . . . whatever it is." Cody got to his feet and went back to the barn. He'd seen a rusty shovel in there. When he returned, Stieger was in the same place but had gotten to his feet.

"Let's find out, shall we?" Cody said, hefting the shovel.

"Can we? Shouldn't we call CSU or something?"

"Yes, we should, but it'll take them an hour to get out here and we're already losing the light. I'll disturb as little as possible, but I want to know if we're dealing with more bodies."

Twenty minutes later, Cody had uncovered an entire skeleton. It was barely as big as his two fists together.

"What is that?" Stieger asked from over his shoulder. "Squirrel?"

Cody shook his head. "Groundhog, I think. Not too many squirrels out here." The animal was small with a delicate skeletal structure. An obvious deformity in the spine hyper-extended the head and neck back toward the tail.

"Looks like its neck was broken," Stieger said.

"Yeah."

"So these are a bunch of animal graves?"

Cody glanced around and did a quick count. "Twelve, to be exact."

Stieger's eyebrows climbed. He turned in a circle, lips moving silently as he counted. "You're right," he said when he'd finished. "Definitely a creature of habit."

Cody glanced back toward the vacant house and barn. The wind fluttered through the meadow's grass, and the blue flowers swayed gently. Suddenly the place felt lonely.

"This is where his psychosis was born." Cody straightened his legs. "He was out here torturing and killing animals under Alastair's nose for . . . who knows how long? At some point, he escalated to human violence."

"You think it was Charles, then? Or Jonathin?" Stieger asked.

Cody shook his head. "Hard to say which yet. But it's sure looking like it was one of them."

Stieger nodded.

Voices brought Cody's head around and he turned in time to see two teenagers, a boy and a girl, come around the Landes barn. It took them several seconds to notice Cody and Stieger, but the instant they did, they both froze, looking like deer that had just wandered into a semi's high beams.

"Hey! You two! Come here."

The two teenagers glanced nervously between Cody and Stieger. Then they shared a look, turned, and took off.

"Hey! Wait!" Cody chased them. When he came around the barn they were fifty yards ahead of him, but still clearly visible. There was a stand of aspen trees a quarter mile up the road, but other than that, the property didn't have many trees, only low desert shrubs and sagebrush dotted the terrain. "Mt. Dessicate PD. Stop!"

The boy stopped. The girl ran a few more paces before realizing her companion wasn't with her anymore, and followed suit. Cody jogged up to them. Stieger's steady footfalls thudded behind him.

When Cody reached the two youths, they were both trembling with fear.

"We didn't do anything." The boy had long brown hair and clothes that screamed musician.

"Then why'd you run?"

"It's not just us," the girl whined, pushing waist-length black hair over her shoulder. "Everyone comes here."

"Relax. I'm not here to bust you," Cody said. Technically this was public land, so they weren't trespassing, but he didn't say so. They'd have looser tongues if they were afraid of legal consequences. "I just want to ask you some questions. Do you come here a lot?"

The teens exchanged glances, then the boy put his eyes resolutely on the ground. "No."

Cody rolled his eyes. "I told you I'm not here to get you in trouble. I'm interested in the property, not what you're"—he glanced between them—"doing out here. Just tell me the truth. Are you out here a lot?"

The boy looked at Cody, sizing him up. Finally he seemed to decide Cody was telling the truth. He sighed. "I been out here a few times."

The girl's eyes and mouth widened. "With who?"

Suddenly the boy looked more afraid of her than of Cody. Cody didn't know whether to laugh or yell. He didn't have time for teen drama. He waved his hands to get their attention. "All I want to know is if there are any other buildings or structures or places where kids go when they come out here."

The boy shook his head slowly. "Everyone hangs out in the house, or sometimes the barn, but that's it. There is one more place, but it's the opposite of what you said: *no*body wants to go out there."

"Out where?" Stieger asked, stepping up beside Cody.

"There's an old shed of some kind a quarter mile out. You can't see it from here, but it gives everyone the creeps."

"How come?" Cody asked.

The boy shrugged. "It's small, kind of boring, but it's really creepy, too."

"Why?"

"I went out there once," the girl put in. Her boyfriend turned a scathing look on her and she held up her hands. "With my girlfriends. It was two years ago on Halloween. We went out there, but I couldn't get anywhere near the shed."

"Why not?"

"It just freaked me out. It wasn't anything that I saw or anything that happened. It was just this freaky feeling. They say Ol' Man Landes' ghost is out there, and I believe it. It just felt wrong."

Cody looked in the direct they'd pointed, out past the field he and Stieger had been staring at minutes earlier. "A quarter mile, huh?"

"Yes, sir." The boy looked like he wanted to salute.

"Okay, you two. I won't call your parents. This time. But I want you to do something for me. Spread the word to your friends that the cops are watching this place and we don't want anyone hanging out here for the time being, okay?"

"Does this have something to do with that psycho in the desert?" the girl asked.

Cody had to choose his words carefully. Not that he would mind scaring some sense into these two, but anything he said could get back to the press. "No, we don't think so, but with a killer potentially on the loose, it may not be safe for anyone to be out here. You two ought to stay closer to home. Just spread the word, okay?"

"Yes, sir," the boy said again.

"Good. Get going."

They both hesitated, looking fearfully at him, as though they were afraid he'd throw a hatchet at them when they turned their backs.

"Go on."

They turned and jogged off. Stieger came to stand beside Cody.

"You grew up around here, didn't you detective?"

Cody nodded.

"Did you ever come out here as a teenager?"

"I came out with a group of friends on Halloween once, but I'd never heard of this shed. We just played night games in the barn and got buzzed on some beer one kid swiped from his dad's cooler. I always thought it was a little creepy for a make-out spot." He glanced at the two retreating teens. "Obviously not everyone feels that way."

Stieger chuckled. "So you want to go check out this shed?"

"Yeah. We'd better hurry. It'll be dark before long."

Only a sliver of light blue sky remained in the east when Stieger finally spotted a dark, squatting shadow among the aspens. The tree population rose considerably as they moved away from the house, and Cody hoped they didn't get lost in the white-pillared forest.

As they approached the small shed—no more than ten feet by ten, with a slanted roof—Cody thought he understood what the girl had meant about feeling creeped out. He didn't feel afraid, but he had a sensation of adrenaline, as though his heart was racing and his muscles were trembling, only they weren't. It wasn't a physical sensation. Cody didn't know what it was, but it was odd.

The only time he'd ever felt anything like it was when he'd come nose to nose with a pedophile in a barn. The parallel of the two situations chilled him.

Clicking on his flashlight and raising it to his shoulder, he pushed the door inward. The hinges protested loudly, and the smell of decay entered Cody's nose. He stepped forward, Stieger right behind him, and Cody was glad for the other man's company.

There was barely room for both of them. The girl had been right about not many people coming to the shed. There were a few shoe prints inside, but not many. Though there was evidence of trodden paths to and around the shed, Cody didn't think anyone had actually ventured inside for months, possibly years. An ancient spade was half buried in the dirt in one corner and a long, rusty, manual saw with many of its teeth missing leaned against the far wall. Other than that, Cody's flashlight revealed only what the barn and house had: dust and mothballs.

Plenty of spiders had decorated the corners and crannies with silvery webs, but Cody didn't see any of the actual critters. Even they had abandoned the shack.

"What do you think?" Stieger asked, making Cody jump. The older man cleared his throat. "Sorry."

"I don't know what to think. There's nothing here."

"Maybe anything that's here really is supernatural."

"Maybe," Cody murmured. He felt like he should explore more, but there was nothing else to investigate. He could see every part of the one-room shed, and there was nowhere to go without bumping into Stieger.

Cody took a tentative step toward the wall and something beneath his feet creaked. The sound was so soft he wondered if he'd imagined it. He turned back.

"Did you hear that?"

"Yeah, I did." Stieger was looking at Cody's boots. Cody stepped back. He stepped all around the area, trying to re-create the creak, but there was only silence. The ground felt solid beneath him. Rising onto the balls of his feet, he tried to thrust his weight downward, into the ground. He did it several times, unsure what he was feeling. If there *was* movement, it was so subtle, he could barely detect it. It certainly wasn't a visible thing.

"What is it?" Stieger asked.

"The dirt feels hard-packed, but I think it's giving a little."

"You think something's buried?"

Cody got to his knees. "Let's find out."

The ground was packed densely enough to be like stone. Cody used the butt of his flashlight to break it up, while Stieger retrieved the old spade from the corner to help. After twenty minutes and six inches of dirt clods, the point of Stieger's spade hit something that *clunked.*

"What was that?" Cody asked. "A rock?"

Stieger shook his head. "Felt more like wood. I think I almost broke through it."

Further digging revealed an old pine box, but ten minutes later, they still hadn't found the edges of it.

"How big do you think it is?" Cody wiped sweat from his eyes.

"Can't be any bigger than the shed, right?"

"You said you almost broke through before? *Can* you break through it?"

Stieger gazed steadily at Cody. "Do you want me to?"

Cody sighed. Was he marring a potential crime scene? Yes. But this wasn't the city; they were out in the middle of nowhere.

"We need to know what we're dealing with," he said. "This could be Gertrude Landes' hope chest. If that's the case, there's no point in dragging everyone out here. If on the other hand . . ."

He didn't need to finish the thought. Stieger nodded and raised the spade over his head, point toward the ground. With a mighty heave, he thrust it downward. The third thrust produced a loud *crack* as the wood splintered. Cody pulled a pair of work gloves from his pack—perfect for guarding against splinters—and pulled away broken chunks of wood.

When a basketball-sized hole had been cleared, Cody shone his flashlight into the box. Stieger peered in with him. Cody let his head drop, suddenly exhausted. He fell back onto his buttocks and leaned his forehead against his arm. He wasn't spooked by what looked up at him from the hole, just saddened.

Not for the first time since this whole thing began, he wondered how his Uncle Clyde would have handled it. Cody felt like he was falling down a rabbit hole—one with smooth sides and no way to tell how deep it was or which way was up.

Rivulets of sweat ran down Stieger's cheeks and his chest moved more deeply than usual. "The plot thickens," he said quietly.

"I don't think we're discovered the plot yet. I think we're only scratching the surface." Cody pulled his camera from his pack and snapped a picture to send to the captain. The skeletal face staring up at him could almost have been sporting a morbid smile. Cody was no coroner, but the long, undecayed locks of hair sprouting from the skull suggested a small woman or girl.

Stieger reached into the splintered coffin and pulled out a book. When he gingerly let it fall open, faded handwriting could be seen. It looked like a journal.

Cody's camera flashed again. Pictures were supposed to be mementos, usually of something good. Cody didn't think he'd ever get used to photographing the dead.

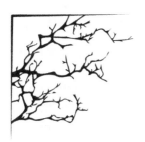

Chapter 25

WHEN CODY ARRIVED BACK at the station two hours later, the captain, Frank, Court, and Tom were all waiting for him. He'd called the appropriate people, and it didn't take long for what was once Alastair Landes' property to be cordoned off. Reporters showed up and Cody thanked heaven for the extra cops in town. Linda arrived in a coroner's vest to take the bones away, and Stieger promised to keep in touch.

"Well, where is it?" Frank asked.

Cody produced the sealed plastic bag that contained the journal Stieger had found. "It needs to be printed. If we're lucky, this guy'll be in the system."

"Did you read any of it?" Court asked.

"No. It was too dark out there. Pretty much just chicken scratch anyway, but look at the inside cover." The plastic bag was wrapped loosely enough that he could partially open the book and let them look inside. The white part of the inside cover was dirty and creased. The faded blue ink constructed only two words: *Shakespeare's Girls*.

Despite the different mediums, the style and shape of the writing was unmistakably similar.

"Okay." The captain removed his glasses and rubbed the bridge of his nose. "That's enough to assume that whoever buried the bodies in the desert also wrote this journal."

"Agreed," Cody said.

"I'm going to call in a criminalist."

"What?" Frank and Court said at the same time.

"Like a profiler?" Tom asked.

"I'm not any happier about it than you,"—the captain replaced his glasses—"but I think it's the best thing. The mayor's leaning on me, because the governor's leaning on him. I've had offers of help from every major agency in the country, all the way up to the FBI, and quite frankly, I think we're out of our league here, unless one of you has worked a serial killer case I don't know about?"

Silence followed.

"I'm not bringing them in to run the show, but we have too many leads to follow to sit around trying to interpret the psychotic scribblings of a madman. I'll give the journal to the experts and let them figure out the psychosis. That way we can focus on catching the guy."

Cody rifled around on his desk, looking for the real estate document he'd read earlier about Alastair Landes's land. He glanced up to find the captain and his fellow detectives staring at him.

"Do you know that little convenience store on fifth and Center called *Janet's?*"

"Sure," Court said. "My wife likes that place. A bit out of your way, though, isn't it?"

"No. I try to avoid the traffic on Main during certain hours of the day, so I take a detour that takes me right past *Janet's*. I drive by it all the time. Earlier today, I read a report about none of Mt. Dessicate's stores knowing of any customers that bought a lot of blue food coloring, but you're right Court: *Janet's* is a bit off the beaten path, both geographically and in terms of business visibility. An out-of-towner uniform might miss it, so I decided to stop in, and guess what?"

"They knew of someone?" Tom's voice always rose in pitch when he was surprised.

"The owner remembers a transient that used to buy blue food coloring by the case. This was at least twenty years ago. This guy apparently gave everyone the willies and he worked for a man named Alastair Landes."

"Landes," Frank said. "*Landes*. Why do I know that name?"

Cody held up the report. "Because he's the one who last owned the land the mass grave is on."

Tom let out a low whistle. "So what happened to this Landes guy?"

Cody sighed. "He died in '87. He didn't leave a will, so the county liquidated his ranch and absorbed the real estate. It's part of county public lands now. The owner didn't know what happened to the transient, assumed he left town when Alastair died. He did suggest that someone who knew Alastair more personally could tell us more about the transient."

"And maybe give us a better idea of where he went after Alastair's death," the captain finished.

Cody nodded.

"Well, it's a place to start. You stay on that, Cody, and keep me updated." The captain looked down at his papers, shuffling them. "Does anyone else have anything of import?"

There was a brief silence before Tom spoke. "I did manage to get the report about Alex being found on the highway."

Cody's head snapped up. "And?"

"It's about like she says. Not a lot of details. There is one thing of note, though: guess which highway she was found wandering?"

Cody raised his eyebrows in question.

"*This* highway, about a mile north of that historical monument."

The silence stretched as that sank in.

"Obviously *that's* not a coincidence," Frank muttered.

"Keep digging," the captain told Tom, who nodded. "All of you keep at it. Bring anything important directly to me, and it goes without saying that this is your priority. Everything else is on the backburner. Beyond that, I've got the mayor breathing down my neck and the press to deal with. I'll be in my office."

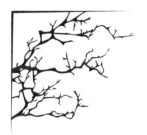

Chapter 26

AN HOUR LATER, CODY'S phone rang, making him jump. He'd made fourteen calls in the past hour, trying to confirm what Stieger had found on Alastair Landes and fill in the holes. Landes was proving a difficult man to learn about.

"Cody Oliver." Cody cradled the phone's receiver with his shoulder so he could work while he talked.

"Detective Oliver? This is Officer Shaffer. I'm with Ms. Thompson at the safe house?"

"Of course. Is anything wrong?"

"Not with her, sir. Ms. Thompson is resting. She's fine. The problem is that my captain just called and ordered me back to Gunnison. He wants me back there tonight. I need someone to come and relieve me so I can head back."

Cody glanced at his watch. It was a quarter past seven. Most of the extra cops in town would have retired for the evening. He didn't know who to contact to assign another uniform to Alex. Frank was the one keeping track of how many extra men had come from which towns and where they were at any given time, but Frank and Court had headed out for dinner ten minutes ago. And when Frank was ripping into dinner, he generally didn't answer his cell phone—at his wife's request, but Frank gleefully used it as an excuse to ignore work while he ate.

"Well, Shaffer, it'll probably be an hour or two before I can get another uniform over there. Do you need to leave right away?"

"As soon as possible, sir. My captain insists."

"All right. I'll come and relieve you myself. Be there in fifteen."

"Thank you, sir."

Cody stood and gathered up his things. He was waiting to hear back from all of the calls he'd made, but he'd given his cell phone number in each instance, and he could read his boring reports just as well at the safe house as he could here. Might as well let the young man get home and appease his captain.

"Cody."

Cody skidded to a halt beside the front desk. "Yes, Rose?"

"Lab reports on the vics came back."

"Where?"

Without taking her eyes from her monitor, Rose stabbed her pen in the general direction of a manila envelope on the corner of her desk.

Cody snatched it up, noting his name on the front. "Thanks, Rose."

"Mmm-hm."

On the way over, he called Frank. As he suspected, the call went straight to voicemail. He left a message for Frank to find a uniform to spend the night at the safe house with Alex, and to call and let Cody know when the officer was on his or her way.

The safe house was a small, red brick rambler that snuggled in perfectly with every other house on the street. The grass was cut but not landscaped; the front and garage door paint was faded but not chipped; the driveway was pocked but not potholed. It looked lived-in without drawing attention to itself—the perfect location for a safe house.

Shaffer opened the door. "Thanks again, sir."

"No problem. Heading home right away then?"

"Yes. Well, I have to take the unmarked car back to the station and swap it for my squad car, sir, but after that, yes."

"Stay alert out there. Apparently the highway isn't safe at night."

"Going the other direction, detective, but I'll be careful anyway."

Cody chuckled, then raised a hand in farewell as Shaffer backed out of the driveway.

He took his files into the kitchen and spread them out on the table. The house was quiet, and the bedroom door was closed. Alex must still be sleeping.

For the next hour and a half, he sifted through the reports. He found a few interesting details, but nothing jumped out at him.

A surprising amount of the land outside the city limits was either still privately owned, or had been up until the eighties. Apparently, quite a few people or companies had bought parcels over the years, planning to develop it. Developing so far into the desert was difficult, though, and in most instances, plans fell through and the property rights lapsed or were simply abandoned. The county then absorbed the land.

There was some talk of underground springs in the area the bodies were found. That might explain the wet soil in the graveyard. Perhaps the spot was a natural oasis, and that's why the killer picked it. If underground streams laced that mountain, a person might be able to survive out there, away from civilization, without much trouble.

Cody couldn't stop thinking about that passageway above the graveyard. He'd started to explore it, but it simply hadn't been feasible when he was out there by himself. As far as he knew, no one else had explored it any more than he had. The CSI team had put a camera down it, but they hadn't found any evidence that suggested it was anything more than a natural fissure. Cody made a note to set up an exploration of that spot.

A few papers later, he came across a CSI report that corroborated his theory. It said that water was seeping up through the ground in the place the corpses were found. It was also kept in the shadow of the mountain during the hottest part of the day. That meant that it was probably the best spot for miles to get something to grow.

Unfortunately, the lab reports on the bodies didn't help a whole lot either, other than to make him more disgusted than he already was. There was precious little tissue to deal with, but analysis of what they did have, along with bone marrow analysis, showed a neuromuscular agent present in the tissue. That meant that they had been paralyzed, but awake, while the torture was going on.

Cody set the report down and rubbed his eyes. This was all interesting, but it didn't tell him how to find his killer. The answer was out in the desert somewhere. Or possibly in Alex.

As though thinking of her was a summons, the bedroom door opened somewhere beyond his sight. He heard footsteps on carpet, the sound of a light switch being flipped, and then a door shutting. He could only assume she'd wandered into the bathroom.

A few minutes later, he heard running water. The door opened, and she appeared around the corner. Her eyes brightened when she saw him.

"Hey. It's you."

"Yeah."

She walked over to the cupboard and took out a glass. "I didn't think babysitting was part of a detective's job."

Cody laughed. "It's a protective detail, not a babysitting job. Please don't go around telling people that my job is to babysit witnesses all day."

"Why not?" She laughed, filling the glass with water.

"Because this is a small town. It'll probably get back to my father."

Alex smiled. He could see her intelligent eyes picking up on the implications of what he'd said and making deductions. Her gaze wasn't judgmental, though, just mildly curious.

"Actually." He casually returned all of the reports to the folder and closed the lid. "Frank's supposed to find me a replacement. I'm kind of surprised I haven't heard from him yet." He looked up at her. "How're you feeling?"

She shrugged. "Fine. Sore, but not bad. I was going to make something for dinner. You want some?"

"Sure. Although, maybe I should do it. You're supposed to be resting."

"I'll be fine. No offense, but it's obvious that men stocked this place. It's all Easy Mac and scrambled eggs and hot dogs."

Cody tried to hide his laugh. That sounded an awful lot like Tom's favorite foods.

"Do you have a preference?" she asked.

He shook his head. "No, you choose."

He continued reading while she worked. Her phone rang, and she talked with her father for a while. He could tell she was structuring her words very carefully to keep from alarming him. Cody couldn't help but admire her. He thought she ought to tell her parents the truth, but he could tell she was looking out for them.

She'd found some vegetables in the fridge and made them both what turned out to be surprisingly good omelets, accompanied by toast. Before she ate, she said grace, another thing that surprised him. It wasn't that she didn't seem the type—she didn't strike him either way—but she was so no-nonsense, so independent, that he wouldn't have thought her religious.

The vague awkwardness as they began to eat lasted only a few minutes. It was broken by Alex, of course.

"So, your father disapproves of your job?"

Cody's hand froze on the way to his mouth.

"Sorry. Didn't mean to pry. You don't have to tell me; I was just making conversation."

He shook his head. "No. It's all right. It's just that most people don't pick up on it so quickly. Or exactly."

"Well, you said you didn't want people telling him that you babysit witnesses all day. So it's either that, or he's a cop too and just really hard on you."

"No, not a cop. My dad is *definitely* not a cop. My uncle was."

He could see the wheels turning behind her eyes. "Is he the man in picture on your desk? You're, like, six or something."

"*Fifteen*. And yes, that's my uncle. That was the last picture I took with him before he died."

Alex's playful expression turned serious. "In the line of duty?"

"Yeah." She didn't press but the question hung in the air, and he found he was comfortable sharing it with her. "He surprised a couple of drug dealers peddling their wares and it got ugly. He was shot in the crossfire."

"No vest?"

"No. But it wouldn't have mattered. He took one to the head. Never woke up."

Alex sighed. "Cody, I'm sorry."

He shrugged. "It was a long time ago."

"Is he the reason you became a cop?"

"Yeah. I idolized the guy. He was a decorated hero in this community before he accepted a detective's position up north. Just wish he would've lived long enough to see me follow him."

"So why doesn't your father approve?"

"I don't know. My dad and my uncle seemed close. Some of my earliest memories are of spending weekends with my dad and Uncle Clyde. They always got along. We'd go fishing or watch sports, or work on the house for my mom. We even went up north once or twice for a big-deal ball game. But for some reason my father didn't want me to take up my uncle's profession. Tom thinks they must have had a falling out as adults."

"Makes sense."

"Not to me. Even if they did, that doesn't mean that cop work is bad. I might as well have gone into the street side pharmacist business, for all my dad's pride in my profession." Cody stopped and cleared his throat, realizing he was venting.

Alex didn't seem to notice. She was studying her food. "I think Tom must be right, though, about the falling out."

"Why?"

"It's just odd. Police work is a really noble profession. Unless your dad is a . . . some color-collar criminal—"

Cody chuckled.

"—he should at least be *okay* with it. Something must have happened to give him a grudge."

Cody shrugged. "Maybe. Probably. He won't talk about it, though." He waved his hand at her. "It's an old argument anyway. I went through the academy six years ago, and he still tries to talk me out of it."

Alex's eyebrows went up, and she laughed. "Six years later and still trying, huh?"

Her amusement dissipated the anger he'd been nursing for the last few days, and he found himself grinning back at her. "Yup. Always concocting schemes to get me to work with him, join other companies, overnight millionaire scams."

"Really?" She laughed harder.

"Yeah."

After a moment, her smile faded a bit. "Sorry, I guess that's probably not funny to you."

"No, it's nice to laugh about it. Easier than being angry, anyway."

Alex nodded.

"What about you? Your parents hate photography?"

"No. I haven't had too many problems with my parents—at least, not of that nature. They've always been supportive of anything I want to do."

"Well then, of what nature *are* your problems with them?"

"Well, there was the whole adoption-deception thing."

Cody's gaze dropped to his plate. He'd forgotten. "Right."

"Other than that, my mom can nag with the best of them, and my dad is pretty overprotective. He scared away a few boyfriends in high school. But that's just normal family stuff."

He nodded and they were silent for a few minutes. "You know," he finally said, "I've gotta say, I'm impressed with the way you're handling all of this. Most other people wouldn't be nearly so calm about it."

Alex studied the table for a moment before answering. "First of all," she said, "I think you're giving me too much credit. I'm only pretending to be calm. It's totally an act."

He grinned. "Noted."

"Other than that—" She lifted a shoulder. "Between the shock of the adoption news and some . . . other realities of life, I suppose I've just learned to take things in stride. Fight for what you want, of course, but being angry about things you can't control—there's just no point to it. Like my adoption—my aunt in Arizona made me see how blessed I actually was. Especially considering how I was found, who knows what kind of biological parents I had. Or if I had any by that point? I was put in a good home with loving parents. I couldn't have asked for better." She shrugged again. "Whatever happens, especially if it's not something you choose, I think there's a reason for it. I think there's a reason I'm here. Whether just to help catch this guy or to have an experience I'll grow from or"—she glanced up at him—"some other reason, I don't know. But I believe it just the same."

She was sounding more like the praying type, now, but Cody respected her for it. "I hope you're right."

They finished the meal in silence, and she got up to clear the table.

He stood. "Uh-uh. No way. You cooked. I get to do the dishes."

"'Kay. It'll take you all of three minutes. Um, assuming the dishwasher works, that is."

"I think it does." They found some dishwasher soap under the sink and assumed that meant the appliance worked. They only had six or seven dishes to put in, so they wouldn't run it anyway.

"So," Alex said when he was done, "are you still working on that stuff?"

He glanced at the file. "No, I'm pretty much done, except I need to call Frank. Why?"

"There are some decks of cards in the living room. You up for a game?"

Cody smiled. "Sure."

He followed her into the next room where they sat on opposite sides of the coffee table. He decided his call to Frank could wait.

SITTING IN HIS OFFICE, Captain Brecken rubbed the bridge of his nose while pressing the receiver to his ear. The shock of the revelation the caller had made had worn off, but a dull ache brewed behind the captain's eyes.

"And they're certain?" he asked.

He barely registered what the tinny voice talking in his ear answered, except that it was an affirmative. He supposed the question had been mostly rhetorical anyway. Minutes later, he put down the phone. This case was becoming more complicated by the hour, and that worried the captain. A lot. Mt. Dessicate didn't see many things like this, and he wasn't sure they were equipped to deal with it.

He sighed as he walked into the room where his four lead detectives' desks faced one another. They were all working overtime on this case, which meant they went home for dinner, but then came back for a few more hours. Cody, the only one not married, barely bothered to go home at all, which was why the captain was surprised that he wasn't at his desk. Of course the one he needed to talk to wasn't there.

"Tom, where's your partner?"

"Dunno, captain. I haven't seen Cody all afternoon. Assume he's out chasing a lead."

"Ope!" Out of the corner of his eye, the Captain saw Frank slap his palm to his forehead. From Frank, that was admission of guilt.

"Frank?"

"Sorry, captain. He's at the safe house with Alex."

"Why?"

"The uniform assigned to her had to leave—called back to duty by his captain in Gunnison. I was supposed to send a replacement hours ago, but I got busy with this and totally forgot."

The captain sighed. It wasn't really Frank's fault. A criminalist by the name of Tandy was being sent out to deal with the journal Cody and his PI friend had found. The captain didn't have the time or inclination to deal with all the red tape, so he'd made Frank his liaison until Tandy arrived. Frank had been on the phone making travel arrangements and giving instructions, directions, and information to half a hundred people all afternoon. No wonder he'd forgotten something as mundane as a spare unie.

"Find a replacement now, Frank, and I mean *now*. If you can't get one over there in less than fifteen minutes, one of you go. Cody has other business."

All three detectives stopped what they were doing to stare at him.

"What's going on, Captain?" Tom asked.

"I just got a call from the Point of the Mountain. Jagar Resputa wants to see Cody. Says he has some information about our case."

"And you believe him?"

The captain glared at Court.

"Uh, I mean, should we believe him, sir? He's just trying to waste our time—torment Cody some more."

The captain sighed again. He was doing that a lot today. "Just before the prison called, I got another call, from one of the search teams. Twenty minutes ago, they found another mass grave."

The silence was so uncomfortable, it was prickly; the detectives squirmed in their seats.

"Is it one through eleven?" Tom asked.

"No," the captain said. "It's thirty-six through forty-eight."

Court gasped; Frank's mouth dropped open; Tom shut his eyes, expression pained. The gravity of the situation settled on each of them. The captain saw it. He felt what they felt as well. Unless the killer had numbered his plots randomly, there were nearly fifty victims here. And who knew how many more?

"I don't want to deal with Resputa anymore than you do, and I'm certain Cody won't either. But we can't afford to not hear what he has to say if it means information on this case."

"But how would Resputa know anything about our guy, Cap?" Frank asked.

"Resputa was caught in the same general area. Criminals often know of one another's work."

"I think he's just seen *Silence of the Lambs* too many times," Frank grumbled. His face shifted with renewed attention as the person he'd been dialing picked up. "Hello, yes. I need a uniform . . ."

"Why tonight, Cap?" Tom asked quietly. "Can't this wait for tomorrow?"

"Resputa's holding our time hostage. He wants Cody there before midnight. At midnight, his offer of information expires, and he won't give it to us for any price."

"You know he'll try to negotiate a deal."

"Cody won't be authorized to give him any deals, unless it's to convince the warden to supply Resputa with an extra roll of toilet paper each week."

Tom smiled but without humor.

"Resputa came to us with this, Tom. He knows no one's going to cut him any deals. That alone makes me wary. I know we're busy here, but I think it's dangerous not to know what he's up to."

Tom nodded. "I'll call Cody."

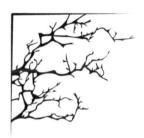

Chapter 27

ALEX SQUEALED WITH delight when her hand beat Cody's for the fifth straight time. Cody laughed. She thought his smile was beautiful.

"You are *way* too good at this, Alex. Who taught you to play poker?"

"Ex-boyfriend. It's how he made his living."

"And you conveniently forgot to mention that?"

"Don't worry. I'd never take your money. Just your candy." She unwrapped a tootsie roll and popped it in her mouth. They'd found a stash of mixed candy in the pantry, divided it evenly, and used it to bet with.

"Maybe we should switch games." Cody feigned worry with his eyebrows, though he was grinning broadly.

"Hmm," she said, with mock seriousness. "Well there are the classics: Go Fish? Old Maid? *Memory?*"

Cody shook with quiet laughter but before he could answer, his cell phone buzzed.

"Maybe Frank finally got you a replacement." Alex tried to sound more chipper than she felt at the prospect.

Cody answered his phone. "Hey Tom, you guys finally remember—"

His face froze, then slowly fell.

The area around Alex's heart turned chill. Something was wrong.

Cody got to his feet and walked to the window, turning his back on her. Not wanting to look as though she was trying to eavesdrop, Alex picked up their soda cups and took them into the kitchen, but she could still hear his voice.

"Now? Tonight . . . are you sure?"

Alex turned on the faucet and rinsed the cups before placing them in the dishwasher. Before she finished, Cody came into the kitchen, looking more serious than he had all evening.

"Everything all right?"

He frowned. "I have to go talk to someone. Tom's gonna come stay with you."

Alex studied Cody. He was obviously distraught. She was curious, but she also knew that police business was none of hers. If she asked, he would be well within his rights to tell her to butt out.

"A lead in the case?" She clapped her hands together in mock joy. "Is it solved?"

He didn't laugh as she'd hoped, but smiled a bit. "No. It's a guy in the state pen. Says he might have some information for us. Captain wants me to go talk to him."

"Any reason it has to be you in particular?"

"Yeah. He asked for me."

Alex frowned. Someone *in* the state penitentiary asked for a particular detective? "Why?"

"He sort of knows me."

"Did you help put him away or something?"

Cody stared at her levelly for a few seconds. "Yes."

"Oh."

After that, Cody clammed up, and the silence got awkward. Twenty minutes later, Tom's unmarked car pulled into the driveway beside Cody's.

"See you tomorrow," he said over his shoulder as he headed out the door. He and Tom conversed in the driveway briefly before Cody got into his car, and Alex tried to read their expressions. Tom looked . . . was that sympathy? The lines around Cody's eyes tightened as they spoke, and his lips pressed into a thin line. Then, looking supremely annoyed, he drove away.

Tom moseyed into the room. "Ms. Thompson." He grinned at her.

"Alex, remember? So you stuck here all night with me?"

"Maybe. For a few hours, at least. Frank's trying to track down a uniform, but it's getting late and most of them have gone home. He may not be able to find one to assign to you until morning. We'll see. But no worries. I called my wife. She's cool with it." He grinned again, and Alex returned it.

"She's cool with you not coming home all night?"

"Told her I was protecting a beautiful woman half her age."

"Tom! You should be nice to your wife."

"Why?"

He was teasing her and she knew it, but she couldn't help but return the banter. "Because she cooks your dinner."

Tom laughed. "You have a point there."

"Speaking of"—Alex glanced toward the kitchen—"have you eaten tonight?"

"Actually yes, but"—he followed her gaze—"whatcha got back there?"

Alex was glad he'd asked. In her experience, food often loosened a man's tongue. "I'll make you something."

When he was digging into a plate of microwave pasta, she sat across from him and asked, "So, am I allowed to ask what's going on, or not?"

"Going on with what?"

"Cody. Where'd he go?"

Tom studied his uneaten pasta for a full minute before answering.

"If it's police business, you don't have to tell me, Tom. I'm just wondering." She secretly hoped he'd tell her anyway.

Tom shook his head, and she was sure he'd refuse to say anything. "It's not police business. It's a closed case, so it's not illegal for me to tell you about it. It's just that it's something I think Cody should tell you about." Tom heaved a great sigh. "But then I suppose he won't do that. It's not something he cares to talk about much."

Alex leaned forward and rested her chin on her fists.

"All right. A few years ago, we had a really awful case. Actually, it was a federal case, made the news, so you might remember it. A pedophile went on a rampage. Guy by the name of Resputa started in Washington. He was driving south through all the states, snatching kids as he went."

Alex swallowed. "And doing what to them?"

"All kinds of things. Molesting, assaulting, terrorizing."

"But not killing them?"

"Not according to him. Most of them were picked up at truck stops, rest stops, or gas stations along the highway, exploited, then dropped off a few hundred miles away. We had to double our highway patrol presence because kids were being found wandering on random, desolate stretches of highway."

"How awful. But you said most, not all?"

"Seven children who were snatched from similar locations while this was going on were not dropped off anywhere or ever found alive. The bodies of three of the seven were found sometime after we caught Resputa, and they were all buried not far off the highway. They'd been sexually exploited, in some cases tortured, and then killed."

"And you think he's the one that took them, too?"

"Yes. I'm sure he did. Just couldn't ever prove it. He left no DNA on them."

"Did he on the others? The ones he let live?"

"No, but they all identified him."

"Why would he do that? Let some live that could I.D. him?"

Tom sighed. "I don't know, Alex. Resputa is a sick, twisted man. Once we caught him, we all interviewed him numerous times. We couldn't get an answer as to his motives that made any kind of sense. He's a criminal. Only he knows why he does what he does."

"So what's this all got to do with Cody?"

"The entire country was on alert, but Resputa's pattern was headed due south. Once he realized he had the FBI's attention, he made a break for the Mexican border. Figured he could lose us there, and he probably would have. He just had to keep to the back roads." Tom waved his arms about to indicate everything that was around him. "Enter the great metropolis of Mt. Dessicate.

"This was two years ago. Cody had only been a detective for a few months. One day an elderly rancher that Cody had known for years—friend of his uncle's, I think—called Cody to say that he thought someone was squatting in his barn. The rancher was too old to be chasing trespassers off his property anymore. Because they were friends, Cody offered to just go over himself and have a look around, rather than dispatching a uniform. I think he expected to find some teenagers screwing around in there or something."

"Was it Resputa?"

"Yeah. He had four kids with him. Cody announced himself as a cop before he realized it was Resputa. He just thought he could scare the trespassers off. Resputa attacked him. He's the one who gave Cody the scar across his face."

"Really?"

"Yeah. Sliced at him with some kind of scythe he found in the barn. Cody was lucky to keep his eye. He got hurt pretty bad otherwise, too—broken ribs, punctured kidney. Despite all that, he managed to cuff Resputa to one of the barn columns; kept him there until backup arrived. I think the thing that really messed with his head were the kids."

Alex inhaled sharply. "They weren't dead were they?"

"No, but they were a mess. Not all of them were clothed. When he tried to help them, they all started screaming. After what they'd endured at Resputa's hands, they were afraid of men. Hell, most of them were probably afraid of their own fathers after that. Terrible situation."

Tom rubbed his eyes, and Alex felt guilty for making him recount a painful experience.

"I don't think Cody was ever the same after that. A case like that makes you grow up real fast, and not in a good way." He paused, lost in memory.

"So," Alex prodded, "is this Resputa guy the one who called from the state pen today?"

"Yeah. He claims to have information on the Shakespeare case. He said if Cody didn't come talk to him tonight, he wouldn't tell us."

"How would he know anything about it?"

"I don't know. He was driving around the desert down here for a while, hiding out, before we caught him. Maybe he stumbled on something . . . but I doubt it. I think he's yanking Cody's chain. He's always trying to get Cody to come down and talk to him."

"What do you mean? About what?"

"Over the last two years, he's tried to lure Cody out to talk to him a handful of times. Cody went the first time, thinking maybe Resputa was ready to confess to something—the murder of those seven children, perhaps? It only took one trip to realize that Resputa just enjoyed toying with him, messing with his head. After that, Cody didn't go again. Until now."

"But why target Cody specifically? Cody stumbled on him accidentally. It wasn't like he was really invested in the case or anything. What's Resputa got against him?"

Tom shrugged. "We've all been trying to figure that out for two years, Alex. Maybe it was because Cody was the one who tangibly beat him. Maybe because they tussled. He nearly killed Cody, but then Cody won. Maybe he thinks they bonded over it. I don't know. This is a pedophile and probably a child-killer."

Tom leaned forward. "You need to understand something, Alex. Cody is . . . a good person. He's an exceptional human being, and an even better cop. Maybe this is my wife's book club coming out in me, but there's something epic about the kind of goodness in Cody meeting the kind of evil in Resputa. I think Resputa saw Cody and knew him for what he was: a good man that refused to be beaten by a lowlife pedophile. I think Resputa can't help himself. He has to try to torment Cody. He hasn't given up yet. Nor will he ever."

"But he won't ever get out of prison, right? He torments because it's his only pastime?"

"Unfortunately, it didn't work out that way."

"What? But after all those kids . . . ?"

"We couldn't get him on the murders. Sex offense laws are always evolving but they aren't as strong as most of us would like them to be. Resputa cut a deal of sorts. He agreed to plead guilty to assaulting all the kids that I.D.'d him in exchange for the prosecutors not seeking the death penalty. It was agreed. The idea was that he would get life, but he has good lawyers. As of right now, he's serving a sentence of fifteen to life, and his lawyers are appealing even that."

"So he *could* serve life."

"Or he could serve fifteen. He won't get out any time soon, but there's a very good chance he could get out someday. When he does, he'll be just as dangerous as when he went in. Probably more so."

Alex shivered. No wonder Cody's mood had turned dark so quickly. She found herself worrying about him, having to go speak to that monster. She wouldn't want to do it.

Her shudder didn't go unnoticed. Tom smiled sadly. "Sorry, Alex. I suppose I've said too much."

Alex shook her head. "No. Don't be. I asked. I wanted to know. It's just a lot to deal with. You and the other detectives are all so happy and . . . goofy, for lack of a better word. How do you do it? How do you deal with all this and still smile?"

Tom leaned back in his chair, looking more relaxed. "We do the best we can. We try not to obsess about our jobs. We work hard, chase the bad guys 'til they're caught, then go home at night. We try to find joy in our families, our friends, the smaller parts of our lives. We have to find it, really. If all you see is sadness in everything, the world becomes an overwhelming place pretty quickly. So we keep moving forward, and know that every scum bag we get off the street is a small mercy.

"Like you said, Resputa might serve life. If he does, we've saved a lot of families a lot of pain. If he doesn't, at least we got him off the streets for a while, and we've established a history that will convict him faster and for longer next time. Optimism, Alex. Optimism is the only way to go through life."

He grinned his floppy grin and Alex smiled back. Cody wasn't pessimistic, but he was more serious than Tom. She could see why they would work well together as partners. Tom's experience and positivity countered Cody's caution and seriousness.

Alex yawned. "I suppose I should turn in. The doctors say I should be sleeping twelve hours a night for the next week."

Tom looked at his watch with concern. "Better hurry, then. It's getting late already."

Alex laughed. "Well then you'll just have to do your own dishes."

"Yes, ma'am."

"Will there be a uniform here when I wake up in the morning?"

He shrugged. "Possibly. You'd better hope so. I'm not as charming in the morning as I am in the evening."

"I think that's true of most of us, Tom. Thank you. Thank you for coming to stay with me, and for telling me about Cody."

"Sure. Sleep tight."

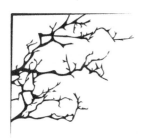

Chapter 28

THE DRIVE TO THE PRISON was grim. And long. Cody wished he could get out of seeing Resputa. He had too much on his mind to be side-tracked by a twisted sex offender.

When he'd first captured Resputa in Coleman Douglas's barn, he hadn't slept for weeks. Cody had only seen him again at the trial, and then the one time he'd visited the prison a few months later. Each time, he'd had trouble sleeping afterwards, as though some of Resputa's darkness had followed him home. Resputa was not a man; he was a creature, slimy and creeping.

As he pulled up to the guard station and flashed his badge to the security officer, he told himself to be calm. If he was at all emotional—positive or negative—Resputa would know it immediately and pounce. The man was a master manipulator and could read body language like a picture book.

Cody's straight-laced and simple nature kept him from excelling in any kind of performance art, but when he went to see Resputa, he had no choice but to become an actor—a different man, with different thoughts in his head, and with sensibilities to entirely different things.

He'd been to the prison enough to know the protocol. After being ushered through the guard station, and assured the warden would be waiting for him, he parked in the appropriate place and headed into the building.

The warden's name was Brett Lincoln. Cody didn't know the man well, but he saw him each time he came to the prison, so they'd developed a professional relationship.

"Detective Oliver." Lincoln clasped his hand firmly. Variegated gray and white wandered through his dark, silky hair, and his bulky, Native American build would have been intimidating had he been an inmate rather than a warden.

"Nice to see you again, Brett."

"Sorry to drag you out here in the middle of the night."

"It's not your fault. Resputa has to play his twisted games, doesn't he?"

Lincoln's eyebrow arched. "Is that all you think it is?"

"I sincerely hope that's all it is."

"And yet you're here."

Cody sighed. "Brett, this case has us in knots and running in circles. If there's any chance he could give us a viable lead, we can't risk ignoring it."

Lincoln nodded. "He's already on his way to the room we've set up for you. He'll be waiting for us there."

Cody followed the warden through the narrow, eternal stone corridors of the prison.

"By the way," Lincoln said over his shoulder as they walked single file through the narrow passages, "you should know that I believe Resputa may be plotting an escape attempt."

"Escape? Is that possible?"

Lincoln guffawed. "Of course not. I just want you to know that he's contemplating it."

"Does he give you any trouble?"

"No. Like all pedophiles he's a people-pleaser. He's a model prisoner, but a few odds and ends that have gone missing have been found in his cell. He's also been reading books about constructing simple machines, and asking to get his hands on books about more complicated ones."

"Why don't you just give him a copy of the Great Escape?"

Lincoln smirked, which Cody guessed was as close to laughing as he'd come. "I'd love to throw that in his face, but then he'd know I was watching him."

"He may already know that. Resputa's intelligent enough that maybe he's not trying to escape at all. Maybe he's trying to make you think that as a way of covering up something else he's doing."

"I thought of that, too. If that's the case, I don't know what his end game is yet. Just thought you should know what he's been up to lately."

Lincoln brought him to something akin to an interrogation room. It wasn't large, but an oblong, metal table sat in the center, and a mirror with one-way glass covered most of one wall.

Resputa sat at the far end of the table, head down, with two guards standing at attention behind him. A chain threaded from his shackles, through a metal ring in the table, down to the manacles around his feet, and into a ring in the floor.

When Lincoln opened the door and he and Cody entered, Resputa raised his head. He got uglier every time Cody saw him, and Cody knew the ugliness was of Resputa's own making.

Resputa had golden hair and olive skin. The combination was seductive, and had he been a happy, smiling person, he might have been pretty; perhaps he'd even have had a life of celebrity. Instead, he used his beauty to lure unsuspecting children into his car, into his perverse fantasies. He snarled so often that his face had become that of a hyena, the skin around his eyes pulled back, his lips thinned and peeling back over straight, white teeth. He had a cross tattooed between his eyes, but Cody knew that with time, Resputa would flag each of the points, as Charles Manson had done, forging the peaceful sign of the cross into the backward, egotistical sign of the swastika.

Careful to keep his face a mask of serenity, Cody strode into the room and sat down across the table from Resputa. The prisoner's stark blue eyes were red-rimmed, and they glittered, boring into Cody's from across the table. But Cody wasn't afraid. Resputa may have scarred his face, but that was only because Cody had been inexperienced and unready. In a fair fight, Resputa would run for the dark corners and cower rather than stand toe to toe with any cop. That was why he preyed on children. They were the only ones he had courage against: those too weak and innocent to have any chance of defending themselves against him.

After several minutes of tense silence, when Resputa was certain Cody wouldn't flinch under his stare, his eyes shifted pointedly to Lincoln. He wouldn't speak to Cody with the other officers in the room.

Cody didn't know why it mattered to Resputa if they stayed or went. He must have known that the mirror was one-way glass, and that they would be watching and listening, whether they were inside the room or out, for any sign that Resputa might try something.

Resputa was taller than Cody, true, but Cody was certain he was stronger. Not that Cody expected trouble from him; Resputa was too intelligent and self-controlled for that.

"Warden, perhaps you can give myself and prisoner Resputa some privacy?"

Lincoln didn't sigh, but his exhale was slightly heavier than it had been a moment before. He didn't like the idea of leaving Cody alone with Resputa, but he wouldn't question Cody's resolve in front of the prisoner, so after only a moment's hesitation, he motioned the two guards out and followed them, shutting the door behind him.

"*Prisoner* Resputa?" His voice was both deep and nasal. "Reminding me of my place, Detective? Or perhaps trying to reassure yourself?"

"Not at all. Just giving you a true name."

Resputa sat back in his chair. He looked impressed, but Cody was sure it was all for show. "You've grown more philosophical since we last spoke."

"I've had more experience dealing with . . . people like you."

"We're something to be dealt with, are we?"

"Yes. Nothing more." Cody made his voice nonchalant.

"Oh, come now. I am simply a man who refuses to deny myself my natural urges. Don't you give into your urges, Detective? The urge to eat, to sleep? To relieve yourself? To . . . copulate?"

"My urges don't exploit and victimize little children, Resputa."

Resputa's lips curved into a sinuous smirk, as though Cody had said something amusing.

"I know well what your urges entail," Cody continued, "and I've not come all this way in the middle of the night to hear a lecture on human biology. You told Warden Lincoln that you have something to tell me about the case I'm working on. Was that true?"

Resputa spread his hands, ducking his neck obsequiously. "I never lie, Detective."

"Then let's hear it."

Resputa leaned back in his chair. He seemed to be savoring the feeling of having Cody's attention. Cody didn't press him. He couldn't let Resputa know that he was having any effect on Cody's nerves, or temper.

"A few days before you and I met in that kinky little barn, I was roving the desert in a four wheeler."

Cody leaned forward in spite of himself. To get to Coleman Douglas' barn, Resputa would have had to leave the main roads. They'd always suspected he'd had an off-road vehicle, but they hadn't found one, and he'd never told them how he got past all the road blocks unseen.

"You must have hidden it well. We never found it."

"Of course you didn't! I didn't want you to." He went from smugness to thick annoyance, then back again in seconds. "Anyway, I was snooping around out there, looking for a place to take my . . . little children for a few hours . . ."

Cody looked down at his hands, willing his face to remain steady. When he looked up, there was glee in the wrinkles around Resputa's eyes, and he knew Resputa could tell how Cody was really feeling.

". . . and I found something interesting, a work of art, if you will."

"What was it?"

"A graveyard, hidden in an out-of-the-way spot."

Cody kept his face entirely placid. That much Resputa might have heard on the news. If he started guessing, Cody couldn't let him know whether or not he was right.

"What made you think it was a graveyard?"

"Twelve mounds, each planted with a single, pale-blue tulip."

Cody's heart sank. The color of the flowers hadn't been released to the press. Cody sighed, but finally nodded. "You could only know that if you'd been there."

Resputa smirked self-assuredly, and Cody wished he could wipe that petulant grin off the inmate's face.

"But then," Cody went on, "we already know that, so I hope you have more to offer."

"Don't you want to know about the man that killed them?"

Cody froze. "Did you see him?"

"Came almost face to face with him."

Cody put on his best earnest face. "Why are you doing this, Resputa? You haven't even asked me for anything."

"Would you give it if I had?"

"Probably not. But I don't believe you'd help the precinct that put you in here out of the goodness of your heart."

"Oh, come now, Detective. My parole date may not come for more than a decade, but when it does, behavior goes a long way. If I cooperate with the cops and help catch an active serial killer, well, that's impressive."

He was right. Cooperation with the authorities was a big plus when trying to convince a parole board to release a violent predator. Still, Cody didn't think any parole board on the planet would let Resputa out, especially if someone showed up at the hearing to re-hash Resputa's crimes in detail, which Cody and each of Mt. Dessicate's other detectives intended to do.

"You really think if you give me a few details, a parole board will just throw the doors open for you?"

"I think it couldn't hurt."

Cody leaned back in the cold metal chair, studying Resputa. There had to be more to it than that, but Cody couldn't imagine what it was. Maybe Resputa was telling the truth. Or maybe these were just more mind games. It had gotten Cody down here to see him, which nothing had done previously. Perhaps when Resputa heard on the news that the mass grave had been discovered, he just couldn't help himself. Still, Cody had a bad feeling, the kind that crept up his spine and made him want to look over his shoulder.

He resisted the urge.

Whatever the reason Resputa was willing to divulge what he knew, at least he was willing to do it.

Cody nodded. "All right. So tell me about this killer."

"What do you want to know?"

"Let's start with what he looks like."

"Tall. Six-four at least. Shaggy brown hair that curls around his neck. Slender in the shoulders but with a gut that comes out over his belt. Imposing."

"Any facial hair?"

"No. But I couldn't see his face."

Cody almost laughed. "Of course you couldn't."

"No, Detective, I don't think you understand. I was looking right at him, but I couldn't see his face because he was wearing a mask."

Cody rested his forearms on the table, studying Resputa's expression. The other man had obviously known that this would be an important piece of information. The question was whether it was real or not. The rest of the description was in line with what Alex had said, but this was new.

"What kind of mask?"

"A mask of mud."

"Mud?"

"Yes. He cakes mud all over his face, leaving only his eyes, mouth, and nostrils uncovered." Resputa leaned forward. "What does that tell you about him, Detective?"

"He hates the way he looks."

"Ah, but it's more than that, isn't it? Everyone hates *some*thing about the way they look. Perhaps you can sympathize with that?" He looked pointedly at Cody's scar.

Cody looked away, annoyed.

"This man, on the other hand, hates himself so much that he covers his face with mud."

Cody let that sink in. When his eyes shifted to Resputa again, he found the other man watching him, as though fascinated.

"You say he saw you, Resputa? Then why didn't he kill you?"

"Even thieves have an honor code, Detective. He knew I was no threat to him. He must have seen me walking among his pretties. By the time he came out, I was two hundred yards away. I waved at him, though, as if to say that I'd keep his secrets."

"Yet here you are."

Resputa shrugged. "Only because his work has already been discovered, and because I'm in here, now, where before I was roaming the open desert."

Cody barked a laugh. "A code of honor that extends to the ends of the earth, I see."

"We're delinquents, Detective, not saints."

"What else?"

"The soil."

"Yes. It was much more fertile than anything else out there. We think he has some kind of irrigation system set up. It's being excavated as we speak."

"An irrigation system? Perhaps, but that soil was darker, woodier than anything this far south. It looked like it could capture more moisture in a day than your desert sees in an entire season."

"You're saying he's importing soil?"

Resputa stared levelly back at Cody, but didn't reply.

"Anything else?" Cody asked.

"You can be certain he has an underground lair somewhere out there. What he does takes time. He grows the flowers specially, so he must have somewhere that he can replicate certain conditions."

Cody nodded, straight-faced. They had already figured all of that.

"Any idea where?"

"Who can say? I never ventured into the mountain, but merely traversed its outer sheath. There will be a link from the lair to each of the grave sites, but it won't be an obvious one."

Cody didn't react, wondering if Resputa realized that he'd just given something away, or was it purposeful and calculated?

"A link?"

"A passage that can be easily traversed without being seen; probably inside the mountain."

"You said grave*sites*? Only one has been found." That wasn't true, but as far as the press was concerned it was.

Resputa stared at him for several seconds before shaking his head. "You're lying. You've found more than one; you just haven't told the reporters yet."

Cody frowned and leaned back in his seat. Could Resputa really read him that well, or was he guessing? Either way, he knew that there were multiple grave sites.

"You said you saw *one*, Resputa. What aren't you telling me?"

Resputa laughed as though it was all a jolly game. "What I told you was true. That was the first one I stumbled upon. And that was when I saw Mudface. After that, I travelled around a great deal more. I saw more of the mass graves. By then, he knew I was not a threat, so he didn't show himself to me again, though I'm sure he was watching."

"How many did you find?"

"Four. I didn't have time to stay and search for others, but they seemed to be arranged in a somewhat circular pattern."

"Around what?"

"Probably his lair. I still couldn't pinpoint that for you, though, because I don't know how many there are. I saw only four, and the pattern was incomplete. They radiate out from a central spot, like spokes on a wheel. If you can find them all . . ."

Cody thought about that. He hated to ask an opinion of Resputa, but he was being forthcoming. Perhaps if Cody was . . . nice to him, he'd reveal more. Cody gritted his teeth.

"How many do *you* think there are?"

Resputa grinned, like he noticed the effort Cody was making and it amused him. "Impossible to say with any certainty. However, there are twelve bodies in each site, so . . ."

"So you think the number twelve has some significance to him? Twelve bodies in each of twelve gravesites?"

"All I'm saying is that it would make sense. And might I point out that, even if all twelve spots have been chosen, not all of them might be full yet."

"What do you mean?"

"He's been perfecting his craft for years. Maybe he's still working up to a certain number. You may not find a complete pattern because it may not be finished."

If that was true, it would make pinpointing the lair harder, but it was still more than he'd had a few hours ago. It was looking more and more as if finding that lair would be the key to catching this guy.

"What do you make of the Shakespeare reference?"

"An interesting detail, that. I've thought a lot about it. I'm not well-versed in medieval plays, Detective, but what I do remember from high school English tells me that Shakespeare's heroines were generally beloved, were they not?"

Cody nodded. "Sometimes." He wasn't well-versed either, but a few plays that had been required reading came to mind. "Yes."

"And very tragic?"

"Sometimes. Not in the comedies."

"Perhaps Mudface sees himself as Shakespeare."

"How so?"

"He is creating stories, is he not? The playwright is very mysterious in history's pages. Perhaps he even wore . . . many faces."

Cody could understand where Resputa was going with this. A fascinating psychology to be sure, but why Shakespeare? Why had that been the trigger? And what did the number twelve represent to this man? There was no way Resputa could know those things for certain. It would have to do with the individual psychology of the murderer.

"Did you notice anything else about him? Were his clothes fine or ragged? Did he have any scars? Did he carry any tools or weapons?"

Resputa grinned his sickly-sweet grin. "Very good, Detective. Now you're thinking. His clothes were middle-class, but not particularly fine. He had on expensive hiking boots, though. Even through the mud mask, I could tell his face was scarred, and his hands were immaculately clean. In his hand he carried some kind of tool. I couldn't see clearly but it was a heavy metal lump at the end of a stick—a meat-tenderizer, perhaps?"

"Were his clothes as clean as his hands?"

"Not dirty, but dusty, as though he'd been working."

"A clean freak that lives in the desert. This guy's making more sense by the minute."

"Don't sneer at the contradictions, Detective. Sometimes they're the hand that tightens the noose."

Cody froze. Something about the way Resputa said it made Cody think he wasn't talking about the Shakespeare case anymore. All this was information he could use, but he'd have to think about it more when Resputa wasn't studying him like a particularly fascinating bug.

"If I hadn't asked about his clothes, would you have told me that?"

Resputa spread his hands. "I fancy myself a teacher, Detective. How will you learn if I tell you everything?"

Cody tried not to laugh at the teaching reference. Instead he nodded. He'd suspected as much: Resputa wasn't saying everything he knew, nor would he. He would cheerfully watch Cody like a rat in a maze, laughing when Cody floundered and trying to look impressed, rather than disappointed, when Cody made the right connections.

"If there's nothing else you want to volunteer at this time, I think I'll go from there."

Resputa ducked his head, as though he was being supremely magnanimous.

Cody raised his voice. "Warden, we're finished here." A moment later the door opened and the two guards, followed by Lincoln, entered. The guards went around behind Resputa and stood there, so he'd know he wouldn't be moving until Cody left.

Cody stood and turned toward the door, where Lincoln waited for him.

"Do me a favor, Detective: don't get yourself killed before my first parole hearing. I fancy a game of . . . cat and mouse."

Cody met his red, glittering eyes for a long time. Then he turned and walked out.

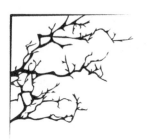

Chapter 29

WHEN ALEX CLIMBED INTO bed in the back bedroom of the safe house, leaving Tom playing cards in the living room, and turned out the light, she fell asleep almost immediately. The dream came again.

She sat on the floor in a room with red walls. She could hear the nearby melancholy wails of a man, juxtaposed with the farther terrified screams of women. Her face was tear-streaked, and the blue dress she wore billowed above her knees while she sat cross-legged. The sickly-sweet smell was in her nose again, and she was afraid.

Suddenly a hulking shadow covered her. She looked to her right and saw a pair of knees. Her eyes traveled upward. She didn't want to see who it was; she was afraid to see. Perhaps it was the wailing man? Perhaps her father, or someone who would take her away from this place? But deep down she knew it wouldn't be. She could feel, as only little girls can, that this was someone to hide from.

When her neck craned so far back she had to lean with her body, she finally found his eyes. They were cruel and peered at her from behind a wet, muddy face. His lips peeled back, revealing yellow teeth. The monster lunged down at her, snarling, and she screamed.

Alex kicked herself awake between the cotton sheets. Her heart pounded in her chest and her hands shook. The wind howled around the corners of the house; the shadows in her room moved.

Telling herself to calm down, she flopped back on her pillow. Why did she keep having these dreams? She'd had some version of them since she was a kid, but they'd come more frequently since she arrived in Mt. Dessicate. Why had this town unsettled her so?

No matter how practical Alex told herself to be, the fear wouldn't dissipate. As she lay in the dark, trying to calm her body, she realized by degrees that something was wrong.

A series of thumps came from somewhere outside the bedroom door, random and unevenly spaced. They sounded close as well, like they were coming from the kitchen.

Alex pressed the light button on her watch. It was 2:30 am. She'd been sleeping for a few hours.

She wondered what Tom was doing out there. She supposed that he wasn't allowed to sleep while on watch. She wouldn't have minded if he had—just having him there was enough for her—but he was probably required to stay awake. Maybe he was rummaging for food to keep from falling asleep.

Alex turned over to try and get back to sleep, telling herself everything was fine, but a niggling worry wrapped itself around her heart. She told herself it was just a dream, and she was too old to be afraid of the dark, but she didn't believe herself.

Another noise from the kitchen sounded like the table being scooted over the linoleum. Just as Alex wondered again what on earth Tom was up to, a loud crash sent her shooting up and out of bed.

She dove into the jeans beside her bed faster than a teenage boy when his girlfriend's father shows up with a shotgun. She pulled her sneakers on, tying them tightly; she felt more in control with her shoes on.

Her gaze shot around the room, looking for a weapon. Her suitcase was too bulky to handle effectively, and what else was she going to do? Throw T-shirts and jeans at a potential attacker? She picked up her book. It was better than nothing, even if it was just a cheaply-bound paperback.

Then she went to the door. She turned the handle slowly, and the door swung soundlessly inward. Everything was silent—eerily so. Sticking her head into the hall, she looked both ways. Around the corner she could see the kitchen cabinets, and a corner of the table, which had indeed been pushed askew, but nothing else.

Deciding against calling out, Alex started toward the kitchen. Her heart threw itself against her rib cage, as if to escape the same terror that made her limbs tremble.

She got to the kitchen doorway, but was afraid to go any farther. The fear from her dream lingered, and her feet felt like lead. She looked behind her. Nothing. Silence. She couldn't go the other way. The noises she'd heard were from the kitchen. She couldn't go back to bed and pretend like nothing had happened either. The only way was forward.

Alex tried to enter the kitchen, but couldn't make herself move. She tried again and failed. Only when she mentally berated herself for being a coward did she feel the blood coursing through her limbs again.

Deciding that if there was an intruder, a blitz attack would be the best method, she jumped the last two feet into the kitchen.

At first glance, the room looked empty. The table and chair were pushed askew, but Tom was nowhere to be seen. Then she heard a soft, huffing noise. Cautiously, she stepped forward. A pair of legs were on the floor on the far side of the table. They were Tom's. Had he simply fallen down?

She came around the table more quickly.

"Tom?"

When his face came into view, Alex gasped, then lunged forward. Tom had one hand on his neck, which was spouting blood like a geyser, and used the other one to drag himself across the floor toward his cell phone, still five feet from his reach. Every time he pulled himself forward, the blood leapt from his throat with renewed vigor.

"Tom, stop! I'll call for help. Sit still. Keep your hand on your throat."

Alex grabbed the phone and a dishtowel, which she pressed to Tom's neck. There was so much blood that she couldn't see the actual injury. Bright red was mixed with dark purple.

With shaking hands, Alex dialed 911. She was already spattered with Tom's blood and, try as she might, she couldn't keep any more of it in his body. It soaked the dish towel and dripped onto the kitchen floor.

"Hold on, Tom. Relax, try to breathe." His eyes were rolling back in his head, and she had no idea if he understood her.

Using her shoulder to cradle the phone against her ear, she pressed down on Tom's neck with both hands. She had to find a balance between keeping the blood in and not crushing his windpipe, and she had no idea what that balance was.

The voice of a soccer mom spoke into her ear. "911, what is your emergency?"

When she answered, Alex was aware that she was shouting, but she couldn't conceive of how to make her voice softer. "My name is Alex

Thompson! I'm in a safe house on Terrance Avenue! The cop that's with me has been stabbed—"

Alex vaguely registered the movement of air behind her before the world went dead.

When she recovered, she was lying on the ground, facing Tom. She shook her head, wondering what had happened, and why her hearing was muted.

A thumping above her head made her to look up. A huge foot was smashing the phone to tiny electronic bits two feet away. Alex struggled to clear the cotton from her mind. Then her eyes fell on Tom. He was unconscious. Nothing was holding the blood in his neck, and it was flowing freely now.

Alex scrambled to her hands and knees and across the floor to Tom, not bothering to see who the owner of the foot was. In truth, she already knew. No one else's presence would have made her feel so afraid.

Just before she reached Tom, strong fingers dug into the hair on the crown of her head. She screamed Tom's name as she was dragged backward. Alex kicked and thrashed and twisted, but the kitchen receded, followed by the living room, entry way, front door, and finally the house itself. The front door shrank as she was dragged down the cement steps and toward the driveway.

Rusty hinges on a car door squeaked, and Alex screamed and thrashed harder. A light went on in the house next door and she could see a man peering out through the window. She'd made enough noise to wake the neighbors.

"Help," she screamed, then realized that was too generic. She was calling as loudly as she could, but already losing her voice. "Murder! Call 911! Somebody's hurt in the house!" The Botanist was trying to stuff her into the back of a blue, rusted van. "Call Detective Oliver! Get Cody Oliver!"

Something crashed into her head. Every muscle in her body went slack, including her tongue. He shoved her the rest of the way in, and she watched him shut the two back doors to the van, but couldn't get her body to respond. Her thoughts wandered along jaded, zigzagging paths. She couldn't make them cohesive.

The van's frame vibrated as the engine roared to life. Then there was the feel of motion, of air rushing underneath her, just beyond the metal barrier, and Alex knew that this time, she was really in trouble.

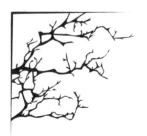

Chapter 30

CODY DROVE SLOWLY BACK from the prison, turning everything Resputa had said over in his mind. The sex offender's information had opened up more questions than answers, and Cody felt a compulsive urge to shower, but it hadn't been quite as bad as he would have thought.

Maybe Cody was finally moving past Resputa, becoming strong enough not to let Resputa get to him anymore.

He ran through a mental list of everything he'd have to do in the morning, and wondered whether to call the captain. Either the captain would be waiting up for him, anxious to hear what Resputa had to say, or he'd holler at Cody for not letting it wait until morning.

Cody glanced at the digital clock below his car's radio. It was nearly 4 a.m. He didn't have any missed calls, and nothing Resputa had said was urgent, so Cody decided it could wait until morning.

Fifteen minutes later, when he was still half an hour from home, his cell phone buzzed. Maybe the captain was waiting up for the news after all.

To his surprise, the name displayed on the screen was Court's. Why was Court calling him at this hour? A soft, creeping dread stole into his stomach. He pushed the green button on his phone.

"Yeah?"

"Cody, where are you?"

"Half hour from town. Why?"

"Come to the hospital."

Cody swallowed, not sure he wanted to ask the next question. "What happened?"

"It's Tom. Someone broke into the safe house. He's hurt."

"What about Alex?"

"She isn't there, Cody. We have people looking for her. A neighbor saw a tall man in a cop uniform shove her into the back of an unmarked van."

Panic rose in his chest. "I have to go look for her, Court. I'll meet the units at the safe house and go from there."

"*No,* Cody—"

"But—"

"This *just* happened, Cody. She managed to call 911 so we got there only minutes after. They can't have gotten far; we'll find her. But you need to get to the hospital. Right. *Now.*"

Cody waited. Panic of a different sort rose up. What was Court getting at?

"Is Tom all right?"

"No, Cody, he's not. It's bad. The captain already went to pick up Margaret and the kids. You need to get here, Cody. Now."

Cody let the cell phone slip through his fingers and slammed his foot down on the accelerator.

SLOWLY, ALEX'S AWARENESS returned. It seemed to her that the van was flying along at an impossible speed, while her limbs took evolutionary eras of time to respond to her brain. After what seemed like years, she began to feel her fingers and toes again, then her feet and hands, her wrists and ankles. Her limbs began to tingle.

With awareness, the pain increased. That was the nice thing about oblivion: you were too out of it to realize how miserable you were. Her heart pounded in her temples and it felt like a fifty-pound barbell was balancing on the side of her head.

Finally, she tried to move a sand-filled foot—and it worked! Alex cautiously turned her head so she could see her abductor. He was staring out at the dark road from behind the wheel of the van. Alex's hair rested over her eyes and it was dark outside, so she didn't think he'd be able to tell she was awake. She had to be careful. If he realized, he might knock her out again.

Without moving her head, she let her eyes roam over the interior of the van. It was mostly empty, but a doorless cabinet had been built into one side. It held random tools and debris.

On the floor was a dark lump. It sparkled with a dull metallic gleam when a streetlight gleamed through the window. A tire iron, perhaps? Alex couldn't tell, but she was sure it was the weapon the Botanist had used to subdue her. He'd left it on the floor, four feet out of her reach. He was certain she'd be unconscious until they reached their destination, wherever that was.

She had to act, but she was still woozy, and her limbs were only sort of doing what she told them. Once she hit him, he'd know she was awake and trying to escape, so she'd have to make it count. She wouldn't be able to kill him with a tire iron; she didn't have the physical strength, or the emotional will power. But then what? Even if she hit him and jumped from the van, where would she go? Cody wasn't nearby to save her this time. The Botanist would just return with the van and get her.

She could take the tire iron with her, but that would be too hard to cart along in her weakened state. Besides, what would she do? Fight him off all the way back to town? They must be miles away. He had the advantage because he had a vehicle.

Alex knew what she had to do. She didn't know if it was possible, but she had to. She *had* to. Her life depended on it. And she'd be damned if she was going to let this lowlife cart her off to the middle of the desert and make a victim out of her. She would *not* be buried in a mass grave—a sob story that evening crime dramas would no doubt rip from the headlines. Alex gritted her teeth, sprang to her feet, and grabbed the tire iron. Immediately the fifty pound weight moved from the side of her head to her forehead, and she became aware that her vision was compromised, but it was too late to back out. The second he glanced in his rearview mirror, she was done for. She let her arm drop all the way back behind her so she'd get a full range of motion. Then she swung the tire iron forward, arcing it toward her abductor's head.

At the last second, he glanced up, his puffy eyes widening. He twisted around and threw a mammoth hand up just in time to catch the tire iron, keeping it from splitting his melon.

Despite that, her effort was not entirely in vain. The tire iron slammed into his outstretched hand, and she was sure she broke something—fingers, if nothing else.

Her suspicions were confirmed when he tried unsuccessfully to hold onto the tire iron, but she pulled it easily from his grip. She whipped around to aim for his head again. He leaned out of the way just in time, but the iron glanced off the top of his head. They swerved, and Alex was thrown to the floor.

Okay, so she hadn't thought about the fact that he could crash the van and kill them both, but she wasn't about to go down without a fight. Her head was still pounding but the adrenaline blocked out most of the pain.

She got to her feet, ready to aim for his head again, but he was thinking fast now, too. He slammed on his brakes, sending her into the dashboard. Before she could push herself up, his fingers closed around her throat. They were rolling forward because he hadn't bothered to put the van in park. His fingers tightened, and Alex knew if she couldn't get away, this would be it.

At the least he was trying to make her pass out, and this time she probably wouldn't regain consciousness. At worst she'd pissed him off enough he would actually strangle her. She kicked and twisted and flailed her arms, but it did no good.

Alex slammed her hand down on the console between the driver and passenger seats, feeling for anything that might help her. Her fingers closed over something long and skinny and hard—a writing pen, maybe?

She told herself to concentrate, but it was hard to focus on what she was doing, tell her lungs to draw breath through the tiny, needle of an airway she had left, *and* fight the panic rising in her gut.

She turned the pen so the pointy side was—she thought—toward her attacker. Then she abandoned breathing all together and threw her entire strength into this one, last-ditch effort, grasping the pen tightly in her fist and thrusting it forward. She felt it stick into something . . . and he let go of her throat.

Alex sucked in a massive, painful gulp of air, then tried to look at him. Her vision still wasn't right, as if blood vessels in her eyes had popped, marring anything directly in front of her. She had to turn her head to the side to see him, as though she were wearing reverse blinders.

He was staring down at the pen she'd stabbed him with. It was sticking straight out, just below his collar bone. He looked puzzled, like he was trying to decide whether or not to remove it. For the first time, Alex could see his entire face, free of sunglasses, false facial hair, or anything else. It was dark outside, but the full moon supplied enough light to see him clearly.

His face was deeply scarred and his jaw was slack on one side, making him look deformed. Even in the moonlight, she could tell his skin was pasty white and everything about him screamed of malnutrition.

His hesitation was enough to spur her into action, though now her head, chest, lungs, *and* limbs all throbbed with pain. Tears of fatigue coursed down her cheeks as she twisted away from him and picked up the tire iron, which had fallen to the floor beneath her. She got to her feet and swung it as hard as she could. This time she connected solidly with the side of his head. He slammed against the driver's side window with a resounding crack. He still didn't pass out, but was too stunned to react.

Alex reached across him and opened his door. Then she perched on the passenger seat and kicked. It took seven or eight savage kicks before he toppled out, but she did it. He hit the ground, but was already stirring, trying to get up, moving as if in slow motion.

Alex got into the driver's seat, yanked the door shut, and slammed her foot down on the gas pedal. She went forward twenty feet, swerved wide, did a U-turn, and then sped back the way they'd come.

By the time she passed him, he was on his feet. He pounded on the side of the van as she passed, and she was afraid he'd grab onto the handle. Terrifying images of him being dragged, but holding on and managing to get inside the van filled her head, but he didn't have the strength. She left him limping after her in the dust.

Alex couldn't see much, so she relied on her peripheral vision and hoped she was driving in a straight line. Actually, if a cop thought she was drunk and pulled her over, it would be a blessing. Well, unless it was *him*. How would she ever trust cops again after this? She tried to keep her mind on Cody. Him, she trusted, and he was a cop, too, albeit not one that would probably pull her over for a traffic violation.

She'd recognize the street lights when she got back to the city. From there, she thought she'd be able to navigate her way to the police station. She just had to pray the road she was on took her back into the city, and not farther out into the desert.

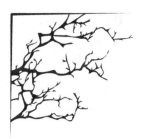

Chapter 31

WHEN A *ka-thud* announced that the dirt road had become pavement, the ride became smoother. The asphalt looked pale in the headlights compared to the surrounding darkness. She reached an intersection. Up ahead was only darkness. To her distant right there was light, but it was too far away to tell what the source was. Still, light spoke of civilization, so she turned toward it.

Twenty minutes later, Alex started to recognize things—a general store, a gas station, a bridge over the highway in front of the school. She was on Main Street, heading through the center of town.

Oddly, when the Botanist took her this time, he hadn't gone back to where he'd tried to abduct her before, near the historical monument. Rather, he went the opposite direction, coming out on the southern side of town. Where had he been going?

When she was almost to the station, lights in her peripheral vision caught her eye. They were red and blue, like cop lights. She put on her breaks and turned her head every which way, trying to figure out where she was. After several minutes she realized she was in front of the hospital. So not squad car lights, but ambulance lights? She wondered if they could have found Tom already. She had no idea how long she'd been gone.

Alex debated. She shouldn't drive any more than strictly necessary, and she needed medical attention. Even if the detectives weren't here, the hospital staff would call them for her. She turned the van onto the narrow road that led to the hospital, but only got half way down it before she had to slow again.

Something was in the road out ahead of her, but she couldn't tell what. It looked like a dark blur to her.

"Stop, ma'am."

Alex jumped at the voice outside her window.

"Where are you going, ma'am?"

Alex realized what she was seeing was a roadblock. The man outside her window was one of the cops assigned to it.

"Can you roll down your window, ma'am?"

Alex tried to find a circular handle—the van was way too old for power windows—but there wasn't one. She fumbled around for a minute, but she didn't know how to get the window down or how to tell the cop that she couldn't, so she opened the door.

She knew it was dangerous to get out of a car when the cop hadn't told you to, but she was too tired to care. Her strength was fading. She tried to step out of the van, but her legs weren't working particularly well. She fell out of the vehicle and stumbled until she could shut the driver's side door and lean against it.

"Ma'am, what are you—?" The cop's voice was guarded.

Alex could imagine how terrible she looked. She was covered with Tom's blood, her hair was a mess, and after wrestling with the Botanist, she was willing to bet her face could be the punch line of a black-and-white-and-red-all-over joke.

"Ma'am, are you—?" His voice had taken on a sound of awe, but to Alex he sounded hollow and far away.

She tried to speak. If they hadn't found Tom yet, she had to tell them to go get him. She couldn't force her voice out any louder than a whisper, though, and she was having trouble stringing full sentences together.

"Tom," she whispered, "Detective . . . hurt . . . the safe house."

She heard the cop step toward her.

"Are you Alexandra Thompson?"

"Alex!"

The voice was familiar, but it took a few more sentences before she realized it was Frank's. His voice was far away and his shoes thumped on the pavement as he jogged over to her.

"Alex, what happened?" There was a moment of shock while he took in her appearance. "Is that your blood?"

"No. Tom's . . . he's hurt."

"We know. He's here, in the hospital."

"Is he . . . okay?"

There was a minuscule hesitation. "The doctors are working on him. Alex, tell me what happened."

"Cop from before. He stabbed Tom; hit me with a tire iron."

"Then what?"

"I woke up, hit *him* with the tire iron, and kicked him out of the van. Came back."

There were several seconds of stunned silence.

"Really?" Frank asked, sounding impressed.

Alex nodded, but instantly regretted it, as it made the world sway violently.

Frank shouted in the other direction. "You, officer! You wanna catch a really bad guy today?"

"Yes, sir."

"Round up as many men as you can. I want at least five squad cars with ten men. Go now!"

Frank stepped closer to her, and she could feel his breath on her face, though she still couldn't see him clearly.

"Alex, this is important. Where did you kick him out?"

"I don't know . . . the highway, south of town."

"How far south of town? Did you see a mile marker?"

"No. Can't see anything. Couldn't even see the mileage gage in the van."

"What do you mean you can't see anything? You were just driving."

"He hit me with a tire iron. It's all blurry."

Immediately Frank's arm was around her waist, holding her up. She sagged against him with relief, not sure how much longer she could remain standing on her own.

"Anything you can tell us, Alex. Anything. He doesn't have a car. We can go get him right now if we know where to look."

"Stay on this road. When . . . get past the lights—way past—a dirt intersection. Turn right . . . went slowly on that road for . . . twenty minutes from where I kicked him out."

"Okay. Officer! When the other unies gather here, tell them to wait for me. I'm taking her up to the ER."

"Yes, sir."

Frank helped her hobble along, though in truth he was almost carrying her. She couldn't get her feet to move the way she wanted them to. She tried to hold her own weight up, but it was exhausting. The distance from the roadblock to the sliding door of the emergency room was probably only a few hundred feet, but it took a lifetime to cross.

Muted voices murmured around her. In the periphery of her vision, she could see blurry forms of men standing around, watching her. Radios spouted voices and static alternately, and everyone was talking on cell phones. Even Frank was talking to someone—to her or was he on a phone, too?—but she couldn't make out what he was saying.

Then there were forms of people coming toward them. One voice stood out of the din and brought Alex's head up.

Her eyes were getting worse, not better, but the voice, height, and vague, blurry features were all recognizable as Cody's. Alex was so relieved to see him she wanted to cry.

"Alex?" His voice dropped to a whisper. "God Almighty."

Cody came up beside her and started to put an arm around her. She didn't know if he meant to take over for Frank or not, but she reached up and wrapped her arms around his neck, clinging to him with what strength she had left. Then his arm was under her knees and she was being carried.

"I've got her, Frank."

"I'm going out with the uniforms, Cody. Tell the doctors she's got a head injury, reported blurry vision."

"I will."

Even Cody's voice became muted as she drifted farther from consciousness. Shapes and colors became more indistinct, until there were only shades of black and white and soft echoes all around. Then, mercifully, the darkness enveloped her.

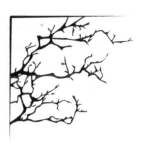

Chapter 32

CODY STARED OUT THE window of the hospital. The sun was out, the sky was blue, birds were singing, and he felt numb. Utterly numb.

The safe house was compromised, Alex was badly hurt, and the units that had gone out with Frank had found nothing—absolutely nothing—in the desert.

And Tom was gone, just like that. He'd been circling the drain when the ambulance pulled into the bay. They hardly bothered with the ER—just rushed him up to the operating room, where he "expired." Cody hadn't even gotten to say goodbye. No one had.

The medical staff cleaned Tom up and covered the gaping hole in his neck with a thick cloth, so the family could say goodbye. Cody sat with the body until Margaret and the kids arrived.

He hadn't cried, at least not right away.

He sat with the man who'd been his mentor and partner since he'd joined the force, and simply couldn't imagine that Tom wouldn't sit in the desk across from his at work anymore. He knew once the tears came they'd be unstoppable.

That moment arrived with Margaret and the kids. The second they entered the room, the wailing began. Cody stepped out into the hall to give them privacy, but the sound of little Hank crying for his father was too much, and Cody had to leave.

Normally, he might have gone out to his car, but hundreds of uniforms were standing around the hospital grounds, so Cody found a bathroom in a quiet part of the hospital and locked the door. He slid down the tiled wall, helpless and impotent, and the tears had come. Sobs wracked his body for more than an hour before he'd exhausted them. Even then, he remained on the floor for a time, unable to stand and face what lay beyond the dead-bolted door.

Finally he pushed himself to his feet. His face was wet, but clean. His eyes were dark red with blood. He splashed some water on his face and left the bathroom.

He walked through hallways with lines of blue-uniformed men and women lounging on either side. Young beat cops in uniforms lined the hallways. Cops, especially when they were all together, tended to be loud and jovial. These were solemn and melancholy. They'd all heard the news. The uniforms straightened up when they saw him coming. So they also knew who he was, that he'd just lost his partner. Many of them took off their hats as he passed. Some even reached out to touch his shoulder as he walked by them. Their faces were filled not with pity, but with empathy and genuine sorrow.

Cody thought he'd cried himself dry, but his eyes watered again at the show of respect and strength they were giving him. He might outrank most of them, but these were his brothers in arms, and they understood Tom's loss in a way no one else in the world could.

Walking the long, blue-lined hallway felt like walking a gauntlet, or a funeral march. It was the opposite of lonely, though no less painful.

Finally, Cody reached the captain, who stood at the end of hallway like a sentinel. He glanced up at Cody, then did a double take and turned his attention full toward him. Cody knew it was obvious he'd been crying, but the captain didn't ask if he was okay, and Cody was grateful.

"What now?" Cody asked.

The captain studied Cody for a moment, then looked past him at the dozens of uniforms still watching. The captain swallowed, and his eyes looked haunted.

"Do you want to make arrangements for the funeral?"

Cody looked up at him, and the captain hurried on.

"I can do it. I'd be glad to do it. But you were his partner, so . . ."

Taking care of the arrangements would be painful. It would be easier to lose himself in the work—go find this bastard hiding in the desert and kill him—but he also knew that if he didn't take the time to pay Tom his proper respects, to do what he owed his partner after so many years, he'd regret it later.

"We should ask Margaret what she wants. I'll take care of it. Is she still here?"

The captain shook his head. "Frank took her and the kids home a few minutes ago."

Cody nodded. "I'll go over and see them, talk to her about it."

"Take all the time that you and she need. When you get done, come to the station. You and Frank and Court and I need to have a meeting."

The profound sadness stole over Cody again. This time he hadn't expected it, and it took his breath away.

"What is it?" the captain asked when he saw Cody's face.

"Just the four of us."

The captain's eyes were suddenly wet, and he looked away. "Yes," he whispered.

Cody cleared his throat. "What do we need to have a meeting about?"

"We need to keep people calm."

Cody frowned. There were plenty of things that had happened in the last twelve hours than warranted fear, but he wasn't sure exactly what the captain meant.

"Which people?"

"The public. The press has the story. They ran wild with it before we could stop them."

"And what are they saying?"

"That the most prolific serial killer this state has ever seen came into town, broke into a residential house, went through a seasoned cop, and snatched someone."

Cody sighed. There was bound to be panic. There might even be a mass exodus from Mt. Dessicate. Cody wouldn't blame anyone who left. Any decent person with a family—which was most of the town of Mt. Dessicate; these were salt-of-the-earth people with children to protect—couldn't help but be afraid.

And could the cops defend them? Obviously not. This guy had killed a detective in a safe house, for heaven's sake. And what could anyone say to persuade the people they were safe? Cody couldn't be sure that they were. Despite the fact that this guy was zeroing in on Alex for some reason they still hadn't figured out, there was no guarantee he wouldn't prey on someone else if she kept getting away from him. Everything about this situation reeked of chaos.

"I'll be there after I talk to Margaret."

The captain nodded.

"ALEX, WAKE UP."

The hand shaking her shoulder yanked Alex from disturbing dreams. It hadn't been the red room this time, but rather one of those dreams where she couldn't keep her eyes open, no matter how hard she tried. In it, she was running from the Botanist, but she couldn't see where she was going, which direction was best, or how close he was. Then she heard Cody's voice, beckoning her to come to him and she'd be safe. The problem was that it seemed to come from every direction and because she couldn't see, she couldn't tell where he was.

Alex sat up. She was in a hospital bed. The room was light—bright, actually. The illumination filtering through the windows was that of midday. She was surprised she'd slept in this kind of light. Normally she needed darkness to sleep well.

"Sorry, honey," the nurse who'd awakened her said. She had auburn hair that was twisted up in a claw, but down would probably fall to her shoulders. "You can go back to sleep now."

Alex wore a white hospital gown and tried to brush away a stray piece of hair she could see out of the corner of her eye. After the third attempt, she realized it wasn't hair. It was the outside of her eye. It was so swollen she could see it.

"How did I get here?" she asked, probing her face gingerly.

The nurse, whose name tag read, "Hi, I'm Tanya," looked at her with concern. "You've been here since early this morning, honey. I've been waking you up every two hours. You don't remember?"

Actually, she did. Was it two hours between each time? It felt like two minutes. Alex vaguely remembered answering questions each time she was awakened, and even remembered seeing Cody sitting by her bed a few times.

"Do I have a concussion?"

"Yeah. Pretty bad one. We have to wake you up every couple of hours to make sure that, you know, we can."

Alex nodded. The previous night came back to her in halting patches. Then she remembered.

"Tom! Is he okay? The detective that was brought in? With a neck injury?"

Tanya studied her for minute, looking torn. "Maybe I should go get the doctor—"

"No! Please, Tanya. Just tell me. I need to know. Is he okay?"

Tanya slowly shook her head. "They took him up to surgery, but he died on the table before they could start."

Alex's heart turned to stone and sank into her stomach. Tom was dead? She couldn't comprehend the idea. How could he be gone? She'd been bantering at the dinner table with him not eight hours ago.

She drew her knees up to her chest and buried her face in them. Hot tears welled up in her throat, but for reasons she couldn't comprehend, they came out of her eyes instead of her mouth.

Tanya came up beside her. "It's not your fault, honey. He was a cop. These things happen."

"Of course it was my fault! He was there to protect me. This guy just . . ."

Tanya perched on the side of Alex's bed. She took Alex's arm and rubbed it compassionately. "What can I do?"

"Tell me what to do. I've never felt so . . . *not*-in-control in my life! This psycho keeps doing things that we can't predict. What if this keeps happening? He'll find me no matter where I go and kill anyone who's trying to help me. I don't know what to do."

Tanya was quiet for a long time, and the scalding tears stung the cuts and bruises on Alex's face as they passed.

"When I was a teenager," Tanya finally intoned, "I was a cheerleader. Junior year, another girl in the squad started a vicious rumor about me. Every time I passed her in the hall, she'd give me nasty looks, point and swear at me. She had a coterie that always followed her lead. Finally, my mom told me that I needed to act, rather than react to her. So, even though the last thing I wanted was to ever see her again, I sought her out, cornered her, and forced her to tell me what I'd done to deserve her behavior. She finally admitted that she liked the boy I was dating and wanted him for herself. That was it.

"I told her that if she liked him, she should approach him about it. He and I were dating, but we weren't exclusive. Well—" Tanya shrugged and studied the afghan that was draped over Alex's legs. "I don't think she ever *liked* me, but it diffused the situation. She stopped harassing me in the halls, and by senior year, we managed to be . . . civil."

Alex thought about that for a few minutes, and Tanya pretended to study Alex's chart, to give her time to think. The last thing Alex wanted was to ever see the Botanist again. And yet, Tanya might have a point.

"Act, rather than react, huh?"

"Yes." Tanya smiled. "If you wait for someone to seek you out, it will always be on their terms. If you want to set the terms, seek them out. Make them face you on your own turf. It's the only way that you can control the situation. Oh, I don't know what your situation is, honey, and I hope this isn't bad advice. But it's a lesson I learned early."

Alex nodded. "Thanks, Tanya."

Cody was gathering his things, preparing to visit Tom's family, when a uniform came into the ER calling his name.

"Detective Oliver? Is there a Detective Oliver here?"

"That's me, Sergeant. What is it?"

"There's a man outside asking for you, sir. He's a civilian so we can't let him in, but he's putting up a bit of a stink. He asked me to come find out where you were. Seems pretty desperate, sir."

With a nod, Cody followed the man outside. A crowd pressed against the police blockades, trying to find out what was happening. It was a small town, after all. Dozens of squad cars with flashing lights, congregating outside the hospital, was big news. The sky was overcast, due to the pending storm, and the gray clouds highlighted the police lights more than normal. There were dozens of officers who were looking to the Mt. Dessicate detectives because they were heading up the case; camera crews from different states and networks wandering around, looking for a good angle; and a crowd of civilians who, even if they didn't know Cody personally, knew he was a detective.

"Cody! Cody, there you are!"

It was his dad. His face was gaunt, his eyes slightly sunken, hair unkempt. Cody had rarely seen him in this state, and certainly never in public. Fear rose in his chest. He didn't think he could take any more tragedy today. He crossed to where his dad was and motioned to the cops manning the blockade to let his father through.

"Dad, what is it? What's wrong?"

His father stepped between the two wooden barriers when the uniforms pulled one of them back to let him in. He crossed to Cody looking incredulous.

"What's wrong? With *me*? What do you mean 'what's wrong?' Why aren't you answering your cell phone?"

Cody's eyes immediately looked for his car, but it was in some random spot in the hospital parking lot. "I must've left it in my jeep. Why? Was I supposed to ... ?"

He wracked his brain, trying to come up with some commitment he'd forgotten about.

"*Cody!* The local news channel has been reporting the murder of a detective for half the night. Your mother and I have been trying to call you for four hours. She's having a fit of hysteria wondering if it was you!"

Cody let out his breath. He closed his eyes as guilt washed over him. He hadn't thought to call his parents. He hadn't thought about the fact that the media would already have reported the incident, which meant his parents had probably heard it. He should have. There were already news crews at the hospital when he'd arrived, which meant a few of them had police scanners and had heard Alex's 911 call when she made it.

"Oh, Dad, I'm so sorry. I didn't think—"

"No you didn't think! I know you and I don't get along, Cody, but your mother doesn't deserve this."

Cody had never seen his father this unhinged before. He was exhausted, both emotionally and physically, and his anger flared.

"I didn't do it on purpose, Dad. A lot has happened tonight and I haven't even slept yet—"

"What could you possibly be dealing with that's more important—?"

"Tell Mom," Cody spoke over him, "that I'm sorry. I didn't mean to worry her, but I'll come see her as soon as I—"

"*Tell* her? Aren't you coming with me now? She's sitting in the car in a puddle of tears."

Though they had long differed over Cody's chosen profession, hitting his father had never crossed Cody's mind. Before now. All his pent up emotions over Alex, Tom, and a soul-numbing situation that was spiraling out his control rose to the surface.

He couldn't do it, though. His father was right about Cody's neglect in calling them. Cody clenched his fists. He couldn't contain the rage, and it seeped out of his pores and his tear-ducts, making his arms shake and his vision blur. When he spoke, his voice was low and barely controlled. He forced his words through clenched teeth, but had to keep stopping so that his voice didn't break.

"No, Dad. I'm *not* coming with you right now. My partner died tonight. And the man who murdered him is . . . hiding . . . somewhere in the desert. I have funeral arrangements to make, the press to deal with, and a killer to catch." Cody hung his head for a moment, letting his hands and lungs release their energy.

His father's taut, angry face had relaxed to the point of blankness.

"Tell Mom I'm *so* sorry." A tear spilled over Cody's lower lid. "I didn't mean to make either of you worry. It was unintentional. And I'll come and see her . . . as soon as I can."

As he spoke, his father's eyes widened with . . . could that be sorrow? Shame? Or just pity?

Cody didn't have the strength to stand around and try to explain why his deceased-partner's family had to come first right now. He stalked away, leaving his father looking forlornly after him.

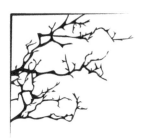

Chapter 33

TWENTY-FOUR HOURS LATER, Alex decided to check herself out of the hospital. The doctor wasn't happy about it, but he said as long as she didn't sleep for more than two hours at a time for the first twenty-four hours after her concussion, she should be fine. She figured she would be awake most of the day, and even when she did sleep, she'd probably be put in the second of the town's safe houses. She could get whichever officer stayed with her to wake her every few hours until morning.

Actually, she was hoping to have an excuse to stay up all night. Now that Tanya had planted the seed in her mind, she couldn't stop thinking about it. When the doctor grudgingly said he'd get her discharge paperwork, Alex turned to the two officers who were guarding her door. She noted that neither of them was young. They were both seasoned beat cops. Their uniforms said they were from a unit in St. George.

"What's your name, officer?" The man she spoke to was six inches taller than her, with dark hair and ears that stuck out like Yoda's.

"Michaels, ma'am. My partner is Hanson."

"Please, call me Alex. Where is Mt. Dessicate's police chief? I need to speak with him."

"I believe he's gone back to the station, ma'am. Now that you're being discharged, I should probably call and get orders from him."

"You can call if you like, but regardless of what he says, I need to speak with him in person. Tell him I want you to take me to the station so he and I can talk privately."

"I'll tell him, ma'am."

Forty minutes later, the squad car Alex sat in the back of pulled into Mt. Dessicate's police station. The number of reporters and camera crews hanging out on Main Street had doubled since the first day she'd arrived. Someone *did* recognize her as the victim of the latest attack, and a barrage of strangers and electronic equipment came flooding toward her.

A dozen uniforms set themselves up in a line between her and the press. Michaels and Hanson each had her by one arm and hustled her protectively into the building.

The captain met her in the lobby and took her hand.

"Alex, how are you feeling?"

"Fine," she lied.

"Come into my office."

Michaels and Hanson took up posts on either side of the door, which the captain shut before helping Alex into a chair in front of his desk.

"All right. I'm listening."

"Captain, I know this is a terribly insensitive thing for me to say at a time like this, when you've just lost one of your own, but I, more than anyone else, need this to be over."

The captain gave her a compassionate look. "I understand, Alex. We all want this to end, but you're the one he's after. You have every right to feel that way."

"It's not just that, Captain. Yes, he's after me for some incomprehensible reason, but Tom was there to protect me."

The captain put a hand up to forestall her. "Alex—"

"Please don't give me the 'it's-not-your-fault' speech. I know it wasn't my fault, in that *I* didn't kill him, but obviously anyone who tries to protect me is in danger. This guy is desperate to get at me. I don't pretend to know why, but maybe we can use that to our advantage."

The Captain's eyes narrowed as she spoke. He looked wary. "What do you mean?"

"Most criminals are cowards, right? They wouldn't walk into a safe house and take on a cop. I mean, Captain, he didn't even have a gun."

"It depends, Alex. Depends on the type of criminal and on how much he wants what's in that house."

"Exactly! I think he's more than just desperate. I think it's some kind of psychosis: he feels compelled to get me. This guy has never zeroed in on a victim before, right?"

"Not that we know of," the captain corrected. "Besides, most of his victims, from what we can tell, never got away from him. He took them off the highway, and they never had a chance."

"But that's my point. He doesn't want one that 'got away.' He feels compelled to come after me until he gets me. I don't think he can help himself, even if he knows there are cops protecting me."

The Captain frowned. "What's your point?"

Alex took a deep breath and settled back in her seat, squaring her shoulders. "I have a plan."

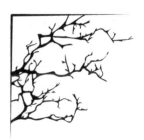

Chapter 34

CODY SPENT SEVERAL hours at Tom's house. As soon as he arrived, almost trembling with how different everything was from the last time he'd been there, Hank threw himself into Cody's arms, sobbing into his shoulder. A fresh wave of tears misting Cody's vision, he picked Hank up and took him into the living room. They wept together, Cody rocking the boy back and forth. He felt like he ought to say something comforting, but he couldn't think of anything. He couldn't make his mind form coherent thoughts. Hank eventually cried himself to sleep and Cody laid him on the couch, covering him with a throw.

Margaret came in and sat down opposite him. She gave Cody a grateful look. Her eyes were red-rimmed and puffy, but she was calm.

Cody had a hard time looking her in the eye. "I'm sorry, Margaret," he finally blurted out. "I'm sorry he was there instead of me."

Margaret shook her head, wiping away a runaway tear as though it were merely a stray wisp of hair. "It's not your fault, Cody. The captain told me what happened—that you had something else to attend to and there was no one else to stay with that woman. What's her name?"

"Alex," Cody whispered, but he didn't think Margaret really heard him.

"Besides, if you'd been there, it would probably be you we would need to make arrangements for."

Cody didn't answer. Tom was a good cop, but he was older than Cody and carried more weight. Cody tended to think that perhaps, had it been him in the safe house with Alex, he could have done more—moved more quickly, had more strength—and that the night might not have ended in tragedy. But Margaret was right: that might not be true. The assailant might have taken him by surprise just as he had Tom.

Running through that line of thinking would only drive Cody crazy, and neither argument would bring Margaret any comfort now.

Cody cleared his throat. "Speaking of arrangements, what can I do to help?"

Margaret shrugged. "Deana and Yvonne and Patricia have already been in touch with me. They're taking care of the pleasantries—flowers, food for the wake, that sort of thing. They'll sit with me and the kids tonight."

"Good." Deana and Yvonne were Frank and Court's wives, respectively. Patricia was the captain's.

A moment later, Margaret met his eyes. "Maybe . . . could you talk to Linda? Find out when she'll have things taken care of, and what she needs from me?"

"Of course. I know she'll need his dress uniform, but I'll ask her what else."

"I'll have it dry-cleaned," Margaret managed thickly. "Then I'll have to iron it, of course. It'll take me a day or two to get it to her."

Cody doubted Tom's fancy uniform needed to be cleaned or ironed. Most cops took prodigious care of their dress blues, and the Mt. Dessicate police hadn't had an occasion to wear them for months. But who was he to contradict Margaret in her grief?

"What else can I do?"

"I think everything else is taken care of."

"I didn't mean the arrangements, Margaret."

She looked at him for a long time. Then her eyes went to Hank, sleeping peacefully on the couch beside Cody.

Margaret shrugged again. "Hank's in love with you, Cody. Always has been."

"And I'll be here for him. Whenever he needs me."

She gave him a small smile, and it was painful to watch. "I appreciate that, Cody, but you have your own life to live. You can't always be here with us."

"That's true. But I can be sometimes. And I will be, as long as I'm not a burden."

"You know you're not. Hank will have a hard time with this. I think he'll have questions about his father, about how he died, about why *this* was Tom's chosen profession. They're questions I don't know how to answer."

Cody didn't think anyone, even most cops, knew how to answer them. The job was a calling, one most cops couldn't get away from even if they wanted to. He didn't know how he could explain that to a boy Hank's age, or how to put such things into words at all. He dreaded the day when he would have to.

"I'll be here to answer them for him. I've been where he is."

"You have?"

"It wasn't my father that died, but my true hero was always my uncle."

Margaret nodded. "He died in the line of duty?"

"Yes."

"Is that why you became a cop?"

Cody considered that. "I probably would have become one anyway, but it instilled a passion."

"Do you think Hank will follow in Tom's footsteps?" She studied the coffee table as she spoke.

"Would it be a bad thing if he did?"

Margaret didn't answer right away, and Cody was relieved when Margaret finally shook her head.

"No. I just hope these tragedies aren't cycles in a family of cops."

"They aren't," Cody assured her, though he really had no idea what the statistics on such things were. "After all, I'm still here."

She smiled appreciatively at him, then looked down at her hands.

They sat in silence for several minutes. Then Margaret's face crumbled, and she hung her head. Cody stood and went to sit beside her on the couch. He wrapped his arms around her, and she cried into his chest.

After a time, Hank stirred. He woke, saw them, and the remembrance of all that had happened seeped back into his face. His complexion went from bright and curious to gray and terrified in seconds. Hank swung his legs over the side of the couch, then crossed to where Cody and Margaret sat. He put one pudgy finger under Cody's eyelid and dragged it gently downward over Cody's wet face and under his chin. Hank watched the tear his finger was pushing along until it left Cody's face. Then he hugged his mother's shoulder.

She put her arm around him, and the three of them cried together.

It was after four when Patricia showed up with dinner for the family. Cody doubted any of them would eat for several days, but with Patricia there to watch over Tom's family, he excused himself to return to the station.

He barely noticed the time or the miles pass as he drove into town. The extra squad cars and news crews lining the streets didn't register at all. It wasn't until he got into the lobby of the station that he took notice of his surroundings.

There was a bustle of activity in the station that was . . . constructive almost. Bodies moved with purpose rather than chaos. Clusters of people stood around various tables and computer monitors, making plans, testing equipment, and going over maps.

A man breezed by Cody. It was Frank. Cody grabbed his sleeve.

"Frank. What's going on, man?"

Frank looked surprised to see Cody standing there. His red-rimmed eyes became wary. "Um . . . maybe you should go talk to the captain, Cody."

Cody's eyes narrowed. "About what?"

"Cody!" The captain called from the doorway of his office, motioning him over. Cody gave Frank a suspicious look, but Frank looked back at him levelly. Cody heard a familiar voice amidst the din and craned his neck to see around Frank. Alex was sitting at a desk with Court. They were pouring over a map of the desert north of the city.

"Frank, what's she doing here? Who let her out of the hospital? Shouldn't she be resting?"

"Uh, first of all, you should know that Alex is not a woman that anyone *let's* do anything."

"But—"

"Just go talk with the captain, Cody."

Heaving a sigh, Cody crossed the lobby. The captain shut the office door behind him.

"What's going on, Cap?"

"Now, Cody, I'm going to tell you right off to calm down." The captain perched on the edge of his desk and indicated a chair, but Cody ignored him.

"About *what*?" What at first had been wariness, then worry, was now panic spreading through his chest.

The captain studied him for a few seconds before answering. It felt like an hour. "We have a plan."

"Great. Best news I've heard all day. What is it?"

"We're setting a trap for the Botanist."

That didn't sound so bad. Suspicious, he asked, "What kind of a trap?"

The captain didn't answer right away, his eyes wandering back toward the lobby. Cody followed his gaze and found Alex, still bent over a map. He was still worried about her. She ought to be resting.

Then it dawned on him. His head snapped back to meet the captain's gaze.

"Tell me we're not using her for bait."

The captain sighed, looking very tired.

Cody sprang to his feet. "Why would you even consider a plan like that?"

"Because it's the only one we have. If you have a better one, Cody, believe me, I'm all ears."

Cody studied the floor furiously.

"That's what I thought," the captain said gently. "I don't need to tell *you* that we need to get this guy. I would have thought you'd be on board with anything that had even a remote chance of working."

Cody looked at the captain. It was true that he, maybe more than anyone, wanted to bring this coward to justice, but not at Alex's expense. Hadn't she been through enough?

"If you really thought that, then why were you afraid to tell me this? Why start by telling me to stay calm?"

The Captain didn't answer right away.

"She's a civilian, Captain. She's hurt, she's traumatized. How can you ask her to do this?"

"I would never ask a civilian to do something like this, Cody. She came to us with it, offering to help."

"And that makes it right?"

"You're right. Under other circumstances, I wouldn't even consider it. But we don't have any idea where this guy is. We have no idea where to start looking. Apparently, he's willing to come inside the city limits and hurt people to get at her. He's an imminent threat to the town, Cody, and we've got to get him into cuffs. Now.

"As long as she's willing, I'm taking her up on her offer. We have to draw him out. And we know he'll come for her."

Cody shut his eyes for a second. The horror of the entire situation was becoming too much for him. Tom's family at home, crying their eyes out; Alex in danger once again; every cop in the southern part of the state wanting so desperately to catch this guy that they were abandoning all protocol.

"And if she changes her mind?"

"I don't think she would have suggested it only to change her mind a few hours later."

"But what if she did?" Cody insisted.

"This isn't something we can force her into. We need her fully cooperative and alert for this."

"But she's not alert. She has cracked ribs and a concussion. She ought to be resting."

The captain sighed and got to his feet. "The decision's been made, Cody. Unless she changes her mind, this is happening. Tonight. She'll be surrounded by cops. We'll keep her safe. And with any luck, we'll have this guy by dawn."

CODY WANDERED OUT INTO the lobby, practically shaking with helplessness. He felt like he was climbing walls, only he wasn't confined. Except that he was. He couldn't find the killer, he hadn't been able to save Tom, and he couldn't stop Alex from putting herself into a lethal situation. The captain could be downright mulish when he put his mind to something. Cody couldn't stand it—any of it.

His eyes fell on Alex, who was being tutored on what to expect from several different scenarios that might possibly play out once they got into the desert. Her face was bruised and her eyes looked tired, but her smile came easily and frequently. Cody had a hard time tearing his eyes from her.

After a while, someone came to stand beside him.

"Hey, Cody."

He turned to Court. "What exactly is the plan, here?"

"We're going to put her in some clothes that look like the same ones she was wearing yesterday. We'll even spatter them with red paint. Then we're going to put her back into his van, and let her drive aimlessly around the desert for a while."

"Seriously? Why would that work?"

Court shrugged. "I don't know if he'll believe the ploy, but Alex has a point: he seems desperate to get at her, and he's escalating, which means he's no longer thinking clearly. Even if he knows it's a trap, I think he'll make a grab at her anyway. He can't help himself."

"And where will we be?"

"Close by. All around. We'll have men hiding in fox holes and crevices; we'll have squad cars and emergency vehicles hidden under nearby overhangs. We're gonna put a wire on her so that we can hear what's happening, and the second she sees him, she'll tell us."

"Yeah, but the media already broke the story."

"Not all of it. They broke the story that a cop was killed by this guy, and a woman was snatched. It hasn't been made public, yet, that she got away. And anyway, if he lives in the mountains out there, he may not have a media outlet. He may not be following the investigation at all."

"We don't know that."

"No," Court admitted, "but I think it's a real possibility."

"Even so," Cody persisted, "what about the fact that he probably *does* live out there? He *knows* all of the overhangs and crevices. What if he watches us get all our guys into place? He may be ten steps ahead of us."

"Maybe, but I think you're giving him too much credit. If he lives out there somewhere, I don't think he has a state-of-the-art security system. You can't plug something like that into red rock. He may know the area better than we do, but he can't watch hundreds of square miles of terrain all at once. We're already moving people into place."

"Now? In the heat of the day?"

"Yeah. Some of them are dressed as hikers. They'll pitch tents and then move into position when it gets dark. Others are driving miles out of their way, just so they can approach from the other side of the range. They'll use night vision goggles to find where they need to be. Trust me, Cody, this will work. He won't know they're there."

"What if he doesn't take the bait?"

Court shrugged. "He may not. But if not, we won't be any worse off anyway."

Cody nodded. He was out-voted. It would be better, now, to become a part of it. It might be the only way he could protect Alex. Unless . . .

"So what can I do to help?"

"Ask the captain where he wants you. When you have a minute, I'll show you the route she'll be driving. It's a loop, but we'll have people placed all along it."

"Will anyone be in the van with her?"

Court turned, looking surprised. "Of course. Four SWAT team guys."

Cody was mollified. A bit. He supposed they were taking every precaution, but he still didn't like it. He searched until he found Alex again. She was still sitting in the same place, but she was alone. The others had vacated the table.

Cody decided that he had to at least try to talk her out of it.

He walked toward her. She glanced up as he got closer, then got to her feet, an expression of genuine concern on her face.

"Hey, Cody. How are you doing?"

He frowned. It took him several seconds to realize she was referring to the loss of Tom. Despite coming over to her with resolve, her sympathy disoriented him.

"Uh . . . fine. I'm . . . yeah, I'm fine. Can I talk to you for a minute?"

She nodded.

Cody looked around. Honestly, all the activity in the lobby ensured their conversation would be private, but he still preferred to find a quiet place where he could focus.

Court had headed toward the front of the lobby, and Frank was zigzagging continually around the room, his arms full of files, so it was a good bet that their office at the back of the building was empty.

"Come with me." He took her hand and led her to the room with the four desks clustered together. Cody did his best to ignore Tom's desk, which was, of course, still full of his stuff: a Styrofoam cup of cold coffee, pictures of Margaret and the kids, a palm tree paperweight from their family trip to Fiji five years ago. Cody pretended not to be affected by any of it.

The door that separated the detectives' office from the rest of the building was propped open. Actually, it hadn't been closed in years. Now, with random people Cody had never seen before parading constantly past the door, Cody closed it for privacy.

Then he turned to Alex. He motioned to the nearest chair, which happened to be Court's. "Want to sit?"

She shook her head. "Thanks, but I've been sitting out there for hours now. It feels good to stand. What did you want to talk to me about?"

"Why are you doing this?"

"Doing what?"

He motioned to indicate the four walls around them and all the activity on the other side of them as well.

Alex sighed. She leaned back to perch on the edge of Court's desk. "Why do you think?"

"You don't have to."

"I know that. I want to."

"But why?"

"Because Tom was trying to protect me."

"It wasn't your fault, Alex."

"Ugh! Why does everyone keep saying that? I know it wasn't my fault, but anyone trying to protect me might be killed, and that's not okay with me!"

Cody was taken aback by her sudden frustration, and she moderated her tone when she saw his face.

"Look, I know I can't have anything to say to you about Tom. I only knew him a few days; he was your partner and best friend. I could tell. But even so, I liked him. He was obviously a decent guy, and he had a family. I want this to be over, Cody. I want to get this guy as much as you do. I really think he'll come for me if I'm dangled in front of him, no matter the consequence. We can get him this way."

"And what if it doesn't go as everyone plans? What if this turns dangerous for you?"

"I'll be virtually surrounded by cops."

Cody huffed and turned away, pacing across the room. That wasn't good enough. He didn't know why; it just wasn't.

"What? Cody, they're *your* colleagues. Don't you trust them?"

"Of course I trust them. That's not the point. This man is dangerous, fatally so. I trusted Tom. I would have put my life and yours in his hands without a second thought, and this guy just—"

It was then that his voice broke. He hadn't expected the emotion to overtake him so completely, but it did, and when it did, he couldn't recover. He was on the other side of the room from Alex, but facing her. It didn't occur to him to turn away. He dropped his head, face toward the floor, trying to hide from her until he could regain his composure.

He was vaguely aware of Alex closing the distance between them. She walked up and put a hand on his chest, bending her knees slightly so that she could gaze up into his face, but Cody wasn't ready, yet. He closed his eyes, refusing to look down at her, until he was sure he could keep his expression tranquil. Then he opened his eyes.

Her face was inches below his, and the concern was back, but it was more than concern. There was something so empathetic, so genuine about the worry in her eyes that he felt like she understood him, and his loss, as no one else could.

Then she did something he didn't expect. She raised up on her tip toes and kissed him. He didn't pull away, but he didn't respond either, taken by surprise. But then he did kiss her back, moving his lips over hers, and as the kiss became deeper, something ignited in him that, despite how impressed he'd been with her over the last few days, was completely unexpected.

He kissed her more deeply still, wrapping his arms around her waist, and her arms threaded up to twine around his neck. He pushed her backward, until the office wall stopped them. Then his lips left hers, wandering down one side of her neck and into the crevice of her shoulder.

She gasped and used her grip on his shoulders to hoist herself up, hooking her knees around his waist. His lips found hers again and his hands roamed down over her sides and legs.

The sound of the doorknob turning and the heavy door being pushed open were only vague impressions, but Frank's voice pulled Cody instantly out of the moment.

"Hey Alex, the captain wants you to—"

Cody pulled back and Alex let go of him, bracing herself against the wall. Cody immediately took two giant steps back from her, but the action came far too late for Frank not to see it.

At first, Frank's face was a comical mask of shock, and he averted his eyes. Then his expression darkened. The tension in the room was palpable.

After several awkward seconds, Frank spoke again. His voice was ominously controlled, masking a quiet fury below the surface. Cody wondered if Alex knew Frank well enough yet to see his anger for what it really was.

"Alex, the captain wants you to go see Rose. She'll take you to our electronics guys. They're going to fit the wire on you and show you how to use it."

Cody looked over at Alex. She stared at him in an intense way, but her expression was utterly unreadable. Finally, she tore her gaze from him and looked at Frank.

"Okay. Where's Rose?"

"I'll take you to her."

Alex nodded. She shot another strange look at Cody before ducking her head and exiting the room. Frank glared at Cody for five full seconds before following her.

When they were gone, Cody let out his breath, feeling exhausted. He rubbed the bridge of his nose. What just happened?

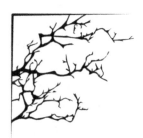

Chapter 35

AN HOUR LATER, FRANK came back into the room. Cody glanced up, but Frank was ignoring him, so Cody went back to his reports, content to let Frank start the conversation.

It took nearly five minutes.

"You okay, Cody?"

Cody sat back in his chair. "I'm fine." It was a lie, but he wasn't going to guilt Frank into not speaking his mind.

"Good." Frank's back was to Cody but as he spoke, Frank spun toward him. "'Cause I just wanted to ask, what the hell is wrong with you?"

Cody heaved a sigh. Here it came, and he completely deserved it.

"What *was* that, Cody?"

"It just happened."

"It just *happened*? Cody, when I teased you about her a few days ago, it was because I saw you looking at her. I was kidding when I did it; she's pretty and I figured you thought she was attractive, but never in a million years did I think you would actually *act* on it!"

"I—" Cody cut off. He'd been about to say that he hadn't, she had, but that was copping out, too. He'd kissed her every bit as much as she'd kissed him. He could have put a stop to it, but instead . . .

"You're a *detective*, Cody!" Frank's voice was more irate by the sentence.

"Stating the obvious, Frank—"

"Then start acting like one! Cody, you can't screw her."

"I'm not screwing her—"

"She's part of an active investigation, and we haven't even cleared her as a suspect yet."

That brought Cody up short. "You still think she's lying?"

Frank sighed, the anger draining out of him like a deflating balloon. "No," he said after a moment, "probably not. I don't think anyone thinks that anymore. There's too much going on here, and she seems too . . . sincere. But Cody, we haven't *officially* cleared her yet, and if anyone in the press gets a hold of the idea that one of us has a relationship with her—"

"But I *don't* have a relationship with her. I told you, this *just* happened." Frank's jaw clenched again, and Cody held his hands up. "And you're right, Frank. I shouldn't have let it happen. But with everything that's going on, and Tom, and . . . and Resputa . . ."

Frank's attention perked up. "I forgot you spoke with Resputa."

"I think everyone has."

"What'd he say? Did he give you any leads?"

"A few, but nothing that will find our guy before tonight. Look, this operation is already underway. We'll try it, and if he doesn't show, we can work on what Resputa told me tomorrow. But I *will* insist on staying close to Alex."

Frank took on a wary look again. "That's a conflict of interest, Cody. If I told the captain—"

"But you won't."

"Why not?"

"Because." Cody got up and stalked toward his friend. "If it was your wife, or daughter, or sister, or anyone else you cared about being used as bait for a sadistic killer, would you be willing to be sidelined?"

Frank gazed at Cody for a long time, frowning. Then his eyes shifted and he shook his head slowly. "No. I'd insist on being front and center." But he still looked doubtful. He ran his hands through his hair. "You can't let your emotions cloud your judgment here, Cody. This guy is too dangerous for that."

"I hear you, Frank, and if you see me doing any such thing, by all means, pull me back."

After a moment, Frank nodded. His eyes shifted to Tom's desk, and a gloom Cody understood all too well came into his face.

"Help! Please, someone, I need help!"

The woman's cry must have come from the front lobby because it was muffled as it reached their ears. Cody and Frank exchanged glances, then hurried out of the room.

The earlier productivity had come to a halt and people were gathering around someone Cody couldn't see up near Rose's desk. He and Frank pushed their way to the front of the crowd. Court and the captain were already there. Alex stood a few rows back, arms crossed over her stomach, looking anxious.

The woman who called out was a plump, twenty-something brunette. Cody recognized her. She was Melissa's best friend. He was totally blanking on her name, but she, her husband, Melissa, and Cody had double dated a few weeks ago.

"I'm looking for Cody Oliver. Is he here somewhere?" Even as she said it, Cody walked into her line of sight, and she turned fully to him.

He cleared his throat. "Hi, uh . . ."

"Jillian."

"Jillian, right. Are you okay?"

"I'm fine. Melissa's not. Something's happened to her."

Cody frowned. "What?"

"The guy you've all been looking for—the killer from the desert? He took her."

A cold stone came to rest at the base of Cody's stomach.

"Who's Melissa?" Court asked.

"She's, um, a woman I've been dating. Here." He took Jillian's hand and guided her toward a chair. She was trembling. "Sit." He crouched down in front of her. "Jillian, why do you think he took Melissa?"

The crowd followed them to the seat and was listening for Jillian's reply with rapt attention.

"I saw him."

The crowd broke into murmurs, which the captain quickly silenced.

"What happened, Jillian?" Cody asked.

Jillian took a deep breath before starting. "Melissa's car is in the shop until tomorrow, so I told her if she needed to go anywhere, to call me and I'd take her. Today I had to run to the market for an emergency pack of diapers, and I ran out of the house without my cell phone. When I got back, there was a message from her. She was frantic. I haven't watched the news in days, but she told me that a detective was killed, and she couldn't get a hold of you. She said she didn't know where I was but that she was going to walk down to the safe house—you know, the old Harrison place?—and try and find you since no one could get into the hospital."

"Whoa," the captain stopped her. "The safe house?" He turned accusingly to Cody. "You told your girlfriend where the safe house was?"

"No! I didn't." Cody looked at Jillian. "How'd she know where the safe house was?"

"She just figured it out. She used to live in that neighborhood. I think a lot of the neighbors have figured it out, but they're upstanding citizens so they don't publicize it."

"But why did she think I was there?" Cody was still incredulous.

"You aren't answering your cell phone," Jillian said. "She kept calling the station and was just told you were out. She said on a hunch she called old Mrs. Jones, who lives across the street from the safe house. Jillian was discreet, but Mrs. Jones reported seeing your car there. I think Melissa was at a loss, so she just decided to walk down and see if she could find you."

"So, she went down to the safe house looking for me . . . and then what?"

"I got back and got her message, so I changed my kid, put her in the car, and went to find Melissa. I figured, even if she was already there, I could at least give her a ride back. I took the route she would have walked from her place, looking for her. By the time I saw her, she was a block up from the safe house. I could see her a hundred yards ahead of me, but I got stuck at a red light.

"Then a police cruiser pulled up next to her. She walked out into the road to talk to whoever it was. I didn't think anything of it. I figured she was asking the cop who was driving where she could find you, or if he knew who'd been killed. She stepped away from the car, like she was afraid or something.

"The next thing I know, the tallest man I've ever seen gets out of the car, grabs her wrist, and wrestles her into the back seat. I'm sure she was screaming, but I couldn't hear her from so far away. If I hadn't been there specifically looking for Melissa, I don't think I'd have noticed the abduction at all. It happened so fast, and there was no one else out on that street."

"No one?" Cody asked, incredulous. "But it was the middle of the day."

"I know, but a lot of the people in that area are elderly. Most of them were probably napping in their sun chairs by that time. I'm telling you, I'm the only one who saw it."

"Did you see which way he went?" Frank asked at Cody's shoulder.

"He drove away from me. I would've had no problem running the red light to help her, but by then there was tons of cross traffic. My two-year-old was in the car. When the light turned green, I sped after him, but he'd already turned several times, and I drove around for a while looking for him, but I couldn't tell where he went. So I dropped my daughter off with my husband and came here."

Cody ran his hand through his hair. This situation was getting worse and worse. He hadn't seen Melissa—or even thought about her—since she'd come to see him two nights before. His head was way too tightly wound around this case. Now, because he hadn't thought to call her, she'd been dragged into it. Literally.

"What does this mean?" Jillian asked. "Cody, is he going to kill her?"

Cody came out of his thoughts to look into Jillian's frightened eyes. He shook his head slowly, but firmly. "Not if I can help it."

"But . . . but you couldn't help the other victims, either. Melissa said there were twelve bodies in the desert."

Cody took Jillian's hands. Her chin trembled and tears squeezed themselves from the corners of her almond-shaped eyes. "We didn't know about them," he said. "We found their bodies a long time after they were killed. We know about Melissa, and have an idea of where to look for her. We also have a plan to try and draw him out. At the very least, it will be some time before he tries to . . . do anything to her. We'll find her before then, okay?"

"You have a plan? What is it?"

That was something they couldn't discuss with Jillian. Cody looked at the captain for help.

"Jillian, why don't you go with this detective," the captain said gently. "We need to take an official statement and see if we can download a picture of Melissa to distribute. Then we'll get you set up with a sketch artist."

Jillian nodded and allowed herself to be led out of the lobby by Court. "All right, everyone." The captain addressed the entire room. "Back to work."

Cody got slowly to his feet. The captain and Frank clustered around him.

"Cody, look at me," the captain said, his voice more serious than Cody had ever heard it. "Could this have something to do with you?"

Cody understood why the captain was asking him that. He was the lead detective on the case, and a woman he'd been dating had been targeted. The captain needed to know whether his own family, as well as Frank's and Court's, needed to be put under police protection. But it was simpler than that, so Cody shook his head.

"This isn't about me; it's about Alex."

The captain frowned. "I don't understand. Did she know Melissa?"

"No. But she *looks* like Melissa."

Both Frank's and the Captain's eyebrows jumped. "They look alike?"

"You wouldn't mistake one for the other if they were side by side or anything, but general features, height, weight, coloring . . . yeah, they look alike."

Frank was giving Cody a knowing look, but Cody ignored him. The last thing he needed was some psychoanalytic discussion about the fact that the woman he was dating and the woman he was falling for looked alike.

"So," the captain said quietly, for Cody and Frank's ears only, "they look alike in the way that serial killers often choose similar victims who look alike."

Cody nodded.

The Captain sighed. "So Alex got away from him, but he stumbles upon a woman who looks a lot like her, who's in the vicinity of the safe house—"

"And who was probably asking him about the case," Frank put in.

"So he snatches her instead. It makes sense."

Maybe it made sense, but the situation was so revolting, Cody turned his back to the captain. He needed to think about something else—anything else—just for a few minutes. He found Alex standing six feet away, observing their little powwow. Her arms were folded tight against her stomach, and her face had a green hue to it.

Cody crossed to her.

Alex's gaze wandered around the room of now-busy people. Even when he stood right in front of her, she continued to run her eyes around the perimeter of the lobby before finally coming to rest on his face. She looked frightened. And vulnerable.

Cody turned her around, put his hands on her shoulders, and guided her firmly through the lobby. He aimed for his office, but upon seeing Frank's gaze go from curious to suspicious, he made a sharp turn and steered her into the captain's office. It was closer, empty, and had a couch.

Cody sat Alex down and crossed the room to where a water cooler sat in the corner. He filled a small Dixie cup and brought it to her. Alex accepted it, but didn't drink.

Squatting down so he was looking up at her, he put a hand on her knee. "This isn't your fault, Alex. We don't even know if this is the same guy."

Her voice was wooden. "He took Melissa because I got away from him."

"We don't know that."

She met his gaze very directly, then. "Don't we?"

He didn't answer her. They both believed the same thing in this matter, and he wouldn't lie to her about it.

"And she's your . . . she's your . . ."

Cody shook his head. "She and I have dated off and on over the last few weeks, but we don't know each other that well. It's not a very serious relationship."

"Yes but you know her. You've spent time with her. That's got to mess with your head."

Cody frowned. "It does, but that's not your fault either. I don't want you blaming yourself for this."

"You keep losing people, Cody. First Tom, now her."

"Alex." He took her hands and sat beside her on the couch. "First of all, no one's lost her yet. I don't intend to let this bastard kill her. And second, the reason so many people I know are caught up in this is because this is a small town. If I'm caught up in it, others I know will be, too. I can't afford to let my personal feelings cloud my judgment. If I do, I'll miss something."

"If Melissa dies, I'll know for the rest of my life that it was because *I* didn't."

"Don't apologize for fighting for your right to not be victimized by a psychopath—and for winning. We'll figure this out."

A tear escaped her eye and slid down her face, leaving a skewed trail of moisture on her cheek. "Don't you get it, Cody? He has someone to torture, which means he's less likely to be wandering around looking for me. This whole plan to bait him tonight might not work."

Cody hadn't thought of it that way, but she was right. If he wasn't desperate to capture Alex right *now*, he might not show tonight.

"Do you want to call it off, Alex?"

At that, she hesitated, then shook her head. "No. I think we should try either way, and I'm willing to. I just think there's a much smaller chance of success now."

"That's true."

Cody looked up to see Frank, Court, and the captain standing in the doorway. The three of them filed into the room, and Frank closed the door.

"I've just spoken with a uniform who was patrolling the area," the captain said. "We radioed out for a unit where she was abducted. They just got back to us with what they found. I brought Court and Frank in here to tell them because I wanted to spare poor Jillian a complete meltdown."

Cody's heart went cold. He held his breath, wondering if they'd found Melissa's body.

"What was it?" Court whispered. He and Frank looked as worried as Cody felt.

The captain seemed nonplussed. "Three houses down from the safe house lying on the sidewalk were three pale blue tulips, just like the ones on the mass graves. There was nothing anywhere near them."

Cody let his breath out, but the relief wasn't total. Melissa wasn't dead—not yet—but this was confirmation that she'd been taken by the Botanist.

"I still think we ought to try our plan," the captain continued grimly. "Everything's in place already, and who knows? Maybe we'll get lucky. If you want to back out, though, Alex, everyone will understand."

Alex sat straighter. "No. If he comes for me, it may keep Melissa alive long enough to give her a chance. We have to try."

Cody suppressed a sigh. He couldn't expect Alex to keep herself completely out of danger, but he didn't have a good feeling about this. Not at all.

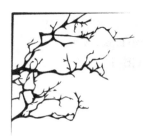

Chapter 36

BEFORE DARKNESS FELL, three SUVs that would serve as a command center for the operation were moved into place. They were hidden under an overhang near where the Botanist had disappeared. The vehicles couldn't be seen from the road, and the mountain above them had been scouted to make sure they couldn't be seen should anyone emerge from a cave or gaze from an outcropping.

Tiny glows from computer screens and low-powered flashlights were the only permitted light. No headlights, spotlights, or Maglites were allowed. The van Alex had driven to the hospital was parked nearby. Four SWAT team members loitered beside it.

"Are you ready for this?" Cody looked down at Alex. She was wrapped in a blanket and holding a still-full cup of hot cocoa. The blanket and cocoa would have to stay behind when she got into the van. In order for the ruse to work, it had to look as if she hadn't received any help since she drove away from him yesterday.

Alex hunched her shoulders against the cold wind. It wasn't ferocious, but it was getting there, blowing a summer storm in. Every so often, the low rumble of thunder could be heard in the distance.

"As ready as I'm going to be."

"If you have any problems, if you get too tired, if you feel funny about *anything*—"

Alex nodded. "I'll be fine, Cody. I'm not backing out. I wanna get this guy. I'm more worried about being out here all night for nothing."

"I'll be nearby."

She smiled up at him in a perceptive sort of way. "I know."

She looked down into her cocoa cup, and for a moment he thought she might actually drink some of it, but she didn't.

"Cody, um." She cleared her throat. "About earlier—"

He shook his head and held up his hands. "Let's not get into what happened earlier. You need to be focused on *this*. Don't worry about it one way or the other. This is happening now. Let's deal with it, and we can talk about everything else later."

After a moment, she nodded, but it wasn't convincing. A blustery wind blew her hair back, off her shoulders, and she squinted against it when she looked up at him. Cody was suddenly overcome with the urge to kiss her again, but they were surrounded by bustling cops. Even in the near-darkness, everyone would see.

As if reading the thought, Alex smiled at him, then looked down, suddenly shy. He smiled back at her, the sweetness of the moment filling him up in a way he rarely felt these days. He wanted to make it last, and the only way he could think of to make it more real was through touch. He rested a hand on her wrist, letting his thumb run over the back of her hand.

"Cody!" It was a yelled whisper.

Cody turned to see Frank and the captain walking toward them. Even in the dark Frank looked suspicious. His gaze went pointedly to Cody's hand on Alex's wrist, but Cody didn't let go of her.

"We're about ready to go," the captain murmured as he approached. "Everything's in place. You'll be stationed up on the ledge there." He pointed to a ridge above them where another cop was already lying on his stomach, readying binoculars and other equipment.

Cody looked at Frank, but Frank's eyes were hooded, and Cody couldn't read their expression. "Why am I staying here?"

The captain looked confused. "Where else would you go? Everyone not assigned to the route is staying here."

Cody didn't answer. He supposed he should have expected that. Hidden fox holes lined the route Alex would be driving, but only SWAT and snipers were in them.

"I would've thought you'd like that post, Cody," the captain continued. "You'll be able to keep eyes on the entire course from there."

"It's fine," Cody said, unable to keep the irritation out of his voice.

The captain frowned, but when Cody didn't volunteer anything else, he turned to Alex. "It's best to get you out there now. The moon's behind the clouds, and we don't want him knowing where you came from."

"Those clouds are holding rain," Alex said, tilting her head back to take in the inky sky. "The moon might not come back out at all."

"That's what headlights are for," the captain said. "Are you ready?"

"Yes." She handed Cody her mug and her blanket. Beneath it, the shirt they'd given her was torn and spattered with fake blood. Her hair was mussed, and they'd even gone so far as to spatter some of the paint as high up as her neck. The effect was a little too realistic for Cody's peace of mind.

Alex climbed into the ancient van; the SWAT team piled into the back. Everything inside had been removed to make room for them. The van had been swept for trace evidence, and it had yielded plenty of DNA, but it would be days before lab results came back.

It was fifteen minutes before Alex was ready to drive out. The concealment of the SWAT team members was carefully checked and rechecked. Equipment was given last minute performance tests. Alex was asked again and again how she felt.

Cody stood by her window and watched her handle it with a graceful elegance that he envied. When she wasn't talking to anyone in particular, she looked out over the steering wheel, and Cody could swear there was fear in her eyes. After she did it a third time, he realized it wasn't just fear, but stark terror. She was petrified, but she hid it well, smiling patiently when they asked for yet another sound check, or inquired yet again if she needed anything else.

Finally, it was show time.

Cody put his hand over hers, which rested on the van's open window. "It'll be over before you know it."

She looked unconvinced, but she forced a smile anyway. "Sure. Thanks."

Cody stepped back as Alex put the van in drive and pulled forward, wishing there was something else he could say. There wasn't. He willed this night to pass quickly.

As soon as the taillights disappeared around the red rocks that concealed the command center, Cody put his ear piece in. Everyone was linked in and could hear what was happening with Alex, as well as the captain's voice.

"How're you doing, Alex?" the captain asked.

"*Fine.* Just approaching the loop."

Cody got into position on the ridge just as Alex reached the pre-plotted course she would drive over and over again. Even from this distance—probably a half mile away—he could vaguely make out the headlights. The binoculars made it much easier.

The route they'd mapped for her was basically a mile-long figure-eight in front of the mountain that the Botanist most often appeared around. She would be instructed by cops who were high up on the ridge to deviate this way or that to make it look random, and somewhat erratic. Hopefully the Botanist would think she was suffering from fatigue, the elements, and her injuries. There would be times she would have to drive almost into the mountain itself, come to a stop, back up, then go again. The hope was that he would think she was confused—altered even—and that when she drove up to a dead end and had to back up, the Botanist would try and grab her. Handfuls of cops were hidden around the designated stop-and-go spots so that if the plan worked, they would easily apprehend him.

Cody sighed. His arms already ached from holding himself up while lying on his stomach, and lifting the binoculars at the same time. Despite what he'd said to Alex about it being over quickly, they were in for a long night. It might be hours before anything happened.

Cody glanced at the middle-aged cop beside him. "I'm Cody Oliver."

"Helam Merriton. From Sigurd."

"You walk a beat?" he asked, though he doubted Sigurd actually had a beat. It was a blink-and-you-missed-it sort of town.

"Nah. I just live there. I'm not really a cop. I'm an equipment specialist for the entire county. Work almost exclusively with law enforcement though. You?"

"Detective here in Mt. Dessicate."

"Ah. Brave girl, eh?"

Cody nodded, peering through the high-power binoculars again. "Yeah. Very brave girl."

Three hours later, nothing much had happened, other than Cody growing dizzy from watching Alex complete the loop over and over again. At the speed she was going, it took about ten minutes to do the entire thing, but still . . .

As she completed it yet again, Cody glanced at his watch. It was after midnight. They were still a long way from dawn. Alex's voice came onto the com, startling him.

"This isn't working, Captain," she said. "He's not falling for it."

"He may not know we're here yet, Alex," the captain's voice intoned. "Once he realizes it, he may act."

"Or maybe he does know, and he's hanging out, watching us, knowing better than to approach the van. He probably knows I'm not alone inside."

"There's no way to know that for sure, Alex." The captain's voice was calm and reasonable. "Just keep doing what you're doing."

Through the binoculars, Cody watched the van's movements. He could make out the vague shape of the van, but only because of the outline of her taillights.

She reached the far side of the route. She was supposed to loop around and head in the other direction. Instead, the van came to a stop. Cody wondered if she would back up, rather than looping around, just to change it up. He waited. Nothing happened.

She was obviously distraught. Cody could picture her, staring out over the steering wheel and thinking. When a full sixty seconds passed and still the van hadn't moved, he pressed the button to speak into the com system.

"Alex, what are you doing? Why have you stopped?"

Nothing. Just dead air.

"Alex? What's wrong?"

When she didn't answer again, Cody went from his stomach to his knees. Then the captain's voice was in his ear.

"Alex, respond please. What are you doing?"

Alex's voice answered almost immediately. "I . . . I'm just trying something."

Cody knew he ought to let the captain take the lead, but he couldn't help himself. He pressed the com button again. "Trying *what?*"

Merriton sucked in his breath beside Cody, but Cody didn't have time to figure out what had caused the man's reaction. He was too preoccupied with what Alex was "trying."

Suddenly the equipment specialist was tugging at Cody's shirt sleeve, frantically whispering his name. "Detective? Detective Oliver!"

Cody swatted him away, still looking through the binoculars.

"Alex, you need to keep moving," the captain said into the com. "If you stop, you need to do it at one of the designated sites. If he blitz attacks you there, our men are a bit far away for comfort."

"Detective Oliver! Detective Oliver!" Merriton's hiss was urgent.

"What?"

When Cody looked over at his binocular buddy with exasperation, Merriton snatched is binoculars from him.

"Merriton, what are you—?"

The other man clicked a small button on the top of the binoculars and they suddenly glowed with a greenish light.

"What'd you do?"

"Turned on the night vision."

"These have night vision? Why weren't we using it all along?"

Merriton got defensive. "*I* was. I didn't realize you didn't know you had it until just now."

Cody rolled his eyes, thoroughly annoyed, but Merriton was flicking his hands out frantically in Alex's direction.

"Look what she's doing!"

Throwing one last glare at Merriton, Cody jammed the binoculars against his eyes, giving himself a mild headache, and looked out over the now-illuminated terrain. When he found Alex and the van, he gasped, simultaneously jumping to his feet and jamming a thumb down on the com button.

"Alex, get back in the van! Right now!"

"Is she out of the van?" the captain sounded alarmed.

"Yes. She's walking twenty feet behind where it's parked!"

"Alexandra Thompson, you get back in that van." The captain sounded like the father he was.

With the night vision binoculars, Cody could see Alex clearly. She turned in the general direction of the command center and folded her arms.

"Do you boys want to catch this creep or not?" She spoke softly, as if trying to mask the volume of her voice and its potential to scare nearby listeners.

"Not if it means compromising your safety, Alex," Cody said.

Alex sighed into the com. "Look guys, he's not going to come at me if I'm in the van. I can feel that much. If I stagger around on my own, he's more likely to think me vulnerable and try and get me."

"That's because you *will* be more vulnerable."

"Cody, lie down," the captain said. "Anyone who looks this way will see you clear as day."

Cody fell into a crouch, but didn't lie back down on his stomach. He had no intention of doing any such thing until Alex was safely back in that van.

Cody cursed softly. How had that happened? He'd thought of the killer's van as a safe place. It wasn't. Nowhere out there was, not for her.

"Alex," the captain was saying, "this isn't what we discussed. It's not a good idea. We can't protect you well enough if you aren't in the van."

"I'll stay on the same route, Captain, only walking rather than driving five miles an hour. Your people will be the same distance away."

Cody's heart sank as the silence on the com stretched. The captain was considering it. When the captain voice came over the com again, it was confirmed.

"Does everyone have eyes on Ms. Thompson? Start with Desert-1 and tell me."

The person in each position called in.

"Desert-1. Affirmative."

"Desert-2. Yeah, I can see her."

"Desert-3, that's a yes."

"Desert-4 . . ."

Only those at the far end of the loop couldn't see her, but they would when she was closer to them.

"Captain, don't let her do this. It's asking for trouble."

"I don't think we have much choice, Cody. She's right. He hasn't tried anything yet, and we need to be realistic about the reasons for that. I don't believe he doesn't know she's out there. Alex, you can proceed, but with caution. And stay on the loop. One more misstep from you and I'll bring up the spotlights and shut this whole operation down. Understood?"

"Yes, sir."

"Captain." Cody knew he was out-voted, but he couldn't accept the situation. "She needs more protection than that."

The captain sounded weary when he responded. "What do you suggest, Cody?"

Cody looked out over the desert, realizing he didn't have an answer. It only took him a minute to think of one.

"Let me go down there. If anything happens, she should have a bodyguard nearby."

"She's surrounded by SWAT, Cody."

"Yes, but they'll be focused on *him,* not her. I can go from foxhole to foxhole and just stay close to her."

Frank's voice came on the com for the first time. "No, Cody. You could be seen."

"I know how to keep to the shadows, Frank. And with no moon, all there *are* are shadows."

"What if he has night vision?"

"If he has night vision we're screwed anyway."

"Okay, enough," the captain broke in. "Go ahead Cody, but keep your distance."

Frank couldn't have told the captain of what had happened between Cody and Alex earlier that day. If the captain even suspected there was a conflict of interest on Cody's part, he'd have sent Frank or Court instead.

Cody turned to Merriton. "Do you have some goggles, rather than binoculars, that have night vision on them?"

Merriton dug around in his bag for a few seconds before producing a heavy-looking pair. Cody secured them to his head. "Thank you." Then he was off, before Frank could spill the beans and the captain could change his mind.

By the time Cody reached the first foxhole, Alex was a third of the way through the loop. It was taking a lot longer for her to walk it than it had been to drive it. Cody jumped into the small, concealed hollow in the ground. The SWAT guy didn't flinch.

"Sir," he whispered when Cody squatted down beside him.

"Where is she?" Cody breathed, winded.

"Ten o'clock, sir."

Cody spotted her, but he was too far away still. He pushed the com button.

"Desert-6, I'm heading to your location. Be there in about fifteen seconds."

"Roger, sir."

He patted the SWAT guy on the shoulder and bolted from the foxhole. When he landed lightly in Desert-6's hole, he was actually a bit ahead of Alex. She would pass by his location in the next minute or two.

As she came level with his position, she stopped. She seemed to be looking at something across from where he was crouching. He was about to ask what she was looking at when she spoke.

"Captain"—her voice came clearly across the com—"I'm looking at a smooth boulder about ten feet south of me. Permission to climb it?"

"Why?" the captain asked.

Cody was close enough to see Alex shrug. "Maybe he'll think I'm tired and looking for a place to rest for the night. Maybe he'll . . . I don't know . . ."

"Think you're a sitting duck?" Cody broke in. "That's off the loop, Alex, and that's exactly what you'll be."

"But it's up higher. If he comes, it'll give our guys a crystal clear shot, won't it?"

Cody looked at the SWAT guy he was squatting next to. The man nodded.

"She's right, sir. If he comes at her from any direction, I'll have him."

Cody sighed—not the answer he'd been hoping for.

The captain must have gotten the same information from someone else near him. "She's right, Cody. Permission granted, Alex, but climb slowly and tell us exactly what you see up there."

"All right."

He watched her deftly climb the boulder. She slid onto the top of it, then spun in a slow circle on her backside, taking in her surroundings.

"I don't see much of anything; it's too dark. I s'pose I'm offering a free meal to any nocturnal creatures who care to venture this way."

Cody rolled his eyes. "Not funny, Alex," he said into the com.

"Oh, lighten up, Cody. I'll admit I was nervous about this operation. Now I'm just bored. The only thing up here is sagebrush, dirt, the wind wafting through the prickly pear. You know, normal stuff."

Cody felt the corners of his mouth twitch upward. "We don't have prickly pear in Utah," he said as seriously as he could manage.

"Really? So what *are* the names of the cactuses here?"

Cody opened his mouth, then clamped it shut again. He glanced over to see the SWAT guy grinning stupidly into his rifle's scope. "What're you laughing at," he muttered out of the side of his mouth. "Do *you* know the names of—?"

"Detective!" The rest of the sentence was forgotten when the SWAT guy suddenly gasped and lifted his gun.

Cody jerked his face forward in time to see what looked like an arm coming up out of the earth and wrapping itself around Alex's waist.

"Cody!" Her shriek came from out in front of him, rather than through the com. It stopped his heart and cinched around his stomach. Cody leapt from the foxhole, sprinted, and scaled the boulder she'd been sitting on in five seconds flat.

When he stood on top of the boulder, she had vanished. There was no trace of where she'd gone. Cody pulled a flashlight from his pocket and shined it out as far as he could, expecting to see her being dragged off. There was nothing.

"Alex!" His voice echoed in the silent isolation of the desert. "Alex!"

In the next instant, a half dozen SWAT team members were standing around him. They produced flashlights and spotlights, and in a matter of seconds, the area was well-lit. Then more people were appearing on and around the boulder. They were digging, knocking, patting, and doing a host of other things to the area Alex had just been in.

Cody recognized the man he'd been squatting next to less than a minute ago.

"Why didn't anyone shoot?" he asked the man.

"All I saw was an arm, detective. I could have hit it, but my ammo would have gone through it and hit her in the abdomen. I didn't want to risk killing her."

"Detective! Over here!"

Cody strode over to where several of the men were digging. When he got there, Frank was standing beside him. The men had discovered a tarp of some kind with dirt clods and desert plants glued to it. It covered what looked like a manhole, blending perfectly into the landscape.

"Open that!" Cody yelled.

They felt around the flat circular hatch for some kind of opening device; they dug around it; they pounded on it with their shovels. It sounded metallic, but didn't give under their efforts.

"I think it's cemented shut, sir."

Cody ran his hands through his hair, panic washing over him. The Botanist had Alex. The sound of her voice screaming his name echoed between his ears and scratched up and down his spine.

"What do you mean it's cemented shut? How is that possible?"

"I don't know, sir. But it's gonna take us some time to get it open."

Cody turned, pacing, barely keeping from tearing his own hair out. He kicked a nearby dirt clod and cursed.

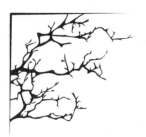

Chapter 37

CODY REMAINED ON SITE until well after sun up. The entire area was being excavated. It was obvious that the Botanist had some kind of underground system to move around the desert without being seen, just as Resputa predicted. Cody didn't want to think about how long it would take to build something like that, or why no one knew about it.

The problem was they were having a hard time breaking into his system. Bulldozers were on the way to help, but it would be nearly ten o'clock before they arrived. Alex had already been missing for hours. When Cody thought of what that animal might to do her—of what had been done to the other victims—panic rose in his chest to the point that he found it difficult to breathe. He pushed those thoughts away, telling himself she'd be all right.

She wasn't the only one he had in his clutches. It was a horrible thing to think, but Cody couldn't help it. It made him feel better to think that maybe the Botanist wouldn't torture Alex right away, that maybe he'd leave her for later, giving Cody time to find her first. Then the guilt over caring more about her safety than Melissa's set in, and Cody's chest started to hurt.

Just as the bulldozers arrived, Cody got a call from the station.

"What is it, Rose?"

"I need you to come back to the station, Cody."

"Why? The bulldozers just got here. They're going to try to break in—"

"The captain told me that even with the heavy metal it might be a few hours, Cody. A man named Vern Thompson just arrived. He's asking to speak with the detective in charge of the case."

"Who?"

"He's Alex's father."

CODY ARRIVED BACK AT the station an hour later, exhausted and scared. He hadn't shaved or showered in two days, and the last thing he felt ready for was meeting Alex's father, especially when he'd allowed a killer to kidnap her only hours earlier.

"Cody?"

Cody turned toward the familiar voice. His eyebrows rose when he saw his father standing beside the station door. Cody eyed him warily. More questions? More accusations? Cody wasn't up to either, but his father merely looked sad.

"Dad? Is everything all right?"

"Yes. I know you're busy, Cody, but I wondered if we might talk for a few minutes."

Cody glanced toward the station. Alex's father and the captain were waiting for him.

"I'd like to, Dad. I really would, but there are people waiting for me."

His father paused, then nodded. "Okay." He turned and headed for the parking lot. Something tugged at Cody's heart.

"Dad, wait."

His father turned, and Cody had no idea what to say.

"How—how's Mom?"

"Fine. Better now that we know you're okay." Guilt washed over Cody again, but his father continued. "I wanted to say that I'm sorry."

Cody's eyebrows jumped. He didn't think his father had ever apologized to him before.

"I was so worried about you that it didn't occur to me that you'd know the detective who died. I'm so sorry."

Cody swallowed, but didn't trust his voice.

"We've been watching the news. They're saying a young woman from up north was attacked, but managed to get away. I'm sure you're working with her. I don't want you to think that I'm angry with you for trying to help her."

Cody winced as though struck, and his father paused, looking at him.

"Cody, what is it?"

Cody swallowed and took a deep breath. Tears of frustration and fatigue welled up behind his eyes. He hated being vulnerable in front of his father, but try as he might, he couldn't completely blink away the tears.

Cody glanced toward the station, but no one was nearby.

"You can't repeat this, Dad. Not to anyone."

His father looked very serious, and he nodded. "All right."

"Alex is gone. The killer took her."

His father's eyes widened in alarm. "What?"

Cody dropped his head, feeling the need to explain. "We were trying to draw out the killer. She volunteered to do it, but I didn't feel right about it."

Cody's father was silent for a few seconds before whispering, "Did you say anything?"

"Yes! I did, but I was out-voted. It was her decision, and I know that, but I still should have fought harder against it. Or I should have stayed closer to her, done something—anything—to keep her safe." His voice cracked on the last word.

His father's hand came up to rest on his shoulder. "Cody," he said quietly.

He didn't say anything else, but it was enough. Norman was a good father, but it had been years since they'd had any kind of tender moment together. Now standing together with a feral wind wafting in from the black desert, Cody felt closer to his father than he had in years.

After a minute of companionable silence, his father dropped his hand. "Cody, there's something I want to tell you. I . . . I know that . . . you've chosen your profession based on a sense of honor, and not just to piss me off, even though it sometimes seems like that's what I think."

Cody nodded and wiped his eyes, his voice quiet. "I'm glad to hear you say that."

"It's just, there are reasons, Cody. Reasons I didn't want you to become a cop."

"I think I know what they are, Dad."

"You do?"

"Yeah. You and Uncle Clyde had some kind of falling out, so when I wanted to do what he did, you didn't like it."

Cody's father sighed. "I suppose I understand why you think that's what happened, but that's not exactly how it played out."

Cody turned more fully to face his father. "Then how did it play out?"

His father immediately withdrew, looking away and stiffening his shoulders. "Perhaps this is a conversation for another time. You have a lot to worry about just now."

"I'd like to hear it now, if you're willing." Cody was afraid if he didn't press for answers now, his father would return to his same old closed-mouth self, and the window for getting answers would be gone.

His father sighed, hesitating again. "Your uncle and I were always close. We didn't have a falling out. I never had a problem with the fact that he was a cop; I even thought it was cute when you started asking for toy guns and plastic sheriff's badges as a kid. Truth is, I didn't have a problem with his job until after he died."

"But why? What happened?"

His father hesitated again, scrutinizing the sidewalk below their feet with an intensity usually reserved only for his wife's cooking.

"Cody?" a feminine voice said.

Cody turned to see Rose's head and shoulders peering around the station door. "They're waiting for you, Cody."

Cody nodded, about to tell Rose he'd be right there, but Norman was already on his feet.

"Dad, what—?"

"Go to your meeting, Cody. Solve your case. We'll talk again later."

"But, Dad," Cody whispered. "I want to hear this."

His father nodded. "I'll tell you whatever you want to know. I should have told you years ago, I suppose. But now is not the time. Solve your case. Bring Alex home. Then we'll have a conversation."

"I'm going to hold you to that," Cody finally said.

"I know."

He and his father hadn't hugged in years, but it felt like they should, and things were suddenly awkward.

"Uh, well, tell Mom I'll come see her in a few days."

"I will. Take care of yourself, Cody. Go get some sleep when you're finished here."

Cody hoped the look he gave his father was reassuring even though he had no intention of sleeping anytime soon.

He watched his father get into his car and pull out onto Main Street.

"Sorry." Rose came up beside him. "I didn't mean to interrupt a personal moment, but the captain stressed urgency when he had me call you."

Cody shook his head. "Don't be. I think he was looking for an excuse to exit the personal moment anyway."

Rose smirked, then turned and led Cody into the station.

Cody had prepared himself for rage, for terror, for anxiety; he prepared himself for every reaction Alex's father might have . . . except the one he actually did. When Cody walked in, he could see the captain speaking with a man inside the door. Even from behind, streaks of gray were visible in the man's hair. Cody took a deep breath and went in.

Alex's father was not tall, but was solidly built. Deep laugh lines had settled around his eyes and mouth, and the gray in his hair swirled with the brown like a peppermint candy. He was not irate or terrified. Though his eyes had a haunted look about them, he held himself with a quiet dignity that Cody had seen in Alex. Though she looked nothing like her adoptive father, she exuded an air that was unmistakably his.

"Mr. Thompson."—the Captain stood as Cody walked in—"this is Cody Oliver, lead detective on the case."

Alex's father stood, shook Cody's hand firmly, and stared at him with a direct, hawkish gaze that Cody found unnerving.

"Mr. Thompson"—the Captain addressed Cody—"has driven most of the night to get here."

Cody looked at Mr. Thompson. "You'll have to forgive me, sir. Alex didn't tell us you were coming."

"She didn't know I was coming," Mr. Thompson said. "I spoke with her two nights ago, right after I got back from a business trip. She assured me and her mother that she was fine, but I had a bad feeling about it. This morning, not long after midnight actually, I had a nightmare. I woke up feeling alarmed. I felt like Alex was in trouble, and she wouldn't answer her cell. I told my wife I was coming down here, and I drove straight through."

Cody's eyes widened as the man spoke, and he couldn't seem to shrink them to their normal size. He'd had a nightmare about Alex just after midnight? That was right when the Botanist nabbed her.

As if reading the thought, Mr. Thompson repeated it. "Your captain tells me that's about the time that this guy took her."

"And that doesn't surprise you? The timing, I mean?"

Mr. Thompson merely looked at him. "No. Why should it?"

Cody exchanged glances with the captain, but didn't answer.

"She's my daughter," Alex's father said. "I know when she's in trouble."

"So, you came out of fear for her safety? You don't have anything to add to the investigation?" Cody changed the subject just to help himself stop staring at the man.

Mr. Thompson hesitated. "I can tell you what I remember of her adoption, and the bracelet she wears. I don't know how much help it will be, but that's what your captain has been asking me about."

Cody blinked. "Of course. Anything you can tell us might be helpful. Please, sit. Tell me what you remember."

They both took a seat on the couch in the captain's office, but the captain's cell phone rang. He glanced at it.

"It's my wife. I think I'll step out and take this. Please give your statement to Detective Oliver, Mr. Thompson."

Alex's father nodded, and the captain left the room.

"First of all, sir," Cody began when they were both seated, "I want to say how sorry I am that it turned out this way. We took every precaution, but—"

Alex's father held his hands up. "Please, son, you don't have to apologize. Your captain has already told me everything, including the part where Alex got out of the van when she wasn't supposed to. That's just her way."

Though he looked far from amused, Alex's father said the last part with affection. "She's always been a proactive person. She gets things done. Of course I'm terrified for her, but Alex is intelligent, independent, resourceful. If anyone can keep it together, get away from a dangerous man, it's her."

Cody nodded, remembering Alex had already escaped from this guy. Twice. Cody elected not to bring it up at this juncture, especially because he couldn't agree more with what her father was saying.

"I believe you're right, sir. What can you tell me about her adoption?"

"Only that it was strange from the get-go. I looked into it myself, even investigated the origin of the bracelet."

Cody arched an eyebrow in surprise. "You did?"

"Yes. I always had an . . . unsettled feeling about it. An investigation was done, but it wasn't extensive. When a child is found wandering on the highway and her parents don't come looking for her, let's just say no one is in any hurry to return her to them."

"Understandable. So what did you do?"

"I tried to find out where the bracelet had come from. The investigators hit a dead end with it, but it was mostly about not having the manpower or resources to investigate further. I'm a curious man, Detective. I can be relentless when I want to find something or someone."

"Sounds like some investigators I know."

Thompson shook his head. "I'm not anymore, but when Alex was four I joined a PI firm, worked there for the better part of a decade."

"What made you leave it?"

"Frankly? Not enough money to raise a family on. But I was good at my job, Detective."

Cody rubbed the bridge of his nose. He tried to imagine what might have been going through this man's mind during that time in his life.

"Forgive me, Mr. Thompson, but what were you hoping to find? Surely, you didn't want to actually find her parents."

Thompson sighed, looking tired. "I don't know, son. I suppose I was just looking for peace of mind. Like I said, I always had a strange feeling about Alex, about the way she came to me. We always believed she was meant to be ours—my wife and I—but I also always had this strange feeling that someone was waiting around every corner, waiting to take her away from me. Even if my investigation had led me to drug-addicted guardians that neither knew nor cared that Alex was no longer with them, I suppose at the least it would have given me closure. It would have been something I could tell her when she was old enough to understand."

"So what did you find?"

"Not much. I traced the origin of the bracelet, based on a partial serial number that was on the back of it. It was part of an exclusive collection—only a hundred or so pieces were ever made like that one. The craftsman who made them didn't keep them together though. We're talking about somewhere between seventy-five and one hundred buyers, who then might have sold them to others. The pieces had all been made and sold ten years before Alex was born, and they weren't worth enough to be traced beyond their first selling."

"We've come across similar information," Cody said, thoughts of Tom making him pause. "One of our detectives traced the partial serial number to a database, but that was the only source of information we could find."

Thompson heaved a deep sigh. "That's my doing, Detective. The pieces aren't valuable enough to be put in that database, but I put it there, hoping that someone would see it and either add to its history or contact me. I left my contact information on the website."

Cody thought about that. Suddenly the database made sense, though Tom hadn't said anything about contact information. Cody wouldn't be able to ask him about it now. His throat felt blocked. He pretended to cough so he could clear his throat and blink away the tears Tom's memory evoked. "So what do you know about the artist that crafted the jewelry?"

"Not much more than I put into the database. His name was Jones. He fell off the face of the earth not long after the pieces were sold. He actually lived in these parts, but there's no paper trail for him after 1991. I never did find a death certificate for him, but for all intents and purposes—financially, legally—he doesn't exist anymore, hasn't for twenty years."

Based on Stieger's information, Cody knew Jones and Landes were the same man, but he wanted to find out what Alex's father knew independent of that information. "You said he lived around here? You mean *here* here? In southern Utah?"

Thompson nodded.

"That's quite the coincidence, considering Alex was found wandering these highways wearing one of his signature pieces."

"I agree, Detective, but I couldn't ever find anything to tell me where he was, or what happened to him. The biographical sources I found were people who worked with him professionally when he was creating the jewelry. They said the man who made those pieces grew up not far from here, on a ranch just outside of Antimony. But when I tried to check up on that, I couldn't find anything anywhere on paper that said he ever lived in these parts. Nothing at all. Trust me. I knocked on every door in this county. No one knew anything about him. Or if they did, they were very convincing liars."

"What do you think that means?"

"Either my source was lying, or perhaps the name is made up. Lots of artists take on different names for their work."

Cody longed to tell Mr. Thompson what Stieger had learned, but he couldn't reveal information about an active investigation. "And from there the trail went cold?"

"It did. After a while, I tired of obsessing about it, gave up after a few years. I tell you, though, even years later, if an unexpected knock came at the door, I would get a sick feeling in the pit of my stomach. I was so sure that someday, someone would try to take my daughter away from me."

When he said it, his eyes grew misty, and Cody understood the haunted look. What he'd been fearing for twenty years was now happening. The man wasn't raging against it. Rather, he was trying to accept with dignity something he'd always known, but had never had any control over.

"Mr. Thompson," Cody said quietly, "I'll find your daughter. She's going to be okay. You have my word."

Thompson looked up at Cody curiously at first, then as though seriously considering what he was saying. A look of awe came into the man's face. "Detective, that's the first thing I've heard in two days that gives me reason to hope."

Cody swallowed hard. He prayed it wouldn't prove false.

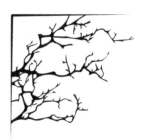

Chapter 38

IT WAS LATE AFTERNOON before Stieger finally drove up to Colleen Hinckle's sprawling ranch house. It was a two-story monstrosity with a wrap-around porch and white siding badly in need of a paint job. Wind chimes tinkled lazily beside a weather-beaten screen door, and an ancient wooden rocking chair faced west.

After visiting the old Landes property with Detective Oliver, he'd spent the last twenty-four hours making a formal request for Jonathin Landes' military records and trying to track down Colleen Hinckle. Eventually, he'd made his way back to Ronnie, who'd let slip that Colleen owned the land she lived on.

Stieger got out of his car, wondering if he should knock or look around first. His question was answered when Colleen suddenly appeared from the screen door, carrying the biggest basket Stieger had ever seen. Knitting needles stuck out of it at different angles and he assumed the colorful lumps rising above its rim were balls of yarn.

Colleen froze when she saw him, looking trapped. As he walked toward her, she took on a resigned look. He stopped when he reached the porch, looking up at her.

"So," she sighed, "you found me, did you?"

"Wasn't easy."

"No?"

"You've got loyal neighbors—wouldn't give your address out to a stranger."

"That's good to know at least. How then?"

"Public records. Got Ronnie to tell me that you owned this place."

"You're a PI aren't you?"

"Yes, ma'am."

She sighed again. "You might as well come in. I'll get us some lemonade and we can chat."

Fifteen minutes later, Stieger was sitting on an ancient couch with a glass of yellow liquid in his hand. It was the good stuff: homemade, sweeter than anything stores had to offer these days, and surrounding three perfectly formed ice cubes. Stieger practically guzzled his first cup.

Colleen didn't say anything, but he saw her smile with pleasure. She poured him another cup. He didn't complain.

"So," he said when he'd downed half the second cup in one gulp. "Did you know Alastair Landes well?"

She shook her head and wisps of white, cottony hair came loose from the bun curled at the nape of her neck. "No. I knew who he was by reputation, but we were hardly acquainted at all."

Stieger nodded but waited for her to speak again. She was studying her cup of lemonade.

"Mr. Stieger, I'd like to tell you some of my history, if you don't mind hearing it. If I'm going to tell you what you want to know, I need you to understand the reasons behind my choices."

"I'm here to listen to whatever you have to say, Mrs. Hinckle."

She smiled. "Colleen, please. No one calls me 'Mrs.' I'm far too old."

Stieger ducked his head in acquiescence.

"You should know I've recently found out that I am terminally ill. I'll be dead within the year."

A stone lodged in Stieger's middle. He'd dedicated his life to the pursuit of law, justice, and the enforcement of them. Death was part of life, and often an integral part of his chosen profession. Still, when you find out someone who is living and breathing and talking right in front of you will be dead soon . . . there's an utter finality to it that's suffocating.

"I'm so sorry."

She looked up in surprise. "Don't be. I'm not. I've lived a good, long life. I've put my affairs in order and made my peace. I'm ready to go. There was only one thing I ever regretted in my life. When the news about my health came, I wished on a star that God would help me make it right. I'm sorry I ran away from you yesterday. I suppose I should have known that righting an old wrong wouldn't be pleasant. Despite asking for it, when the opportunity came, I ran from it." Her smile was far away. "Yet, here you are."

"Here I am."

"More than twenty years ago, Mr. Stieger, I buried my second husband. It was one of the most difficult times of my life. For weeks—no, more like months—I was shrouded in a darkness of my own making. My grief consumed me, and I couldn't pull out of it. Only with time—a lot of time—and the love of my friends and family was I finally able to find joy in life again." She looked up at him, as if to ask if he understood.

"Many people go through similar things when they lose loved ones," he offered.

"Yes, but my experience lasted longer than most. My children were worried that I was suicidal. Perhaps I was, I don't know. They tried to get me on depression medication, but I refused. To cope, I started taking long drives through the countryside."

"Doesn't sound like such a bad way to cope."

"It is when you disappear for days at a time, or forget to show up to work, or run out of gas a hundred and fifty miles from home. Still, it was the only thing that calmed the aching in my chest, so I did it for months.

"It was during this time that Alastair Landes died. I remember hearing that he'd passed but I barely registered it. I hardly knew him, as I said, and I was dealing with my own demons. The thing is . . ."

She trailed off, studying her lemonade intensely.

"Yes?" Stieger prodded after a long period of silence. She looked surprised to see him still sitting there.

"You must understand, Mr. Stieger, that I'm unsure of the timeline. That whole year is a blur to me. It's like I was drunk the entire time. I wasn't, but my grief was such that I wasn't particularly . . . present either. I went through the motions of my life, but didn't make any effort to actually *live* it. Because of that, I'm not sure what order things happened in."

Stieger set his empty glass on the coffee table between them and rested his forearms on his knees. "Okay. Fair enough. Go on."

"One day I was driving aimlessly. I didn't know where I was going—just driving—but I happened to drive past Alastair's farm. This wasn't on the highway. I was on a little-known dirt road that runs between his land and what back then was the McClintock place. Only the land owners and townsfolk ever use those little roads. Outsiders wouldn't know about them.

"The only reason I remember where I was that day—near Alastair's land—is that I had to stop. Some of his sheep were in the road right in front of where I needed to go. It wouldn't have been difficult for me to go around them—I had four-wheel drive and the dirt path was quite wide—but I didn't. Again, it was my mental state. I might have stayed there waiting for those sheep to move all night; I might have run out of gas waiting, and it wouldn't have made an ounce of difference to me.

"I'm not sure how long I actually waited. I'd say ten or fifteen minutes, though I'm not at all certain. Then, a man appeared. I recognized him right away because I'd known him since he was only a child. He smiled at me, coaxed the sheep out of my path, and waved me on."

"Who was it, Colleen?" Stieger realized he was holding his breath, but he couldn't make himself release it.

"It was Alastair's son, Jonathin."

Stieger's body went rigid. He blinked in disbelief. That wasn't possible, was it? "Colleen, you said this was right around the time Alastair died, right?"

She nodded.

"Do you know if it was before or after?"

"No. That's why I explained that everything seems jumbled. I couldn't say if this was before or after I heard about Alastair's death. I was so out of it. I have no way now of sorting out the chronology of events."

"But it was definitely right around the time of Alastair's death?"

"Yes."

Stieger took a deep breath. "And you're sure it was him? You're sure—with your grief and all—that you didn't imagine it?"

Colleen smiled. "I'm sure, Mr. Stieger. In my younger years, I was a teacher. Jonathin was one of my pupils. I'd know him anywhere. I think, when he coaxed the sheep out of my way, he even called me Mrs. Hinckle, as he had when he was a child in my class. That memory has stayed crystal clear in my head all these years. I don't know why, when the rest is so hazy, but perhaps there's a reason for it. I'm positive it was him that I saw."

"Colleen, when Alastair died, people looked for Jonathin. They wanted to tell him of his father's passing and encourage him to make a claim for the land. No one ever found him. No one remembers him being in town. He disappeared years before Alastair's passing, and no one ever saw him again."

Colleen's eyes had taken on a sad cast. They were covered with a misty sheen that bespoke a profound, aching sadness. "I know that, Mr. Stieger."

"Then why . . ." Stieger had to work to keep his voice calm. "Why didn't you ever say anything?"

"To be honest, I didn't think anything of it until weeks afterward when I realized people were looking for Jonathin. At that point, I should have, but it would have required action on my part, and I could barely force myself out of bed in the morning. I have only excuses for why I kept silent, nothing justifiable. I told myself that if he'd been there and hadn't come forward, then perhaps he didn't want to be found. I convinced myself I was doing him a favor by not mentioning what I saw. I even invented grand stories about him coming back, having a falling out with his father, and leaving, and the drama of it all causing Alastair's untimely death. I told myself I was right; I told myself I was protecting him; I told myself whatever I needed to sustain my cowardice.

"In the years afterward, when I finally rejoined the world of the living, I thought about it a lot. But by then, people had stopped talking about the Landes family. The land had been turned over to the county. The town gossip had moved onto other subjects. I still rationalized. I told myself that it didn't matter anymore. Who would care or even believe me after so many years? I was afraid of repercussions. Though, in truth I was less afraid of being condemned by the town for silence, than of finding out that my actions—or lack thereof—would have much greater consequences than a change in my social status in the community." She looked down at her lemonade. The ice cubes had long since melted. "I suppose I've always known how wrong my silence was. I always felt that I'd done some kind of evil by letting the truth slide, though I never knew what it was."

Steiger frowned, feeling a stab of compassion for the woman. "You only saw him on the side of the road, Colleen. How could you possibly—"

"I'm an old woman, Mr. Stieger. And a Christian. If it wasn't a big deal, it would have gone away eventually. It never did. And with each passing year, the nagging weight of what I'd done grew stronger." She smiled at nothing. "I suppose it might be hard for people to understand."

"No, ma'am," Steiger said quietly. "Not hard at all."

"When you're running the home-stretch of your life, the things you've left undone start to glare at you like branches coming up from an otherwise unbroken lake."

She swallowed and met his eyes. "What's this about, Mr. Stieger? Are you investigating those corpses found in the desert?"

There was fear in her eyes, now, but he couldn't bring himself to lie to her. "I'm part of that investigation, yes."

"Is Jonathin Landes dead?"

"That I don't know, Colleen. We haven't found him. You may have been the last one to see him alive, though."

Colleen suddenly looked every year of her age. She lapsed into uncomfortable silence, and Stieger found himself thinking about a certain daughter he hadn't spoken to in almost a decade. She was as pig-headed as he was and had stormed out nine years ago, promising to never speak to him again. She never had. For years, Stieger had wanted to reunite with Kyla, but he always found a reason not to. Now, looking at this poor woman in her misery over a choice made a lifetime ago, under circumstances mitigated by soul-numbing grief, Stieger made himself a promise that he'd call his daughter the second he wrapped up this case, not an instant later. Colleen had a regret that had haunted her for decades. Stieger didn't want to end up the same way. "Do you have anything else to tell me?"

Colleen looked at him steadily, and he took her silence for an answer.

"Well, thank you for sharing this with me. I don't know what bearing it will have on our case, if any, but I appreciate the information. Just one more question. Did you know the transient that was working for Alastair at the time of his death? Do you recall seeing him around the property on your drives?"

Colleen shook her head. "I remember hearing about him, but I don't think I ever met him. And no, I don't recall seeing him. I couldn't even say what he looked like."

Stieger nodded, suddenly unsure how to make his exit. "Well, I think I've taken up enough of your time, ma'am. Thank you for the lemonade. It was the best I've had in years. I do want to reserve the right to call on you again and ask you to give the police a formal statement."

"Of course." She smiled, but it was a melancholy smile, and he felt bad just leaving her to her grief.

"Colleen, don't worry about this anymore. It's understandable, given your state of mind. And you've done your duty, now, by telling me everything. There's absolutely no reason for you to think on this any further."

She looked up at him from her loveseat and a tear leaked down her cheek. "Thank you," she whispered.

He took her hand briefly and she walked him to the door.

"Good evening, Colleen. Thank you for your kindness."

"Good evening to you, Mr. Stieger. I hope you find what you're looking for."

"We all hope for that, ma'am."

He kept an encouraging smile on his face until he'd driven away. The information she'd imparted was valuable, but it also frightened him. How could Jonathin Landes have been in town and no one have known about it? Did he kill his father? Was he their desert killer? Was the town covering for him, Texas-chainsaw style?

Stieger told himself not to let his imagination get the best of him, but something sinister had happened on that land twenty years ago. He could feel it. He would find what he was looking for eventually. He just wasn't sure he'd like it when he did.

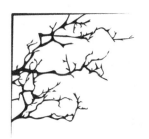

Chapter 39

BY EVENING, SHOCKINGLY little progress had been made at the dig site. The reports Cody got were disheartening. The bulldozers had broken through several weak underground tunnels, but two out of three had collapsed completely, obscuring any pathways that might lead farther in. The third had held, but led only to a dead end—yet another barrier to drill through.

They *were* making progress, and as they found their momentum, the pace of the work had sped up in late afternoon, but Cody still worried. Progress or not, at this pace it would take weeks to find Alex. Who knew how long they had? Days? Hours? There was the possibility that she was already dead.

The thought made Cody want to vomit, so he pushed it away. He had to believe that both Alex and Melissa were alive and would remain so.

Cody spent the better part of the day with Alex's father, teasing out details and clues from her life, and what her father remembered from her childhood, but nothing helpful surfaced. By the time they were finished, darkness had set in, and digging had halted for the night. Huge spotlights were being brought in so that the digging could go on twenty-four-seven, but they wouldn't arrive until the next day. It was too dangerous to dig in the dark, so everyone had gone home, promising to return at the first sign of the sky's lightening.

Cody knew he'd never sleep tonight. He understood the safety factor. It was black as tar out there, and flashlights couldn't compete with the darkness when they were talking about digging underground in an unstable structure with desert night prowlers all around. Captain, Court and Frank had left for a short time, but were back now. They'd gone home, kissed their wives, tucked their kids in, and then returned to grill Cody on what Resputa had said.

Resputa. It seemed like so long ago that Cody visited the prison. His fellow detectives immediately began plugging in leads based on what Resputa told him. Cody appreciated it, and knew he should help, but he couldn't concentrate. He didn't care about puzzles and clues when Alex was alone in the dark with a stark-raving flower-grower.

Frank and Court hurried in and out of the office, working on leads while the darkness prevented them from working at the dig site. Cody tried for the hundredth time to read the report in front of him, but he couldn't concentrate. His phone rang, and he was glad for the distraction.

"Oliver."

"Hello, Detective. My name's Sterling Rogers. I'm with the 4–2 in Cache County."

"What can I do for you, sir?" Cody asked, hoping he didn't actually have to call the guy Mr. Rogers.

"I've got about three dozen unies up here willing to volunteer their weekend to help you down there if you need them. I wanted to make sure that you could put them to work. We're getting reports of more police officers than you know what to do with down there."

"Actually I'm not the one to talk to, Officer Rogers. I couldn't even tell you."

"Aren't you the detective in charge?"

"Yes, but I'm not handling logistics. I'll have to transfer you to my captain. He'll be able to direct you." Frank had handed off logistics duty to another officer so he could help in last night's operation, but Cody had no idea who it was.

"That's fine. And thank you, Detective. What'd you say your name was?"

"Oliver. Cody Oliver."

Rogers barked a laugh. "Not related to Clyde Oliver from up north, right?" He sniggered through the phone line.

Cody froze. Something about Rogers' tone made the hairs on his neck stand up.

"Detective? You still there?"

"Yes," Cody said warily. "Clyde Oliver was my uncle."

The silence that stretched across the phone line was both loud and uncomfortable.

"Did you know him?" Cody asked when Rogers didn't speak.

"I . . . well, not really, no. I knew of him."

"And what did you know?"

"I . . . my apologies, Detective. I simply meant . . . that he had passed. I didn't dream that you were actually related to him. It was terribly insensitive of me. I'm sorry."

Cody played the conversation back in his head. Rogers sounded flippant, even sarcastic when asking if Cody was related to his Uncle Clyde, as though it would be a negative thing for a familial tie to exist. Had Rogers really been poking fun at a fellow officer who'd died in the line of duty? As if to say he was a loser for it?

"Okay," Cody said slowly, "but I'm not sure which part of what you said was insensitive. What were you implying?"

"Nothing, Detective. Nothing at all. If you'll just transfer me to your captain, I'll get my situation straightened out."

Cody didn't answer. He tried to think of what to say to get Rogers to tell him more.

"You know," Rogers said, "I think I have your captain's number somewhere. And I should probably double-check my count of officers. I'll do that and call him back myself. Thank you very much, Detective."

The line went dead before Cody could respond. With a sigh, he replaced the receiver. Frank walked in, trying to read a paper he was holding while also tilting his head back to sip his coffee from a white disposable cup. Cody's worry must have shown on his face because when Frank caught sight of it, he paused. But before he could say anything, his torso was thrown forward, independent of his feet. He stumbled forward, like someone had hit his retard button, spilling coffee on the ground and barely staying upright. He turned to glare at Court, who'd walked right into him, not realizing he'd stopped in the doorway. Court glared back at Frank for stopping.

Cody ignored them, getting to his feet and grabbing his keys.

"Where you going, Cody?" Frank asked.

"To my car. Be right back."

They moved to let him pass. Cody went out the back way to avoid the captain's suspicious eyes, and headed for the parking lot.

FRANK SIGHED AS HE threw back the last of the long-since-cold liquid in his cup. His eyes were ready to fall out of his head. Working at the desk opposite him, Court looked about as strung out as Frank felt. Court's pen was moving at a much slower cadence than usual, and Frank was sure the same slow motion sickness was affecting him. He still had hours of work to do, but he needed to get rid of some of it to feel like he was accomplishing *something.*

He had a small stack of reports he could pass off to Cody. Ah, the joys of being lead detective on a huge case like this—mountains more paper work than anyone else had to deal with. He chuckled an evil laugh in his head. He would have done the laugh verbally—he usually did—but he was too tired to trouble his voice box.

Feeling pleased with himself, he siphoned the reports he could get rid of off his pile and turned toward Cody's desk. Cody wasn't there. Frank supposed he could just leave the reports, but now that he thought about it, he hadn't seen Cody in a while.

Welcoming the excuse to leave his desk for a few minutes, Frank got up and walked out into the lobby. He used his thumb and index finger to stretch two of the horizontal blind slats apart and gazed, blurry-eyed, toward the parking lot. Cody was nowhere to be seen. The parking lot was vacant of Jeeps.

"Rose?"

"Yeah." Rose had perfected the art of talking while not looking up from her work.

"Did you see where Cody went?"

"Left a while ago."

"Do you know why?"

"I assume he's following a lead."

"Why's that?"

"He's a detective."

Frank rolled his eyes. "Rose . . ."

His tone brought her irritated eyes up to his, and she finally turned from her computer.

"Cody paced outside the captain's door for a while. He only does that when he wants to ask a question, but the Captain's been on the phone for hours. Finally, Cody got in his Jeep."

Frank smirked to himself. For a woman who never looked up from her work unless forced, Rose had nearly omniscient powers of observation.

"And which way did he go?"

Rose gazed at him, expressionless, for several seconds before answering. "South. Into the desert."

Frank's smirk faded. Cody lived in the other direction. Unless he was making a run for it, hoping to start a new life south of the border or some such, the only place he could be going was to the abduction sight. Why would he go there now? It was after midnight. The digging would resume in only five or six hours. It wasn't as if Cody could operate the bulldozers himself, especially in the dark. Unless . . .

"Thanks, Rose."

Frank turned abruptly and walked back to his office. He knew Cody too well. He loved the kid, but Cody was a man of action. As detectives, they all were, but Cody could be independent to a fault, and the feeling in Frank's chest was suddenly one of urgency.

"Court," he whispered when he got back to his desk, "we gotta go."

Court looked up from what he was working on, his eyes bloodshot from lack of sleep. "Huh?" His voice was alarmingly loud in the quiet of the station.

"Shhh! Cody just took off."

Court looked completely blank. "Oh . . . kay . . ."

"He went to the abduction sight. I think he's going to try and find this guy on his own."

Court's expression went from confusion to concern. "Why would he do that?"

"Um, well. I gotta tell you something."

Court raised an eyebrow.

"He has a thing for Alex."

It seemed to take Court a long time to process that statement. "Well, we've all seen him staring at her, but that doesn't mean—"

"Trust me, man. I walked in on the two of them going at it yesterday."

Court's eyes widened. "Going . . . at it?"

"Making out"—Frank motioned vaguely to the left side of the room—"against the wall."

"Oh."

"Didn't you see how freaked out Cody was when she disappeared?"

"Yeah, but Cody takes every case to heart."

"Now multiply that by a thousand because he's got feelings for this woman. What would you do?"

Court's mouth drew into a worried line. He nodded, stood, checked his gun in its holster, and came around the desk. "Let's go."

Frank put a hand on his partner's chest to stop him. "The captain won't approve of us going out there in an official capacity. He can't. We should leave him out of it."

Court nodded. "Plausible deniability. Agreed."

"I'll tell Rose I'm going on a midnight coffee run. You sneak out the back and meet me in the parking lot."

Court nodded as he slipped out the door and toward the back of the station. "See ya in two."

THE CAPTAIN HUNG UP the phone and rubbed his eyes. He'd been on the phone with Mayor Thomas Hascomb for an hour. Thomas had ripped him a new one for "letting the investigation get away from him." Really it was because he'd allowed a civilian to get involved in a sting operation that had gone horribly awry. Within hours the press had a hold of it. They were painting the Mt. Dessicate PD as incompetent and practically complicit in Alex's abduction.

The captain sighed. He'd agreed to allow Thomas to send in more experienced reinforcements. In truth, it would be a relief. The captain had no intention of letting anyone else run his investigation or take charge of his jurisdiction, but this was getting too big for him to manage alone.

The fact that the press was getting details not privy to the public within hours of their inception meant that someone, probably one of the unies, was informing them. There was absolutely no way and no resources to commit to finding out who it was and plugging them up.

A soft knock at his office door brought him out of his thoughts. Rose's head and shoulders appeared. The captain looked at the clock. It was well after midnight, which was when her shift officially ended.

"Heading home, Rose? You ought to. If you don't get enough sleep to do your job, there's no hope for the rest of us."

Rose smiled. "I'm almost done, sir, but actually there's something I thought you should know."

"Oh?"

"All three of your detectives just headed for your crime scene."

The captain frowned. At this hour? "Why?"

"I don't know, sir. They don't exactly keep me in the loop. Cody headed off by himself twenty minutes ago. I didn't think much of it. He's been all over the place lately. When Frank realized he was gone, he bolted back to his office. I heard whispering. Then Frank told me—*very* casually, I might add—that he was going out for coffee. I think Court went out the back. They always forget that I have a crystal clear view of the parking lot. They both jumped into the same car and tore after Cody like vampire bats out of hell."

The captain smirked. "I guess we're not all that mysterious to you, are we Rose?"

"When you say 'we,' do you mean men in general, or . . . ?"

The Captain chuckled and got to his feet, feeling every one of his fifty-three years. "Thank you, Rose. I'll take care of it."

Rose nodded and disappeared, but the door froze on its way to closing, and Rose appeared again. "Are you going after them, sir?"

"It's my job."

"Then if you don't mind, I'd like to stay at my desk a bit longer. Just in case you need anything."

The captain considered. He knew he should tell her to go home and to bed. She had five kids to get off to school in the morning, and she'd been a loyal employee for the better part of ten years. Still, he would feel better, should the situation in the desert turn ugly, having Rose at her post. There was no one he trusted more to get things done.

"Don't feel obligated to stay, Rose, but it's up to you."

She gave him a quick nod and left. For good this time. The captain gathered his keys, gun, and cell phone. He'd have to call his wife on the way and tell her not to expect him before dawn.

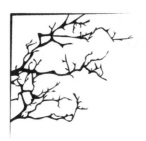

Chapter 40

CODY'S PARENTS LIVED on the outskirts of town, in the same direction as the site where Alex had been abducted. As he neared the turnoff to their neighborhood, he slowed down, contemplating going back out into the desert to look for Alex. If he hadn't wanted so badly to know what his father knew, he might have done it.

Despite the fact that it was after midnight when Cody pulled into his parents' driveway, all the lights in their home were still on. Cody wasn't surprised. Both his parents worked nine-to-five jobs, which meant they didn't need to be in bed early. His father had been a night owl for as long as he could remember, and his mother had chronic insomnia, so they were often up late.

Cody rapped loudly on the front door. It was nearly five minutes before it opened, but he didn't knock again because he could hear his mother rustling around on the other side. He could just picture her, smoothing out her night robe, checking her hair in the mirror in the entry way, and tidying up the sitting room before even considering opening the door.

When she did, her face broke into a smile.

"Cody!" She threw herself into his arms. He stood there on the porch, hugging her for a few seconds. "We've been so worried about you."

"I know, Mom. I'm sorry. I didn't mean to scare you."

"I know that." She pulled back. "Your friend, Alex, told us everything. I'm so sorry about Tom, Cody."

"Thank you," he managed in a whisper.

"Do you want to crash here for the night?"

He shook his head. "No. Actually, I can't stay long. I need to talk to Dad."

"About what?"

"Uncle Clyde."

His mother's face went very still. "That's not a good idea, Cody. You've had a rough couple of days. Your friend died. You should deal with what you have on your plate right now before you—where are you going?"

He stepped past her. She was his mother, and he knew she was trying to protect him, but it angered him that she knew things she wasn't telling him. Some random cop from up north knew more about his uncle—his hero, the reason he'd become a cop—than he did. Rather than yell at her for it, he simply stepped around her.

He walked to the foot of the stairs and listened. Not a sound. He couldn't hear his father moving around up there.

"Cody, listen to me—"

Cody looked down the hallway. Light framed the door on the right. His father was in the den.

"You must understand—" His mother was at his shoulder. "There were things we didn't tell you, and there were reasons for them. You were only a child."

Cody had started down the hall, but that last stopped him. He swung to face her. "I'm not a child anymore, Mom. I haven't been for a long time."

She seemed abashed by that. Her gaze went to the ground, and after a moment, he turned and stalked down the hall.

He didn't bother knocking. His father's den was cramped, but cozy. A huge mahogany desk filled one side. It was surrounded by overstuffed chairs, bookshelves bursting with volumes, and a little-used fireplace on the opposite wall.

Cody's father was hunched over a large book, pen in hand, making notations. Cody recognized it right away; it was his father's account ledger. Norman was a meticulous bookkeeper. He owned his own business, so he had to be, but he never let anything slide.

He looked up with surprise when Cody strode in. "Cody. What's wrong?"

Cody walked to his father's desk and leaned over, resting his palms on the edge of it. "I want to know what you haven't told me about Uncle Clyde's death."

His father's face became still, as his mother's had. "Cody what happened?"

Cody dropped his head in exasperation. "What happened is that I got a call from a cop today who seemed to know something negative about Uncle Clyde. He practically laughed when asking if we were related. Why would he do that?"

Cody's father sighed. He rested his elbows on his desk, laced his fingers together, and leaned his forehead against his hands for a moment before looking up at Cody again. "What was this cop's name?"

With a snarl of exasperation, Cody turned away from his father. Couldn't he answer a simple question? His mother was standing in the doorway, looking scared.

"Markinson?" his father asked.

"No."

"Rosette?"

Cody swung back toward his father. "What difference does the name make?"

"Rogers, then."

Cody swallowed. How had his father guessed that? He felt like he ought to be connecting something, or coming to some logical conclusion, but his mind was so a-swirl with the events of the past week, he couldn't imagine what was going on.

Cody's face must have been a confirmation of sorts because his father nodded. "We've always known you'd figure out the truth sooner or later. To be honest, I'm surprised it's taken this long. I'm surprised you haven't run into anyone, or stumbled upon anything suspicious before now."

"What is there to be suspicious about? Uncle Clyde died in the line of duty."

His father smiled, and it was sad, sympathetic even. It made Cody afraid.

"That's not exactly what happened, Cody."

"That's what the papers said, and the news, and everyone I've ever spoken to about it."

Norman nodded. "Because that's what most people believe happened. They weren't lying to you. They just didn't know the whole truth."

"Which is what?"

"This isn't the time for this." Cody's mother stepped forward. "You're upset, Cody. Your partner died two days ago. You need time to grieve. You need time to figure out your case. Then we can revisit this."

Cody turned to look at her. "Everything in my life—and I do mean absolutely everything—has gone to pieces in the last few days, Mom. I have a right to know this." He included his father in his glare. For some reason, his father was more willing to talk to him than his mother was, and that had *never* happened before.

His father nodded slowly. His mother opened her mouth to protest, but Norman put up a hand. "He's right, Barbara. He has a right to know." His gaze shifted to Cody. "Just understand, Cody, that this won't fix the things that have broken. If anything, it'll make them worse."

Cody considered that, but found he didn't care. How could he just go home now without knowing? "So be it."

His father nodded. "The official story was that you uncle surprised some dealers. It was a glorified drug bust, and he was shot trying to take them down. You've never questioned that story?"

"It's what everyone said. Why *should* I question it?"

"There aren't many details to go on."

"I always thought it was police business. The kind of thing that wouldn't be released to the media."

"Or the family?"

Cody sighed. "There are things that sometimes aren't, Dad."

"And when you became a cop, you never looked into the old report?"

"Sure I did. It didn't say anything different than I already knew."

"I suppose it wouldn't."

Cody waited for his father to speak again, heart pounding.

"Cody." Norman's voice was quiet. "Your uncle didn't stumble upon the dealers. Nor did he do exceptional detective work and figure out where the deal was going down. He was there for a different reason: he was meeting them."

Cody frowned. "What do you mean?"

"He was meeting the dealers purposely. He was part of the drug deal."

Cody tried to make sense of that. "Was he undercover?"

Norman slowly shook his head. "No, Cody. He wasn't. He was crooked."

A cold pit settled in Cody's stomach. He didn't remember bending his legs, but suddenly he was sitting in one of the chairs in front of his father's desk.

"I don't believe you." He'd meant to be vehement, insulted, shocked—how could his father even suggest such a thing?—but it came out as a barely audible whisper.

Norman's eyes dropped to his ledger. He shut it. "That doesn't surprise me."

Cody found his voice again, making it sound more solid this time. "If that's true, why have I never heard it before?"

"Because no one knows. Even back when it happened, no one knew. Clyde and I were very close in the year before his death. We spent every weekend together—watching games, doing yard and house work, spending time with you—and I knew nothing about it. Even Clyde's partner knew nothing about it."

"How could his partner know nothing about it?" Those weekends were what made Cody idolize his uncle. But they were just weekends, not every waking moment.

"From what I understand," Norman said, "his partner was a rookie. If there were signs, his partner was too inexperienced to pick up on them, or just too afraid to report them. They were together all day on the job, but this was something Clyde was doing in his spare time."

"Doing what exactly?"

"It was a type of blackmail. He had an agreement with these dealers. He looked the other way—sometimes even gave them information to make sure they could do their deals without getting caught—in exchange for a cut of the profits."

"But—" Cody ran the information through his head over and over again, trying to make it fit. "What was he doing with the money?"

"Who knows? From what we could tell, most of it was going to an off-shore account. We were never able to trace it, and without his identifying information, we have no way to locate or access it." Norman went on when Cody remained silent. "It was suggested that he was starting a college fund for you."

Cody's head snapped up. "For me? Why do you think that?"

"One of the dealers that survived the shooting was questioned. He implied it. But he was probably full of it anyway. Even if they were partners, I doubt Clyde would have confided in someone like him."

Cody stared at the rug beneath his father's desk for a long time. He felt utterly hollow. How could it be true? Yet the seriousness of his father's face, the fear in his mother's eyes, the tone in Rogers' voice on the phone earlier . . . it *was* true. It had to be.

"And why didn't you ever tell me this? Why keep it from me?"

"You were only a child when he died, Cody," Norman said. "And so heartbroken already."

Cody jumped to his feet. "That's not good enough! Maybe I was a child then, but I haven't lived under your roof for almost a decade. What right did you have to keep this from me when I practically . . . based my life on who he was?"

His mother answered, her voice small. "You idolized him so, Cody. We wanted to preserve your memory of him."

"A memory that was a lie."

"It wasn't a lie," his father said firmly. "Clyde loved you, Cody. He doted on you. His professional misdeeds had nothing to do with how he felt about you."

Cody shook his head and sunk into the chair, rubbing the heels of his hands into his eyes.

"So this," he ventured, looking up at his father, "is why you disapproved of my becoming a cop?"

Norman shrugged uncomfortably. "Clyde was a good man, Cody. And he wasn't always crooked. He was such a good cop, he was offered a promotion—to join the narcotics division. He was going after dealers that were higher up on the food chain. Don't you see? The temptation of money was right in front of him. Before that, he wouldn't have thought of it. You are just like your uncle, Cody, in so many ways . . ."

Rebellion flared in Cody's chest, and he leapt to his feet again. "So you couldn't trust me with the truth. You were certain I'd repeat *his* mistakes! You've tried and convicted me of something I haven't even had the chance to say no to."

"Cody—"

"Don't you think that if you wanted me to avoid his sins, you should have at least told me about them?"

"Cody—"

"Rather than encouraging me to be a better man than he was, you hid the truth from me because you didn't think I could handle it. What kind of parent assumes their child is too *weak* to deal with the darker side of life?"

"Cody!" his father roared, on his feet now.

They glared at one another from opposite sides of the desk. Something tickled Cody's face, and he swatted it away. It was a drop of water.

Finally Norman dropped his glare. "It's not that I think you're weak. No man is immune to that kind of temptation. I wouldn't have thought Clyde could do something like that, but he did. Everyone is capable of giving in to depravity."

Somewhere in the back of Cody's mind, in a place he couldn't acknowledge, his father's argument made sense. Cody straightened his back. He couldn't be here anymore. When his father said the word *depravity*, it only served to remind Cody that Alex was out in the darkness somewhere with that monster. Without a word, he turned and headed for the hallway.

"Where are you going?" his mother asked when he came level with her.

He turned in the doorway and looked back at his father. "I have a job to do."

His mother placed a hand on his arm. "Cody please, won't you just—"

"There's a monster pulling people off the highway and murdering them in the desert."

His mother shuddered.

"I'm sorry, but it's the truth."

"I know," she whispered.

Cody looked from her to his father, his voice laced with bitterness. "I *will* protect this town. No matter what you think me *capable* of."

Without another word, he left the house.

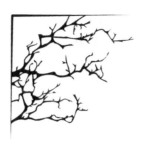

Chapter 41

CODY SLAMMED THE HEEL of his hand into the top of the steering wheel in frustration. He was being followed. He didn't have time for this. It took a while to be sure, but now he was certain. The winding desert road would twist, hiding the pursuing headlights from view, but they always reappeared, staying far enough behind him that he couldn't tell what kind of car it was.

Cody needed to know who it was and what they were up to sooner rather than later. He was not in the mood for games. His adrenaline was so charged after his shouting match with his father, he knew he'd never be able to go back to his desk and stare at reports. Rather, he decided to go check out his lead at the dig site. Sure, it was dark, but now was as good a time as ever. At least he'd have something to report back to the captain.

A particularly deep curve in the road gave him his opportunity to confront whoever his tail was. He put on his breaks, slowing to just over twenty miles per hour, and waited for his pursuer to come around the bend.

Just as he expected, they came barreling around the curb at fifty or sixty miles per hour, nearly slamming into him. The squeal of brakes and the screech of tires on the pavement combined as Frank's car swerved to miss his and spun out into a near-perfect donut across the deserted highway.

With a sigh, Cody pulled onto the opposite shoulder and got out of his Jeep. Frank jumped out of his car like a spry cat.

"Cody, what the hell was *that?* I could have hit you! I could have killed you!"

"And I could have killed you."

Frank blinked and snapped his mouth shut. Both he and Court, who'd come around from the passenger side of the car, looked confused.

"What are you two thinking, trying to be all sneaky and following me in a strange car on *this* highway in the middle of the night? With everything that's going on, what if I'd freaked out and gone all trigger-happy on you?"

Frank's mouth opened, then snapped shut. "I . . . we . . ."

"We weren't trying to be sneaky," Court supplied lamely.

Cody glared at him.

"Okay, maybe a little bit, but where are you going, Cody? We saw you pull out of your parents' neighborhood. What's going on?"

Cody affected a nonchalant expression. "Nowhere. Just a midnight drive."

Both of them glared thunderbolts at him.

"You're allowed to make fun of us, Cody," Frank said, "but don't insult our intelligence. We've all known each other too long."

Cody sighed. Frank was right. He owed them the truth. At least.

"I can't wait until morning, guys. I just can't."

The three of them gazed steadily at one another for several seconds.

"Then let us back you up," Frank said.

"I thought you were pissed at me, Frank."

"No—"

Cody glared.

"Okay, maybe I was, but . . . well I wasn't really mad. I just thought you handled things in a . . . less than professional manner."

"And now?"

"We all lost Tom, Cody. We're all dealing with it. Besides, this bastard is hurting people in *our* town. Don't you think we want to get him just as bad as you do? Don't you think we want to find Alex alive, for *your* sake, if no other?"

Cody was touched by that, though his pride wouldn't allow him to say so.

"We're your friends, Cody, and the three of us are the detectives in this town. Protect and serve, right? That includes the town as a whole, individual citizens, and any outsiders who might happen to be here."

Cody didn't know what to say.

"Look, if you're going after this guy, we're going with you. Either that, or we can cuff you, throw you in the trunk, and cart you back to the captain as excess baggage."

Cody rolled his eyes. "All right. I know where I'm going. Just follow me."

Frank and Court followed Cody out into the desert, but Cody didn't go to the dig site where Alex had disappeared. Rather, he led them to where he had first discovered the mass grave. Since then, makeshift roads had been set up for the coroners and other emergency vehicles, so this time he drove right up to it.

He got out of his Jeep and pulled an emergency pack from behind the back seat, complete with a water bottle, beef jerky, a flashlight, a coil of rope, and a few other supplies. He crammed his arms through the straps as Frank and Court pulled up behind him and parked.

"What're we doing here?" Frank asked as they exited the car.

"Looking into something I found just before I discovered the grave. I haven't thought much about it since. It seemed irrelevant."

"And now?" Frank asked.

"I think it may be a way into his lair. I think the tunnel I saw may be how he was moving around and tending to the graves." He hadn't really formed the thought until Frank asked, but he'd suspected it for a while now.

"But if it's big enough for him to travel through, why haven't we explored it? Why hasn't anyone even mentioned it?" Court clicked the flashlight Frank had given him on and off, checking the batteries.

"It doesn't look big enough for a person to fit through. But up until Alex was taken, we didn't realize he had some kind of underground passageway either. No one would have thought of it. And, honestly, I could be wrong. I just haven't been able to stop thinking about it since he snatched her. This way."

They followed him in silence. Alex's abduction site was half a mile south and fairly well lit. Here, the only thing they could see was what their flashlights revealed.

"Who goes there?"

All three men swerved toward the voice. Cody wrenched his Glock from its holster and pointed it in the direction of the sound. Frank and Court's hands went to their guns, though they didn't pull them.

Cody's flashlight found a frightened-looking man who seemed familiar. The second the man saw Cody's gun, his hands flew up in front of him.

"Whoa, whoa! Don't shoot." He peered at them through the darkness. "Detective Oliver, is that you?"

Cody was taken by surprise and it took him a moment to answer. "Yes."

"Mike Ware. We met yesterday. I'm the foreman at the dig site."

Cody did remember him, now, and lowered his gun. "What are you doing out here, Mike?"

"There are a lot of extra people running around town, Detective. Plenty of them are trying to get a peek at the crime scene. That's your arena, and I'm sure your men are efficient, but if anyone should slip past your cops, there's a lot of expensive equipment out here. I've been sleeping out here the past three nights. Just have to protect my livelihood, you understand?"

Cody supposed he did, but he wasn't sure how to feel about Mike sleeping out here with a potential killer nearby. He didn't know if the man was a little dim, a little arrogant, or just insanely brave. At the least, he was another civilian who could potentially get hurt, and Cody didn't want the responsibility for him.

"My apologies Mike. For the gun. We didn't know you were out here. We're just checking into something."

Mike pressed his thumb and forefinger to different buttons on his watch. "At this hour?"

"It couldn't wait."

Mike shrugged. "I'm just dozing in the cab of my truck if you need anything."

"We won't," Cody said quickly. "Please, go back to sleep."

Mike nodded and got back into his truck, closing the door loudly. Cody hoped the man would stay in his truck and out of harm's way.

He led Frank and Court over the now-familiar path to the mass grave. The bodies had been removed, of course. The site had been photographed, sampled, and searched a dozen different ways. It now looked like brown mulch—soil that had been recently turned and was ready for planting. He shuddered at the thought.

Cody easily hoisted himself up to the shallow outcropping. Once there, he pulled the soil away from the wooden planks and removed them, shining his light down into the narrow tunnel.

"This is it?" Frank asked from beside him once he and Court had made it up. "Cody, I don't think *we'll* fit in there, much less a guy who's supposedly twice our size."

Cody unwound the rope from his pack and tied the end of it around his wrist. "I think I'll fit; it'll just be tight."

Frank played his flashlight over the narrow tunnel. "But it curves to the right and disappears. How do we know it doesn't dead end two feet after the bend?"

"We don't. That's what I have to find out. Here. Hold the rope. If it's nothing, you can hoist me back out."

"And what would you have done if we weren't here?" Court asked, sounding falsely casual.

"I'd have tied it to something."

Court looked around at the smooth, lumpy angles of the mountain. "To what?"

Cody's annoyance flared. "I'd have managed."

"Uh-huh."

Brushing it off with a roll of his eyes, Cody grasped the upper lip of the tunnel and swung his legs into it. "All right, going in."

"Wait, Cody." Frank put a hand on Cody's shoulder. "We need to have more of a plan than this. After you go around that bend, we'll be able to hear you for a few feet at most. How are we supposed to know if you're in trouble, or if you need us to pull you out?"

"I suppose we'll have to go with rope-tugs. You tug once to ask how I'm doing. One tug from me means I'm fine, but gonna keep going. Two tugs means pull me out. Three means . . . you two should come down." He glanced at his friends; both wore worried frowns. "Any other contingencies?"

They both shook their heads and Cody slid into the tunnel. Though he'd never been prone to claustrophobia, this was one scenario where he could imagine it. It wasn't tight over his legs or hips, but his shoulders brushed both sides. He took a deep breath, filling his lungs and telling himself that he could breathe; no problem. He managed to make himself believe it, but the illusion of breathlessness was definitely there.

Cody scooted downward in the tunnel by straightening his legs, digging his heels in, then wriggling his butt down until his bent knees brushed the top of the tunnel. Then he'd straighten his legs and scoot some more.

The going was agonizingly slow. It felt like hours before he reached the bend. Once he got around it, he wanted to shine his flashlight down the tunnel, to see if he could tell how far it went. But his flashlight was in his hand, above his head, and there wasn't enough room between the top of the tunnel and his head to bring the flashlight or his hand past his face. He settled for turning the light toward his toes and trying to see what he could. The tunnel didn't look like it ended any time soon, and up ahead, Cody could swear it got bigger.

Looking forward to that, he scooted down farther. Five minutes later, the tunnel opened up considerably. Cody couldn't sit up completely, but he could come up on his elbows. He scooted a few more feet, then tried to sit up. Straightening his legs, he found nothing. His feet had gone over some kind of precipice. He panicked. The tunnel was wide enough for him to turn over now, which he did, digging his fingers into the dirt below him to keep from going over the edge, even though he wasn't in real danger of falling. Only his feet and the bottom of his calves hung over the edge of the tunnel. He pulled his feet back and sat up. He couldn't sit up to his full height, but if he hunched his shoulders and ducked his neck, he could almost attain mobility.

Sitting on his backside, Cody pulled his knees into his chest and ducked his head. He brought his flashlight up to see what he could see. His mouth dropped open. This was not the edge of a cliff he'd found; the tunnel emptied into a large room. The "precipice" he'd been afraid of was merely the end of the tunnel, with the floor three feet below him.

Cody scooted to the edge and hopped down into the cavern. It was huge—easily the size of his entire apartment—and black as tar, other than what wandered into the beam of his flashlight. A passage hewn out of the rock on the other side of the room led deeper into the mountain. It was spacious, closer to the size of a sewer than to that of the tunnel he'd just exited.

Cody turned and called up the tunnel. "Frank, can you hear me?"

A muffled response came, but Cody couldn't make it out. Instead, he grasped the rope and yanked distinctly three times. Several minutes passed before the indistinct tugs of someone descending came. When they did, Cody untied the rope from his wrist and went to explore the perimeter of the chamber he was in. There wasn't much to see.

When both Frank and Court slithered unceremoniously out of the tunnel, Cody went to stand by them. Frank let out a low whistle.

"No offense, Cody, but I really hate it when you're right."

Cody shook his head. "Right there with you. You guys want to keep going?"

"We're here," Court said. "We might as well."

"Do you think both women are down here?" Frank asked.

"I do," Cody answered. "The question is how big *here* is. It might take some time to explore all of it."

Frank un-holstered his gun, turned off the safety, and pointed his flashlight at the passageway on the opposite side of the room. "Then we'd better get started."

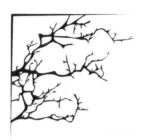

Chapter 42

THE FIRST SENSATION Alex had upon waking was that of her pounding head. The throbbing reached from her forehead, just above her nose, all the way around to the nape of her neck. She had no idea where she was, or how she'd gotten here. She couldn't string together enough thoughts or images to even gather what her most recent recollection was.

Her muscles were stiff and uncooperative. She rolled over and groaned. Whatever she was laying on was rock hard and had absolutely no give. After a few minutes, the pounding in her head became less violent, though it didn't subside altogether, and Alex pulled herself into a sitting position. The wave of dizziness that washed over her forced her to the ground again. She landed on her elbow, stubbornly refusing to lie back down. She had to figure out where she was.

"Are you okay?"

Alex jumped, inhaling sharply at the voice on her right.

"I'm sorry," the woman said quickly. "I didn't mean to scare you. Actually, I'm relieved you woke up at all. You've been out since he brought you here, and I was afraid you were dead."

Alex looked around the room. It was dark, with a bit of light filtering in from somewhere, though she couldn't identify the source. Then she realized there was a door into the chamber. An outside light spilled into the room through the bottom crack. The musty smells of dirt and plants and desert rock were all around them. Something smelled sweet as well. Sweet . . . and familiar, but Alex couldn't put her finger on it.

The room was round, though irregularly shaped, and the walls were made of rock. Alex was lying on the hard-packed dirt ground beside a boulder that was roughly twice her size. Her right arm felt heavy, and she lifted it to find a metal shackle clamped around her wrist. It was attached to a chain that coiled near her feet, then disappeared underneath the boulder.

All she could see of the woman the voice belonged to was an indistinct silhouette, lying on the ground six feet from her on the other side of the boulder.

As she looked around, the memories came crashing back, memories of being in the desert, driving the van in grandiose figure eights. She'd gotten out. Why had she done that? She knew exactly why: because she was on the verge of a meltdown at the time. True, she'd volunteered to be bait, but as the night wore on and there was no sign of him, the stress began to grate on her.

She'd felt like the walls of the van were closing in on her. She'd had to get some air. She'd given the cops a lecture about how he wouldn't attack her in the van, and this was a better way to catch him, but it was all crap. She'd gotten out of that van because she needed the fresh air to keep from losing it, and because she'd been feeling rebellious. Besides, the desert was full of cops, and she'd see him long before he reached her, or so she thought. Never in a million years did she imagine he would rise out of the landscape like some desert ghoul.

She'd gotten onto the boulder because from up there the breeze felt good, and she could see most of the countryside. The moon had shone eerily over the arid region, and Alex had felt calmer, more in control. She'd bandied with Cody, trying to ease his mind. She knew he was worried for her, and she felt like she was causing him way more stress than he deserved. In truth, the conversation had made her feel lighter as well.

Then something had been creeping up behind her like a giant arachnid. She'd turned to see the killer coming at her, slithering forward on his belly, using his arms to propel him forward. He'd covered his face in some kind of muck, and he'd looked like a red-eyed demon emerging from hell.

She'd screamed and tried to lunge away, but he was too close. He'd yanked her down into the earth with him, and she'd seen the surface receding, getting smaller and smaller. She'd had the sensation of the earth swallowing her whole. Then there was nothing.

Alex groaned and, confident she wouldn't pass out again, let herself lay down on the ground. "Cody," she muttered.

"What?" The woman's voice was alarmed. "What was that? Did you say Cody?"

Alex sat up onto her elbow again. "Yeah. He's probably having a coronary by now. Are you Melissa?"

"Yes! How did you know that?"

The awkwardness set in all at once. Here she was, talking to one of Cody's girlfriends. They were in a dire situation, but Alex didn't see why it had to be awkward for Melissa, too. She was aware of the cop-out on her part, but at this particular juncture, she didn't care.

"He's looking for you. Well, everyone is."

Melissa let her breath out in a whoosh. "Well that's a relief. The street I was nabbed on was so quiet, and I couldn't think of a single date or appointment I had over the next few days. I had this terrifying notion that no one would realize I was missing for a week or more."

"Don't you have a job?" Alex asked.

"No. Full-time grad student. Don't get me wrong; my professors would worry if I didn't show for class, but it still might take them a week to realize anything was really wrong."

Fully realizing that this was the most inappropriate situation imaginable in which to feel jealous, Alex pushed away her deep urge to be neurotic over whether or not she could compete with this woman for Cody's affections. Alex was no grad student. She'd barely graduated junior college.

"Your friend—the one who was giving you rides while your car was in the shop?—she got your message and came to pick you up. She got stuck a block down at a red light but she saw him force you into his car."

"Well that's good." Melissa sounded hopeful. "Uh, you know, that people are looking for me. So what happened to you?"

Alex sighed. "I was bait."

"You were . . . and he *got* you? That's awful."

"It was kind of my fault actually. I did something stupid."

"Still, that sucks. I'm sorry."

"I am, too, but here we are." Alex pulled herself into a full sitting position. "Has he hurt you?"

"No. He keeps walking by, but since he stashed me here, he hasn't touched me."

"That's good."

Melissa cleared her throat. "What he did to those other women, do you think he's planning on doing that to us?"

Alex paused before speaking, telling herself not to say anything snippy. Both she and Melissa had to remain calm if they were going to make it out of this alive.

She settled on, "It doesn't matter."

"It doesn't?"

"No. We aren't going to let him *do* anything to us, good or bad. We're going to get out of here."

"But how?" Melissa's voice already sounded stronger than when she'd asked the question.

"Are you shackled like I am?"

"Yes."

"Where does the chain attach to?"

"It runs under this boulder behind me."

Alex nodded. "Mine, too." She got up on her knees and started digging, trying to free the chain her shackle was attached to.

"What are you doing?" Melissa asked.

"Maybe we'll get lucky."

"How?"

"Maybe he put the boulders on top of the chains because he couldn't attach them to the ground any other way. If that's the case, all we have to do is free the chain."

"What if it *is* attached under the rock?"

"If what it's attached to is small enough, we can just dig it out and take it with us. Better than waiting here until he has the urge to fulfill one of his twisted fantasies with us."

Melissa was silent a few seconds. Then Alex heard the unmistakable sound of her digging around her own chain. The earth was hard-packed, but Alex used her thumbs, and it soon crumbled aside in chunks.

"Try to dig in a straight line," she told Melissa, "following the chain."

"Why?"

"The goal is to free the chain, not displace the weight of the entire boulder."

"Right."

They dug in silence.

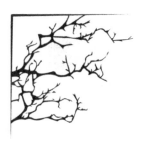

Chapter 43

AFTER TEN MINUTES OF walking through the dark tunnel that led out from the cavern, Cody, Frank, and Court had found nothing. There weren't even any obvious signs of animals, though Cody was sure plenty of insects and arachnids took shelter from the desert's harsh climate down here. He tried not to think about it.

Then his flashlight illuminated something strange up ahead. At first, he thought they'd hit a dead end. Then he realized the wall in front of them was a septum. The tunnel forked, one branch leading off to the right, the other straight ahead. He turned to his friends.

"What do you think?" Frank asked.

"I think we should look everywhere."

Frank nodded. "I'll go down this side tunnel. With any luck it will dead end before long. When it does, I'll double back and keep following the main drag."

"You don't want me to come with you?" Court asked.

Frank shook his head. "If there are more forks like this one, you two will have to split up eventually. Each of us should explore as far as we can. When we're satisfied that there's no women, or killers, down the branch we're in, we can find each other and keep going."

Cody played his light along the floor until he found a white rock that fit easily in his hand. He scraped it along the wall in the direction Frank would be going. It left a white, chalky scratch. He handed the rock to Frank.

"Use this to mark where you've been so you don't get lost. I can't imagine these tunnels go for more than a few miles in either direction. It shouldn't be hard to find our way out again, but we can't be sure. Once the Botanist realizes we've made it into his terrain, he may purposely try to turn us around."

"Yeah," Court muttered, "if he doesn't just kill us instead."

Cody swallowed, and a loud silence stretched between them until Cody cleared his throat. "Be careful, Frank. He's going to see us before we see him, and these tunnels are his home. Use all your senses, not just your eyes."

Frank nodded. "You two do the same. This guy doesn't get to kill any more of Mt. Dessicate's detectives."

He started down the tunnel that branched to the right, and Cody and Court moved forward. Like a prophetic fulfillment of Frank's words, another fork loomed up not three hundred yards further on.

"I'll take the right, you take the left?" Court asked.

Cody considered for a moment. The tunnel Frank had taken had been smaller and led off to the right. It had seemed to Cody that the route he and Court continued on was the main thoroughfare, if there was one. Now the two tunnels were the same size and led away from each other in equal, opposite directions. Cody had no idea which one was more likely to have Alex and Melissa at its end.

"Sure. Be careful, Court."

"You too. Cody?"

Cody had taken a few tentative steps to the left, but he stepped backward so he could see Court.

"Frank says you're involved with Alex."

Cody studied the ground, but there was no point in denying it. "What of it?"

Court studied him for a moment. "If you've got feelings for her, I get why you're here. I do, but you can't let it impair your judgment. You have to be a cop down here; a determined, pissed off, but impeccably careful cop."

Cody smiled sadly. "I know."

Court studied him for another moment before nodding. "Okay. Good luck."

"You too."

Cody moved forward.

AFTER FIFTEEN MINUTES of digging, Alex's fingers found the end of the chain, and her heart sank. It was attached to some kind of square object.

"Okay, Melissa. Looks like we'll be digging out a box of some kind."

Melissa sighed. "Is it heavy?"

"I won't know until I unearth the entire thing."

Melissa was silent. She didn't resume her digging.

"Something wrong?" Alex asked.

"I just don't like the idea of trying to find our way out of here while dragging a heavy object behind us."

"We might not have a choice. If we *can* drag it, we should."

"But we won't be able to run."

"Maybe not," Alex admitted, "but at least it would be a rebellion. Even if he catches us again, at least it would throw him off. We wouldn't be where he wanted us to be. Why should he make all the rules?"

"But it might make him mad. He could kill us faster."

Alex sighed. "Melissa, there were a lot of women in that grave. I'm sure at least a few of them were submissive and did what he wanted in the hopes of living longer. All of them are dead. Doing what he wants us to do isn't going to keep us alive."

Melissa was silent. Then her breathing sped up. A lot. She was panicking.

"Melissa?" Alex stopped digging. "Melissa, take a deep breath."

"No doubt some of those women fought back, too, or tried to escape. What you're saying is that we're going to die no matter what, so we might as well go out fighting."

"That's not what I'm saying. We're going to get out of here."

"You don't know that!"

Alex took a deep breath. "Of course I do. We have a lot of advantages those other women didn't have."

Melissa had begun sniveling, but she stopped at that. "Like what?"

"When they were taken, no one knew who this guy was or what he was doing. No one was looking for these women. Cody—actually most of the state—is looking for us. They're coming for us, Melissa. I know they are. But we have to help them."

Alex scrubbed a hand over her eyes, thinking fast. "I've been along this stretch of highway more times than I'd care to admit. If we can get topside, I know I can figure out where the highway is and head toward town. Actually, if we come up anywhere near where he snatched me, there will probably be a herd of police cruisers in sight. We just have to get there. And in order to do that, we *have* to keep our heads."

Melissa's breathing slowed down again, and, though Alex still couldn't see her face, she could tell Melissa was nodding in the darkness. Alex hung her head in relief when Melissa turned over and went back to digging underneath her own boulder.

Her first hunch had been right; she'd have to keep Melissa busy to keep the other woman from freaking. Melissa's fear was contagious. As soon as her breathing sped up, Alex's adrenaline, her panic, had spiked. She needed to keep Melissa calm as much to keep herself calm as anything else.

Feeling weak, Alex started digging again. She tried to dig along the edge of the box she was chained to. If she could uncover one side, she'd get an idea of how big it was.

Three minutes later, Alex heard a faint scratching sound. "Did you find what you're chained to, Melissa?"

"No. Not yet."

Alex frowned. The scratching sound was getting louder. "Melissa! Shhh. Listen."

Melissa stopped digging. An instant later she jumped to her feet and started scooping all the dirt she'd dug up from around the chain back into place.

"What is it?"

Melissa's voice was a high pitched squeal. "He's coming!"

Alex watched Melissa scoop everything back into place and plop down next to the boulder as though she hadn't done anything mutinous at all. Alex couldn't judge her. Their captor was a killer after all. Alex didn't get to her feet. She didn't replace the dirt she'd moved. She sat up on her backside, crossed her legs, straightened her spine, and relaxed her shoulders. Despite a pounding heart and cold fingertips, she refused to show fear.

The door opened, the light from the adjacent room blocked almost completely by his shadow. When he entered, he was much smaller than his shadow suggested, but still one of the largest men Alex had ever come face to face with.

Slimy mud covered his face, and Alex wondered what its purpose was. He was dressed in worn denims and a colorless button down shirt. His left foot dragged a bit when he walked, which made the scratching sound she'd heard, and his hair hung, long and greasy and limp, to his shoulders.

He walked forward until he was standing between Alex and Melissa, looking down at them. He stared at Melissa for a long time before turning his head toward Alex.

"It's you." His voice was raspy as ever.

Alex felt annoyed, or at least she tried to feel it beneath her trembling hands. "Who? Who do you think I am?"

He turned his head slightly to the side without taking his eyes off her. "His."

That left Alex genuinely confused. *"Whose?"*

He jerked his head to the side, as though indicating a person standing next to him, but the three of them were the only ones there. "His."

Alex looked down at the ground, telling herself to stay calm. Then she lifted her chin and met his eyes again. Her voice trembled only a little. "I don't know who you mean."

He stared at her for so long, her entire core started to shake. She didn't want to look at him anymore, but she didn't dare look away.

"Now that's sad," he whispered. "Cordelia." He raised one long arm to touch her face. Alex tried to lean away from him, but there was nowhere to go. His fingers lingered on her cheek. His thumb traced her lips, then gently pressed on her bottom one to part them slightly.

Alex jerked away. "Why do you keep calling me Cordelia?"

"Because your father loves you. So much."

Alex huffed in frustration. What kind of answer was that? She was afraid to know.

"It's a pity," he said.

"What is?" she whispered, just to have something to say.

"Because you're his, I'm not allowed to touch you."

His hand dropped, and he turned toward Melissa.

Melissa's form stiffened, shrinking back against the boulder, and Alex started talking, grasping for a way to stall him.

"No, it's me you want. It's me you've been looking for, trying to catch all this time. You've finally brought me back here."

"Yes." He turned his head to look at her. "Back for safe-keeping."

"But why bring me here if you aren't gonna . . . do anything to me?"

"I never should have lost you in the first place."

Turning back to Melissa, he pulled something long and sharp from his belt. It glinted metallic in the moonlight.

Melissa started screaming.

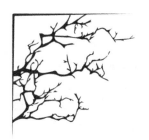

Chapter 44

CODY DIDN'T KNOW HOW long he'd been traveling through the dark tunnels. He was losing track of time in this place. He wasn't wearing a watch, but knew the cell phone in his back pocket would have the time. He didn't bother to check. In truth, he didn't care. He *did* wonder whether anyone had noticed their absences yet, but that was not something he had the luxury of checking on.

He'd only come across one other fork since leaving Court, but when he'd shined his flashlight down it, he could see its end. It was really more of a nook. He'd taken the time to walk its length, just to be sure there were no bends or hidden tunnels that he couldn't see from the main one. There weren't.

As he'd come back to the main tunnel, a fat mouse had run across the ground in front of him. It was the first sign of life he'd seen, and it came at the perfect time. Because his flashlight was on the ground, following the mouse's progress, he'd seen the tripwire.

Upon closer examination, it looked like simple string, but no matter where Cody shined his flashlight, or how close he got to the walls, he couldn't figure out what kind of booby trap it triggered. Perhaps it was just meant to strike fear into the hearts of any intruders; perhaps it was some kind of alert system, so the Botanist knew when outsiders had entered his lair; or perhaps, had Cody walked into it, a sharpened stake would have swung down to pin him against the wall, Rambo-style. There was simply no way to tell.

Cody's first worry was for his friends. He stepped carefully over the tripwire and pulled out his phone, wondering if he would be able to text the others and warn them about booby traps. He couldn't. His phone was in roaming mode and wouldn't even let him access the text menu.

With a sigh, he slid the phone back into his pocket and moved forward, sweeping his flashlight in broad circles over floor, walls, and ceiling. Up ahead, he could see another fork. He wondered how he would choose which way to go.

It was then that he heard it: a far, echoing shriek. Cody's head snapped up. Someone—a woman—was screaming. He ran to the fork, and waited. It was twisted to hope that she'd scream again, but it was only way he'd be able to tell which way to go. A moment later, she did. The sound unmistakably came from the right.

Forgetting to be cautious, Cody tore down the right tunnel, the beam of his flashlight jumping and bouncing ahead of him. The screams continued, but he had no way of knowing which woman was making them. There was white light coming from up ahead.

As Cody barreled down a particularly long, straight stretch of tunnel, a hulking, dark figure stepped out in front of him, blocking his way. Cody skidded to a stop and raised his gun to point at the man's chest.

"You're going the wrong way," the man said. His voice was urgent, but solid.

The light was coming from behind the man, leaving his features in shadow, but of one thing Cody was absolutely sure: this man was African-American. Alex had sworn up and down that the killer was either Caucasian or Latino. She was a reliable witness. Could she have been so wrong about the killer's ethnicity?

"W-what?" Cody stammered.

"You're going the wrong way. If you want to save her, go back to where the tunnel forks and go left."

Cody regarded him suspiciously. "The screams came from this way."

The huge black man shook his head. "The killer has the place rigged. There's a small opening into the room she's in. That's why you can hear her screaming. But the opening is the size of a basketball. You won't be able to get through. To actually find a way into the room, you have to go left and take the long way around."

"Who *are* you?"

"It doesn't matter who I am." The man stepped toward Cody, and Cody had to stiffen his legs to keep from stepping back. The man was considerably taller than he was and twice as wide through the shoulders. "Look," the man said, "you need to go and get her. She's the woman you love. You're supposed to be with her. Go now or she'll die!"

Cody's adrenaline was through the roof, and for some reason he couldn't explain to himself, he wanted to believe the man. He wanted nothing more than to fly back through the tunnel and to the left.

Still, the cop in him stood rooted to the spot. This could all be a ruse to let the killer, or if not that, the killer's accomplice, escape. Something told him he wouldn't see this man again.

"Who are you?" he shouted.

"Go now!"

"Not until you give me a name!"

"Karl! Now go!"

Knowing he'd regret it later, Cody spun on his toe and fled back the way he'd come.

ALEX VAULTED ONTO THE killer's back. She'd planned to wrap the chain she was shackled with around his neck, but it wasn't long enough. By the time she clutched his shoulders, the chain was taut.

He did little more than thrust his shoulder back, but it was enough to throw her off of him. The small of her back slammed into the boulder her chain was under, and the air was knocked soundly from her lungs. She rolled onto her side in the dirt, gasping for breath. By the time she got her bearings and looked up, his hands were on Melissa's neck, thumbs pressing down into the delicate hollow at the front of her throat.

Alex refused to watch a woman be strangled to death. Still unable to draw a full breath, Alex scuttled around in the dirt with her hands, looking for a weapon. Her hand closed around a rock. It's wasn't large, or sharp, but it was all she had. She knew she'd only get one shot, so she let her adrenaline build for a few extra seconds. She turned onto her side and sat up on her elbow, putting one foot flat on the floor.

Throwing all her energy into her left arm, she leapt up and swung the rock at the killer's face.

It was never going to cause him severe damage, but she connected with his cheek, striking bone and scraping mud and skin. It knocked him off balance, and he let go of Melissa.

The breath Melissa sucked in sounded raw and painful.

The Botanist swung around, backhanding Alex. She flew a short distance before hitting the ground and skidding to a stop, the hard-packed ground scraping the tender skin from her back. Panting, Alex sat up on her elbow.

He moved toward her. There was stark rage in his eyes. He said only minutes before that he wouldn't touch her, but his face said all bets were off; she'd pissed him off, and he was coming for her.

She rolled onto her stomach and tried to crawl away, but he grabbed her ankle and easily dragged her back, flipping her over. He stood over her, knife raised over his head, about to come down.

Alex shrieked . . . and nothing happened. He cocked his head to the side, as though listening for something. If he hadn't done that, Alex would never have heard it: a soft clattering sound, constant and repeating.

The killer slowly lowered the knife. Blood dripped from his cheek where Alex had struck him with the rock. Some of it fell off his jaw and landed on her jeans. He got to his feet, then slowly backed out of the room. When the scratching of his dragged foot could no longer be heard, the soft clattering sound stopped.

Alex lay on the floor on her back, panting, for several minutes before she could find the will to rise. Then she remembered Melissa, who was utterly silent.

"Melissa? Melissa, are you okay?"

Melissa seemed like she might be unconscious, but she groaned and turned her head toward Alex. Alex let her breath out, relieved that Melissa was alive, but her chain wouldn't allow her to get close enough to tell how bad the other woman's injuries were.

Alex pulled herself into a sitting position, wrapped her arms around her knees, and tried to still her shaking hands.

Minutes later, Alex became aware of footsteps heading toward the room. They were much quicker than the killer's slow gait and came from the opening on the opposite side of the room from where the killer had exited.

Unsure what to expect, she got to her feet, but remained in a squat, and found the same rock she'd attacked the Botanist with minutes before. In truth, she wasn't sure she would have the strength for another fight with him.

It took interminable seconds for the owner of the footsteps to reach the room. When he did, it was immediately obvious he wasn't the killer. He wasn't big enough. This guy had a flashlight and a gun. The flashlight roamed around the room before coming to rest on her. She couldn't see beyond the blinding white light.

"Alex!"

Alex let her breath out in a whoosh, falling forward onto her hands in relief. "Cody."

Cody skidded to his knees in front of her, throwing his arms around her. Alex wrapped her arms around his neck and buried her face in his shoulder. He pulled back to kiss her several times, his hand running through her hair, then down her back. They stayed in the small of her back, pressing her against him, but he managed to find the exact spot where she'd fallen on the boulder, and she shuddered, inhaling softly.

"What's the matter?" He took her face in his hands. "Are you hurt?"

"Just a bruise, I think. Cody, Melissa's right over there. The killer attacked her. She needs a doctor. She's unconscious."

Cody crawled over to Melissa, taking her face in his hands. "Melissa, can you hear me? Wake up."

It was too dark for Alex to see Melissa, but it didn't sound like she was waking up. In the semi-darkness, Alex saw Cody raise one hand to his face, studying it.

"What's wrong?" Alex asked.

"Blood. The back of her head is bleeding."

Alex groaned. That wasn't good. "How bad?"

"I can't tell. It's too dark. I can carry her if you can walk."

"How? We're shackled."

"What?"

Alex raised her chained arm in explanation. Cody ran his flashlight beam over it.

"I've been trying to dig it out, but there's some kind of box under this rock. I don't know how heavy it is."

Cody came over to kneel beside her. Together they dug at the chain, feeling along the edges of what it was connected to. Three minutes later, Cody stopped, shaking his head.

"Can you tell what it is?"

"I think it's concrete," he said. "It's huge—gotta be a hundred pound block."

Alex's shoulders fell. "I can't drag that amount of weight. And you certainly can't carry her while dragging that behind you. What do we do?"

"We've got to find something to get you out of the chains."

"What about your gun?"

He shook his head. "The chains are too thick. The bullet would ricochet off; it could hit one of us, and you still wouldn't be free." Cody ran his flashlight over the room, running it along the walls, the ceiling, and into the corners. He stopped somewhere up behind her.

"What is it?" she asked. "Did you find something that'll help?"

"Not with the chains, but I think there's a light switch up there."

"A light switch?"

Cody got up and walked over to the wall behind her, climbing up on some boulders. He fiddled in the darkness with something she couldn't see, and a moment later, the room was flooded with light. Soft orange bulbs were strung around the perimeter near the ceiling. Compared with the darkness Alex had been sitting in, it was blinding.

She squinted and grimaced for several seconds before her eyes adjusted. As Cody jumped off the boulder and landed behind her, she got her first real illuminated look at the room.

She gasped, hand flying to her mouth. Horror and revulsion were not strong enough words to describe what she felt. Her entire frame trembled.

Cody was instantly by her side. "Alex, what's wrong?"

She wanted to answer him, but she was so shocked by what the dim lights revealed that she'd forgotten how. The walls of the room were hewn from the red rock of the mountain. *The room with red walls.* It was the room from her dreams. The smells and feels, which hadn't registered in the dark, now reverberated with an intensity that made her spine ache. The sweet smell she'd awoken to was sickly sweet, but she hadn't realized it at first.

The fear she felt was different from what she'd felt before when she was wrestling with the killer. That was a fear of something real, something tangible. If she couldn't get away, he'd kill her, but that was the here and now. Alex could fight until he *did* kill her.

This fear was different. It was psychological, something that had happened in her childhood that she'd never understood; the paralyzing fear of a vulnerable, innocent child, returning to attack her during one of the most terrifying experience of her life.

"Alex, what is it?"

She looked at Cody, mouth open, eyes fearful, hearing his questions but not comprehending them. She had no idea how to explain, or how to utter a sound.

Cody turned her fully toward him, put his hands on her shoulders and shook her. "Alex, snap out of it!"

It worked. Alex shut her mouth, looked down at her knees, and shut her eyes. She was in an underground cavern with Cody. And Melissa. There was a killer here. She had to keep it together.

She opened her eyes and looked back up at Cody. That was no longer concern in his face, but stark fear.

"What's the matter?"

She swallowed. "This room. I've been here before." Her voice quavered violently as she spoke, but she no longer cared.

"You have? When?"

"I don't know. I've had dreams about it for . . . ever since I can remember."

He was looking at her strangely now, as though she were something dangerous, or worse, something to be doubted.

She felt compelled to explain. "I thought they symbolized something. I didn't think it was a real place!"

Cody put a hand on her shoulder. It was a calming, reassuring influence. "It must have been when you were a child."

She shook her head. "My parents would have known—"

"It was probably before they adopted you. You were found wandering on the highway not far from here. You were just a toddler, Alex. Why *would* you remember?"

Alex thought about the things the killer had said: he'd brought her back for "safekeeping;" he "never should have lost her to begin with." She shivered. Could she be the offspring of a killer? It was looking more and more that way, but Alex turned her head, hiding from the thought.

"Cody, get me out of here. Please," she whispered. "I can't be here anymore."

He cupped her face in his hands, using a thumb to wipe away a tear that escaped down her cheek. "I will. I promise. But there's nothing in this room that will break these chains."

"So what do we do?"

"I have to go and find something that will."

"Like what?"

"If nothing else, the Botanist has the keys."

"You can't just go looking for him!" Her voice was shrill.

"Alex, I can't get you out of these by myself. If I can find something else—a sledge hammer, an ax, even a crowbar to pry the links apart—I will, but I have to go find *some*thing, okay?"

Alex ran her hands through her hair, feeling her nerves fray. She was sure Cody was a competent cop, but after the confrontation she'd just had with the killer, she wouldn't wish for her worst enemy to come face to face with him. What if he killed Cody? The thought made her want to throw up.

"Here." Cody pulled up his pant leg and produced a small gun. It was a nine mil.

Alex shook her head, pushing the gun away when he thrust it toward her. "No. If you're going looking for him, you need to keep your gun."

"I have mine." He showed her his other hand which held his state-issued Glock. "This is my backup piece. Look. Load the magazine here, safety, hammer. Got it?"

She took the gun from him, too numb to speak.

"Alex, if he comes back, if he tries to do anything to either of you, kill him. Do you understand me?"

She nodded.

Cody reached down and kissed her again. Alex clung to him for a moment, needing his touch. She let go when he did.

"I'll be back as soon as I can."

Then he was gone. And Alex was left alone in the red room, shivering.

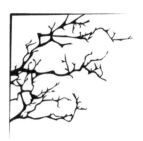

Chapter 45

CODY MOVED THROUGH the murky corridors as swiftly and silently as he could, sweeping his flashlight over everything, looking for something that would free Alex. There were plenty of rocks, but none that would help him. The chains the two women were shackled with were old and rusty, but they were also large and solid enough he didn't think simply hitting them with a rock would do the trick.

He hated leaving them in there, especially Alex. At least Melissa was unconscious and therefore oblivious to the situation for the time being.

He knew Alex would be able to defend them. She was independent and capable. Actually, it was that independence that was the problem. Alex was a woman who was used to having her life in her own hands. Now she was chained up and at the mercy of a brutal killer. The helplessness was starting to unhinge her. He had to find something to free them quickly, for Alex's sanity as well as her physical safety.

As Cody moved along the dark passage, he noticed tiny mounds strewn sporadically around the cavern. He stopped to study one of them. It looked like putrefying fruit, though he couldn't be certain. Whatever it was, it was rotting, causing the sickly-sweet smell that permeated this part of the caverns.

The passage he was in opened into a bigger room. There was nothing in it, but there were several adjoining caverns beyond, and the air was cooler. He continued on, and was soon convinced there was an opening nearby that led to the outside. The air was no longer the stale, dank air of the underground. A refreshing desert wind was blowing through from somewhere.

He reached a cavern the size of the entire Mt. Dessicate police station, and knew he'd found something significant. He stood in the doorway longer than was prudent, running his flashlight over every corner and cranny. He didn't want to enter and have the killer jump him.

In the center of the room, roughly twelve feet apart, were two beds, if they could be called that. They looked anything but comfortable and were furnished with leather straps, the kind used to restrain combative medical patients. From the ceiling hung an assortment of knives, scythes, sickles, hooks, pincers, and even a pickaxe.

In the left wall was an opening to a narrow corridor. The right wall had a huge hole in it that Cody could see led to open air. Cody move forward cautiously, trying not to notice the dried blood and...other things he didn't want to identify on the various weapons hanging from the ceiling.

Careful not to turn his back entirely on the dark passage that led from the room—unbidden, his mind conjured images of the Botanist hiding just beyond his line of sight—Cody advanced to the opening. It was like the mouth of a cave, looking out over the black desert and dropping off sharply inches in front of where he stood. The desert air was a relief after so long in the close confines of the mountain, and though the sky was still black, the stars twinkled in a way that could make one forget the dire situation at hand.

Cody edged forward until he could look straight down. They wouldn't be able to get out this way. The drop-off was severe with jagged rocks below. It was a form of psychological torture for any victims the killer brought into this room: the outdoors—and escape—were tantalizingly close, but to jump from this height would mean broken bones, if not death. Even if they survived, the killer would simply go get them. No one can run through the desert with broken legs. Cody sighed, then turned back to the torture chamber.

He wondered if he could use the pickaxe to free Alex. None of the knives would do him any good, and even the pickaxe he was unsure about. If it had a broader blade, maybe, but with just the pick . . .

A scratching sound on his left made him jump. He spun on his toe, landing in a squat, with his gun pointed at the noise, his pulse pounding painfully in his temples. In the shadows, only feet from the drop off, was a dark, round mass. He hadn't noticed it before. It was tucked away in a pocket of shadow, and Cody couldn't tell what it was. A small boulder perhaps? Certainly not large enough to hide a killer. Of course, this guy apparently had secret passageways and hatches all over the place, so maybe the scratching sound had been him trying to shift the boulder to the side. The thought made the hair on the back of Cody's neck stand on end.

He crouched there, scrutinizing the boulder for a full two minutes before lowering his gun. Perhaps it had only been a rodent, scurrying by, but he had to be sure. Staying in a crouch, gun lowered but at the ready, he inched forward.

There was some kind of...material on top. So not a boulder, but a bundle of rags? What on earth was it? He nudged it with his gun...and it moved!

Cody stumbled backward, barely keeping from landing on his backside, and raised his gun again, pointing his flashlight as the thing moved again, groaned, and raised its head.

It was a person. Cody's mouth fell open. If not for the full beard and intelligent, if faraway, eyes, it wouldn't have even looked human. The man was filthy and emaciated—rotting away. He was so thin, he'd huddled himself into a sleeping bag-sized ball. It took several seconds for his eyes to focus on Cody. When they did, the skeleton of a man pulled himself into a sitting position. The motion looked painful, and revealed a chain shackled to his arm.

This was another of the Botanist's victims. But why would he take a man? And keep him alive up here? Cody couldn't close his mouth. He sat for several seconds staring in shock.

"Who are you?" The man's voice was surprisingly solid considering his physical condition.

"Cody Oliver. I'm a detective in Mt. Dessicate. The town a few miles from here," he added when the man looked confused. "I . . . who . . . how long have you been here?"

"Probably since around the time you were born."

Cody doubted that was true. Even a few days in place like this would seem like an eternity, and for this degree of emaciation, the man must've been here for months. It probably seemed like decades to him.

"Do you know where the killer is?" Cody asked.

"You mean old Mudface? He hasn't come through this room recently."

"Mud face?"

"He smears mud all over his face when he's here, so I've taken to calling him that."

Cody nodded. These were details for another time. "Look, he's got two more victims in another room. I'm going to get you all out, but I have to find something that will break these chains. Do you know if he has any other prisoners down here?"

"Have you seen my daughter?" The hope in the man's voice chilled Cody's heart.

"Your daughter? Who's your daughter?"

"She's just a toddler—probably too scared to tell you her own name. Have you seen her?"

The panic rose from Cody's chest to his throat. There was a child down here somewhere? He still didn't have a way to free the now three prisoners, and the killer could be anywhere. Now would be a fantastic time for Frank and Court to show up.

"No, I'm sorry. I haven't seen her. When was the last time you saw her?"

The man's eyes looked far away. "It's been a really long time."

"Which way did the . . . Mudface take her? Did you see?"

"Back that way." He pointed in the direction Cody had come from. Cody sighed. He hadn't seen her, but it was dark. There could easily be other rooms or passages he'd missed. He hoped the child wasn't dead. He didn't know enough about this killer to know whether he was likely to hurt such a small child. The youngest victims they'd excavated from the mass graves had been young teenagers, and that was horrific enough, but a toddler was another thing entirely.

"Please," the man said. His face was a collage of hope and desperation, and his iridescent blue eyes sparkled with a sheen of moisture. "You must find my daughter. He said he'd keep her alive if I helped him. She must be here somewhere."

Cody swallowed, wondering what to do. He preferred to get everyone out and come back en force with plenty of men and guns. He didn't relish searching for a tiny child that could be hidden anywhere and, if they were being realistic, might not even be alive. Yet, he doubted this man would be willing to leave without his daughter.

Then something occurred to Cody. In his grimy, emaciated state, the man looked like he was eighty years old. He was probably twenty or more years younger that, but being kept prisoner had made him look older than he was.

Still, he had to be at least fifty. Why would a fifty year old man have a toddler with him? Cody was in no position to contradict the man, but he wondered if captivity of this sort hadn't driven the man over the edge, if he wasn't a bit delusional.

"Sir, if your daughter is here, I'll find her."

The man looked relieved.

"For now, I need to try and get you out of here. Who are you?"

"I'm an artist."

"What's your name?"

"Jonathin."

Cody had started to turn away, but he froze, turning back slowly. "Not Jonathin Landes?"

The man looked confused. He searched the dirt in front of him, before nodding his head, slowly at first, then more quickly. "Yes. Yes, that's my name. How did you know?"

Cody was at a loss. Landes disappeared more than twenty years ago. What was he doing here now? Suddenly Cody was sure that between what he knew and what Stieger had found out, he had all the pieces of the puzzle, but he couldn't see the picture in his mind.

"I . . . I've been looking for you."

Landes' reaction was the last thing Cody would have expected. The man's eyes filled with tears, which spilled down over his cheeks. "You're looking for me? Why?"

"You're still on your father's land. Do you know that?"

Landes nodded, his body shuddering with unmitigated sobs.

"We looked into the prior ownership of this land, trying to figure out how . . . Mudface might be tied to it. No one's seen you in . . ."

Cody realized that Landes' assertion that he'd been here for most of Cody's life was not so farfetched. Could he have been out here this entire time? Since the eighties?

Landes' body was still wracked with sobs. Cody leaned forward to put a hand on the other man's shoulder. Carefully. Landes was so frail-looking that Cody was afraid too much pressure would break his arm.

Finally, Landes spoke. "For many years now, I've been convinced that I would die here, that no other soul on earth would ever see me, or know my name, or that I ever walked the earth." He looked up at Cody, and gave him a pathetic, heartbreaking smile through his tears. "But you've been looking for me."

"I'll get you out of here," said Cody. "I promise." He sighed, turning away to collect his own emotions, before speaking again. "I'm going to try and break these chain links with that pickaxe."

He got to his feet, but Landes raised a hand. "Wouldn't a sledge hammer work better?"

Cody looked down at the emaciated man with surprise. "Yeah. Do you know where one is?"

"The bed on the right; there's a trundle that opens at the bottom. He keeps heavier tools in there."

Cody went to the bed and found a drawer near the ground that opened when he got his fingernails under the right grooves. Inside was an array of hammers, maces, heavy steel balls, even a meat tenderizer.

Cody shuddered but removed the sledge hammer.

It occurred to him that slamming a sledge hammer into a chain was going to make a lot of noise. He could only pray that it worked. If it didn't, it would probably bring the killer running, and Landes still wouldn't be free.

Landes laid out a two foot length of chain, then sat back against the wall so Cody would have plenty of room to swing without hitting him. He pointed to a series of particularly rusty links. "I think this will be the weakest section."

Cody nodded, impressed at how clear-headed Landes was. His clarity suggested that perhaps he was telling the truth about his toddler. Cody hoped not. This whole thing might go much easier if Landes was just a bit delusional.

Letting the sledge hammer drop back behind his shoulder, Cody concentrated on the length of chain Landes had indicated, then swung the hammer up over his head with all his might. It clanged loudly against the chain, but failed to break it. Both men froze, listening. There was no sound but a soft moaning as the wind blew in through the opening beside them and wandered through the narrower caverns.

Cody repositioned the hammer and swung again. This time, the chain broke, one link shattering into four pieces while the side links sprang left and right. Relieved, Cody held out his hand to help Landes to his feet.

The other man was staring at the end of the broken chain like he'd never imagined such a thing before. He looked up at Cody. "I'm free?"

The man was in shock, but they didn't have time for shock. The killer could appear at any instant. "You're no longer chained," Cody said, "but we won't be free until we get out of these caves. Come. We have to hurry." He held out his hand again.

Landes glanced at the hand as though it was of little consequence, then went back to staring at the broken end of his chain.

"Please, sir," Cody implored, "if we're to find your *daughter,* we must go."

That got Landes' attention. He gripped Cody's hand and allowed himself to be pulled up. Landes was shaky on his feet, so Cody put one shoulder under his arm, and grabbed the sledge hammer with his other hand. He would need it to free Alex and Melissa.

It was then that he noticed the markings on the wall where Landes had been chained. At first glance they had looked like scratches and dirt streaks that were fading into obscurity. Cody had barely noticed them. Now he could see there was more to them. There were drawings; many of them looked like plants. There were equations, both mathematical and chemical. There were even what looked like some sort of genetic pedigree charts.

Cody looked over into Landes' haunted blue eyes, only inches from his now. "He's not the Botanist," Cody whispered. "You are."

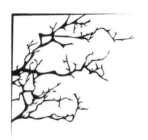

Chapter 46

ALEX PACED BACK AND forth next to her boulder, for lack of anything better to do. Cody hadn't been gone long, but it seemed like an eternity. It was utterly quiet in the caverns. She supposed that might be a good thing; if Cody and the killer came face to face, they were sure to make some ruckus. But if the eerie calm meant nothing was happening, then where had the killer gone?

Her heart pounded violently in her chest. No matter how many times Alex told herself that everything would be okay—Cody had found her and they'd all get out alive—she couldn't make herself believe it. A cold foreboding squatted in the pit of her stomach, refusing to budge. Something was about to happen; she could feel it.

"Alex?" Melissa had been coming to by degrees since Cody left. At first her eyes fluttered open, but she seemed unable to speak. Then she started muttering half-coherent words and phrases. Now she sat up on her elbow, holding her head. "What happened?"

"The killer attacked you. You hit your head pretty hard."

"But you stopped him?"

"Sort of. Cody's here."

"What? Where?"

"He had to go find some tools to free us."

"He *left* us here?"

"He'll be back, Melissa. Our chains are connected to big slabs of concrete. We can't drag them. If he's going to get us out of here, he has to find some way to break the chains."

When Melissa spoke again, it was in a frightened whisper. "What if the killer finds him?"

Alex didn't have an answer. The echo of her own worst thoughts made her feel like she would explode. "He won't," she said, her voice small.

"But he knows these passages better than any of us."

Alex turned away, not wanting Melissa's rising hysteria to infect her. Then she heard a soft scratching sound coming from the corridor Cody had disappeared into less than half an hour before.

"And what if he can see in the dark down here?" Melissa's voice was getting shriller by the syllable.

"Quiet, I hear something." The scratching sound, like a foot dragging, was getting closer.

"But what if he sneaks up on Cody, and Cody doesn't see him and—"

"Melissa, *shhh!* Someone's coming!"

Melissa froze, looked toward the sound, and gulped. The two of them waited, statue-still, as the scratching sound got closer and closer. A shadow fell across the light spilling into the room, then a shoulder thrust its way into Alex's field of vision. Two more steps, and Alex let her breath out in relief.

Cody was half dragging—hence the scratching sound—another person along with him. In his free hand, he held a sledge hammer.

"Who's that?" Alex asked when she found her voice.

"Jonathin Landes."

"Who?"

"I came across his name during the course of the investigation." Cody set the frail-looking man on the ground on the side of the room, then crossed toward Alex.

"And he was down *here?*"

Cody shrugged, hefting the sledge hammer absently. "No doubt it's a long story, but let's get out of here first and deal with explanations later."

Alex nodded.

"Cody," Melissa breathed from the side of the room.

"Melissa," Cody said. "How do you feel?"

She gave him a weak smile. "I've been better."

"Let's all get out of here. Then we'll get you to a hospital."

"Did you see anyone?" Alex glanced at Melissa and dropped her voice to a whisper. "Did you see *him?*"

Cody shook his head. "Only Landes." He took a knee and examined Alex's chain.

"I don't understand. Where'd he go?"

"You said you injured him, right? Maybe he went to bandage his injury."

"It wasn't that bad an injury, Cody—a scratch. It bled, but it wouldn't slow him down."

Cody shrugged straightening his legs. "Then we'd better hurry. Either way, he'll be back soon. Stand back."

He'd laid out a rusted length of chain. Alex stood as far back from it as she could while Cody positioned the sledge hammer behind his back.

"Ready?"

She nodded.

He planted his feet, gripped the far end of the handle with both hands, and held it over his head so that it would come down onto the chain with a vengeance.

He didn't get that far.

Alex felt more than heard something rush by her. Then a black mass tackled Cody. He and the Botanist went down as one and rolled.

Alex gasped. Melissa screamed. The two men rolled in the dirt, fighting for the upper hand. Punches were being thrown. All of them seemed to be connecting solidly, but in the semi-darkness, it was impossible to tell who was winning. Of course, the killer was much bigger than Cody, so if all punches were connecting, then . . .

Melissa was alternately screeching and sobbing, but Alex barely registered it.

"Alex!" Melissa screamed. "Shoot him! You have Cody's gun!"

"I'm not that great a shot," Alex yelled back. "I don't dare while they're wrestling so close together. I might hit Cody."

They rolled closer to her, and Alex could see more clearly. She looked for an opening, a time when there was enough space between Cody and the Botanist that she could shoot the killer without injuring Cody.

It never came.

They staggered toward her, both trying to get the upper hand. Alex tried to get out of the way, but didn't move quickly enough. They slammed into her, knocking her gun out of reach.

Cody tried to use his gun, but the killer slapped it away. The killer then landed a right hook to Cody's nose, which crunched, and Alex was sure it was broken. It was enough to momentarily stun him. The killer leapt to his feet and retrieved the sledge hammer, which had landed a few feet away.

"Cody, watch out!" Alex shrieked.

Cody recovered just in time to throw himself to the right, barely getting out of the way before the hammer slammed into the earth where his face had been an instant before. He had to roll away from two more hammer swings, but he finally got to his feet. When the killer raised the hammer over his head once more, Cody threw his shoulder into the killer's abdomen, knocking the wind out of him. The killer dropped the sledge hammer as Cody threw him back against the rock wall.

The hammer landed close to Alex. She slid forward onto her knees in the dirt, but her chain kept her from reaching it; her fingers were just inches shy. Changing tactics, she slid onto her hip and reached out with her feet. Cradling the handle of the tool between the curved arches of her sneakers, she dragged it toward her. It took precious time because the metal part of the hammer was distal to the handle, difficult to move without actually gripping it, but she finally got it close enough to grab with her hands, and leapt to her feet.

Cody's fight was growing desperate. Even in the semi-darkness, Alex could tell his face was a collage of bruises and blood streaks.

Alex straightened out the same length of chain Cody had, and swung the hammer at it with all her might. She was not nearly as strong as Cody would have been. He probably could have broken the chain in two or three swings.

The killer looked up in surprise at the first clang of the hammer, but Cody tackled him before he could react further. Alex swung it again and again, connecting with the chain, until her back and shoulders ached and her neck was cramping. The killer hit Cody in the head with what looked to be just his hand, but Cody hit the ground. Hard. Only then did the killer drop a donut-sized rock that Alex hadn't seen. He knelt down hard on Cody's chest—enough to make Cody grunt—and then used both his hands to push Cody's chin upward.

Alex swung harder at her chain while Melissa's crying subsided into a high pitched whine. She sounded like a wounded animal.

On the eighth swing of the hammer, Alex's chain broke.

In the dim light, Alex couldn't see where either gun had ended up. Instead, she grabbed the broken end of her chain from where it connected to her right hand. She vaulted onto the killer's back, looped the chain around his neck, and yanked back hard.

He gasped and lurched to his feet. Reaching up and behind him, he groped for Alex, and she had to dodge his meat hook of a hand. His other hand dug into his throat, trying to get a finger under the chain so he could breathe. Stunted whining noises came from his throat as he tried—and failed—to draw breath.

Alex caught a fleeting glance of surprise on Cody's face, but then there was only a blur of images as the Botanist stomped and thrashed around the room. It took all her energy to keep the chokehold with the chain. Her arms shook and her biceps ached with the strain.

She had a vague impression of Cody feeling around frantically in the dirt.

Then the killer smartened up.

He staggered backward and slammed into the rock wall, pancaking Alex between him and it. Pain pulsed through every nerve in her body, and the air whooshed from her lungs. Her arms and legs went numb, her hold on the chain limp.

The staggering psychopath grabbed her chain in one hand, a handful of her hair in the other, and flipped her over his shoulder, slamming her into the ground.

Something in her abdomen cracked.

High above her, the killer raised his fist. She tried to dodge out of the way, but pain lanced through her torso, and she didn't make it. His blow glance off her cheek, and her right eye went blind. She didn't think she'd be able to move even that much again.

The killer produced a blade no larger than a steak knife, but it looked sharp. Using a hand on her neck to anchor her down, he raised the knife, aiming for her chest.

Gore exploded outward from the killer's chest in four small, round spots. Alex jumped, but didn't have the strength to scream. The killer looked down at the four bullet holes in his chest, seeming to forget she was there, then raised his eyes.

Alex followed his gaze, craning her neck painfully. There stood Cody, feet planted, both hands wrapped around his glock, barrel smoking.

The Botanist got to his feet, then staggered backward several steps. He studied his wounds. His face was expressionless, though his eyes held a vague sense of confusion. He looked at Cody. Then his eyes fell on Alex. His expression hardened, and he lunged toward her.

Cody raised his gun a quarter inch and emptied his clip.

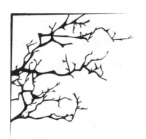

Chapter 47

WHEN THE BOTANIST WENT down, he landed partially on top of Alex. She pushed at the ground with her feet, trying to crawl away, but gasped in pain. Cody rushed forward, grabbed her under the arms, and dragged her back. She grunted when he moved her.

"Alex, where are you hurt?" He knelt beside her, looking down into her face. "Alex?" Her breathing was labored, beads of sweat dotted her face and neck, and she didn't seem to be able to answer. Then he realized she was holding her ribs.

"I'm going to lift up your shirt, Alex, so I can see how bad it is."

She still didn't answer, but jerked her head forward, trying to nod.

He put a hand on her forehead. "Just relax." He lifted her shirt up to her sternum...and gasped. He shut his eyes, horror radiating through him. From sternum to belt line, her abdomen was a mass of blue and purple and black bruises, which tapered to a sickly yellow hue at the edges. No wonder she was having trouble breathing.

"Try not to move, Alex. We'll get you some help."

"Cody?" Melissa's voice from behind him was thick with tears.

He turned. He'd almost forgotten her. Near the door, Landes was still sitting where Cody had put him, his face blank despite the violence that had just transpired in front of him.

Alex's hand shot out and grabbed Cody's wrist. Her eyes pled with him to stay with her.

"Are you okay, Melissa?" he asked over his shoulder.

"I . . . I just want to get out of here."

"I know. We will. It's all right. He's dead now."

He became aware of footsteps coming toward them from the outside corridor. His mind filled with visions of another attack from the killer, or perhaps the black man he'd seen earlier, who had been almost as big. He jumped to his feet, wanting to put himself between both women and the threat, but Alex and Melissa lay fifteen feet apart. To be in front of both, he'd have to stand almost *at* the doorway, and he couldn't meet the threat like that.

He settled for standing midway between the two women, ready to spring in either direction if necessary. He'd already loaded a second magazine into his gun. Now he raised it.

His breath, along with all the tension, seeped out of his body when Frank and Court ran in, guns raised.

"We heard the shots," Court said, breathing hard.

Cody nodded to the killer's corpse, and both detectives lowered their guns.

"So the threat is neutralized then?" Frank asked.

Cody started to nod, then stopped. "Actually, I did see someone else down here earlier."

Frank arched an eyebrow. "Who?"

"I don't know. Another man. Actually, he helped me. I don't know who he is, or where he went."

"You mean *that* guy?" Court was looking behind Cody.

Cody spun and raised his gun before realizing that Court was talking about Landes.

"No. That's Jonathin Landes."

"The jewelry guy?"

Cody nodded, but turned back to Alex. "We need to get these three to the hospital. Let's save stories for later."

Frank nodded.

Cody retrieved the sledge hammer and handed it to Frank. "See if you can break Melissa's chain."

"Keys." It was Alex. Her breathing was still labored, but she seemed to be adapting to the pain enough to take in what was happening around her. She had raised one hand to point at the killer, lying five feet from her. "He . . . has . . . keys." She gasped between each word.

Cody went over and, squatting down, put a hand on her shoulder. Then he looked where she was pointing. Sure enough, a small ring with a dozen keys was attached to the killer's belt. He retrieved them and tossed them to Frank.

Frank went to squat by a shivering Melissa to work on her shackle. He put a hand on her arm, and Cody could hear him murmuring comforting words to her. Cody knew Melissa deserved his attention, but he couldn't bring himself to leave Alex. He knelt beside her again and took her hand. Court came to kneel by him.

"What about him?" He nodded at Landes. The old man was staring at them, but not really seeing.

"I'm not sure he's all here," Cody whispered. "I think he's been a prisoner down here for a long time."

Frank frowned at Landes, looking about as disturbed as Cody felt.

"Why don't you take him, Court? Frank can help Melissa. Get them both out of here and send help back in for me and Alex."

"You don't want to just bring her now?"

"I don't want to move her."

Court's face turned stone-serious. "Her neck?"

"No, that's not it. I don't think." He reached down and lifted Alex's shirt again. She watched them without reaction, still focusing on her breathing. Court had roughly the same reaction Cody did when he saw Alex's abdomen. "If we try to carry her," Cody said, "she'll be in a lot of pain."

"I understand, Cody, I do, but there's a problem."

"What?"

"While I was exploring, I found a way out. It'll be a lot easier than the way we came in—these three won't be able to crawl up that skinny tunnel. The way I found lets out about half a mile and . . . around the corner, if you will, from where he abducted Alex the other night. When I got there, I checked my phone. Had six missed calls from the captain."

Cody sighed. "He knew we were gone."

"I guess Rose saw Frank and me leave, ratted us out. Anyway, he was on his way out here with reinforcements anyway, so I told him where the outlet was. Told him I was coming back in for you and Frank, but he said he'd meet us there."

"So what's the problem, other than me maybe losing my job?"

"Like I said, it's a much easier way out than the tunnel, but there's still a bit of climbing involved—scaling large boulders. The opening is up high. I think the three of us can get these guys out." He glanced around at Landes, Alex, and Melissa. "Even carrying Alex, we could hand her up in succession and get her through without too much trouble, but no way we're getting a gurney down here. Not right away anyway. We could always call in more people and do a rope-and-pulley sort of thing, but that'll take time. If we just carry her out, we can have her to the hospital in ninety minutes. If we wait, it could be hours."

Cody sighed. More dilemmas. Then Alex squeezed his hand and he looked down at her.

"It's okay," she breathed, "Cody. Take me out"—*breath*—"now. I don't want to be" —*breath*—"down here"—her eyes went around the room, then rested on the killer's corpse—"anymore."

After a moment, he nodded.

"You guys ready to go?" Frank had successfully freed Melissa from her chains. Cody and Court nodded, and Frank reached down and scooped Melissa into his arms. She laid her head against his shoulder and cried softly.

Court helped Landes to his feet. He leaned heavily on Court but looked at Cody. "What about my daughter?"

It was the first time Landes had spoken since Court and Frank had entered the room, and both of them seemed surprised to hear him.

Cody had forgotten about the man's daughter.

"Sir." Cody addressed Landes, voicing a suspicion he'd had since discovering who Landes was. "Did you have your daughter with you when you first came here?"

"Yes." Landes nodded. "It was the only way he could get me to help him."

"But if you've been down here for twenty years, then she wouldn't be a toddler anymore. She'd be grown, now."

Landes frowned. Cody could see the wheels turning in his head as he tried to make what Cody was saying compute. He shook his head, frowned, and tried again, but he couldn't accept it. "She's just a little girl," he whispered.

"She *was* a little girl," Cody said gently, his gaze going to Alex. "A little girl who might have . . . escaped out onto the highway."

Alex had been listening to the conversation passively. When Cody said the last, her eyes flew open, and she twisted her neck around to stare at Landes in awe.

Landes looked confused, as did Court and Frank.

"What?" Court asked.

"What?" Frank said from behind him.

Cody shook his head. "Look, Jonathin, there are people waiting to help us just outside these caves, but we have to make it there. If you'll come with us now, I promise I'll send rescuers back in to look for your daughter."

Landes looked downright terrified, but when several seconds passed and he didn't respond either way, Cody nodded to Court, who nudged Landes forward. The two of them followed Frank, carrying Melissa, out of the cavern.

Cody bent and, as gingerly as he could, picked up Alex. Her face contorted in pain and a groan escaped through her clenched teeth, but she slung her arms around his neck and laid her head against his shoulder.

"Is that man my father?" she asked when they'd moved out of the cavern and into the corridor.

Cody bent his head slightly so he could whisper in her ear while still keeping his eyes ahead. "I can't be sure, but I think so."

She nodded and as the minutes passed, Cody became aware of the spot on his shoulder where her cheek rested becoming damp.

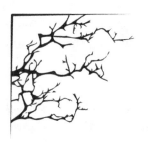

Chapter 48

NORMAN OLIVER GLANCED at his phone. He stood behind a police blockade, staring at a mountain in the middle of the desert. How had it come to this? He'd sworn that he would never do this again: stand on the sidelines, foot tapping, praying for the best but expecting the worst. Yet here he was. Again.

The sun was not yet up, but the sky had turned light blue over the last half hour, and the opaque of pre-dawn was receding imperceptibly, minute by minute.

Norman was a man who prided himself on being right *all* of the time. He was a business consultant, and he loved his job because it was something he could control. Any problems had solutions. Norman was very good at ferreting out a problem, and then posing and implementing the solution. It was very satisfying work.

Which was why, when his only son chose to follow his brother into a law enforcement career, Norman simply didn't understand. Truth be told, it frightened him. Criminals were unpredictable people. They lived by their own set of rules, and often no rules at all.

But it was more than even that. Norman had watched his kid brother, with whom Cody shared *so* many traits, fall into a pit of his own making. And there had been nothing Norman could do about it. He couldn't save his brother. He'd accepted that. And he was a father who'd been in love with his son from the first time Cody had wrapped his tiny, infant fingers around Norman's thumb. He didn't want the same end for Cody as his brother had experienced. And Cody just couldn't understand that. Worse, he never tried. Why would a man want to put himself into a world of utter chaos?

The only way Norman knew to bring his point across was to not be seen to support Cody at all. And he'd done a good job of that, he thought. What Cody didn't know was that Norman kept a police scanner hidden in his den.

Cody had been a detective for several years now, but back when he was a uniform, Norman would sit up on nights that Cody worked the graveyard shift and listen to it. If his son had ever gotten into a dangerous situation, Norman might have beat EMS to the scene, but it had never happened.

There was the incident in the barn with that pedophile, but Cody had been a detective then. Norman had been out of town when that went down and didn't hear about it until hours after it was over. By then, the only news was that Cody was a bit beat up, but all right. He had a few injuries, including one to the face that would result in a scar, but that was all. And what did Cody do? The day after getting out of the hospital, he simply went back to work, with no fears and no regrets.

Now he was after a serial killer, which posed a much bigger threat than the pedophile had been. Despite the massive relocation looming in his future, Norman had taken to sitting up nights listening to the scanner again, ever since Cody discovered the mass grave in the desert.

Last night, Norman hadn't been able to sleep, so he'd slipped into the den around midnight and turned it on, playing solitaire on his computer while he listened. Then the captain's voice had come across the radio, announcing that three of Mt. Dessicate's detectives had gone into the mountain and needed backup. Only someone close to the force would know that three detectives were all Mt. Dessicate had left, and that the "mountain" was where they believed the killer had taken his two female captives.

Norman had flown up the stairs, scared the daylights out of his wife while yanking his clothes on, and rushed out the door. Now he stood between two cruisers, wondering for the hundredth time why no one was going into the mountain looking for them. They seemed to think the detectives would come out, but what if something had happened? What if they were hurt?

Norman sighed and glanced at his phone again. His wife was texting him every ten minutes, and each time he had to tell her that there was no news.

He decided to go talk to the captain again. He knew Cody's boss was supremely annoyed with him, but he was too restless to stand here any longer. Besides, the captain had let Norman stay, despite his civilian status, so he was somewhat sensible.

Norman started around the barricade, eying the side of the mountain. The exit from whatever underground labyrinth the killer had built was up high, the slope down from it steep. A line of rescuers had taken up position from the mouth of the cave to the ground, where three squad cars and two ambulances waited. They stood like a human assembly line down the rock-faced slope to make sure no one tumbled.

But what was the point? The call to help the detectives had gone out not long after midnight. It was nearly dawn. Why wait around to see if they'd make it out?

Norman was about to put a hand on the captain's shoulder when the cry went up from the man standing closest to the mouth of the cave. "They're coming!"

All the rescuers turned full attention to the opening. The EMTs, who'd been lounging against their buses, stood up straight and readied their stretchers. The captain glanced back to see Norman standing right behind him.

"Behind the barricade, Mr. Oliver."

Norman nodded but couldn't make his feet move. It was another ten minutes before anyone emerged from the mountain. Norman recognized one of Cody's fellow detectives, but couldn't recall the man's name. He was sweating and covered with a layer of dust. A second man Norman didn't recognize leaned on the detective for support. The second man was elderly, painfully emaciated, and looked like he would break at the slightest provocation. The two of them made their way slowly down the slope, helped by the line of rescuers, until they reached the ground.

The old man was immediately taken to the ambulance. The EMTs asked the detective if he was hurt. He assured them he wasn't, but Norman didn't hear any more because more people were coming out of the cave.

This one, Norman remembered, was named Frank. Frank was dirtier than the first detective had been. He carried a woman whose clothes were stained with blood. Even from this distance, Norman could see tears glistening on her face. He wondered what had been done to her.

One of the rescuers offered to take her from Frank, since Frank was sweating from exertion, and she was passed to a solid-looking man who wore a uniform with "Salina Fire Department" embroidered on the sleeve. He carried the young woman to the nearest ambulance, with Frank on his heels.

Finally, Cody emerged. He carried a second woman in his arms. Another of the rescuers offered to take her, but Cody shook his head and continued down the steep slope, steadied by the line of rescuers. They followed carefully down the slope after him, which meant there must not be anyone coming after them.

Norman studied his son. Cody was caked in the same grime his comrades were, but he looked much worse. His nose was obviously broken. Purple bruises and trails of dried blood covered his face. His eyes were bloodshot and haunted. Even what Norman could see of his arms were scraped and bruised.

The young woman in Cody's arms was in no better state. She was covered in muck and her wrists, twined around Cody's neck, had blood on them. He couldn't see her face because it was buried in Cody's shoulder, but she was shaking so violently Norman could only surmise that she was in a lot of pain.

When Cody was three quarters of the way down the slope, he caught site of Norman and did a double take. His eyes widened. He paused at the base of the slope for a moment to stare at his father.

Norman stared back, unsure what to say. The young woman was gasping in agony, so Cody took her to the waiting ambulance. He laid her gently on a gurney, but she seemed unwilling to let go of him. She clung to his shoulders, shuddering. The last of the rescuers made it down the slope, then converged silently around the ambulance. Alex was the last victim to be loaded in, and all those who had assisted huddled around in silence to see the bus off. Those wearing caps removed them and watched Alex and Cody with reverence.

Cody placed his hands softly on her head and whispered something in her ear. She nodded and let go of him. Not until Cody stood up, away from her, did Norman realize that this was the same woman—Alex, he thought her name was—that he'd met only a few days before. His heart went out to her.

Cody spoke quietly with the other two detectives, who seemed to be trying to convince him to get in the ambulance. Norman hoped he would. He ought to be seen by a doctor. Cody nodded his head and turned toward the ambulance. Then he looked at Norman again.

The haunted look in his eyes was one that Norman would never forget. *Now do you see?* his eyes asked. Then he climbed into the ambulance. One of the paramedics closed the back doors before hurrying to the driver's seat.

The first ambulance, carrying Melissa and the old man, had already taken off, lights and sirens blazing. Norman hadn't noticed. He watched Cody's ambulance until it was out of sight.

And for the first time, he understood.

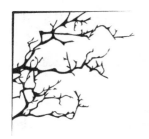

Chapter 49

TWO DAYS LATER, CODY talked with Alex's doctor. He needed to understand her medical condition so he could finish his case reports—which was true, and provided a good cover for his relentless questions about her well-being. He knew she'd had surgery, but was hazy on the actual prognosis.

"What did she need surgery for?"

Dr. Malcolm was tall and lean with ash-blond hair quickly fading to gray. "She had a flail chest," he said, then continued quickly upon seeing Cody's expression. "Uh, that means several broken ribs. The jagged edges of the bones caused tiny tears in her diaphragm and the walls of her abdominal cavity. The tears were bleeding and needed to be repaired surgically."

"She was bleeding internally?"

"Essentially, yes."

Cody sighed, guilt washing over him. He shook his head.

"Are you all right, Detective?"

"Her condition is at least partially my fault. I carried her out of the cave after her injuries occurred. I thought it would have been better to wait for a rescue team to come in, but my colleagues disagreed because that would have taken several hours. I should have pushed harder for that option."

Dr. Malcolm frowned as he listened. Then he slowly shook his head. "No, Detective. I think you did right bringing her out when you did. The tears may have worsened by carrying her, but I believe at least some of them came from the original injuries. Had she waited several hours to seek care, it might have been too late."

Cody wondered if the doctor was just trying to make him feel better. His skepticism must have shown on his face.

"Truly, Detective." The doctor placed a hand on Cody's shoulder. "You did right by her."

"Thank you."

The doctor turned to go, but Cody stopped him again. "The other woman, Melissa Adams, what room is she in?"

Dr. Malcolm had to confer with a nurse at the station, but then he turned to Cody. "Room 234."

"Thank you."

Cody headed for the elevators. He'd tried to visit Alex several times, but had been less than successful. Alex's mother had driven up after her rescue. More than once, when Cody had gone to see her, he'd found her curled up in the hospital bed weeping, her mother holding her hands while her father rested his palms on her shoulder. They were a tight-knit family, and Cody had tiptoed backward out of the room, not wanting to disturb them.

Melissa had a broken ankle and a cracked cheekbone, but her mental state was much worse. Because Frank had carried her from the darkness into the daylight, she'd latched onto him. Frank was still with her, but Cody wanted to speak to her before her family came.

He knocked on room 234 and Frank's voice called out an invitation. As soon as Cody was through the door, Frank stood and silently exited the room. Melissa stared at Cody for a few seconds, then turned her face toward the wall. He went to her bedside and laid a hand over hers, but she jerked her hand away.

"I'm sorry, Melissa," he said quietly. "I'm so sorry."

When she refused to so much as acknowledge him, he sighed and turned to leave. He couldn't be angry with her for it.

He closed the door softly behind him. Once he did, a sound he thought was Melissa crying filtered through it. He sighed again.

"You okay?" Frank asked, coming over. He'd taken one of the narrow, hard chairs that lined the wall a few feet down from Melissa's door.

Cody shrugged. "I don't blame her for it."

"For what?"

"Being angry with me. She's got every right to be."

"Why's that?"

"I chose Alex. I wasn't there for her like she wanted me to be."

"Are you sorry about that?"

Cody shook his head. "No, but that doesn't make it any fairer to her."

"Maybe it's all for the best. It does say something about how you feel about her, about both of them."

Cody nodded. "I don't expect to have a relationship with Melissa, but the idea of her being mad at me, hating me . . . I wonder if she'll ever forgive me. For anything that happened in those caverns. I'm going to see Landes. Care to join me?"

"I told Melissa I'd stay with her until her folks arrived. Did you see Alex?"

"No. She's with her parents. I don't want to disturb them. I'll see you back at the station."

Frank nodded and Cody started down the hall.

"Cody?"

Cody turned back toward Frank.

"Don't be too hard on yourself. It was an impossible situation."

Without responding, Cody turned and walked away. Perhaps Frank was right, but that didn't make it any easier.

Landes needed nearly as much medical care as Alex. He was unhurt, but dehydrated and direly malnourished. His DNA was sent to the state lab, where it would be compared to Alex's, as well as to a distant relative of Alastair's living in Cedar City to establish that this was, in fact, Jonathin Landes. Even with a top-priority rush, the results wouldn't be back for a couple of weeks.

When Cody arrived at Landes' room, he was surprised to find that the man sedated and in restraints. "What happened?" he asked the night nurse. Her name was Tanya.

"He kept screaming at us, being combative. I'm not actually supposed to be here. Got called in on my night off because he attacked the nurse that was here."

"Is she okay?"

"Nothing serious, but he bit her arm and sprained her wrist. Doctor sent her home with an ice pack."

"What was he screaming about?"

"She said he kept calling her Mudface. Said if she'd murdered his daughter, he wouldn't make the flowers grow anymore."

Chills ran down Cody's spine. A living victim of a serial killer, especially one who had lived side by side with the killer for so many years was a rare find, but Cody was less and less sure that Landes would be able to tell them anything coherent.

"Detective? Does that mean anything to you?"

Cody gave the nurse a tight smile. "Thank you, Tanya." He handed her his card. "Will you call me if his condition changes?"

"Sure."

Rubbing the bridge of his nose, Cody turned and walked away.

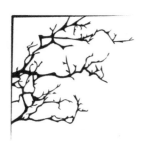

Chapter 50

TWO WEEKS LATER, CODY stood outside an interrogation room, looking in at Landes through two-way glass. The doctors had allowed Landes to be brought to the station to speak with the police, but they weren't releasing him. After several rounds of psychiatric evaluation, it was clear that Landes would spend some time in an institution. He needed real care.

Being the lead detective, Cody had the privilege of conducting the first comprehensive interview since bringing Landes out of the caves. They'd tried to speak to him in the hospital a handful of times, but he was too erratic to say much.

The DNA test results had come back from the lab only the day before. Although DNA tests are never one hundred percent, Alex had enough alleles in common with Landes to give a paternal probability of 99.998% +. She was his daughter.

Stieger had shown up not long after Alex's rescue, towing an elderly woman named Colleen. Her recollection of seeing Landes in Mt. Dessicate after Alastair's death was interesting, but not definitive. It seemed to support Landes' story that he'd been here all along—more than twenty years. Anything else Landes himself would have to corroborate.

"You ready for this, Oliver?"

The question came from John Tandy, the FBI criminologist who'd been called in to assist on the case. He'd been prepping Cody for the interview; it was his belief Landes would be more open with Cody than with a man he'd never met before.

"I think so, sir." In truth, Cody didn't think he'd ever be ready to interview Landes. He didn't think he—or anyone else—truly wanted to hear the story Landes had to tell. It was sure to be macabre, and Cody was too close to this case, too close to Alex.

"Above all, remember to keep your face serene. That's going to be harder than you think, but if you show too much emotion, you'll spook Landes, and he'll clam up."

Cody nodded, but Tandy continued.

"I'm serious, Oliver. This story has an insidiousness to it; we've all felt it, but Landes has a wealth of information not generally available to criminologists locked away in his head; the history of a serial killer from a man who witnessed it firsthand. You *must* keep him talking."

"I understand, sir."

Tandy studied Cody for a few moments. Finally he nodded.

The outer door opened and Frank, Court, and the captain entered. The captain had said they'd be having a quick pow-wow before the official interrogation began. No one spoke. The last few weeks had been too trying for small talk.

"Agent Tandy," the captain said, "why don't we start with you? What has the journal told you?"

"As I was telling Detective Oliver, here, it's a gold mine of information. I'm sure I've only scratched the surface in what time I've had. The Botanist went by the name Charlie, but he doesn't mention a surname in the journal, so it's hard to tell much more than that. He talks about his life on the Landes ranch, but not about anything before he went to work for Alastair, so I still have no idea where he came from or what kind of upbringing he had."

"So what do we know?" Court asked.

Tandy sighed, looking weary. "This Charlie was obsessed with Shakespeare's heroines. He believed they ought to be worshipped and immortalized."

"That by itself isn't *so* uncommon, right?" Frank asked. "Actors believe that sort of thing."

"But the Botanist believed it literally. He believed they ought to be preserved and revered in their dead and tragic state. With his victims, he was creating shrines to these dead women of literature. He believed them to be an homage and a work of art."

The silence stretched while they all frowned at the ground.

"What's the significance of the number twelve?"

"There is none that I can find. Shakespeare wrote more than twelve tragedies, and that's aside from the histories which happened to have a lot of tragedy in them. From what I can tell, that is simply the number that struck his fancy, the one he obsessed about. I'm sure the ones he connected with have something to do with his particular psychopathy, but it will take me months, maybe years to figure it out."

"So"—the captain rubbed the bridge of his nose—"we're saying this man was educated? That he read a lot of English literature?"

"He definitely knew the stories." Tandy nodded. "The way he talks about some of them, it almost seems that he'd grown up with them, like someone had read them to him at some point. Any chance Alastair Landes is responsible for that?"

"I doubt that," Cody put in. "Landes wasn't a man much given to the arts. He would have seen it as less than masculine."

"How about Jonathin? Did he and Charlie know each other long before Jonathin left town?"

"I'm not sure about that," Cody said. "If they did, it wasn't for long—a few months at most."

"Well," Tandy said, "however he learned them, he used them as frames of reference for how he killed his victims. You said your coroner couldn't pinpoint one particular cause of death in the victims? That's because he did different things, depending on which heroine he believed that particular victim to be. He drowned the ones he imagined were Ophelia, strangled those playing the role of Desdemona, you get the idea."

Court rubbed the back of his neck. His face had turned the color of fresh cream. Cody knew how he felt.

"Why isn't 'Shakespeare's Girls' written on the other grave sites?" Frank asked.

It was a good question. Two more sites had been located so far. Resputa's theory about them being arranged like spokes on a wheel was proving accurate. They were using the wheel pattern to triangulate where other sites might be. If Resputa's other theory—that the Botanist's pattern was incomplete—also proved to be true, then those sites might not hold bodies. Then again, if they were full, or even near to full, the Botanist would become one of the most prolific serial killers on record.

"Well," Tandy went on, "I don't think he stuck solely with Shakespearean literature. Near the end of the journal, he starts using other names I couldn't find Shakespearean references for. It took some digging, but I realized they were names out of classic literature of other eras and countries. Simply put, he branched out, looked for other tragedies to model his victims on."

"But"—Court threw up an index finger—"how was he finding these stories? It was one thing when he was living with Landes, but since then, from what we can tell, he's been living out in the desert. No internet, no books of any kind. He's been out there for twenty years. Where is he getting his information?"

It was then that the light bulb went on in Cody's head. "From the library."

They all turned to look at him, Frank and Court with eyes that said he'd finally lost it.

"Tom's maggot case, remember? The librarian said various books would disappear, then reappear in odd places. She thought the place was haunted."

"But how would he have gotten in there?" the captain asked.

"They're still exploring the extent of those tunnels, Cap," Frank said. "Some of them come right up to the edge of town. He could have walked right into town without bothering with the highway or the intervening land—not topside anyway—and we haven't followed even half of the passageways to their exit. Maybe one of them lets out in the basement of the library. It's an old building. Has a bomb shelter and everything."

"The librarian told Tom over and over that she felt an icy cold presence," Cody said, thinking back to what Tom had told him about the case. "She thought it was a ghost."

"We thought it was early-onset dementia . . . " Frank put in with a grin.

"But really . . ." Cody trailed off.

Court let out a frustrated spiral of breath, running his hands through his hair. "Creepy."

Cody thought back to what Stieger had unearthed. "Actually, they said he just wandered into town one day, looking for work. No one had ever seen him before or knew where he came from. Who's to say he wasn't out there even before he worked for Alastair?"

There were several loud swallows as that sank in. "Detectives." Tandy removed his glasses and rubbed his eyes. "Of course we'll scour every inch of those underground passages, and I'll personally read every line of this journal—and between them—dozens of times, but you must accept the fact that there are certain things about this man which we may never know."

Cody nodded, though he was the only one.

"Just one more thing, though not about the journal," Tandy continued. "Do any of you know who a lady named Janie Turner is?"

"Yes," Cody said at the same time Court said, "You mean Crazy Janie?"

"Who?" the captain asked, and Frank's expression mirrored the question.

It was Cody that answered. "Janie is an older woman that lost her daughter twenty-five years ago. The little girl drowned the year the river was insanely high. How do you know her, Court?"

"She's my mother's third cousin, twice removed. How do *you* know her Cody?"

Cody smirked. "My buddy Blaine owns a bar she frequents. We went to high school together, still get together for a drink every so often, and he's told me about her."

"I take it Mrs. Turner never believed her daughter's death was an accident?" Tandy asked.

Cody's eyes narrowed. "No, but the way she raves . . . it's not kind, but people call her Crazy Janie for a reason, Agent Tandy."

"Mrs. Turner came in with dozens of others, volunteering her DNA and demanding to know if her daughter was amongst the dead."

"And was she?" Frank asked.

"She wasn't in the mass grave, no."

"But?"

"The bones you found in the shed on the Landes property, Detective?"

It took Cody a moment to grasp what Tandy was saying. When he did he gasped. "That was Janie's *daughter?*"

The others mirrored his reaction. "But." Court took two giant steps backward, as though to distance himself and get a clearer picture, but it didn't seem to help. He looked just as confused as before. "Wait, *what?*"

"Yeah," Cody said. "What?"

Tandy held up his hands. "The smaller mounds in the field on the Landes property have all been excavated. They are all full of animal bones. My theory is that they are evidence of this killer's progression. I don't think the Botanist had done murder to a human being before the little girl's death. Even while he lived with Landes, though, his homicidal tendencies were already present. His MO was developing; his . . . ceremony was evolving. He buried the animals in flowered mounds, much as he would the women later on, but he hadn't come fully into his own psychosis yet.

"I checked the records; the report was filed on Janie's daughter only months before Alastair's death. I believe Janie's daughter was his first human kill. He snatched her from the river bank at an opportune moment. Her friends heard her cry out, but she was there and gone so fast, the only explanation was the river. It was the perfect cover for our killer because other children had already gone into the river that year. Part of the evidence the river theory was based on was that articles of Julie's clothing were found miles downstream—too far for a child her age to get on foot. Mother Nature's fury was the only explanation anyone considered, and perhaps rightly so. But a full-grown man, carrying the child and taking articles of clothing off her to throw into the river as a decoy . . . it's just not a scenario that anyone imagined."

"But how is this possible?" Frank pounded the table with his fist. "How could no one have known? Traces of this man have been around for decades but no one noticed! He snatched a child from the riverbank; he may have murdered Alastair Landes for all we know; he held a man captive for twenty years—a man who had a toddler that wandered out onto the highway—and no one connected the dots?"

Frank's voice rose in pitch as his tirade went on. Cody suspected that it was the story of the little girl on the river bank—Frank's daughter was about the same age Janie's daughter had been when she disappeared—that was unhinging him. Suddenly Mt. Dessicate didn't seem like the safe, family-friendly place they'd always believed it to be.

Tandy spread his hands. "Please try to understand, Detective"—he directed his remarks to Frank—"it's not that shocking when you look at the whole picture. The assumption that the little girl went into river was a good one. Why wouldn't they assume it? Alastair was an old man when he died. It's highly likely that he died of natural causes. As for Jonathin, I think there was a history in that house—an unhappiness, the full truth of which may have died with Alastair. Jonathin is certainly in no mental condition to disclose it, and the Botanist is dead.

"We must also keep in mind that most of this went down more than twenty years ago. Detective work, DNA, fingerprints, everything was so different back then. I'm not sure anyone *could* have connected all the pieces; no one had them all. Mostly, though, understand that our killer was insanely intelligent."

"Insane being the operative word," Frank muttered.

"Exactly," Tandy said quietly, and Frank looked up in surprise. "He was educated, resourceful, and probably a master manipulator. If he was coming into town to borrow books and put them back again without being seen, he was probably present in other ways as well. He's a chameleon. He's perfected the act of hiding in the light. He hasn't been caught before because, well, he didn't want to be."

"But he did now?" Court asked.

Tandy leaned back in his chair, lacing his fingers behind his head. "I'm not sure I'd go that far. All I mean is that he's smart, and because of that he managed to keep from being found for so long. It's not anyone's fault but his. I will say that I think his being brought to justice has everything to do with this young lady I keep reading about, uh, Alexandra Thompson?"

"How so?" Cody asked.

"Intuitive young woman. Strange, isn't it," Tandy asked, "that a young woman who probably experienced something terrible as a child, and never even found out what it was, who could have lived a full and happy life otherwise, was somehow drawn back to the very spot it all happened? That she was randomly pulled over on the highway by the very man who had her biological father captive? I don't think that's a coincidence. She said she had a strange experience; she reported it. Most people wouldn't have done so much. Granted, it took four years for all this to come out, and she had to return yet again, but still . . ."

"What are you saying?" Cody asked, wondering what shape Tandy's conclusions had taken.

Tandy shrugged. "I'm not sure myself. I don't pretend to understand how it all works. I don't have a chain of cause and effect to show that her actions led to the Botanist's exposure, but I think they must have. She had a strange feeling; she acted on it, rather than just brushing it aside and being happy to have it behind her, as most people would have. Now we're here."

Cody let his head fall back to rest against the wall, thinking of Alex. She really was the key to this entire thing.

"What was the rotting food in the caverns about?" the Captain asked.

As it turned out, it wasn't just fruit rotting, but all manner of food, and even some small animal carcasses. The smell of the fruit masked the smell of the animal decomposition.

"We aren't sure yet," Tandy said. "Could just be stuff he discarded and didn't bother to dispose of. It occurs to me that perhaps he did it purposely to mask the scent of bodies if he had them down there for any period of time after he killed them. We're hoping Jonathin can give us some insight on that count."

"Let's talk about Jonathin's story," the captain said. "Cody, what did your PI friend find out?"

"Stieger finally got Jonathin's military records. He joined at age twenty-two and served his obligatory four years. He was honorably discharged and never contacted the army again. Stieger tracked down a woman who's lived here for forty years. She swears she saw Jonathin on his father's property right around the time Alastair passed."

"Define 'right around,'" Frank said.

"Even the woman isn't sure of the timeline, but possibly within days. What that tells us is that Jonathin did hear about his father's illness and Alastair's pleas that he come home. No one knew he was here and no one heard from him or saw him, courtesy of the Botanist. If Jonathin knew that this Charlie had some hand in his father's death, that may explain why the killer held him captive."

"But why not just kill him instead?"

They all turned eyes on Tandy.

"Hard to say," he answered. "The Botanist kills women—men aren't his cup of tea. But then there's this flower thing."

"Yes." Cody nodded. "Stieger found out Jonathin's mother was an amateur horticulturist. Now, she died giving birth to Jonathin, but he was just like her. If he knew his mother was a botanist, perhaps he taught himself. If the killer was at all acquainted with Jonathin, he might have known of Jonathin's abilities. He kept the man captive and promised not to hurt his daughter as long as Landes kept making the flowers grow. Meanwhile, he was forced to watch the torture of many of the victims."

The captain shut his eyes and shook his head. "Poor man."

"I don't think Landes will ever be the same again," Tandy said quietly. "I don't think he'll ever have his sanity—at least, not the way we all do."

"Do you think he'll be able to tell us anything today?" the captain asked, nodding toward Landes who sat in the interrogation room, expressionless and staring straight ahead.

"I guess we're about to find out," Tandy said.

The door opened and the room filled with those who would watch the interview: all those who'd played key roles in the investigation. Of course Frank, Court, and the captain would remain along with Rose, Stieger, several of Landes' doctors, and Alex's father. Alex probably would have been present except that she was still in the hospital.

The captain nodded at Cody and Cody entered the interrogation room.

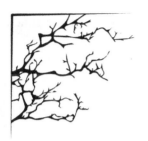

Chapter 51

TWO WEEKS' CARE HAD definitely made an impact. Landes was still painfully lean, but no longer emaciated. The wild look had gone from his eyes, replaced by resigned melancholy. Though he often forgot what Cody's question was before managing an answer, he was able to sit calmly and have a direct conversation. Cody had much the same impression of Landes that he'd had in the cave; despite the horrors the man had seen, he spoke firmly and eloquently, as though he'd managed to keep most of his sanity. It was present but fluid; a few key parts had been chipped away. He would speak of something with quiet authority, then simply trail off, as though he had a hard time keeping himself in the moment. It was an unsettling combination.

At first, Cody tried to keep Landes focused, but it soon became clear that letting him ramble produced more information than making him focus on specific questions.

"So you came home *before* your father had passed?" Cody asked.

Landes nodded, studying his own fingers, clasped together on the tabletop. "I got married. My wife was . . . unstable. She left when Mercy was still just a baby. I brought Mercy back here. I wanted to reconcile with my father. I wanted him to meet his granddaughter."

Cody gathered that Mercy was the name Alex had been given as a baby.

"And did you?" Cody kept his voice soft and steady.

"Yes. I knew there'd be talk when the townsfolk found out I was back. I wanted a day alone with my father first."

Cody nodded. "So you were alone with your father for a day or so? No one else knew you were in town?"

Landes looked up. He seemed surprised to see Cody sitting in front of him. The surprise quickly faded into far away resignation, though. "No," he said. "Charlie was there."

"Did Charlie have a last name?"

Landes' eyes wandered around the room. They fixated on the small, battery-operated clock up near the ceiling on one wall.

"Jonathin?"

Landes looked at him.

"What was his last name?"

"Whose last name?"

"Charlie's."

Landes frowned. "Who's Charlie?"

Cody sighed. Landes had already lost the thread of that memory.

Cody looked back down at his notepad, trying to gather his thoughts for his next approach. Over the last two weeks, Stieger had dug up a few others who remembered Landes. They vaguely remembered a man who'd worked for Alastair before his death. None of them had known his name. They said he kept to himself but that Alastair was fiercely protective of him. They'd all said that something "just wasn't right" about him. All three people Cody talked to had used that exact phrase. Did they think he was mentally handicapped? No. Was it something specific he said or did? No, just a feeling they got from him, like rotting leaves or a cold, dead room. The only other thing they could say for sure was that he was a transient. No one knew who he was, where he'd come from, or where he'd gone after Alastair's death.

"What happened next, Jonathin? You spent some time with your father and Charlie. Then what?"

"Charlie was crazy."

"Why do you say that?"

"I found bones in the barn."

Cody scarcely breathed. "Where did the bones come from, Jonathin?"

"I don't know." Landes gave a dismissive wave. "Mostly animals, I think, though some of them looked human."

"Did your father know about them?"

Landes gave him a tight, sad smile. "My father was a sick old man. He loved Charlie because Charlie took care of him and ran the farm. He had no idea what Charlie did in the barn at night."

"Did you tell him?"

"I tried. I confronted Charlie and tried to tell my father how twisted he was. He flew into a rage."

Landes trailed off, lost in memory.

"Then what happened?" Cody whispered.

Landes' eyes were suddenly misty. He swallowed. "He killed my father."

Cody's head snapped up.

"He . . . Jonathin, are you sure?"

"I watched him do it."

Cody looked toward the mirror, unsure how to respond. This had always been a possibility, but several people had said Charlie was out of town when Alastair passed. He thought back to the report he'd read and what Stieger told him. A report had been filed because Alastair died alone and no one was sure how. Obviously the "alone" part was untrue. Cody wondered if the report had been doctored. Perhaps—Cody sighed—perhaps a lot of things. He doubted there was any way to corroborate Landes' story. Even if they could dig up Alastair's body, it would be too decomposed to tell them anything.

"How did he do it, Jonathin?"

"With a pillow. By the time I got there, it was too late. He took me and Mercy hostage, drove us into the desert, forced us into the caves."

"How did he know about the caves? Did he . . . build them?"

"I don't know," Landes said. A fly was buzzing softly up near the window, and Landes seemed to be looking for it.

"Why did he take you into the caves, Jonathin?"

"He wanted me to grow flowers for him."

"Why did he need flowers?"

Landes shrugged. "He thought they were pretty."

"But why did he think you knew how to grow them?"

"Because I did."

Cody smiled, telling himself to be patient. "But you're a jewelry designer. How do you know about flowers?"

Landes smiled. "My mother. She had a green thumb. She knew how to make flowers grow, even in the desert. I found her botany journals and taught myself. Charlie saw me working with some in my father's house. He was mesmerized." Landes frowned. His face contorted and he looked up at Cody, as though seeking answers in Cody's face.

Cody shrugged self-consciously and looked down at his notepad. He didn't know how to meet Landes' gaze.

"What happened next, Jonathin?"

Landes' face became very still. All the emotion drained away from it. Cody thought he would have to repeat the question, and nearly did, but then Landes opened his mouth.

"He took Mercy, screaming, out of my arms. He said if I didn't grow my flowers, to put over *his* flowers, he'd kill her."

Cody cleared his throat. "Your flowers over *his* flowers? What were his flowers, Jonathin?"

"The women. He called them his flowers, works of his own genius."

"Works of art."

"Yes."

Landes lapsed into silence, and Cody took a few seconds to gather his next question.

"Jonathin, the room I found you in; it had . . . restraints and . . . certain tools—"

"The torture room." Landes was remarking on a simple fact.

"Yes," Cody whispered, fighting to keep his voice from quavering. "Is that where he always kept you? Or were there other rooms you saw?"

"I was always there. Always. Looking out over the desert. That was where he chained me the first day. It's where you found me. Only there. Sometimes I could see people down below, cars on the highway, hikers in the distance."

"And did you ever call out to any of them?"

Landes slowly shook his head. "He would have killed Mercy."

"But Jonathin." Cody leaned forward, resting his forearms on the table. "Did he ever let you see her? After taking her from you, did he ever bring her back?"

Again, the slow head shake. Landes' hands were in his lap now, and he hunched his shoulders, as though a cold wind was at his back.

"But how did you know he would keep his word? That she was alive at all?"

"He told me she was. He would bring messages. 'Mercy says good morning.' 'Mercy is drawing pictures today.' 'Mercy is being bad. Work, or I'll punish her.'"

Cody dropped his eyes and expelled his breath.

"Detective."

Cody looked up at Landes.

"Do you have children?"

Cody dropped his eyes. "No."

"The only thing a man can do is believe that his child still lives. As long as there was any hope of that, I did whatever he asked. Besides, he had other ways of keeping me in line."

Cody swallowed, sure he didn't want to hear this. He struggled to keep his face passive. "And what were those?"

Jonathin looked away from Cody. "Like you said detective: restraints, tools." He was suddenly fidgety and twitching. "He brought them there. All of them. He made me watch." His voice didn't quite break, but with the last word it dropped to a whisper. "He made me . . . listen . . ." It did break then, and tears coursed down his cheeks. He sniffed and seemed to regain himself. "He said if I didn't obey, he'd do the same things to my daughter." He looked back up at Cody. "How could I not spare her that?"

Cody's knee bounced up and down under the table. Because showing too much emotion in his face where Landes would see it was out of the question, it was his only outlet. He sensed that he was pushing Landes too far. The man was nearing his breaking point. Still, Cody had to try. He had to get as much information as he could while Landes was here. Unfortunately, the only place the story had left to go was down, into the killer's depravity.

"And what did he do to them, Jonathin?"

Landes looked up at Cody. His eyes held terror. His head jerked from side to side. At first, he was just shaking his head, but it got more and more violent. Soon his entire body was convulsing. His hands came up and he hit himself in the head, emitting the strangest sound Cody had ever heard. It was both a low guttural growl and a soft keening moan.

Cody jumped to his feet, but the door to the interrogation room banged open and Landes' doctors were at his side before Cody could get there.

It took them ten minutes to calm him down. The psychiatrist produced what looked like a miniature Christmas present from his pocket. It was a red box with a white ribbon painted on, but was only the size of a golf ball. Cody thought it might be a paperweight.

"Find your focus, Jonathin, remember?" The psychiatrist had to yell at first to get Landes' attention. "What do you see?"

It worked fairly well. When he saw the small box, Landes' movements calmed, slowed, then stopped all together. The keening sound stopped. When he started describing the box, he seemed much more himself. After several minutes of calm description, Landes put his head in his hands and began to cry softly.

"I was always there," he moaned, then raised eyes that were nearly identical to Alex's to meet Cody's gaze. "Detective, I will always be there."

Cody hadn't realized he was backing up until he reached the wall. It was cool and solid and Cody felt more grounded leaning against it. As Landes' body shuddered with sobs, the psychiatrist put his hand on his arm and looked up at Cody.

"I think we're done here."

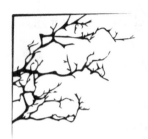

Chapter 52

CODY SAT AT HIS DESK staring out the window a week later. He watched the wind blow gray clouds around an overcast sky. A storm had camped over Mt. Dessicate for the past week. It refused to rain *or* to leave; it just sat there.

Cody knew the feeling. He'd spent an inordinate amount of time staring out windows over the past seven days. The case was barely over, but already he looked back at it as though it had happened years ago, wondering if this would be the case that defined his career. Would it define him as a cop? Would it define him as a man?

A knock at his door brought him out of his thoughts. Frank and Court were around, but they were out tying up loose ends for the case that couldn't be tied from the station, so Cody was alone in the back office. Lars Stieger filled the doorway. He hadn't seen the man for most of the week.

"Stieger. Please come in." The two men clasped hands.

"I hope I'm not disturbing you, Detective."

"Not at all. I'm glad for a break. What brings you out?" He pulled Frank's chair out from under the desk and motioned to it. Stieger sat and Cody pulled his own chair around so the two men could face one another.

"Came to say goodbye actually. I'm heading back up north this evening. I wanted to tell you that I was glad to meet you and glad to work with you. I respect the hell out of what you did here, Detective. It was a job well done."

Cody was touched. Stieger had been on the job for thirty years. That kind of praise didn't come lightly from a man like him. "Thank you. Of course we wouldn't have known the details without your help. The criminologists will study that journal for years. The Botanist's psychopathy was . . . unique. You're a good PI"

Stieger ducked his head at the praise and gave a hint of a smile. Cody suspected Stieger was not the sort who smiled much.

Cody cleared his throat. "I never heard; was your client's daughter among the dead?"

The smile disappeared and Stieger nodded. "She was."

Cody sighed. "I'm sorry for her."

Stieger nodded. "Thank you. I'll tell her you said so, but I think it's high time she got the . . . closure she needs. Maybe now she can move on."

"Closure," Cody repeated, "but not peace?"

Stieger studied the carpet before answering. "I'm not sure that with this type of crime the families ever find peace, not completely. But burying a body is a step in the right direction."

Cody nodded.

"Have you heard about Colleen Hinckle?" Stieger asked.

"No. What about her?"

"She died yesterday."

Cody gaped. "Was it the cancer?"

"Officially, yes, but it was the case, too. We tried to tell her gently, but when she learned that Landes had been out there all these years, that this torture was going on, she took it hard."

"That wasn't her fault," Cody protested. "Even if she'd come forward the day after she saw him, chances are that Landes had already been dragged into the desert. No one knew where this place was. No one would have had any idea where to look. I doubt it would have made any difference at all."

"Agreed, but Colleen couldn't be convinced of that. She took to her bed and stayed there. Until yesterday."

Cody closed his eyes and shook his head. "There are so many things about this case that are just . . . just . . ."

"Not right," Stieger finished for him.

Cody nodded and they sat in silence for a time.

"How's Ms. Thompson doing?" Stieger asked.

"As well as can be expected. I haven't spoken to her much. Her family is here, and I haven't wanted to intrude. The doctors tell me she's healing just fine, though with broken ribs it'll be a month before she's back on her feet."

Stieger nodded.

"She's a strong person," Cody continued. "I think she'll come through all right. She may never speak to *me* again, but . . ."

Stieger cocked his head to the side. "Why do you say that?"

Cody shrugged, wishing he hadn't. "She was traumatized by what happened."

"That's not your fault."

"No, but she'll always associate me with this experience."

Stieger frowned, and Cody could tell he didn't understand. "Didn't it ever bother you, Stieger, when you were on the job? This is what we do, and the work can be rough." He glanced out at the dark clouds. "Sometimes *very* rough. But even if the people we help trust us, even if they're grateful to us, they'll still always associate us with the worst of the experiences of their lives. Didn't that ever get to you?"

Stieger regarded Cody in a calculating way for several seconds before speaking. "You have feelings for this woman."

Cody sat back with a soft laugh. Cody supposed he shouldn't be surprised that the PI had figured it out so quickly.

"I barely know her. But I think it might have been possible . . . in some lifetime."

Stieger heaved a deep breath. "After a big, horrible case like this, you'll always question things, Cody. Sometimes only small things, sometimes everything from one end of your life to the other. And when the questions come, sometimes there *are* no answers. I've always been a believer in God. The only advice I can give you is to know that everything you did in the desert had to be done. You brought down a killer and saved lives—maybe a lot of lives if you consider how many more victims the Botanist may have taken had he been allowed to operate for years longer. Colleen may not have been meant to save Landes back then, but maybe she was meant to shed some light on the mystery now. For myself, I choose to believe that everything happens for a reason, and that God knows what he's doing. That said, let the chips fall where they may."

Stieger was right. Though Cody's parents had never been particularly religious, he too had been raised to believe in a benevolent higher power. What else could he do? Follow the questions in circles until he lost his sanity?

"Well." Stieger rose after a short silence. "I have a few loose ends to tie up before I hit the road. I just wanted to shake your hand one more time."

Cody got to his feet, and the two men shook.

"Thank you again, Mr. Stieger. For everything."

"If you're ever up north, look me up."

"I'll do that."

With a final nod, Stieger was gone.

Cody slid his chair back to its normal place behind the desk and fell into it, feeling drained. Resting his head in his forearms, he closed his eyes. He didn't realize how close to sleep he was until the ringing of the desk phone next to his ear jolted him upward.

Irritated with himself for being so tired—and so jumpy—Cody answered the phone with more gruffness than usual. "Oliver."

"Detective? Warden Lincoln here, from the prison?"

"Of course, Brett. What can I do for you?"

"I have some . . . unfortunate news."

Cody's hackles rose. "I assume it's about Resputa."

"Yes. Detective, he's escaped custody."

"What?"

"We were doing a routine transfer. There was a vehicular collision, which we're pretty sure was staged. The officers performing the transfer were ambushed. One of them's dead."

"Why haven't I heard anything about this yet?"

"It just happened, not an hour ago. When I found out, my first calls had to be to the political channels. My next call was to you. We think he'll just hightail it for Mexico. Every law enforcement agency in the state will probably be called up in the next few hours to try and head him off."

Cody sighed, feeling dizzy. "Thank you for the call, Lincoln. I appreciate it. Is there anything at all I can do?"

"I'll keep you posted, but as I said, requests for your help probably won't come through me. I just wanted you to hear it before the press informed you."

"Thank you."

"Of course. Goodbye, Detective."

Cody hung up the phone. One step forward, two steps back. The Botanist was dead and couldn't haunt anymore highways, but now Resputa was loose again, and there was a good chance he'd pass somewhere close to

Cody's jurisdiction. He knew there'd always be another monster in the world to chase, but he, for one, needed a respite between the hunts. Evidently, he wouldn't get that this time around.

"Cody?"

Cody turned his head and then was instantly on his feet. "Alex!" The chair Stieger had used was still near the door, so Cody motioned Alex toward it.

Her limp was profound but he knew it was more about her ribs than her legs. He took her elbow and guided her to the chair, which she sank into. Her face was peaked and dark circles adorned the lower lids of her eyes. Even her labored breathing betrayed the pain she was in.

"When did you get out of the hospital?" he leaned against Frank's desk.

"Today. About an hour ago."

"Should you be walking around?"

She managed a tight smile. "Probably not, but the drive back will be pretty miserable, so I might as well get what exercise I can."

He returned the smile. "You're driving back with your parents?"

"Yes."

"When?"

She looked self-conscious. "Now."

Cody studied the carpet, hoping his disappointment didn't show. Today, it seemed, was a day for goodbyes.

"I wanted to thank you, Cody."

Cody grimaced. "Please don't thank me, Alex. This has been one long nightmare for you from start to finish."

Alex gazed at him steadily, her green eyes bleak. "True. But you got me through it. You saved my life, Cody, more than once. I won't forget it."

The finality with which she said the last sent a pang through his chest.

"Anyway, it wasn't just me this was a nightmare for. You lost things, too."

Cody didn't reply to that. He didn't know how, and he didn't trust his voice. He'd avoided thinking about Tom for nearly a week. The funeral was tomorrow and Cody had decided to deal with his grief as little as possible until then.

"How are you doing?" he asked quietly.

Alex studied her hands in her lap, "I know there's this . . . thing between us, but . . ." she clasped her hands together so tightly that they trembled. Her voice grew thick. "I have so much to figure out now, Cody. I have so much to wade through." She looked up at him with glistening eyes. "I can't stay."

He nodded, the sadness stealing in softly. "I think I knew that."

Her brow dimpled in distress, and her gaze returned to the ground.

"What will you do?" he asked.

"I have no idea. I don't know how to even begin to move past this. How do I . . . deal . . . ?" Her voice dropped to a whisper. "How do I . . . ?"

Cody came to squat in front of her chair and put a hand on her knee, wishing he knew what to say to make her feel better. "It'll get easier," he finally managed, swallowing the lump in his own throat. "You're the bravest woman I've ever met, Alex. You'll figure it out."

When she looked up at him, her eyes were green pools of melancholy. "He's been out there, Cody, this whole time—most of my life. And I didn't even remember him. All the time I was being raised—and loved—and educated—he was . . ."

"That's not your fault, Alex. None of it is. You were just a baby." Cody wiped a tear from her cheek with his thumb. "The life you've had—it's what he would have wanted for you. If he could have known that you were safe all this time, it would have helped him—"

"But he didn't know it! He still doesn't know who I am or . . . He can't wrap his head around anything that's . . . *real*."

"You have nothing to feel guilty about, Alex."

Alex looked at her hands again and more tears fell onto them. "I know. But knowing that doesn't change how I feel." Her face crumpled and she covered it with one hand, leaning forward and resting her forehead against his shoulder.

Cody put his arms around her, but rested them there rather than pulling her close. She was still fragile, and he didn't want to cause her more pain.

After a few minutes she sat back. She took a deep breath, straightened her spine, and squared her shoulders. Despite the moisture on her face, she suddenly looked regal.

"My parents are waiting for me."

Cody helped her to her feet and put an arm around her waist, allowing her to lean on him as they walked. When they emerged from the station, both Alex's parents were leaning against the side of their gray rental sedan.

They came forward and each took one of Alex's arms, helping her to the car. Getting her situated her in the back seat was a painful process. When she was finally squared away, her head resting against the seat and gazing out at Cody, her mother came to stand in front of him.

Cody had never been formally introduced to Alex's mother. He realized he didn't even know her name. She was middle-aged, perhaps a few years older than his own mother, and petite. She opened her mouth several times, but then shut it. Cody didn't know what to say to her either. He felt shame, in the face of Alex's parents, that he'd let their daughter come to such harm. He knew that, like Alex's guilt, his was illogical, but he still couldn't imagine an appropriate thing to say to her mother.

Finally the little woman reached up and wrapped her arms around his neck. He hugged her awkwardly, and when her body shuddered a moment later, he realized she was crying. "Thank you so much," she whispered, then let go.

As she made her way around to the passenger-side door, Alex's father came forward. He stuck out his hand, and Cody shook it.

"Thank you, Detective"—Vern's solid, bass voice was grounded as ever—"for keeping your promise."

"Of course," was all Cody could think to say.

Vern got behind the wheel, both he and his wife fastened their seatbelts, and then the car was pulling out of the lot.

Cody watched the car until long after it had disappeared from his view. Thunder sounded in the distance, but somewhere high above him, the sky cracked open.

Finally, after a week of waiting, the rain came.

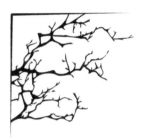

Chapter 53

"OW!"

Cody looked up at the desk in front of his to see Mason scowling and rubbing the back of his head.

The young man glanced self-consciously at Cody before going back to his report.

Cody rolled his eyes. "Frank, stop throwing pencils at Mason. You'll give him a welt."

"Don't know what you're talking about." Frank's muffled voice came from the hallway. This was the first slow night they'd had in months. Frank and Court were making the most of it. Cody gave Mason an encouraging smile before going back to his paperwork.

Mason McLeod was hired to take Tom's place as Mt. Dessicate's newest detective. Of course, if the town kept growing, more would follow. Mason was a quiet, serious man about Cody's age. He could hold his own against Frank and Court, but he got irritated when they wouldn't stop joking, and he was still trying to find his niche.

Cody had only worked with the man for two weeks, but he could already tell that Mason would be an excellent detective. He had a quiet dignity, patience with people, and a knack for making connections faster than anyone else.

Of course, Frank and Court couldn't help themselves but play pranks on the newbie. They had been merciless the first few days of Mason's employment, and Cody wondered how and if Mason would settle in. He'd missed Tom terribly those first few days, so much that it was hard to breathe, but that, too, had passed. When on the third day, as Frank announced he was headed home, Mason nonchalantly stuck his foot out and sent Frank sprawling, Cody knew he'd fit in just fine.

Three months had passed since the Botanist case was closed. Cody's work load was finally lessening, though it would never be as light as it once had been. All the reporters had finally moved out of Mt. Dessicate, but the Botanist had put their tiny, desert community on the map, and more people were moving in daily.

Cody didn't feel like abandoning his town just because of all that had happened, but why a person would want to move to a thirsty little community right after a sadist had ravaged it was beyond him. Still, people continued to show up. The mayor was forecasting major growth for Mt. Dessicate over the next five years.

Cody couldn't care less.

He'd tried hard to stay busy over the last twelve weeks and, in truth, it hadn't been very difficult. He'd worked cases, tied up loose ends, and helped his parents move up north.

Much of his time was spent with Tom's family, especially little Hank. Each of the children was dealing with their father's death in their own way. Cody could only hope that his presence helped, rather than hindering their grief process.

Cody had broken down and called Alex once, a month after she left. He only got a voicemail. He'd left a lame, ridiculous message. She hadn't called him back. When he'd been up north helping his parents, he hadn't bothered to try and see her. She was obviously trying to move on with her life; he needed to forget her.

Resputa hadn't been found. He was long gone now, probably hiding some place in South America. Cody hoped he'd have a chance to put Resputa back in prison, to keep him from exploiting any more children. He also hoped he'd never have to see or deal with Resputa again.

Cody looked back down at his report. He'd read the same paragraph five times. He resolved to get through this last one and call it quits for the evening. He was looking forward to going home and spending the night on the couch in front of the T.V. Actually, the thought made him lonely, but at least he wouldn't be working.

Ten minutes passed without any harassment from Frank or Court, and Cody had the vague thought that it was some kind of record. Then he heard Court's harsh whisper.

"Psst! Mason! Come here!"

Cody glanced up but otherwise ignored the situation.

With a long-suffering sigh, Mason got up and went out into the hallway. Cody could hear excited whispers, but he ignored them.

Next came Frank's voice. "Hey Cody, would you come out here?"

Cody didn't move. He didn't want to screw off with the others; he wanted to finish his report.

"What's the matter, Frank?"

"Just come out here a minute."

"I'm busy. What do you want?"

Something stung Cody's ear. "Ow!" He brought his hand up to his ear and looked down to see a pencil rolling away from him. "What was that for?"

Frank stood in the doorway, looking annoyed. "Cody," he said through clenched teeth, jerking his head to the side and widening his eyes. "Get *out* here. Now."

He disappeared behind the wall, not allowing Cody a reply. With an annoyed sigh, Cody got up. Resolved to give Frank a piece of his mind, he strode through the door and came face to face with . . .

"Alex!"

He practically screamed her name. Frank and Court stood a few feet down the hall, pretending the baseboards were the most interesting thing they'd ever seen, snickering loudly. Mason, standing behind them, looked utterly confused.

"Wha—what are you doing here?" Cody managed.

Even Rose decided that now was the perfect time for some coffee. She got up from her desk in the lobby and came to stand at the coffee pot, which just happened to be much closer to where Alex and Cody stood facing one another than her desk was.

Alex was resplendent in fitted blue jeans and a mauve cotton top. Cody had never seen her look more alluring. She stepped forward so that she was looking up into his face. "I'm here to see you."

Cody glanced back at his office, wondering why he'd been so upset a moment before. What had the report he'd been reading been about? He couldn't remember.

"Have you eaten?" he blurted.

She shook her head. "I've been on the road for a while, so . . ."

"You wanna go to Faye's Diner? It has awesome French fries."

Alex's smile broadened. "I'd love to."

"Give me a second?"

She nodded, and Cody went back into his office. He grabbed his jacket, since autumn was now in full swing, turned off his computer, and snatched his keys from the desk. He went out and held his hand out to Alex. She took it, and he pulled her toward the front of the building.

"Who is that?" he heard Mason whisper as he towed Alex past a grinning Rose.

"It's his future baby-mama," Court answered.

Slap!

"Ow!"

"Don't say that when she can hear you," Frank whispered loudly.

"Would you quit hitting me?" Court didn't bother to whisper at all.

Beside him, Cody felt Alex shake with silent laughter. Allowing himself a small smile, he slipped his arm around her waist and guided her out into the night.

THE END

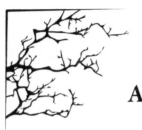

Acknowledgements

I NEED TO THANK EVERYONE I bugged with my questions about real-life crime solving and law enforcement—first and foremost my sister, who has a degree in criminal justice and was always willing to discuss it with me.

I must thank the team at Jolly Fish Press for their relentless hard work, support, and honesty. And all the JFP authors. We all have a camaraderie I haven't found anywhere else, and their support and encouragement is priceless.

And of course, there are my family and friends, who are eternally loving, supportive, and enthusiastic. I love you all! Thank you so much for being exactly who you are!

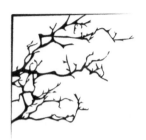

Author's Note

THANKS FOR JOINING Alex and Cody on their adventure. Here's what you can do next:

If you have a spare moment, I would really appreciate a short review. Your help in spreading the word is gratefully received. I'd especially love reviews on Amazon, Bookbub and/or Goodreads.

As an indie author, every review I get helps my visibility, which means I can spend more time writing and less time marketing. If you want me to get more books and sequels out faster, giving me reviews is the way to make that happen!

Advice on reviews: Don't overthink it. Even a line or two about your experience with the book would be perfect! Just be careful not to give spoilers for other readers. ;D

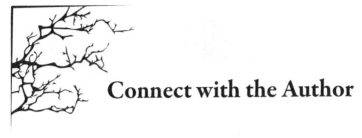

Connect with the Author

WEBSITE: WWW.AUTHORLKHILL.com
Facebook: facebook.com/lkhillbooks
Twitter: twitter.com/lkhillbooks
Pinterest: pinterest.com/lkhillbooks
My Blog: musingsonfantasia.blogspot.com

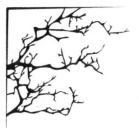

Also by L.K. Hill

Hungry for more serial killer/crime fiction?
Check out my urban crime fiction series, Street Games!

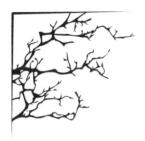

Dark Remnants[1] (Street Games #1)
Would you face down a serial killer to save your brother?

Kyra is already undercover in the murder-capital of the country, and she prefers to go it alone. When she stumbles on a plot to kill most of the city's cops, she has a decision to make.

After shouting her warning at a ~~handsome~~ random detective, she's sure that will be the end of it. Until the same detective shows up at her employer's estate...where there happens to be a dead body in the pool.

But that's not the only corpse in this city. Prostitutes keep turning up dead, and Kyra suspects everything is connected. If she can't figure out how, more than one person might disappear into these shadowy alleys, and never be seen again...

If you love, dark, gritty urban reality, complete with clandestine serial killers and brooding detectives, you'll want to join Kyra and Gabe on this pulse-pounding sprint through Abstreuse City. Because darkness lurks in us all.

"Intriguing storyline. Good fun...Highly recommend!" –R.V.P.

---

1. https://www.amazon.com/dp/B00EXR3II2

**Download here:
https://www.amazon.com/
dp/B00EXR3II2**

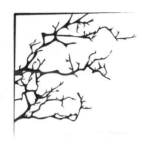

Free Book Offer

Dystopian Romance   Historical Romance   Crime & Mystery   High Fantasy

I'm giving away a FREE Starter Library!
Click the link below to get your FREE reads!

http://www.authorlkhill.com/storysquad

About the Author

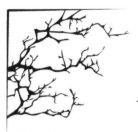

L.K. HILL IS AN AWARD-winning author who writes across three different genres. Her historical fiction is published under the pen name, K.L. Conger. Her sci-fi, fantasy, and dystopian are written under her full name, Liesel K. Hill. And her crime fiction is written under L.K. Hill.

A graduate of Weber State University, she comes from a large, tight-knit family and lives in northern Utah. She is a member of the Church of Jesus Christ of Latter-Day Saints and cherishes her faith, her family and her country. (http://www.lds.org) She plans to keep writing until they nail her coffin shut. Or the Second Coming happens. You know, whichever happens first. ;D

. . .

CPSIA information can be obtained
at www.ICGtesting.com
Printed in the USA
LVHW092208140321
681550LV00022B/55

9 781393 899563